HONOR
RECLAIMED

A HORNET NOVEL

HONOR RECLAIMED

A HORNET NOVEL

TONYA BURROWS

Entangled Publishing, LLC
2614 South Timberline Road
Suite 109
Fort Collins, CO 80525

Visit our website at www.entangledpublishing.com.

Edited by Heather Howland and Sue Winegardner
Cover design by Heather Howland

Print ISBN   978-1-62266-254-8
Ebook ISBN   978-1-62266-255-5

Manufactured in the United States of America

First Edition May 2014

Out of suffering have emerged the strongest souls; the most massive characters are seared with scars.

\- Khalil Gibran

CHAPTER ONE

KUNAR PROVINCE, AFGHANISTAN

Tehani Niazi knew the bomb strapped to her chest was set to explode. The knowledge was right there in the eyes of the warriors left to guard her—they stared at her like she was already dead. And maybe she was. She died a little inside every time her husband stopped her attempts to escape him.

A cold sweat raised bumps on Tehani's skin and chilled her to the bone, but she didn't dare shiver, too afraid of triggering the device. She didn't want to end up like Bita. Their husband had strapped a bomb to her last week and had sent her to the American embassy in Kabul as punishment for her barrenness, even though none of his wives had yet to become pregnant and Tehani was beginning to suspect the problem was on his end and not theirs. Still, he'd said the only way for Bita to reclaim her honor was to become a martyr. And Bita had believed him. Had all but begged him to allow her to prove her loyalty.

Poor, stupid Bita.

But Tehani wasn't Bita and she didn't believe his word was

law. He was nothing but a horrible man who took wives when they were too young, and thought of them as objects to be used until he tired of them.

She wasn't disposable. She wasn't an object. She was Tehani Niazi, sixteen years old. She had a brother, a sister-in-law, and a nephew. She wanted to go to school and study the law to make sure men like her husband were punished. She had dreams, goals, and none of them included dying for Jahangir Siddiqui.

Except how would she escape this time?

Wind whistled through the hallways of the old military compound Jahangir had claimed when the Americans abandoned it. She clenched her teeth, refusing to shudder as the cold abused her exposed skin. The thin red dress wasn't suitable for winter in the mountains, and she'd lost her head scarf long before her husband's men captured her. If she ran again, the cold would end her as easily—if not as fast—as the bomb.

Besides, running wasn't an option this time. Two men had been left to stand guard at her door overnight. They were the ones who had awakened her fifteen minutes ago and fitted her with a vest holding the bomb. Now they stood at their posts again, backs turned against her pleas for help. They both believed in her husband's goals and soon they would load her into a car and take her to a restaurant in Kabul popular with foreigners.

They wanted her to kill people.

Tehani stared at the tangle of wires and round metal objects that made up the vest. She couldn't make sense of any of it, but the thought that she'd soon be responsible for the deaths of dozens of people turned her stomach to acid. She swallowed a sob.

Maybe she could set it off here. At least then she'd only kill the men loyal to her husband and not innocent people expecting only to have lunch at a restaurant.

Yes. That's what she'd do.

If she was going to die one way or another, she preferred to spite her husband on her way to heaven.

With a shaking hand, she touched one of the colored wires, following its path from a cylinder to a small box at the underside of the vest. If she pulled this one, would the bomb detonate? She gripped the wire, but released it without pulling and glanced toward her guards. Maybe she should wait until more of the men surrounded her. Two men wouldn't hurt her husband's plans. In his mind, warriors were just as disposable as misbehaving wives. But if she took out a dozen or more? His plans wouldn't be ruined, but it would take him time to replace the men he'd lost.

She rather liked the thought of stalling him.

Movement at the door caught her attention and she dropped her hand away from the wire, stuffing it underneath her thigh lest one of her guards realize what she was up to. Out in the hallway, the two were talking to someone. The conversation was muffled, but she had little doubt this was the order to take her to Kabul.

Again, she gripped the wire as her guards moved away and a shadow filled her doorway. She imagined Jahangir standing there, closed her eyes, and yanked the wire.

Nothing happened.

Tears burned trails down her cheeks and she grabbed another wire and another.

Still nothing.

The shadow in the doorway swore under his breath and strode into a beam of light cast across the floor by the rising sun. He crouched in front of her and caught her wrists. "Tehani, don't. It's not active."

She blinked until the shadow's blurry face came into view.

Zakir.

Unlike some of the other men, he kept his dark beard neatly trimmed and took care of his appearance. His eyes were such a rich, dark brown; they appeared black, but they weren't soulless like her husband's. She'd always liked him and betrayal left a bitter taste in her mouth. How could he have been involved in this newest torment?

"It's not active," he said softly again. "I made sure it wouldn't hurt you."

He checked over his shoulder, then surged to his feet, moving so fast it took her brain a solid second to catch up to him. He scooped her into his arms and had her halfway out the window before she even thought to fight him. She sent a fist flying and he dodged it, but wasn't fast enough. It glanced off the side of his head.

"Fuck!"

Tehani froze and stared at him, torn between shock and terror. She didn't know many English words, but she'd heard that one often enough. And the way he said it reminded her of the American soldiers who had visited her village. Same accent and everything.

"Who are you?" she whispered.

"You need to trust me," Zakir said in flawless Pashto, and she wondered if maybe she'd misheard him a moment ago. He'd never spoken English before. As far as she knew, he didn't understand any more of the language than she did. Maybe he'd picked up the swear word from the soldiers, too.

At the sound of voices in the hall, he glanced toward the door and swore again. This time, there was no mistaking the language.

She struck out at him. "You're American!"

He avoided the blow and caught her wrist before she could try again. "Tehani, stop it. Do you want to leave here?"

She stared at him, barely comprehending his words. Leave? Of course she wanted to leave, but she had already tried multiple times and it was impossible. He had to be playing a trick.

"Do you want to go home?" he asked, staring straight into her eyes. There was no deception in his gaze and her instincts told her she could trust him even before he added, "I can help you."

She nodded, her heart thundering in her throat at the possibility.

"I'm going to lower you out the window," he said. "Run for the trees. I'll be right behind you."

· · ·

Sergeant Zak Hendricks lowered the girl to the ground and vaulted after her, cursing as he landed hard on one foot and his ankle twisted. Tehani skidded to a stop halfway across the kill zone between the compound and the tree line. She looked back at him with wide, frightened eyes. He waved her on ahead and limped after her, moving way too fucking slowly.

He'd be lucky if he didn't get his ass shot.

Man, he was going to catch hell for putting the mission at risk like this. If he hadn't felt the need to play knight in shining armor before making his escape, he'd be long gone by now. Problem was, he liked the girl. And, like Siddiqui's other wives, she *was* just a girl. At sixteen, she was one of the older wives, but still too young to be married. Too young to become a martyr for a cause she probably didn't even understand. But unlike the other wives, she was smart and had spine. Afghanistan needed more girls like Tehani if it had any chance of moving into the modern era. So, reckless as it was, he'd decided she was leaving with him. It meant he had to bump up his plans, but that was all good with him. He was over playing adoring minion to Siddiqui's evil genius. He had the information he needed. Time to cut and run.

If he could run. His ankle sent spikes of pain through his calf with every step and he felt it swelling inside his boot. Not broken, but definitely sprained.

At least nobody in the compound had raised the alarm yet.

Even as the thought crossed his mind, shouts rang out at his back.

Well, fuck. So much for that.

Tehani waited for him just inside the tree line, trembling and white-faced. It tugged on his heartstrings, but he couldn't take the time to comfort her. Nor could he pick her up. He grabbed her arm and dragged her along behind him until he reached the spot on an overgrown road where he'd stashed a vehicle last night.

Ignoring the throb in his ankle, he hauled Tehani inside, then jumped into the driver's seat. As soon as they were bumping along down the mountainside at a good clip, he reached for the glove box and his sat phone. When he dialed, all he got was an earful of static. He waited until they cleared the trees and tried again.

"This is Zak. I need an exfil now."

More static, but he thought he heard a voice underneath it.

"I repeat, this is Sergeant Zak Hendricks. I've been made. Get me the fuck outta here."

"Sergeant," the warped voice said. "Need—coordinates—"

He rattled off his position, but didn't think it had gone through because now he didn't even hear the static. He thunked the piece of shit phone against the steering wheel.

Tehani made a sound of distress and he glanced over. She huddled against the door, staring at him like he was a snake in the grass. "Are you American?"

"Yes, I am."

Her shoulders relaxed a little. "Are you going to stop my husband?"

That was the plan, but it wasn't going to happen if he didn't make it back in one piece. "Yes. He's a bad man. He can't be in power."

"I know. He needs to be stopped."

He smiled at her. "Brave girl." But the smile faded as he got a load of what was waiting for them down the mountain. Siddiqui's second-in-command had already pulled men together to set up a roadblock.

Goddammit.

Zak pulled the vehicle to a stop and drummed his fingers on the wheel. He couldn't go down there. Not with Tehani in the car. Siddiqui would kill him and use her to kill civilians.

Problem was, Zak couldn't take off on foot either. With the way his ankle throbbed in beat with his heart, he wouldn't get far, and if he never showed up at that roadblock, the men would start combing the mountain. Even though Tehani's village was only a few miles away, they'd never make it.

Unless…

He could buy her some time.

Guess he was going to do the knight in shining armor routine again. He reached under his tunic and brought out the files and flash drive he'd strapped to his chest. "Do you know where you are?"

She glanced at their surroundings. Nodded. She pointed to the southeast. "My village is that way."

"Can you make it home?"

"By myself?" she asked, a tremble in her voice. "I think so, but what about you?"

"I'm going to distract these men, make sure you have time to get away." He pushed the files into her hands. "Take these with you and give them to the first American soldier you see. It's very important. Can you do that?"

Nodding, she tucked the flash drive away in her dress, then clutched the files to her belly. He leaned across the seat to push the door open. "Go on. Be safe."

"Zakir." She hesitated. "Is this about the nuclear bomb?"

Surprise coursed through him. "How do you know about that?"

"I don't know what it is," she admitted. "I've heard the men talking and they are excited about it. I think it's going to hurt a lot of people."

"It will if Siddiqui gets his hands on it. That's why it's so important to give those files to the American soldiers, all right? They'll be able to stop him."

She bit her lower lip. "I'm not going to see you again, am I?"

"No." Zak swallowed the sudden lump blocking his throat. "You're not."

"Are you going to die?"

"Probably."

Her shoulders straightened. "I won't let you down."

"I know. Go on now." Zak watched her scramble out of the vehicle and duck behind a boulder beside the road. He pulled the door shut, drew in a breath, let it out slowly, and shifted to drive. He'd told Tehani the truth—there was a very good chance he wouldn't survive the next few minutes.

And even if he did, he was going to wish like hell he hadn't.

CHAPTER TWO

FLORIDA EVERGLADES
TWO WEEKS LATER

Seth Harlan's boot squished into soft earth where seconds ago there had been solid ground, and his foot slid out from under him.

Aw, shit.

He saw the fall coming but had zero chance of stopping himself in the slimy swamp scum. Barely had time to react beyond lifting his rifle so that it didn't end up jammed with mud. He landed sideways with an ungraceful splash in a pool of stagnant water. The stench was incredible, the taste even worse, but he stayed put. Listened. Told his heart to calm the fuck down before it beat out of his chest and gave away his position.

Water sloshed around him. Insects buzzed, birds cawed. In the distance, a woodpecker tapped out a staccato rhythm on a tree. Closer by, a frog let out a bellowing croak. He strained his ears, struggling to pick out footsteps, voices—any sign that his position had been compromised. But the natural noises drowned out the unnatural, so he was as sure as he could be that his fall hadn't drawn any unwanted attention.

The other member of insertion team Alpha, Jean-Luc Cavalier, crouched behind foliage on dry turf, obviously waiting for him to get his act together. They were still a good two klicks from the target. They'd have to haul ass if he was going to get into position before the opposition force arrived with their "hostage."

He could *not* fuck up another training mission.

"Alpha Two, coming to you," he said into his radio because the last thing he needed was to startle Jean-Luc and end this mission with friendly fire before it even began.

"Roger, Alpha One," Jean-Luc's voice answered.

He hauled himself upright and slogged through the mud, careful not to make any more sound than necessary. It cost precious minutes they didn't have, but eventually he made it to Jean-Luc, who fell in behind him, and he picked up the pace to make up for the time lost. This was his show, another test thrown at him by Gabe Bristow, HORNET's commander, and he wasn't going to screw it up by missing their deadline to get into position.

Using satellite images of the area, he and Jean-Luc had gone over the plan forward and backward, inside and out, before leaving the security of their forward operating base. About a half mile out from the target, he motioned for Jean-Luc to go left, and he moved to the right. He knew exactly where he had to set up his hide, knew exactly where Jean-Luc would be positioned, and how their raid would go down if the intel Gabe had given them was correct.

As he closed in on the target, Seth kept low and advanced slowly. Five hundred meters ahead, a shack rose up out of the swamp, looking like something out of *Deliverance*. He'd be so unsurprised to hear banjo music starting any second. If he were with his old team, Bowie, his spotter, would have even hummed a few bars from the famously creepy "Dueling Banjos" scene and they would have shared a silent laugh over it.

But Bowie was dead.

So was the rest of his old team.

Now here he was, slogging through a swamp without a spotter, doing what was normally a two-person job by himself. All for a new team that didn't accept or trust him.

Yet, he reminded himself. They'd come around.

The shack was quiet. No movement. Intel said two HTs—hostage takers—were supposedly arriving with their principal at 1400. Their mission was to neutralize the HTs and get the hostage out. It had to be quick and quiet, and they had to be en route to their exfil before dark.

Seth shimmied closer, now less than four hundred meters from the place, and found a good firing position behind a thick, half-rotted log. Stretching out flat on his belly, he used some of the local flora to cover himself and his rifle.

Then he settled in for a wait.

The buzzing of bugs got louder, almost deafening, and he suspected a swarm had gathered over his head, but he didn't look away from his scope to confirm his suspicion. A half hour into the watch something with many legs crawled across his back, and the mud coating him from head to foot started to really fucking sting. Still, he didn't move a muscle.

He waited. Watched. Listened. Just as he'd been trained to do in sniper school.

Remaining alert and vigilant during long stretches of inaction was always the hardest part of a sniper's mission. He'd never had much problem with it before, but…well, yeah, that was before. Now it took everything he had in him not to fidget or give in to the creeping sense of paranoia that made him want to glance around. He *knew* there was nobody behind him. Every sense he had told him so. But his heart raced and his gut told him he had to check, had to make sure. He hated having his back open to attack. That was how he'd lost his original team.

The sound of a motor caught his attention, drawing it away from the constant, nagging paranoia. Relief coursed through him. Finally something else to focus on. He scanned the trees through his scope.

Nothing. No boat, although the sound continued to get closer. And then, there it was. An airboat skimming over the murky water, clearing a copse of trees and easing up to the shore near the shack.

Two HTs, just as their intel had said. One operating the boat, one scanning the surroundings holding an AK-47, both wearing camo and face paint.

"Alpha One to Alpha Two," Seth whispered, finally breaking the radio silence. "I have eyes on two HTs arriving by boat. No sign of the hostage."

"Roger that," Jean-Luc's voice said in his ear.

"Are you in position, Alpha Two?"

"Affirmative."

"Hold your position." And just like that, as the words left his lips, they transported him out of the swamp. He heard himself screaming those words, the command echoing around between his ears. *"Hold your positions!"*

The heat surrounding him no longer moved through his lungs like soup—instead, it was a dry heat, like breathing sand, parching his throat with each inhale. The buzzing in his ears wasn't from bugs, but from bullets as they rained down on his stranded Humvee from overhead. His remaining men—Bowie, Link, Rey, Cordero—scrambled to find cover and return fire. Lance Corporal Joe McMahon was already dead, slumped over the steering wheel.

"Seth!" Omar Cordero's panicked voice filled his head. "We're

under attack. Holy shit! There's hundreds of them."

"I got no comms, sir," Link shouted.

"Your orders?" Rey asked. Young and terrified, he was all but shaking in his boots.

Seth hadn't expected the ambush, hadn't prepared his men for the possibility of it. And with their vehicle disabled by an RPG, they were sitting ducks as another wave of insurgents swarmed down the mountain.

Dammit, they couldn't hold their positions. "Fall back! Get to higher ground!"

"Go," Bowie said. *"I'll draw their fire. Go, go, go!"*

"Alpha One? Alpha One, do you copy?"

Jean-Luc's voice in his ear brought Seth slamming back to the here and now with dizzying force. His breath sawed in and out of his lungs and a cold, sticky sweat coated his skin, raising goose bumps despite the muggy swamp air.

Fuck.

By sheer force of will, he quieted his breathing, quashed the lingering fear and horror. His paranoia had amped up to terror alert level red, but he was not going to give in to his mind's games and look behind him. At this point, any unnecessary movement could give him away.

He. Could. Do. This.

"One to Two," he said and his voice sounded like he'd scoured his throat with glass shards. He didn't bother clearing away the hoarseness. "I didn't copy. Say again. Over."

"I have visual confirmation of our hostage. Do you want to engage?"

Seth refocused on his scope. The two HTs pulled a hooded figure up out of the boat and all but threw him over the edge. He stumbled when he landed and face-planted in the swamp mud until his captors yanked him upright again. The guy jerked against the ropes binding his hands, tried to break free and run. His shoulders heaved under a wet and muddy business shirt like he couldn't catch his breath.

"Alpha One, do you want to engage?"

Another breath. In and out. Goddammit. He had to focus. He was not the captive here, but if this was a real situation, he was the only thing standing between the hostage and the kind of memories that kept a man up playing online poker all night. He scanned the distance, calculated, and wished like hell he had a spotter to double-check his calculations. He had a shot.

"One to Two, move in."

All right. Moment of truth.

Seth's heart pounded so hard he heard nothing but the thudding rush of blood in his ears. Cold sweat ran like a river down his spine, but he forced his hands to steady as he checked the scope, adjusted the dials one last time, and sank into his prone position until his bones held him up rather than his muscles. His rifle rested in a natural groove on the log in front of him. Ready. Waiting for his command to do its job.

He took aim, breathed deep. In and out. In and out. He had the HT directly in the crosshairs. All he had to do was breathe and let the rifle take over. Breathe and tighten…his…finger.

Something round dug into the base of his skull.

Arctic water spilled through his veins, sending racking shivers through his body. He knew the feeling of a gun barrel against his head all too well, had lived with it day in and day out for fifteen months, wondering every time if it would be the last time his captors tormented him with the possibility of death.

"Bang," his attacker said, and he flinched. The muzzle lifted away from his head and Ian Reinhardt stood over him, usual scowl firmly in place. "You're dead, Harlan. So's your team. Again. You gotta hold the record for most teams killed by one operator."

The door to the shack burst open and Gabe Bristow limped out into the clearing without his cane. "Reinhardt, enough."

Ian grunted and shouldered his paintball gun. "Boss man's coming to your rescue yet again, noob. When will you grow some fucking balls and stand up for yourself?"

Seth climbed to his feet. "Back off, Reinhardt."

"Or what? You'll put a bullet in me? You miss half the damn time." Ian scoffed. "Where's the Hero Sniper the media went on and on about? 'Cause I sure as fuck haven't seen him."

A sour taste filled Seth's mouth as it always did when someone mentioned the extensive news coverage of his rescue. Half the news outlets had lauded him as some kind of hero and the other half had rifled through his past, looking for any speck of dirt they could find. Some of the more heartless tabloids—one in particular—had even insinuated he had gone AWOL and killed his men, and the whole rescue was all a giant government conspiracy to cover up his crimes.

Fucking reporters. He had no love for them.

"Reinhardt!" Gabe said again, his voice all Navy SEAL commander. "Hit the deck and give me a hundred. Now."

"Yes, sir." Ian flashed a grin full of malice and almost cheerfully dropped into the push-up position right there in the mud.

As Ian counted out the reps, Seth scanned the remnants of their training mission as the rest of the team converged on the clearing.

Harvard, who had been playing the part of the hostage, stood beside Marcus Deangelo and Jesse Warrick, the two HTs. Jean-Luc emerged from the underbrush without any paint on him to indicate he'd been hit, but that wouldn't have lasted. Seth was supposed to have been Jean-Luc's lookout and also provide cover fire. Without him, Jean-Luc was as good as dead.

"All right, gentlemen," Gabe said, addressing the group as

Quinn, the team's XO, came out of the shack where he and Gabe had been watching from monitors. "What went wrong?"

"The Hero Sniper wasn't aware of his surroundings," Ian said between push-ups. He paused in the up position and added, "I'd been tracking him for two klicks, ever since he bit it in the mud. Stood right behind him for a good ten minutes. He never noticed."

Seth's stomach dropped as Gabe's gaze landed on him. He lifted his chin and faced his commander, careful not to let any of the guilt swirling around inside him show on his face. "I fucked up."

"Yeah, Harlan. You did."

"I didn't listen to my instincts. Won't happen next time."

Gabe made a noncommittal sound and addressed the entire team. "Pack up, gentlemen. We're done here for today."

There were a lot of good-natured jabs, some cursing, and some laughter as everyone headed toward the boat. Seth shouldered his rifle and followed in the group's wake. Nobody spoke to him, which was A-okay as far as he was concerned. He got the feeling deep in his gut—and fuck him if he'd ignore it again—that Gabe's dismissive attitude meant he'd screwed up one too many times for the former SEAL's liking.

He was done.

CHAPTER THREE

NIAZI VILLAGE, AFGHANISTAN

As the sun sank behind snow-frosted mountain ridges in the distance, Phoebe Leighton raised her camera and stared through the lens. Her finger hovered over the shutter release, but she didn't snap the photo. It wasn't the right shot. Not yet.

The valley below was dry and cold with the approaching winter, and the pink-gold rays of the sun caught on particles of dirt in the air, streaking the sky with wide dust motes. Shadows cast by the mountains lengthened, spilling darkness over the valley. Still, she waited. She didn't know what for—never did until she saw it.

There.

A lone farmer trudged up the hillside to the skeleton of an abandoned tank left over from the war between the Soviet Union and the mujahideen fighters. A scruffy herding dog bounded in his wake, and when he paused to tie the animal up to what was left of the main gun, her gut told her that was the shot she'd been waiting for. She pressed the shutter release and snapped several quick photos in succession.

Dramatic. Haunting. A dichotomy of past and present, perfectly representative of this beautiful, rugged country caught in a war between tradition and modernization.

Lowering the camera, she stared past the man and his dog at the village. Somewhere down there, a very brave sixteen-year-old girl was standing up for her rights, rights that little girls in America took for granted. Already Phoebe was amazed by young Tehani Niazi and she had yet to meet her.

"You ready? We don't want to be up in these hills after dark."

Phoebe glanced over her shoulder at Zina Ojanpura, an American relief worker who planned to take the girl to a shelter in Kabul. Zina was a pretty woman with long pale-blond hair and vivid green eyes made all the brighter by the red-and-gold scarf wrapped around her head.

On impulse, Phoebe lifted her camera, her gut telling her this was another photo she'd been waiting for.

Snap.

Against the backdrop of the rocky, ragged landscape, Zina was a striking picture. A collision of East and West—just like the war that had ravaged this country for far too many years.

Zina made a face. "I really wish you wouldn't do that."

"Then stop being so freaking gorgeous. I mean, seriously, nobody should look like a runway model after trekking through the mountains for three days." Phoebe tucked her camera away in her bag and adjusted her own scarf to recover the mess of kinky, frizzy red hair that she'd given up trying to tame two days ago. "All right. Let's go meet Tehani."

Zina nodded and led the way back to their guides, two of the local district's police officers, who waited impatiently with their little caravan of horses. Phoebe wasn't entirely comfortable on horseback but there were no roads in this part of the country so the only available mode of transportation had four legs and hooves. And a horse was definitely preferable to a donkey.

"I'm glad Tehani's family contacted us," Zina said as they guided their mounts down the hill. "It's progress at least. They could have just as easily forced her to go back to her husband."

Sixteen years old and already married. It was disgusting and happened far more than the rest of the world knew. But maybe Tehani's story would be the one to finally reach Western ears. Maybe this brave girl would be the vehicle for change.

"Thanks again for inviting me along," Phoebe said, pulling her mount up alongside Zina's mare. "I really appreciate it."

"No, the appreciation is mine. I admire your work and what you're trying to do for these women. You tell their stories with no bias, no agenda. Honestly, it's refreshing. Nowadays, wartime journalism is almost as corrupt as—well, the Afghan government."

"*My* work?" She scoffed. "Girl, I'm just a storyteller. It's your work that's making the difference here. Girls like Tehani wouldn't have anyone to turn to if not for you. The things your group has accomplished in such a short time are amazing. Courageous. Selfless. And that's why I take your picture. When I look at you, I see all that and I want my audience to see it, too."

Zina's cheeks filled with a pretty shade of pink and dang it, she wished she had her camera out. Talk about selfless—a photo of that fleeting moment would have perfectly captured the essence of Zina Ojanpura and the women's shelter she'd single-handedly founded.

Oh well.

Some moments were too perfect to capture in a photo.

Phoebe scanned the mud homes as they emerged into the village by the community well. The houses were almost stacked one on top of the other, often with little more than a blanket covering each front door. Still, this wasn't a sleepy place with everyone tucked up inside out of fear. Kids raced up and down the hill, kicking a ball. Mothers sat in doorways watching their older children with weary eyes while soothing fussy infants and sewing. In front of one of the homes, old men huddled together around a well-loved chessboard, smoking and laughing. She didn't see many able-bodied men and assumed they were up in the hills with their goats. Or, possibly, they had joined the Taliban, which was still very much alive in these hills. Or, even worse, they had become opium runners.

How many of these exhausted women were opium widows? She hated to guess.

"Here we are," Zina said after a quick conversation with their police escorts, and stopped her horse in front of one crumbling house. A man stood in the doorway, his skin tanned and wrinkled, leathered from the unmerciful Afghan climate. He eyed them both with suspicion.

"Salaam alaikum," Zina said and dismounted. Phoebe followed suit, but let the relief worker take the lead. She was only here to document what happened and did her best to fade into the background.

"Are you here to take my sister?" the man asked.

Phoebe felt her eyebrows climb toward her hairline. Sister? Wow. She'd pegged the man for an uncle from the looks of him.

She lifted her camera. "May I?" she asked in Pashto.

He eyed her with open suspicion, but then his face lit up when he spotted the camera. He nodded and grinned, striking a pose against the door. His gap-toothed smile showed his youth in a way that his weathered looks couldn't.

Snap.

"We've come from Kabul. From the women's shelter," Zina explained.

The old-looking young man nodded, his smile vanishing. "She will be safe there."

Their conversation started drawing attention from the others in the village. The group of old men had stopped laughing and watched them with disapproving frowns.

Under the weight of their stares, Tehani's brother shuffled his feet nervously. He motioned to the house. "Come. It's not safe to talk here."

The main room was small with an ornate carpet spread over the floor and pillows scattered along the walls. A woman sat on one pillow, her chador wrapped around her head to cover all but her eyes. In her lap sat a toddler boy, watching everything with innocent fascination. She poured chai into small cups and passed them out to everyone in the room. Usually the chai ritual included small talk before getting down to business, but they were apparently nervous enough to eschew that part of the custom.

"My wife, Darya," Tehani's brother said. "And son. I am Nemat. I will get Tehani. We've been hiding her." He disappeared through a doorway draped with a floral-printed sheet.

Phoebe took the opportunity to ask the woman if she would mind having her picture taken. She nodded, but was shy about it and wouldn't look directly at the camera. Nothing usable for the story, but the photos would make nice additions to Phoebe's personal collection.

Nemat returned with a girl in a stained and torn red dress. Uncovered dark hair swung around her shoulders and she appraised everyone in the room with one sweep of dark eyes much too world-weary to belong to a girl her age. Unlike her sister-in-law, she wasn't shy. She strode right over to Zina and lifted her chin in a gesture of defiance. "I don't want to be married," she said in Pashto. "I want to go to school."

"You will," Zina replied in the same language, her face lit up with delight.

Oh, now *there* was a shot…

Phoebe lifted her camera. *Snap.*

Tehani's gaze shifted to the camera and in that instant, she looked so very young and vulnerable. "Are you taking my picture?"

"I am," Phoebe said, also in Pashto. "Is that okay?"

"I don't know. What are you going to do with it?"

"Show it to other girls like you who are in bad situations so they don't give up hope, so that maybe they will speak up for themselves."

Tehani thought about it for a moment, then a brilliant smile crossed her face. "I like that."

"I thought maybe you would."

"I want to help other girls like me." She again turned to Zina. "Can we leave tonight?"

"Tomorrow morning. Your brother has agreed to host us for the night."

She nodded and focused on Phoebe again. "What about my husband? Will you tell other people about his crimes? About the bombs?"

"Shh," Nemat scolded, his easy brotherly smile dissolving into an expression of real fear. "I told you not to speak of that."

Phoebe glanced over at Zina, who sank her teeth into her lower lip and even though she stayed silent, she didn't need to voice her worry. Her expression said it all.

Crap. This conversation was going nowhere good. Phoebe knelt down to the girl's level. "What bombs, Tehani?"

"Lots of bombs, but—"

"We will not speak of this anymore," Nemat declared, his voice rising with panic.

Tehani frowned at her brother. "I will so speak of it. Zakir died trying to warn the American soldiers. He told me it was very important."

Heart pounding high in her throat, Phoebe set down her camera and focused all of her attention on the little girl. "Who is Zakir?"

"I don't know for sure. I think he was American. He helped me escape, but he might be dead now."

"Shh!" Nemat said. "Tehani, enough. We do not speak of it. Do you want your aunt and baby cousin to be killed? Do you want me to be killed? After we've protected you?"

"No, I'm sorry." Her eyes filled with tears as she shook her head. "I only wanted to help. I don't want anyone else to die." She turned her pleading gaze to Phoebe. "My husband used to strap bombs to us. Sometimes they were active, but most of the time they were not. We never knew for sure, but when he tired of one of us, he'd send us somewhere and blow us up. He still has other wives."

Phoebe wanted to reach out and hug the girl, comfort her, but wasn't sure enough of the local customs and didn't dare overstep her boundaries. At least not until Tehani was safe at the shelter in Kabul. Then all bets were off.

"You *did* help," she assured. "Just by telling us about it, you helped."

"I think we had better leave tonight," Zina said in English and Phoebe nodded. As dangerous as it was to be out in the mountains at night, from the sounds of things, it was a hell of a lot more dangerous to stay in this village any longer than they had to.

It didn't take long to pack Tehani's things. She had little more than two dresses and a few head scarves, one of which she used to cover her hair. She also carried a stained folder that she refused to part with, as well as the vest she'd been wearing when she made her escape. Someone had removed the explosive material, but still the sight of the vest was like a kick in the stomach, leaving Phoebe breathless as she photographed it.

Zina tried to talk Nemat and his wife into joining them, but he steadfastly refused.

"My wife is pregnant. She cannot make such a journey. I will not allow it."

Nemat's wife merely averted her gaze and said nothing, offered no opinion of her own, but Phoebe caught the glimpse of longing in her expression before she dipped her head.

As they said their good-byes, pity swelled in Phoebe's heart for the young woman, who really wasn't all that much older than Tehani. Maybe eighteen and already married with a baby and another on the way.

She didn't speak again until they were headed out of the village with their police escorts and Tehani hiding underneath the *chadari* Zina had donned.

"It's a vicious, never-ending cycle, isn't it?" she asked in English. "That poor girl is pregnant again and she's barely an adult herself."

Zina gave a heavy sigh that moved her shoulders. "You can't save everyone, Phoebe."

But that didn't stop her from wanting to try. Her fingers tightened on her horse's reins, the old leather creaking in her grip. "Who is Tehani's husband?"

Zina's head turned, but because of the *chadari*, her expression was unreadable. "She won't say and I don't want to know. Neither should you. That kind of information will do nothing but put us and the shelter at risk."

Phoebe nodded. She knew that. But dammit, she hated this feeling of utter impotence. "If he's as powerful as I think he is, people need to know he's dangerous."

"These villagers already know."

"But what about the rest of the world?"

"If it doesn't affect them directly, most people won't care. You know that. It's human nature."

As they crested the hill by the ancient tank where the dog was still tied, Phoebe brought her horse to a halt and glanced back at the little village. None of this sat right with her and, gut churning, she took out her camera.

Snap. Snap. Snap.

That old cliché about a picture being worth a thousand words was absolutely true. The awe-inspiring power of a photo was one of the reasons Phoebe had given up her career muckraking for a tabloid, where she'd been on the fast track after writing a controversial piece about one of the country's war heroes. Her marriage had been falling apart at the time, but that didn't matter because Phoebe was finally getting the attention she thought she'd deserved. Never mind that her article launched an investigation and vilified a man who hadn't deserved it.

The thought sent a familiar stab of guilt through her and as she tucked her camera away, she pulled out the magazine cover she kept in her bag as a reminder of why she'd turned to photography in the first place. A reminder of Kathryn Anderson, the ambitious, heartless journalist she used to be, and why she'd separated herself from that person by going back to her maiden name and adopting her middle name as her first.

She ran her fingers over the crinkled print of Seth Harlan kneeling at the grave of one of his fallen men. He looked... haunted. Alone. And she'd done that to him, had turned the world against him with her words.

The first time she'd seen the cover, it had been like having a duct-tape blindfold ripped off suddenly—painful, disorienting, frightening. She'd gone home that day, had taken a hard look at herself in the mirror, and hadn't liked what she'd seen at all. She'd called and quit her job right then and somewhere along the way, she'd found her true calling.

Pictures could make people change their minds. Make them

laugh. Cry. And, yes, even care when they normally wouldn't.

She looked up from the magazine cover and watched as the last rays of sunlight played over the village. Zina was probably right. The world didn't care about Tehani or girls like her, but Phoebe could change that, couldn't she?

All it would take is the right photo.

And she knew better than anyone the power of photography.

CHAPTER FOUR

KEY WEST, FLORIDA

Someone was in his house.

Seth dropped his bag just inside the door and the *thunk* of the duffel hitting tile echoed through the room. A fresh surge of adrenaline jolted him out of the zombielike daze he'd been functioning in since the training mission ended. The team had made it out of the swamp just as darkness fell and then it had been another hour's drive to the hotel in Miami where everyone was staying. He could have gotten a room for the night instead of making the three-hour drive home to Key West—but no. He'd wanted to be home, had needed the comfort of his own space.

Except someone was in his house. How was that possible? In deference to his constant state of paranoia, he'd bought the best home security equipment on the market, and the panel on the wall beside the door was lit up green. All systems go.

He scanned the interior, picking out the familiar dark shapes of the dining table, couch, chairs, TV, piano…

There.

A shadow blotted out the square of pale light thrown across the floor from the patio doors. Not inside the house, then. Out by the pool.

Seth crouched and found his weapon in his bag, never taking his eyes off the shadow. His heart hammered, but his hand stayed steady as he edged across the living room toward the sliding glass doors. The shadow passed by again and he made out the silhouette of a man pacing across the patio.

He lifted his weapon and yanked open the door, setting off the alarm he'd reset upon entering the house. "Get the fuck out of here or I will shoot you."

The man paused, then slowly lifted his hands, locked his fingers behind his head, and turned around. Greer Wilde, his best friend Jude's oldest brother, met his gaze evenly with bloodshot eyes. "I'm unarmed."

"Holy fuck, Greer." Exhaling hard, he lowered his weapon. "I thought you had more sense than to sneak into a psychotic man's house."

"You're not any more psychotic than I am," Greer said, dropping his hands to his sides.

Seth grunted and strode inside to turn off the wailing alarm.

Having lived with PTSD for two years, he'd spotted the signs of it in Greer at Jude's wedding two weeks ago. He'd offered to be the guy's sounding board should he need to vent—no judgment, no questions asked. Greer had since called him only once after a particularly bad nightmare, but had clammed up as soon as he'd calmed down enough to think straight. Honestly, Seth hadn't expected to hear from the former Army Ranger again after that last call.

Seth motioned him inside and went to the kitchen to start a pot of coffee. "I doubt you came all the way to Key West to talk about a nightmare."

"No," Greer said. "No more nightmares. I'm good now."

"Bullshit. You look like hell. When was the last time you slept?"

Greer release a long breath and rubbed a hand over his face. "Going on thirty-six hours now."

"Jesus Christ." Seth had been reaching for a set of mugs in the cupboard by the fridge, but stopped short and went for the cell phone in his pocket instead. "That's it. I'm calling Jude and telling him what's going on with you. Your brothers will get you the help you need since you're too stubborn to get it yourself."

"No. Fuck, don't do that," Greer said. "I swear I haven't had any more nightmares. I've just been too busy to sleep."

"Busy doing what?"

Greer said nothing more for a solid five seconds. Then, with an exhausted curse, he muttered, "You have no idea how many laws I'm breaking right now. I'm here because I need you to put me in touch with Gabe Bristow. I know he's somewhere in Florida and I need to speak to him. Tonight."

"Isn't your brother friends with him? Why not just get his number from—"

"Because Vaughn's in the hospital and even if he wasn't, I couldn't talk to him about this. I shouldn't be talking to you about this, but I need HORNET's help. One of my men is in trouble and the government's not doing a damn thing to help him. It was a fully deniable op."

Fully deniable.

A black op.

Seth groaned. "Do your brothers know you're still active duty?"

"No, they don't, and they don't need to."

"Yeah, well, I don't want to be around when they find out." The shit was really going to hit the fan when Greer's brothers discovered he was still drawing paychecks from Uncle Sam, and

Seth sure as hell did not want to get in the middle of that brewing Wilde family feud. "I don't get it. Why lie to them?"

Greer's jaw tightened. "Can you put me in touch with Bristow or not?"

"Yeah, I can. Hang on." He scrolled through his contacts until he found Gabe's number, then passed the phone over the counter.

Greer punched the number into his own cell and without another word, he left, ghosting across the patio and vaulting over the six-foot fence surrounding the backyard.

Seth stared after him.

Damn fence was too easily breached. Why hadn't he considered that before?

Motion sensors, he decided. He'd top the fence with motion sensors at his first opportunity.

The coffeemaker beeped as it finished brewing, reminding him he'd started a pot. He fixed himself a mug heavy on the sugar for that extra jolt of stay-awake. Hell, might as well pour a 5-hour Energy shot in there, too. He sipped, testing the concoction. It kind of tasted like super-sweet grape-flavored day-old coffee sludge, but it worked. He'd rather be a jittery mess than risk closing his eyes.

Yeah, he'd called Greer out on not sleeping. Didn't mean he had to take his own advice.

He grabbed his laptop from where he'd left it plugged in on the kitchen counter, and carried it and his cup to the patio because he sure as fuck wasn't going to feel safe inside the house when he knew the backyard was open to attack. In the moonless night, the water in his pool was as dark and uninviting as the swamp had been. Somewhere nearby, a guitar strummed out a lively song.

He chose one of the poolside loungers and fired up his laptop, settling in for his nightly routine of taking other insomniacs to the cleaners playing poker. Countless sleepless nights had morphed the man who'd never gambled in his life into a poker shark, and he fell easily into the rhythms of the game. Time passed. He lost himself in the cards on the screen until his cell phone rang, startling him into knocking his mug over. The cold dregs of coffee spilled across the table and he swore as he mopped it up with a towel left from his last swim, the closest thing handy.

But hey, he had to give himself credit for not jumping out of his skin at the unexpected sound.

Progress.

Another ring. He tossed the now-wet towel in the outdoor hamper on his way inside, then eyed the phone as it jittered across the kitchen counter. His father used to say nothing good ever came from a phone call after midnight, which was why his curfew growing up had been 11:55 p.m. and not a second later. His father never wanted to get an after-midnight call.

Dad had gotten one, though. An after-midnight call that happened to come in the middle of the day, in the form of a visit by uniformed Marines, telling him his only son was a prisoner of war.

Nope. Seth shut down that thought almost before it completely formed. Not going there. Not thinking of the fear and pain he'd caused. Not thinking of the fear and pain he'd endured. Nope. Nope. Nope. He was past all that now. Progress, remember?

Because of the whole after-midnight thing, he considered ignoring the phone. But he wasn't his father with children to worry about, and he wasn't a coward who hid from bad news. A neurotic, traumatized mess? All right, he'd cop to that. Coward? No fucking way.

Gabe's name showed on the caller ID. He thumbed the answer button.

"Hello?" Shit, he really needed to start talking more often, even if it was just to himself. His voice sounded like he'd swallowed a box of nails and washed it down with a glass of sand.

"Harlan," Gabe said—no, more like demanded. The tone reminded Seth of a drill sergeant, took him back to the good old days in basic training. Jesus, he'd been such an idealistic, arrogant sucker back then, with no inkling of how fucked up his life was about to become.

How he wished he could go back.

He sucked in a breath. "Yeah, I'm here." So this was it, the ax falling on his fledgling career as a private military contractor. Except…why did Gabe wait until almost 3:00 a.m. to call? Didn't make sense unless he was about to get chewed out for giving away Gabe's private cell phone number.

"I'm sending a helo to you. Get on it and get your ass back to Miami a-sap."

Wait. What? This didn't sound like a firing. "Sir?"

"We have an op."

Holy shit. They *weren't* sending his ass packing? "Uh, thank you, sir."

"Don't call me sir," Gabe said for what had to be the thousandth time during their short acquaintance. "And if you thank anyone, it should be Quinn. He went to bat for you—again. You're still on probation as far as I'm concerned and I still have doubts about your ability to function in combat, especially now."

While that wasn't a ringing endorsement, it was better than he'd expected, and he swallowed the urge to thank Gabe again. "Does this have something to do with Greer Wilde?"

"Yeah." He paused and in that heavy moment of silence, it seemed the world held its breath. Seth sure as hell did. He had a feeling he wasn't going to like what was coming next. Gabe wasn't usually the hesitating type, and when he spoke again, his tone was as gentle as Seth had ever heard it. "We're going to Afghanistan."

Oh, fuck no.

The words plowed into him like a high-speed train and the

phone nearly fell from his numb fingers. He shook his head even though Gabe couldn't see him. Probably a good thing Gabe couldn't see him, because he wasn't holding it together. A lump the size of a tank swelled in his throat, solid and choking, as a tremble worked down his back, the icy claws of real fear digging into his spine. *You can't fucking ask this of me,* he wanted to scream.

Instead, the only sound that came from his throat was a croaked, "Afghanistan?" It was the first time he'd spoken the country's name aloud in two years, and it scraped across his vocal cords.

"I know the enormity of what I'm asking you," Gabe said softly, all but reading his mind. "And under any other circumstances, I'd be the first to say hell no. But these aren't normal circumstances and this isn't a mission I'm willing to refuse. So are you up for this?" he asked after a long stretch of silence. "Tell me right now if you're not."

Seth swallowed. He was not broken. He could do this. "Yeah. Yeah, I'll be ready."

CHAPTER FIVE

The team wasn't happy to see him. Nobody said so out loud, but the good-natured ribbing and off-color jokes he could hear from where he stood in the hallway stopped when Seth finally entered the hotel conference room. Not that he blamed them. After the botched training mission, he wouldn't be happy to see himself either if he were in their shoes. The silence in the room fit like a too-tight boot.

Finally, the door opened and Gabe strode in with Quinn, and Greer Wilde.

Greer looked no better than he had last night. If anything, the bags around his dark eyes were more pronounced, the lines etched into his forehead speaking of massive amounts of stress.

"All right, gentlemen, let's get started." Gabe produced a folder from his pack and opened it on the table, then motioned to Greer with his chin. "Most of you probably already know him, but for those who don't, this is Greer Wilde. He'll be in charge of this briefing. Greer?"

Greer nodded. As he came forward, Jesse Warrick leaned back in his seat and tipped his cowboy hat in greeting. "Thought you left this kinda work, Wilde."

"Not for lack of trying," Greer muttered. "How are you, Jesse?"

"Better than you from the looks of it."

"Been a bad week." Greer stopped at the front of the room and stared down the length of the table, his eyes landing briefly on Seth before he picked up a photo from the open folder. The picture showed an unsmiling man in a turban with dark, unreadable eyes and a neatly trimmed beard. "This man is Zakir Rossoul." He produced another photo and held the two up side by side. The second showed the same man, beardless and grinning, wearing the tan beret of an Army Ranger on his close-cropped hair. "Also known as Sergeant Zakir 'Zak' Hendricks. He's a second-generation Afghan-American, decorated former Army Ranger, and—" Greer paused and cleared his throat before continuing. "For the past eighteen months, Zak has been working deep undercover in Afghanistan. He was supposed to stay there until April, but two weeks ago we received a call from him via sat phone." He withdrew a small recorder from his pocket and hit play. Static filled the room, broken intermittently by a deep, unaccented voice.

"I repeat, this is Sergeant Zak Hendricks. I've been made. Get me the fuck outta here."

"This is the last contact we received from him," Greer said and spread a map across the table. "He tried to give us his coordinates, but the call failed. Best we can figure, his last position was here." He fingered a spot high in the mountains near the Pakistan border, then looked up at the team. "We want him back and we tried to find him, but since it was a fully deniable mission, our government is doing fuck-all to help bring him home. It's not acceptable."

Several of the guys murmured agreement.

"What was his mission?" someone asked.

Greer hesitated, obviously weighing his next words, considering how much to divulge. "In five months, Afghanistan will be electing a new president. What happens during that election will affect the timetable for the withdrawal of American troops. Now as much as we'd like to see all of our guys come home, we don't want to leave the country in the hands of an extremist leader with a hard-on for the U.S. And unfortunately, several of the candidates for presidency are exactly that. Most don't have a snowball's chance of winning, but there is one man who has Washington worried. His name is Jahangir Abdul Rab Siddiqui. He's Pashtun, and popular with religious conservatives. He already has the ear of the current administration and has spent the last several years stacking the Supreme Court and National Assembly with his buddies. There are rumors of his Taliban sympathies and suspicion he's behind several suicide bombs that have killed foreign peacekeepers and anti-Taliban leaders. Zak's mission was to get in close to Siddiqui and dig up all the dirt he could. His secondary mission, in case Siddiqui did get elected, was to make sure the man never made it into office, but something went wrong. We don't know what or how. All we know is what you heard on that recording. Zak called for an exfil, but by the time we got men in the area there was no sign of him."

As Greer spoke, the pictures of Zak Hendricks circled the table, both finally landing in front of Seth. He stared down at the grinning man, his stomach churning. "How do we know he's not already dead?"

"We don't," Greer admitted. "But I seem to remember another situation not all that long ago, where a team of SEALs went into the mountains on questionable intel, all to rescue a lost Marine…"

Every eye in the room swung in Seth's direction. He set his jaw. "That was low, Greer."

"Yeah, but I'm not playing fair. I'm already breaking all kinds of laws by bringing HORNET into this, but fuck it. Zak is one of my best friends and I can't leave him there."

Gabe Bristow stood and clapped Greer on the shoulder. "You'd better head back to DC before anyone notices you're gone. We've got this. We'll bring Zak home."

"Thank you," Greer said tightly and headed out. He paused beside Seth's chair. "I'm sorry for bringing up your situation, but you have to see the similarities."

Seth did, but resentment still burned inside his chest and he couldn't give any more response than a curt nod. If Greer Wilde was looking for forgiveness, he'd have to keep searching.

Gabe waited to continue the briefing until after the door shut behind Greer, then he passed a thin stack of papers around the table.

"This is all the information we have on the key players right now," he said. "Granted, it's not actionable intel—yet—but we'll have a better chance at getting something of use in-country. Once we're airborne, Harvard will gather what information he can on Sergeant Hendricks and Siddiqui and prepare an in-depth report I expect you all to read and know by heart." He glanced to Harvard for confirmation.

The ex-CIA analyst and all-around computer genius nodded. "Got it."

Gabe continued. "Jean-Luc, when we land, you'll take Seth to make contact with HumInt's local asset, a man by the name of Hamid Fahim."

"Wait," Jean-Luc said. "Why Seth?" Then he winced and tilted his head in semi-apology. "No offense, Seth, but I'd rather have one of the guys I know at my back in case things go fubar."

"Too bad," Gabe said. "Seth is just as much a member of this team as the rest of you. He's to be treated as such. We're not frat boys and there will be no hazing of every new guy I bring on. I won't put up with that shit. Am I understood, gentlemen?"

"Yes, sir," everyone answered, albeit halfheartedly.

Gabe gave them a moment to let that decree sink in. "After Jean-Luc and Seth have secured supplies and a safe house from Fahim, we'll set up a forward operating base with internet access so Harvard can continue working. From there, our first course of action will be locate and plant a GPS tracker on Jahangir Siddiqui's vehicle. He's the key to the actionable intel we need. Any questions?"

Some of the guys tossed out questions, but they were working off limited information and Gabe admitted he didn't have the answers.

Marcus Deangelo, a former FBI agent, drummed his fingers on the table. "You know, I hate to be Debbie Downer here, but I'm not real comfortable with stepping on the military's toes. The FBI in Colombia was one thing," he said, referring to the team's first mission together, which Seth hadn't been a part of. "They were in the wrong. Hell, even my ex-partner thought so, which is why he risked his career to help us."

"Yeah, when is Giancarelli gonna give up the Bureau and come over to the dark side?" Jean-Luc asked.

Marcus snorted. "He's considered it, but it's not happening unless his wife says it's okay. And she won't."

Jean-Luc made a *tsk tsk tsk* sound. "Man's pussy-whipped."

"Can you blame him?" Marcus asked. "You have *seen* his wife, right?"

"Good point. If I had a woman as gorgeous as Leah Giancarelli in my bed every night—"

"You'd ask her sister to join you for a threesome," Quinn said, deadpan.

Jean-Luc grinned. "Fuck yeah. Common sense, *mon ami*. Common sense."

Even Quinn cracked a smile at that.

Seth stayed silent through it all and flipped through the handouts. Zak Hendricks's stats, service record, family history... Nothing that would help them find the man.

He closed the folder and pushed it away. "The military won't do anything until Sergeant Hendricks shows up bleeding on an Al Jazeera news feed. And if it was a black op, probably not even then."

"That's the general consensus, yes," Gabe agreed after a beat of silence, then looked at Marcus. "Which is why I'm not all that concerned about stepping on the military's toes here. If Sergeant Hendricks was captured by Siddiqui's Taliban buddies, they plan to make a very public, very graphic example of him. They don't take prisoners. To date, there are only two known POWs in A-stan. One soldier has been held captive since 2009 and is being used as a bargaining chip for the release of Taliban prisoners. And one Marine—" He broke off abruptly. Clothing rustled and the seats creaked as everyone shifted to look at Seth.

All seven stares crawled over Seth's skin like needle-legged spiders, and a bead of sweat trickled down the back of his neck. He hated it, hated being the center of attention, hated that Gabe had just boiled his life down to nothing more than an example in a briefing. But he wasn't a coward and if they wanted to use him as an example, then so be it.

He gulped down the rising panic, shoved up out of his seat, and very deliberately lowered the hood of his sweatshirt. Then he jerked the thing off over his head, tossed it on the table, and held out his arms. He always wore long sleeves in public, but if they wanted to stare, they might as well get the whole fucking picture, right? Scars and all.

He met each of their gazes with a challenge in his own.

Harvard visibly swallowed and looked away first, adjusting his glasses and taking a great interest in his laptop screen. Marcus looked at him with pity, Jesse with the assessing eye of a medical professional. Jean-Luc shifted uncomfortably and for a moment, Seth almost took pity on *him*. The Ragin' Cajun didn't do well with heavy stuff and right now, a thousand-pound elephant sat in the middle of the table. Quinn nodded once in his direction, a gesture of respect. Gabe stood at the front of the table, silent and stone-faced. Ian, one arm draped over the back of the chair beside him, rolled his eyes.

Seth dropped his arms, but didn't reach for his sweatshirt. "I know how these militants work. If they haven't already cut off Sergeant Hendricks's head and they haven't yet issued a ransom demand, then they're torturing him." He couldn't help the crack in his voice on those last two words, but plowed onward, determined to be of some use to the team. "Maybe they're trying to get info out of him, maybe not. Either way, Gabe's right. They're making an example of him—'Look at the infidel, so weak, so broken. These are the men who want our country, who want to corrupt our women and our culture. See? We can beat them easily. We are powerful. Allah is on our side'…and so on. Even better if they can keep him alive and make a hundred examples out of him, day after day after day."

Nobody spoke.

Seth grabbed his sweatshirt from the table, but paused before pulling it on. "Honestly, for Sergeant Hendricks's sake, I hope we're going in after a body. I hope it was a quick and easy death because I wouldn't wish this"—he motioned to his chest—"on anyone except the assholes who did it to me."

CHAPTER SIX

KABUL, AFGHANISTAN

The bazaar was a vibrant place, full of movement and color that put Seth's teeth on edge. Vendors who could afford tables stood under bright umbrellas, shaded from the sun and wind. Those who couldn't just spread their wares out on blankets on the ground or in rusted wheelbarrows, selling everything from sheep heads to dried fruit, fabric, and even toys.

The sounds were just as much an assault on Seth's overwhelmed senses as the sights. Vendors called out in rapid-fire Pashto or Dari. Or, occasionally, even broken English when they spotted a Westerner. A lot of chatter, haggling. Laughter. Yelling. Honking from the crowded street as cars weaved around pedestrians. The putter of motorbikes zipping through stagnant traffic. Traditional music filled the air, seeming to come from everywhere and nowhere at the same time.

It all combined into a quagmire in Seth's mind that had him about ready to jump out of his skin. He couldn't help but glance over his shoulder every time someone pressed in too close behind him. Couldn't control the jitter that made him tense up at every contact or loud noise.

Fuck, he had to get over this. Kabul was a relatively safe place—or at least as safe as any city in this godforsaken country could get. Logic dictated he had nothing to fear here. These were just everyday, average people going about their lives. Just like citizens in America, some of these people had no interest in politics and only wanted the endless warring to end. Not everybody had a political agenda. Or even a religious one.

They weren't all the enemy.

This was another test, he reminded himself, and sucked in a calming breath through his nose, inhaling the scents of people, spice, smoke, garbage, and exhaust. Of all the men Gabe could have sent to the market to meet Fahim, he'd selected Seth to go with Jean-Luc, even though several of the guys had done tours in Afghanistan and they all had at least a basic understanding of Pashto. Certainly enough to go to the market and meet with an asset who supposedly spoke perfect English.

So of course this was a test. With good reason, Gabe wanted to see if he could handle being back here, and he'd be damned before he failed.

Had to pull it together. Stay alert. Stay focused.

And most of all, stay fucking calm.

As they weaved their way through the market, Jean-Luc was his usual cheerful self, just as comfortable halfway across the world as he was in his beloved New Orleans. Laughing, joking, conversing with the locals in flawless Dari. At the moment, he carried on a spirited debate with a teenage boy over the price of a scarf.

Seth kind of hated him for his blasé attitude.

"Little thief," Jean-Luc said good-naturedly and returned to Seth's side with his hard-won scarf.

"You paid too much for it."

"I know. Like I said, kid's a little thief." But he smiled as he looped the scarf around his neck. "Gotta admire him for it. Besides, what am I goin' to do with a handful of afghani bills if we end up running around in the mountains? Up there, it's only good for toilet paper. But a scarf? Now, *mon ami*, that's useful."

"Good point." So there was a method to Jean-Luc's madness after all. Because of his propensity to joke around more than anyone on the team, it was sometimes hard to remember he housed genius-level intellect behind that mischievous grin.

But still, these little shopping excursions were taking too much time. And Seth got twitchier with each passing second. Time to get their job done and get the fuck out of here. "Now let's find Fahim and—"

"Ooh. Shiny." Jean-Luc strayed from the path to another vendor's blanket of goods.

Seth stopped walking and heaved a sigh. "You're as bad as a crow feathering its nest."

A sudden memory of Emma bobbed to the surface of his mind. She'd *ooh*ed and *ahh*ed over the sparkly shit when they'd picked out an engagement ring before his deployment. Actually, kinda the same way Jean-Luc was now.

"Scratch that," Seth said. "You're more like an engaged woman in a jewelry store."

Jean-Luc held up a hand, his knuckles adorned with different rings of varying sizes. "Aw, see, you have much to learn, grasshopper. Women adore sparkles. I adore women. Therefore, I buy sparkles to give to women and I get laid."

"Jesus Christ. Does your every thought revolve around getting laid?"

"Pretty much. Doesn't everyone's?"

"No." He hadn't thought about sex since…well, since that

night after he bought Emma her ring. And in all honesty, the idea of getting naked and sweaty with anyone ever again had bile surging into his throat. Hell to the no.

"See, that's what's wrong with the world today," Jean-Luc said. "Everyone's so…repressed. Politically, religiously, emotionally, sexually. Everyone needs to say fuck it, let it all go, have some fun, and just live."

"Yeah, sure. *That's* the problem with—" Paranoia crawled up the back of Seth's neck and he turned to scan the marketplace. Was it him, or had the crowd thickened? He glanced from face to face, looking for the slightest hint of malicious intent. Save for one woman who seemed to be staring at him—it was hard to tell for sure through the veil of her traditional blue *chadari*—nobody paid any undue attention to him. So maybe it was nothing. Hell, with his track record for paranoid outbursts, it probably was nothing. But he swore he'd felt unfriendly eyes on his back moments ago and he wasn't going to ignore his gut instinct again. Not after the way Ian had gotten the drop on him in the swamp back in Florida.

He tapped Jean-Luc's arm. "We need to go."

"Yeah?" The Ragin' Cajun's easy smile faded, but unless you were up close and personal with him, nobody else would have noticed the slight shift in his demeanor. He continued to examine the ring selection like everything was still hunky-dory. "What did you see?"

"Nothing." And didn't that make him feel stupid? "Just…gut feeling."

"You don't have the best track record with gut feelings, you know."

"Yeah, but—" Seth cut himself off, spotting a man standing off to the side of the crowd, a cell phone raised to his ear. He carried on a very intense conversation with someone on the other end of the line and kept glancing in their direction.

Well, shit.

All kinds of alarm bells sounded in Seth's head. It was more than a gut feeling now. It was a goddamn fact and a strange sense of calm settled over him, the likes of which he hadn't felt in years. "Hang on. Something's going down at your eight. We need to find cover. Now."

"Roger that." Jean-Luc didn't argue and dropped the rings, much to the vendor's disappointment. He nodded to the indoor portion of the bazaar and, without another word, they made a beeline toward the awnings spread out like colorful fans from the side of the mud building. The man with the cell phone's curse carried over the ambient noise and he tried to follow them, shoving his way through the crowd.

"You see him?" Seth asked.

"Yeah, good catch. Guess being a paranoid bastard has its uses." They found cover behind an empty vendor booth just inside the building and waited, backs pressed against the wall.

The man jogged past, now shouting into the cell phone. His voice faded as he disappeared into the crowd.

"*Merde.*" Jean-Luc reached into his pack for the sat phone he'd gotten from Harvard before leaving the plane. "We don't have long before they figure out we're still inside. I'm gonna give Gabe a heads-up. Something about this whole sitch is fucked. Nobody should know who we are or why we're here. Keep an eye out, grasshopper."

As Jean-Luc tried to reach their commander, Seth edged out of the booth far enough to see what was going on around them. He kept his eyes moving like he'd been trained, always scanning, watching, assessing. He saw the woman in the blue veil again — at least he thought it was the same woman — but he didn't see the guy with the cell phone. Still, that didn't mean they were free and clear. Obviously their number one fan had buddies willing to join the party.

Whatever the party was.

Jean-Luc hung up the phone. "Piece of shit. I got nothing. We're outta here. The only person who knew we would be here was Fahim, so either someone got to him or he was never on our side to begin with."

"Damn. We *need* supplies." Since it was usually much easier to secure supplies in-country than go through the international hassle of bringing their own, Fahim had been the mission's lifeline. "Going up into the mountains, we'll be wading deep into enemy shit. Without weapons, it's suicide. And I've been there, done that, got the fucking bloodstained T-shirt, and I'm not up for a repeat, thanks."

"We'll find another supplier," Jean-Luc said without much concern. "Trust me. Gabe's backup plans have backup plans and if there's one thing this team's good at, it's improvisation. Are we clear?"

Seth checked the area. There was the woman again. Was she…following him? "Clear."

"All right." Jean-Luc dusted his hands together. "So what do you say to some escape and evasion?"

That woman…

Something niggled at the back of his mind. Most likely paranoia again, but he had to be sure. "No, not yet. Wait here a sec."

Jean-Luc snorted. "Fuck that. You ever see a horror movie? The pretty one always dies first when they split up and I'm too young to bite it. We're sticking together."

Seth rolled his eyes and ducked into the crowd.

Jean-Luc was right on his heels. "Whoa. If I didn't know you any better, I'd think you just smiled. Did it hurt?"

He flipped off the Ragin' Cajun over his shoulder. But, yeah, he was smiling. It felt really damn good to be part of a team again.

...

It couldn't be him.

Phoebe shook her head and stared down at the eggplant she was holding. What the hell? She didn't need eggplant. She set it back on the table and, distracted, she continued past several other vendors offering different kinds of veggies.

Could it be him?

She glanced up at the same moment the man in the hooded sweatshirt looked in her direction and for a breathless heartbeat, she thought their gazes locked. Of course, that was silly. Her face was covered by the *chadari* and although she could see out, he couldn't possibly see in. Still, his blue eyes stayed on her for a beat longer than necessary before he continued his scan of the crowd.

Dammit, she just couldn't tell with that hood up over his head. It looked like him, but why would he be back in Afghanistan? No doubt this was the last place on earth he'd visit.

Her mind had to be playing tricks on her. It wasn't the first time she thought she'd seen Seth Harlan in a crowd, and it wouldn't be the last.

Guilt was nasty like that.

The man and his blond friend disappeared indoors, where bread and dried fruit were sold. She didn't need either, but…

She followed.

Because if it was him, she could finally—do what? Apologize? Yes, that'd go over well. *Hi, Seth. You don't know me, but I wrote some really horrible things about you two years ago and I just wanted to say I'm so sorry for ruining your credibility…*

Right.

It most likely wasn't him anyway, but at least now she had a distraction from the frustration roiling under her skin. She'd taken her photos of Tehani—face blurred to preserve the girl's identity, of course—and the bomb vest to the Ministry of Women's Affairs and had gotten nowhere. It was like nobody cared that Tehani's husband, obviously a man of power, was using his young wives as suicide bombers when he tired of them.

She just didn't get it. What was the point of having a Ministry of Women's Affairs if she couldn't even get past the front desk to talk to the minister? She'd just have to try again tomorrow. And the next day. And the day after that. All else failed, she'd take it public herself. If there was one thing she could do well, it was creating a media firestorm.

Which, of course, brought her mind back to Seth Harlan.

Pausing just inside the door, Phoebe searched for the man in the hooded sweatshirt. The two men should be easy enough to spot. Blonds like his friend tended to stick out here in a land full of people with brown skin and dark hair. For that matter, so did men with blue eyes.

Except she couldn't find them. A lot of people wandered up and down the aisle, but none were the blue-eyed man or his companion.

She frowned. Now hold on a second. They couldn't have vanished.

Unless her mind really was playing tricks.

She wandered back outside and looked around. Nope. Whoever he was, he'd given her the slip. Sighing at herself, she decided she was too tired and frustrated to continue shopping and cut through the market with the intention of returning to the shelter.

Crossing streets in Kabul was a bit like a real-life version of *Frogger*. One wrong move and *splat*! Game over. Getting to the other side in one piece always took patience and no small amount of skill. Unlike natives who darted out no matter what was barreling their way, Phoebe preferred to play it safe and wait for a break in the traffic. Sometimes it took a while, but waiting was better than ending up a road pancake.

As she stood on the curb, she sensed a presence looming too close behind her. Alarm crawled up her spine and she toyed nervously with the strap of the bag on her shoulder. She usually didn't have problems going out alone in Kabul—as long as she wore the *chadari*, men saw her as a modest Muslim woman and left her alone. It was when she wore only a head scarf that she ran into trouble. Her light-copper hair and pale skin stuck out in a crowd, so as much as she hated the *chadari* as a symbol of oppression, it also provided a modicum of safety. She understood why many women feared to give it up even after the Taliban regime fell.

Finally, there was a lull in traffic and she nipped between a lumbering bus and a taxi. Whoever was behind her stayed on her butt and his shadow fell over hers as the sun sank to their backs.

Probably just someone going in the same direction as her. Nothing to get worked up about. And yet she couldn't shake the feeling of eyes locked on the back of her head. Her heart kicked into a panicked gallop and sweat trickled into her eyes under her veil.

Oh crap. If she was being followed, she couldn't lead this person to the shelter.

Making a split-second decision, she darted back across the road, barely avoiding a motorbike that jumped onto the sidewalk to get around the stalled traffic. With a squeak of surprise, she dropped her basket and stumbled backward.

An arm clamped around her waist from behind and jerked her against a lean, hard body as a big hand clamped over her mouth.

CHAPTER SEVEN

That eerie calm returned, almost as though a sheet of ice had dropped between Seth and the world. He hauled the struggling woman into an alcove. He heard Jean-Luc call his name and order him to stop, but fuck that. This woman knew something and he was damn well going to find out what.

"Who's after us?" he demanded, turning her around and shoving her against the wall. He hadn't spoken Pashto since his rescue twenty-one months ago and the words felt at once foreign and familiar on his tongue. This was one language he doubted time would ever erase from his memory. "Who are you? Why were you following us?"

Behind him, Jean-Luc swore in a long string of Cajun French. A hand gripped his shoulder. "Jesus Christ, Seth. Let her go. You keep this up, you're goin' to have some pissed-off husband or brother or father comin' after your head."

"Nah. They'll just punish her." And he would not feel guilty about that. He would not. She was the enemy.

The woman stilled. He hated not being able to gauge her expressions and yanked up the veil. A pair of pale eyes stared at him, rounded in shock. Interesting color, somewhere on the border of green and blue. He bet in better lighting, the blue of her *chadari* brought out the blue in her irises.

He gave his head a quick shake to dislodge the utterly unimportant thought. Christ, his mind was all kinds of fucked up.

"Oh my God. It *is* you," she said. In English. With a slight accent hinting at...upper-class New England.

Wait. What?

He let her go and backed up a step as she shrugged out of the *chadari,* folded it, and tucked it into the bag on her shoulder. She was a petite thing with curly hair that, like her eyes, wasn't quite one color but balanced between a light brown and red. She wore it pulled back in a low ponytail, the end of which brushed the middle of her back.

Okay. Not exactly what he'd expected.

She watched him like she'd come face-to-face with a ghost. "I can't believe you're *here.* I thought maybe you were you—I mean, of course you're you. But when I saw you, I—" She broke off, shook her head. "I'm not making sense."

"No, you're not and you need to start. Who are you?"

She drew a breath and threw back her shoulders. "My name is Phoebe Leighton. I'm a freelance photojournalist working on a story about the women's shelter here in Kabul." She motioned vaguely toward the street, but he didn't take his eyes off her.

"Jesus. Should have figured you for a fucking journalist."

"Excuse me?"

"You act like you know me," he said, ignoring her outrage. "But I've never met you."

"Of course I know you."

"How?"

And there was that look, the concerned one that came across people's faces when they were wondering if he was crazy. He gritted his teeth against it. "How?"

"Because," she said slowly, "everyone in the States knows who you are. Or at least every journalist in the States worth her salt does. You're Seth Harlan, the Hero Sniper. The only POW ever rescued from Afghanistan. Which brings up the question, why are you here?"

Hero Sniper. Christ, how he hated that ridiculous media-issued nickname. "I'm vacationing."

Phoebe snorted and raised an eyebrow toward Jean-Luc, who had surprisingly kept his mouth shut all this time. "Now you, handsome, I don't know."

Jean-Luc grinned. "I'm more than willing to help ya out with that, *cher*."

She laughed. "I just bet you are. So. Seth." She refocused those amazing blue-green eyes on him. "Are we done assaulting innocent women now? Because thanks to you, the shelter's groceries are sitting in the middle of the road and I need to go back and buy more."

"I don't think so." He caught her arm as she tried to make an escape. She was fast and almost got away from him. He pushed her against the wall again, this time keeping his hand clamped to her thin shoulder. "What do you have to do with the men following us?"

"What men?" she asked in exasperation, trying to shake him off.

"That's what we'd like to know," Jean-Luc said. Must be he decided to play the good cop in this interrogation, which suited Seth just fine. He didn't like the way his stomach jolted every time she turned those eyes on him, and treating her like a bad guy somewhat dampened the sensation. He again caught her as she tried a duck-and-run maneuver.

She made a small distressed noise in her throat. "I don't know what you're talking about."

"Those men were following us and so were you. Are you telling me there's no connection between you at all? Because I'm a paranoid bastard—"

"He is," Jean-Luc said.

Seth ignored the interruption. "—and I have a hard time with coincidences."

She fisted her free hand on her hip, obviously changing tactics and going on the defensive. Again, fine by him. In his football days, he'd been known for his ability to break through defensive lines.

She scowled at him. "Well, that's just too damn bad because I don't know the men you're talking about. I already told you why I was following you. I thought I recognized you."

"And you often follow the people you recognize?"

"I didn't know for sure until just now and—what can I say? Curiosity killed the Phoebe. It's a curse."

Jean-Luc gave a choked snort that sounded suspiciously like a laugh. Seth glared back at him.

Jean-Luc merely shrugged. "What? She's feisty. I have a thing for feisty women."

"You have a thing for all women." He looked at Phoebe again, found himself staring at her pursed lips. Which was wrong. He made himself meet her eyes, noticed a flicker of...

Panic.

The little fucking liar.

He couldn't begin to guess why that pissed him off so much. Maybe because the shriveled nub of humanity left in him had wanted her to be telling the truth.

He tightened his grasp on her arm until she sucked in a sharp breath. "We should take her back with us. She's hiding something."

She tried to jerk her arm free. "I'm not!"

They both ignored her.

"How do you know?" Jean-Luc asked.

"It's in her eyes." If one good thing came out of his captivity, it was his ability to read people and judge motivations. There were some days his ability had been the only thing keeping him sane. He could always tell when his captors were in the mood to hurt him and was able to separate himself from his body to a certain extent, lock himself deep inside his own head. He could also tell when they'd leave him alone and even estimate how long he'd have before they came back. He'd cherished the days they'd left him shackled in a dark room and held on to—

Memories.

Jesus, the memories.

His grip loosened and Phoebe took the opportunity to break free, using her petite stature to her advantage and ducking underneath his outstretched arm.

"Shit! Grab her!"

Jean-Luc tried, but she was already forging a path into the crowd.

Cursing, Seth gave chase, except his bigger size hindered him. She was able to duck, squeeze, and dodge around people while he could only shove them aside or plow over them. But at least she was easy to keep track of with that tail of copper hair streaming behind her, glinting in the last pink rays of the setting sun. And another plus—the men in the market noticed her immodest clothing and were now trying to stop her as well, finally detaining her next to the frantic jewelry vendor's blanket.

The commotion created a void in the crowd and Seth put on a burst of speed for the last twenty yards. Which, shit, was a big mistake. By the time he reached her, he was moving too fast, didn't have enough room to stop, and the laws of physics kicked in. His forward momentum sent them both skidding across the blanket of trinkets as gunfire cracked the air over their heads. Her bag flew up and smacked into his side like a brick as he threw his weight sideways. Even though he took the brunt of the fall, she still gave a muffled whimper of pain when they landed. Hot wetness spilled over his hand from her arm. Her face, inches above his, had gone white, her pupils wide in shock. Her pulse fluttered wildly at the base of her throat.

She was bleeding.

Some fucker had taken a shot at her.

All around them, chaos erupted. The crowd screamed and scattered as the gunshots continued in the *tat-tat-tat-boom* of an automatic weapon.

Seth's heart lodged in his throat, which was a damn good thing because it kept his stomach from revolting at each shot.

His men screaming.

Dying.

"You shot me," Phoebe whispered in disbelief and the tremble in her voice brought him slamming back to the present just as fire peppered the ground feet away from them.

Phoebe screamed. He hauled her to her feet and pointed her in the direction of the nearest buildings. "Move!"

Bullets danced at his heels as he followed. When she turned in a blind panic to run in the opposite direction, he grabbed the back of her shirt and hauled her out of the fleeing crowd toward a narrow opening between two buildings. There was barely room enough for the both of them to stand side by side and the alley reeked of piss, but cover was cover. He'd take it over standing out in the kill zone.

Seth pinned her against the wall with his body and pressed his face into her hair, hoping the hood of his sweatshirt would hide the copper glint from passersby. With any luck, the deepening shadows of evening and his dark sweatshirt would completely conceal them.

If the bad guys didn't have night vision. Or thermal capabilities. Fuck, fuck, fuck.

His hands shook and he flattened them to the wall on either side of Phoebe's head. Adrenaline after-burn. Just adrenaline. He'd be fine in a second…

Yeah, right.

He was one more gunshot away from completely losing his shit. His throat closed, his lungs seized up, and pain squeezed his heart like it wanted to pop the thing out of his chest. The wall was the only thing holding him up. The wall…and the woman trapped trembling between it and his body.

He sucked in a breath and the sweet citrus smell of her hair invaded his senses, intoxicating and strangely calming. Even as Phoebe's heart thundered against his chest, his slowed and he focused on the dueling sensations. Her rate was way too fast and—yeah, it probably made him a prick—but her terror relaxed him. She was frightened so he couldn't be. She needed him.

"You shot me," she muttered into his sweatshirt, her voice little more than a dull accusation.

Seth leaned back to take stock of her condition. She wore a cotton button-up open over a tank top, and the sleeve had been slashed open by a bullet's path, leaving a gouge in her upper arm. Her pale flesh was angry and inflamed around the wound, but the blood flow was already slowing to a trickle. Painful, but not serious.

"I didn't shoot you."

"Who else would it have been?" she demanded, her shock boiling away into temper.

"Good question."

"*You* were the only one chasing me." She shoved him, but he didn't move. "You tackled me!"

"And I saved your life. That bullet was meant for your head. Who have you pissed off lately besides me?"

"Nobody!"

"Call me cynical, but I find that hard to believe. Why did you run from me in the first place?"

"Why did I run?" Her tone dripped with disbelief, even as tears cut streams through the dirt smudging her face. She cradled her wounded arm to her belly. "Seriously? You were manhandling me. Why would I *not* run?"

Seth clenched his teeth and let go of her, backing up as far as their narrow space allowed. The commotion in the market had quieted and he needed to get a handle on the situation out there. "Stay here."

"Where am I going to go?"

He pointed a finger at her nose. "Stay."

Her chin hitched up. "I'm not a dog."

"Stay. Here," he repeated. She harrumphed. Figuring that was the best response he was going to get, he crept to the mouth of the alley and checked around the corner. The shooting had stopped and the crowd had mostly disappeared. Police sirens wailed in the not-too-far-off distance. Several bodies lay on the ground, but thank fuck none of them were Jean-Luc.

Phoebe peeked out under his arm as the first squad car pulled up to the scene. "Oh, thank God. It's the police." She tried to squeeze past him.

"Goddammit." He caught her shirt and yanked her back, once again pinning her with his body weight. "This is not a good thing."

"Are you kidding me? If you didn't shoot me—which, by the way, I still kind of doubt—then I need to report the incident so they can find the person who did."

"They won't give a fuck someone shot at you."

"Of course they will. They're the police."

He stared down at her in disbelief, but her mulish expression didn't change. "Jesus. You really don't get it, do you? How long have you been in Afghanistan?"

Finally, a flicker of uncertainty showed in her blue-green eyes. "A couple weeks."

Figures. He hated to be the one to bust her rose-colored glasses, but someone had to do it before she got herself killed. "You can't trust anyone here."

"Including you?"

"Especially me, but between me and the cops, I'm the lesser of two evils."

"Call me cynical…"

He ignored having his own words thrown back at him. "We need to get out of here. You said you're staying at a shelter. Where is it?"

She shook her head. "I can't take you to the shelter. Most of the women who live there are petrified of men."

He sighed. "Fine, then you're coming with me. Unless you want to tell me what you're hiding…?"

"I'm not hiding anything."

"Yeah, I don't believe you." He clasped a hand around her good arm. "Let's go. And act natural."

• • •

Act natural, he said. Like it was completely natural to be a hostage.

Phoebe tried to pull free from his grasp, but it was no use. Pain throbbed from her wound up into her temple and her stomach churned with nausea, sapping her strength. Not that she would have had any shot at escaping him while at full strength. Whatever his mental issues, the man was built like a warrior, all whipcord muscle.

Which made him all the more dangerous.

She could scream. Attract the police officers' attention that way. As he firmly guided her up the street in the opposite direction of the market, she glanced back. There were several police cars around now and they had the whole area blocked off. At least two ambulances sat in the street and just beyond, gawkers and media had begun gathering around the barricades.

If she screamed, she'd bring a lot more attention to Seth than just the police. Good.

She opened her mouth, but closed it again without making a sound. A man stood near one of the barricades and scanned the crowd as he spoke on a cell phone. She'd seen him once before. Or, no. Twice. The first time was right before she noticed Seth and his blond friend. The second, when she was trying to escape them. This guy had been one of the men trying to stop her.

Was this one of the men Seth had been questioning her about? Seth thought the men had been following him, but if that was the case, why had they been so intent on stopping *her*?

The man spotted her and pocketed his cell phone in the inner lining of his jacket. And his hand stayed there, resting on something as he broke into a jog.

Oh God, he had a gun.

"Uh, Seth?"

He glanced back at her, then noticed the man. "Fuck. Move." Lengthening his stride to just short of a run, he all but dragged her in his wake. She struggled to keep pace until a furtive glance over her shoulder showed the man gaining on them. He carried the gun in plain sight now.

Fear was a damn powerful motivator.

She raced ahead, staying at Seth's side, zigzagging through narrow alleyways, darting across busy streets. When he took a sudden turn to the left, his grip on her arm slipped and she staggered. She dropped to her hands and knees in the hard-packed dirt, chest heaving, lungs burning from overexertion. Blood trickled from her wound and her arm ached down to her fingertips.

Seth reached out to help her up. "C'mon."

She noticed her surroundings for the first time since they started running, but had no idea where she was, had never seen this empty four-way intersection before. The buildings around her looked residential and run-down and if she had to guess, this wasn't part of the city many Western eyes saw. She looked back the way they'd come. The man with the gun was nowhere in sight.

Seth stood there, hand outstretched, panting as hard as she was. He wiggled his fingers. "Phoebe. We have to keep moving."

She could try to run, get away from him. But the street ahead, narrow and soaked in unwelcoming shadows, didn't look like any place she wanted to be on her own. The sun had completely disappeared behind the mountains now and with thick gray clouds rolling in overhead, it promised to be a dark, cold night.

God help her, she didn't want to face it alone.

She accepted his hand.

CHAPTER EIGHT

Jesse Warrick tapped on the door to Gabe and Quinn's bunk and waited. He heard no movement inside, but he knew his commander was in there trying to get some shut-eye before this new clusterfuck of an op. He just hoped Quinn wasn't in there too, or else this was going to make for a damn awkward conversation. Hell, it might even end in a fistfight between him and Quinn again like a similar convo had back in May.

The door opened. Gabe had his phone to his ear, but waved Jesse inside the tiny room. More out of habit than manners, he took off his cowboy hat as he stepped over the threshold. Ran a hand through his hair and glanced around.

The jet had been gutted and redesigned this summer by HumInt Inc. to better suit HORNET's needs and now included a decked-out war room, a galley, and six of these small rooms. It was a typical dorm setup with two surprisingly comfortable beds—a mirror image of his and Marcus's room next door. Except where his looked lived-in with his bed rumpled and a few clothes spilling out of his bag, Gabe's room was immaculate. His bag sat unpacked on the tightly made-up mattress and his boots waited by the end of the bed as if a pair of feet already stood in them at attention. Quinn's side of the room was just as precise.

Not a surprise. Guys didn't get much more fastidious than the two former SEALs.

"It will be a while before I can get in touch again," Gabe said into the phone. "You know how things get when they start moving." A pause. His lips curved into a little smile. "Yes, ma'am." Another pause, and everything about the big guy softened. "I love you, too, Aud. Stay out of trouble while I'm gone, okay? And you can tell Raffi that goes double for him. Brother or no, I'll kick his ass if he doesn't take care of you."

A hollow ache opened up in the center of Jesse's chest and he focused his attention on his hat, dusting imaginary dirt off the brim. Listening in on the husband and wife's conversation, he felt like a voyeur, an intruder on their intimate moment. And damn if it didn't remind him of the similar conversations he used to have with Lacy, back when he'd been with Delta Force and they could still talk to each other without it devolving into an argument. Not that he really missed his ex-wife. There was too much bad blood overshadowing the good memories for him to miss her. But he did miss having someone besides his horses waiting for him at home.

And God, he missed his son with an intensity that hurt.

In that moment, as he tried not to eavesdrop on Gabe and Audrey's conversation, he started making plans to take Connor to Disneyland as soon as he got back stateside. He'd only been promising the kid the trip for years. Well past time to step up and make it happen.

Gabe finally hung up, slid the phone into the leg pocket of his cargo pants, and limped over to the end of the bed. He scooped up his boots. "So what's up, Jess?"

"How's the wife?" Jesse cursed himself as the question left his lips. That hadn't been what he meant to say and he covered by adding, "Isn't it a little early in Costa Rica?"

"0700, but she says she's been up for a while. Inspiration struck." Gabe shrugged, but an indulgent smile played around the edges of his hard mouth. "What can I say? Artists keep stranger hours than SEALs."

"She's worried about you."

Gabe exhaled, the sound something close to a resigned laugh. "Yeah. She's not going to sleep until we get home. She thinks I should be riding a desk because of..." He trailed off and tapped a hand to the cane propped against the wall.

Jesse decided not to comment. Gabe knew full well he agreed with Audrey. The big guy wasn't doing his foot any favors by running around playing hero, but sayin' so would only make the coming conversation more difficult.

Jesse motioned to the bag on the floor. "Where's Quinn?"

"He and Marcus are tactically acquiring a vehicle for us."

Good. Meant Quinn wouldn't be walking in anytime soon. "Are you worried we haven't heard back from Jean-Luc and Harlan yet?"

"Getting there," Gabe admitted. "Yeah."

"Do you think it was good idea to send Harlan out?"

"He *is* a part of this team," Gabe said flatly, but it was hard to miss the unspoken *until I decide otherwise* in his words.

"Yeah, 'course he is. But don't ya think he's kinda..." He'd planned on finishing that sentence with "broken," but trailed off. He didn't want to be the asshole talkin' shit about a guy who had lived through hell and come back out swingin'. And despite all of Seth Harlan's issues, the sniper wasn't the person he'd come to talk to Gabe about in the first place. "Nah, forget that."

"So," Gabe said after a second of silence. "What do you need?"

Like he didn't know. "To talk to you about Quinn."

Gabe pulled the laces of his boot loose and slid his foot in. Trying to remain casual, but Jesse saw the way he tightened up as he asked, "What about him?"

"Honestly, he's not the guy I'd be sendin' out for anything rougher than a pony ride. Probably not even that." The look he got in response would have singed a lesser man, but he wasn't about to back off. Not about this. "I'm sorry, Gabe. I know he's like a brother to you, but Quinn's medical history makes him a liability. We can't have him in the field. I'm already gonna have to keep an eagle eye on Harlan in case he can't deal. What happens if Harlan experiences a psychotic break and Quinn blacks out on us? We'll be down two men. If it happens in the middle of a firefight…" He didn't finish that thought. He didn't need to. His meaning came across loud and clear: they'd all be fucked. Hard and without foreplay.

"I hear what you're saying, Jess. I do," Gabe said and tugged his laces tight, making quick work of the knot before grabbing his other boot. He took more care about sliding that one onto his bad foot. "But I've been watching Quinn since you voiced your concerns back in July. I haven't seen any indication of lingering effects from his brain injury. Have you? Beyond that one time he blacked out in Colombia?"

Jesse pressed his lips together. He should lie. He had been keeping his eyes peeled for another blackout like the one he'd witnessed in Bogotá and hadn't seen a damn thing, but to his way of thinking just because the moon disappeared during the day didn't mean it no longer existed. Quinn's medical issues were very much a real thing, even if no symptoms presented themselves right now.

Yet he couldn't bring himself to flat-out lie to Gabe. He respected the guy too much. "An injury like his won't spontaneously heal itself," he hedged. "I told you before, it's a damn miracle he's alive and functioning. After gettin' thrown through a windshield goin' seventy? His brain should be mush."

"But have you seen any more indications that Quinn is unfit for this op?"

"Christ, Gabe. You know what kind of position you're puttin' me in? I can't okay him for active duty. It goes against everything I've been trained to do."

"Have you seen any more indications that Quinn is unfit?" He enunciated each word.

"No. I haven't."

Gabe didn't so much as blink. "So I only have your opinion—which I do value—but in this case it's based on an incident that happened one time six months ago, correct?"

"It's my professional medical opinion," Jesse said between his teeth. Heat blazed up the back of his neck, but he sucked in a breath through his nose and exhaled hard to dispel the anger. He'd been kicked out of Delta Force for his temper. He wasn't going to get kicked out of HORNET for the same reason, even if his commander had his head so far up a horse's ass, he was tasting hay.

Then again, if Jesse's ten years of loyalty to the Army had taught him nothing else, it was that usually, in the case of commanders, horse's asses were the norm. It was up to the rank and file to bite their tongues and follow orders, no matter how stupid.

'Course, he'd thought Gabe Bristow was better than that.

He straightened and jammed his hat on his head. "Are you orderin' me to ignore my training?"

"I'm telling you I can't order my XO to stand down just because you think he's a liability. Especially because *you* think he's a liability. I have to take into account your history with him. You two have never seen eye to eye and I need something more than your say-so. I need to see proof."

"Frankly, sir, it's not *my* judgment clouded by personal feelings here. I won't give my okay. If he endangers himself or someone else, that's all on you." Jesse strode to the door, but stopped halfway out and tipped the brim of his hat in a sarcastic kind of salute. "And fuck you, Gabe."

He stalked back to the war room, where Harvard was hard at work at his laptop trying to pin down Jahangir Siddiqui's whereabouts. The rest of the team must still be in their bunks. None of them had slept more than three hours in the last twenty-four and Jesse was starting to feel the strain of exhaustion. He probably should have bedded down for an hour while they were stuck here twiddling their thumbs, but he was too worried about the Quinn situation. The guy was going to get himself or someone else killed. Jesse sure as hell didn't want a narcoleptic watching his six in a pucker situation.

"Hey," Harvard said, gazing up from his screen when Jesse kicked an abandoned rucksack in frustration. "Something wrong?"

"No," he muttered. They only had a boss with a bum foot, a second-in-command with a traumatic brain injury, and a sniper with severe PTSD. Nothing wrong at all.

Jesus.

Jesse sank into a chair opposite Harvard and scowled across the table. If Gabe wouldn't do anything about Quinn, maybe he needed to take matters into his own hands, tell the rest of the team what was goin' on. It went against his training to divulge a man's medical issues, but he couldn't see any other way to force Gabe into taking action.

He opened his mouth, but a rattle at the plane's door stopped him. He got up to unlatch the door, expecting to see Jean-Luc and Seth returning with HumInt Inc.'s local contact, Fahim. Instead

Jean-Luc staggered inside, bruised and bleeding, his clothes torn. He all but collapsed into Jesse's arms.

"What the hell happened to you?" Jesse lowered him to the floor and ordered Harvard to retrieve his medical bag.

Jean-Luc winced and slung a duffel off his shoulder. "Someone shot up the market."

"Jesus Christ. Are you shot?"

"No. I caught up to one of the shooters and we had a go-round until he got me in the kidney and left me to be trampled by the crowd." He swore in Cajun and gripped his side. "And trample me they did."

"Where's Seth?" Harvard asked, returning with the medical kit.

"Dunno." Jean-Luc sat up and spit out a mouthful of blood. "Before all hell broke loose, we were being followed by the two shooters and a woman. Seth seemed to think the woman was hiding something when we questioned her. She got away from us, he chased her, and that's when the shooting started. I lost track of him."

"All right," Jesse said after giving Jean-Luc a quick examination. "You're gonna be sore, but nothing appears ruptured or broken. You get dizzy or start to have any pain or swelling in your abdomen or you start pissing blood, you tell me, Cajun. No toughin' it out. Got it?"

Jean-Luc offered up a weak, bloody smile. "*Oui*. I'm a wimp when it comes to pain."

"Good." He grabbed several antiseptic wipes and started cleaning the superficial wounds when a shadow blocked out his light.

Gabe stood over them and took in Jean-Luc's condition, grim-faced. "And Seth?"

"MIA," Jesse answered.

"What about Fahim? Did you meet up with him?"

"No," Jean-Luc said, hissing at the sting from the antiseptic pads. Guy really was a wimp. "I found him slumped over the steering wheel of his car a block away from the market. Shot through the head at close range. This was in his trunk." He shoved the duffel bag toward Gabe's feet.

Gabe bent over to unzip it. Weapons. Radios. "Well, it's a start." He held out a hand and between him and Jesse, they managed to pull Jean-Luc off the floor. "Let's get the guys out here for another briefing. We need a new game plan."

CHAPTER NINE

When she refused to take Seth to the shelter, Phoebe thought they'd go someplace else with amenities like water and heat. She certainly hadn't expected to climb into the skeleton of a building in a deserted, bombed-out portion of Kabul.

"What are we doing?"

"Nobody will look for us here." Seth held out a hand to help her over a pile of rubble. She hated accepting anything from him, but she was in pain and still shaking from her earlier brush with death and she didn't trust her footing.

A skinny stray dog with feral eyes lifted its head and growled as they passed. She shivered. "Looks like nobody has lived on this street in years."

"That's the point." He shot her a narrowed-eyed look over his shoulder. "We lost the shooter, but I need to make sure he doesn't have some sort of tracker on you before I take you back to my team. If he comes looking for you here, I'll know he's got you tagged because he has no reason to be here otherwise."

They climbed another rubble pile and entered a room that appeared to have once been a living area, with tattered tapestries still covering the mostly intact walls. Seth crossed to the street-facing wall, which sported a giant hole. He checked the street, watching for a long time. He didn't seem inclined to talk, so she kept her mouth shut.

Talking to him was dangerous anyway. She couldn't let her guard down or he might find out…things…she'd rather he not know. Like that she'd used his personal tragedy to further her career.

Finally, his posture relaxed and he sat on a chunk of concrete. He searched his pockets for something. "Fuck. My phone's gone."

Phoebe sank down the wall until her butt hit the dusty floor, suddenly too tired to remain standing. "I don't have one either."

"Then what do you have in that bag?"

She pulled the bag around in front of her and lifted the flap. "Just my camera. I don't even have my wallet or passport with me."

"Of course you'd have a camera," he said, censure thick in his voice. "Don't even think about taking my picture."

She winced. "You really hate that I'm a journalist, don't you?"

"I have no love for the media."

Right. After everything he'd gone through—everything *she'd* put him through—who could blame him for that? Guilt tightened her throat, all but strangling her, and she opened her mouth to say—what? "I'm sorry" wasn't going to cut it. "It's all my fault" would probably be a good place to start, but what if she confessed and he left her here, alone? She really didn't want to be alone in a strange place when there were men with guns chasing her. So instead, she leaned her head back and shut her eyes. "Zina's going to worry about me."

"Zina?"

"A friend. The shelter's founder, Zina Ojanpura."

Seth made a sound of disapproval. "That's going to get you

in trouble."

Her eyes popped open and she squinted through the darkness at him. "What is?"

"You're too open. You didn't have to volunteer all that information. You could have just left it at 'friend.' Instead, you told me her name and her occupation. Now if I wanted, I could track down Zina Ojanpura and the shelter. If I was a bad guy, I could do a lot more."

"You're not a bad guy." A bad guy would have saved his own neck at the market. A bad guy would have left her to fend for herself when she fell at that crossroads, and she had a feeling Seth would have stayed with her even if she'd made the decision to run in the opposite direction.

"Just crazy, huh?" he said with a hint of self-deprecation coloring his tone.

She let go a nervous laugh. "Well, no, but—"

"It's okay. I know what I am." He pushed to his feet again. "Let me see your arm."

Phoebe recoiled. "It's fine."

A penlight switched on, illuminating his face before he flicked the small beam over her arm. With his brows drawn together and lips flattened in a grim line, he looked...concerned. "You're still bleeding."

"Only a little."

He stood still for a second, then doused the light. She sensed movement in the darkness, heard clothing rustling. Her imagination filled in the blanks. He had a hard body, but not as bulky as it had been in the pictures she'd seen of him when he was a Marine. She pictured lean muscles flexing as he pulled the sweatshirt off over his head.

Good God, she found that mental image far more appealing than she had any right to. Even though it was all in her head, she lowered her gaze to her lap. The fluttery sensation in her belly wasn't a tingle of sexual awareness. Nope, not at all. It was hunger. For food. She hadn't eaten since breakfast, after all.

The penlight came on again and she found his boots planted directly in front of her. She took in the long lines of his legs, his narrow hips, and the definite outline of his penis at the front of his pants. Not aroused, just…there. And large.

He shifted his weight on his feet.

Shit. She was gaping at his crotch, wasn't she? Heat rushed into her face as she struggled to find something — anything — else to look at. Problem was, with the penlight offering only a meager beam, he was all she could see. At least he still wore his sweatshirt, thank God. In his hand was a white T-shirt that he must have been wearing underneath.

Either he didn't notice her blatant perusal of his body or he chose to ignore it. He knelt in front of her and got to work ripping a strip of fabric from the shirt. When he reached for her wounded arm, she again flinched away.

"Phoebe." Exasperation colored his voice. "I'm not going to hurt you."

Oh, she knew that, but she wasn't about to let him do something as intimate as bandage her wounds. While he wouldn't hurt her, she would most definitely end up hurting him.

She snagged the fabric from his hand. "Thanks, but I can do it."

"Yeah? How do you plan on tying it?"

Without missing a beat, she one-handedly looped the strip around her arm, fashioned a loose knot, then gripped the end with her teeth and tightened it.

His brows lifted in surprise. "Okay. Didn't expect that."

"Girl Scout," she admitted. "I'm not a completely helpless damsel in distress."

"And I never attacked your abilities to take care of yourself. Your honesty, yes. Abilities, no." Shutting off the light, he picked his way back to his seat and settled into silence. Minutes ticked by.

"I'm not hiding anything," she blurted. At least nothing he thought she was hiding.

And there was that guilt again, chewing at the back of her conscience.

"Your eyes say otherwise," he said after a yawn. "But I do believe you have nothing to do with the men at the market. They were after you, not us. It just appeared they were following us because you were."

"Why would they follow me? I was grocery shopping."

"Obviously, you pissed someone off." Another yawn, and his voice took on a drowsy mumble in the darkness. "Someone with enough power to make you conveniently disappear."

She started to protest, but her mouth went dry. Tehani's husband. She'd suspected all along he was a man with power. Could he have found out about her attempts to discover his identity? Her blood clotted with ice. She knew what the man was capable of, and the idea he could be after her made her very glad she wasn't alone right now.

"Seth?"

No answer.

She squinted toward him, making out his slack features in the pale moonlight streaming in from a hole in the ceiling. His chin rested on his chest and his hand hung limply off the edge of his concrete seat. He breathed slow, steady.

Out cold.

Shivering, Phoebe hugged herself, careful not to jar her injured arm, and settled in to wait the night out.

• • •

Jahangir Siddiqui hated the necessity for this trip, hated returning to the mountains that had bred him. It was a desolate place, full of memories of the dead, and coming back to it after all these years still settled a weight in his stomach.

In the driver's seat, Askar, his soldier, ended a call on a satellite phone and glanced in the rearview mirror. "Sir, the men have checked in from the market."

Finally, some good news.

Since leaving the comfort of his city home, he'd been so wrapped up in a sick sense of nostalgia, he'd almost forgotten about the American journalist, Phoebe Leighton, who had been asking far too many of the wrong questions of the wrong people. When one of his loyal soldiers in the Ministry of Women's Affairs contacted him this morning to say she claimed to have photographic evidence linking a public official to the rash of suicide bombs, he'd decided it was time to dispose of her. The men he'd sent to follow her had orders to kill or capture—he didn't particularly care one way or another.

"Is she alive?" he asked.

"Yes."

The news shot a thrill of power through him and he hardened in response. So maybe he did care, after all. "Good. Have them take her to my home in Kabul. I'll deal with her myself."

Askar remained silent. Too silent.

The sexual buzz faded and his blood pressure inched skyward. He sat forward in his seat. "They *did* capture her."

A statement, but Askar answered as if he'd asked a question. "No, sir. Two American men intervened."

Siddiqui leaned back again and rubbed a hand over his beard. A hard bump in the road made him glance out the window at the sheer drop into the valley below, mere inches from the vehicle's tire. The height didn't bother him. He'd grown up in these mountains, had cut his teeth on this rugged terrain. What bothered him was that beyond the valley, the mountains pointed toward the sky like giant white breasts. He thought he could see the scar of dead land on the far side that used to be a village. *His* village. His hands began to tremble and he closed his fingers into a fist.

Fucking Americans.

Askar glanced in the mirror again, his features still completely impassive. "The men did, however, find Fahim."

"Ah." Siddiqui shook out his hands and made himself turn from the window, some of his anger dissolving. "The traitor's friend. I assume he's been dispatched for his lies."

"He's dead," Askar confirmed without a flicker of any kind of emotion in his black eyes.

"I wonder how Zakir will feel about that. I want to speak to him first thing."

"Yes, sir."

Up ahead, the road dead-ended in a mud wall and dented metal gate. The compound. He sighed as the gate swung open. It did his heart good to know he now had possession of the same American outpost that had ordered the attack on his village ten years ago.

Once inside the courtyard, Askar shut off the vehicle's ignition, but didn't move from his seat.

Siddiqui paused before opening his door. "Is there something else?"

"Niazi Village. Do you still want them punished?"

He paused and took several seconds to consider it, since decisions made in haste rarely turned out well. Niazi Village sat on a spit of rocky land that wasn't even good for poppy farming. Its only value lay in the stopover it provided for his drug runners en route to and from Pakistan, which was the only reason he bothered to claim it under his protection. However, the villagers negated that protection when they hid his wife from him.

"Yes," he finally answered. "And it must look like the Americans did it." He needed a sufficient reason to initiate a war when he was elected in a few months, and there was none better than the deaths of peaceful, innocent mountain people. "You can make that happen, yes?"

"Yes, sir." Askar pushed open the door and grabbed his rifle from the passenger seat. He circled the car and opened Siddiqui's door.

The sounds of struggle caught Siddiqui's attention from the other side of the main building. And then came the screams of pain. He strode through the courtyard toward the noise, Askar following in his shadow, and found Zakir Rossoul stripped bare, hands and feet tied spread-eagle to a set of posts. The men took turns slapping a cane across their prisoner's backside and each lash brought about another anguished cry from his parched lips.

"Has he talked yet?" Siddiqui asked as he watched the spectacle.

"No," Askar said.

"I suppose that means we're not trying hard enough." He watched the torture for a moment longer. "Who do you think he is, Askar? Who do you think sent him? The Americans?"

"If so, he's very good. He hasn't said a word of English."

"Maybe he belongs to one of my competitors then. We need him to start talking." He stepped forward. "Enough."

His men backed away, heads bowed. One offered him the cane. He took hold of it and strolled over to Zakir Rossoul. The traitor. The liar. The thief. The infidel who posed as a righteous man.

Using the tip of the cane, he lifted the prisoner's chin. "Are you ready to tell me who sent you to spy on me?"

Zakir's head rolled toward his shoulder as if his neck was too weak to hold it up. His bloodshot brown eyes were bleary but still defiant, and he spit in Siddiqui's direction. Or he tried to, but his mouth was too dry and he only made a pathetic *pfft* sound. Still, that kind of behavior would not be tolerated. Siddiqui jabbed the cane into his stomach and his knees gave out. His body swung forward, catching on his bound arms.

Siddiqui gripped his chin and forced his head up. "Your friend Fahim spoke so highly of you when we first met. He assured me you were a righteous man, a soldier ready to die to see Afghanistan rise from the ashes and take back the power the West has stolen from us. Fahim has paid for his lies."

Zakir winced, but said nothing.

Stepping back, Siddiqui wiped his hand on his tunic and fixed a contemplative expression on his face. "Askar, didn't Fahim have a family?"

"Yes, sir. A wife and two young daughters."

"We should send them our condolences."

Zakir jerked against his bonds. "No!"

Patience frayed, Siddiqui jabbed his prisoner with the cane again. "Then tell me who sent you!"

Zakir stayed silent.

With a shake of his head, he turned away from the pathetic excuse of a man. "I've seen enough here." His helicopter was waiting to take him back to civilization and he planned to be on it in the next fifteen minutes. "Askar, I want you to stay and manage this interrogation. And send some men to kill Fahim's family."

Askar trailed him back to the car like the loyal dog he was. "Would you like me to kill Zakir as well? We could record his execution, stir up the masses."

Siddiqui grinned, pride filling his chest. Askar was stone-cold and unapologetic about it. The perfect soldier. "No. Not yet.

Sooner or later, he *will* talk."

"And if he doesn't?"

"If he doesn't..." Siddiqui stopped before climbing into the driver's seat and looked to the south, where Niazi Village sat, quiet and unassuming. He smiled. "Then he'll die with the villagers who helped him steal my wife."

CHAPTER TEN

Phoebe jerked awake to screams, the bloodcurdling sound of a man suffering the most horrible atrocities imaginable. She didn't remember falling asleep and at first her unfamiliar surroundings sent panic skittering over her skin. She sat up, cold to the center of her being, her injured arm stiff and protesting any kind of movement. Soft early-morning light filtered through the hole in the wall, burnishing dusty motes as Seth thrashed so hard he fell off the concrete block he'd been sitting on. But instead of waking him, the jarring impact only increased his struggles.

Phoebe leaped to her feet and started toward him, but thought better of it when her shadow fell over his face and he started screaming again. She jumped away from his swinging arm, heart lodged in her throat. She'd once heard it wasn't good to wake someone up in the middle of a night terror, and honestly, the idea of getting close enough to touch him right now tightened her chest until she had trouble drawing in a breath. But dear God, he was suffering. His handsome face contorted in very real pain as he relived something nobody should ever have to live through once.

How could she stand back and do nothing?

She eased forward. "Seth?"

He screamed.

Forget caution. Sucking in a fortifying breath, she knelt beside him, wrapped her arms tight around his bucking torso, and just held him. His heart sounded like it was about to explode underneath her ear and each jerk of his body sent pain through her wounded arm. Tears blurred her vision, but she held on, whispering a litany of comforts. Meaningless, but all she could think to do. "Shh. It's okay, Seth. You're safe now."

He stilled.

She kept talking. "It's all right. Wake up and look at me. You're safe."

Slowly, his eyes opened against the morning light and darted around the room. His breaths came in ragged pants and his face was bone white, coated in a thin sheet of sweat.

"See? You're safe now." He seemed to be holding his breath, so she added, "Breathe. It's okay. Open up your lungs and breathe."

He exhaled hard and the strain went out of his muscles.

"There you go. Breathe through it."

He lifted his hand, the tips of his fingers lightly brushing her cheek before he caught himself. Cursing under his breath, he rolled away from her and climbed to his feet. With dirt smeared on his clothes and face, and his eyes showing too much white, he looked like a feral creature from long ago, more animal than human.

She wanted to comfort him, but when she reached out, he shied away.

"Don't touch me," he said in a strangled voice that didn't sound like his own. He held up a hand as if to ward her off.

"Okay. I'm sorry." Phoebe wrapped her arms around herself. Blood seeped from her reopened bullet wound, making her shirt stick to her arm. She ignored it. "You had a nightmare."

"I fucking know that."

She recoiled at the venom in his tone. "Are…you okay?"

He laughed, but it was a nasty sound. "I'll never be okay again."

Oh, damn. Heat stung her cheeks. "I'm sorry," she repeated because she didn't know what else to say.

His gaze snapped to hers and she thought she saw a hint of softening in the icy blue. At least his eyes didn't belong to a wild animal anymore.

"No." Sighing, he rubbed the back of his neck. "It was a legit, polite question you ask a person who has woken up from a bad nightmare," he said, almost as if reminding himself of the fact. "I'm just a bastard who doesn't know how to carry on a civil conversation anymore. I apologize."

"Don't." She wasn't fully aware of speaking the word aloud until he swung around and faced her again. "I mean, you don't have to apologize for anything."

His features darkened. "And you don't have to give me any special treatment just because you know my sob story. If I'm being an asshole, tell me. It's the only way I'll—" He stopped short and edged past her. "We need to get moving."

She wasn't quite sure what made her reach out and catch his hand, but his whole body went rigid. She drew away and clasped her hands together, lest she keep finding ways to touch him. "It's the only way you'll…?"

Seth stared for a long moment, his eyes sweeping over every inch of her face like he was trying to figure her out. Or memorize her features—especially her mouth, which he focused on for a beat longer than necessary before looking away. She moistened her suddenly dry lips.

"Seth? It's the only way you'll…what?" She could only see his profile, gilded by the morning rays. Despite myriad scars, he had a surprisingly pretty face. No other word for it, with those long dark lashes and big blue eyes that probably got him out of all kinds of mischief when he was a boy.

His throat worked. "It's the only way I'll learn to be human again."

He walked away, leaving her to gape after him in stunned silence. Did he really believe he wasn't human anymore? Yes, he'd lived through the unimaginable, and going by his screams while in the grip of the nightmare, she didn't want to imagine it. And, yes, he was ragged around the edges, a walking open wound with psych issues galore. But he still had a beating heart. Thoughts, feelings, fears. He was still human, and someone should prove it to him.

She took two steps in the direction he'd disappeared before catching herself. No. It wasn't her job to help him. As Zina often pointed out, she couldn't save everyone, as much as she wished otherwise. And after what she'd done to Seth, it'd be foolish to even try.

Distance. She had to keep her distance.

Hardening her heart against the need to fix him, she grabbed her bag, climbed over the pile of rubble, and met him on the abandoned street below. Ruins of other bombed-out buildings similar to their hideout cast forlorn shadows across the pitted road and it seemed there was not another living soul for miles. Amazingly, this ghost town existed within the bustling city limits of Kabul—a sad reminder of the wars that had ravaged the country for too many years.

"It's beautiful in a sad, haunting kind of way, isn't it?" She took out her camera and captured a few shots of the hopeful pink rays of morning sunlight playing through the destruction. She couldn't wait to get these pictures into Photoshop. She'd desaturate the crumbling buildings and bring out the reds in the light, varying the shades from pink to orange…

Seth grunted.

She glanced away from her viewfinder. "You don't think so?"

"No."

She studied their surroundings again. He was wrong. The ghost town possessed the same kind of beauty as a desert. Desolate, ravaged by the elements, and awe-inspiring. "How can you look at this place and not see it?"

"I see war. Destruction. Death."

"Of course. But underneath all that…"

"No. There's nothing in this country I find beautiful."

"Nothing?" She turned to find his gaze fastened on her, hot as a caress, and her belly jittered with a nervous kind of excitement. He really did have the most gorgeous eyes, the same intense color of a cloudless Caribbean sky in the middle of summer.

But then he noticed her arm and winced, breaking the intensity of the moment. She'd forgotten about the bullet wound, but now that he'd drawn her attention to it, she became acutely aware of the throbbing pain. She was also bleeding again.

He started walking. "Let's go."

"Where?"

"Somewhere I can get in contact with my team."

His strides were long, filled with purpose, and she struggled to keep up. "Your team? You're still in the military then?" She couldn't see how that was possible, though. Sure, she didn't know much about how the military functioned, but she was certain they wouldn't allow a man with Seth's history to rejoin.

"No," he said and seemed to be making a conscious effort not to look at her.

"So you're a mercenary. Or, wait, I believe the preferred term is private military contractor?" His lip didn't even twitch toward a smile like she'd hoped. She huffed out a breath in exasperation.

"Where's your team?"

"No idea. I doubt they're still in the same place, which is why I need to contact them."

"Great." Her stomach let out an embarrassingly loud grumble. "Well, can we at least get some food first? I haven't eaten since breakfast yesterday."

He stopped moving and blinked at her like she had spoken in ancient Greek. "Food?"

"Didn't even cross your mind, did it?"

"No." His shoulders hunched, curling toward his center, giving her a glimpse of the tortured soul she'd seen during the nightmare. Then he straightened to his full height again. "I don't enjoy eating anymore, so no, I didn't think of it. I'm sorry."

He didn't enjoy eating? How was that possible? Everyone—every*thing* with a pulse liked food. And if he didn't eat, what did he survive on?

Her slack-jawed expression must have broadcast her thoughts because he said, "Protein shakes, mostly. And I do eat. I just don't like it."

"But…why not?"

He shrugged and started walking again. "I don't have any Afghan money, but we'll find something for you."

Okay, so he wasn't going to answer. Fair enough. They were practically strangers, after all. He didn't have to tell her anything. And besides, she was supposed to be keeping him at a distance, not getting to know him better. That path only led to trouble. As it was, every time he looked at her, she was terrified he'd see through her, would somehow know the horrible things she'd done.

So distance was good.

She wrapped her arms around herself, feeling the cold again for the first time since she woke up. Despite all logic to the contrary, it still stung that he wouldn't confide in her. Which, yes, she knew was a completely ridiculous way to feel, but there it was.

Her stomach growled again.

God, she was starving. And cold. And her arm stung like hell.

"Am I still your prisoner?" she called after him.

Seth's breathing hitched and he halted as if he'd slammed into an invisible wall. When he whirled to face her, his complexion drained of color. "You're *not* a prisoner."

He looked so stricken, Phoebe silently cursed herself. She was trained as a journalist and although she dealt primary in photography now, she should still have enough command of the English language to keep from sending the poor man into a panic attack.

C'mon, girl, what's with the verbal diarrhea? Get your act together.

Since acknowledging his panic would probably only embarrass him, she shrugged it off and strode past him like nothing happened. "Then follow me. I'll take you to the shelter."

He hesitated. She imagined he was taking the moment to regain his bearings, but soon enough, he was at her side again, silent and stone-faced. With his scars and that carefully blank expression, he looked downright menacing.

Crap. Zina was going to be so pissed.

CHAPTER ELEVEN

Oh boy, had she ever been wrong. "Pissed" didn't even begin to cover it.

Phoebe had never seen the usually mild-mannered woman so livid and honestly, it was a bit frightening. Zina may have looked like a runway model but she sounded more like a lioness protecting her cubs. In a tone that dared Seth to argue, she ordered him to give her his team's contact info and stay in the courtyard. Then, with a fuming glare at Phoebe, she stormed inside. She didn't slam the front door—that would be too undignified and would scare her girls—but the soft *click* of it closing behind her was somehow even worse.

Phoebe bit her lip and glanced over at Seth, who had borne the gale force of Zina's rage without so much as a blink. "I'm sorry. I knew she'd be angry, but I thought she'd take it out on me."

He nodded. His jaw was clenched so tightly she swore she heard his back teeth grind—but not out of anger. A fine sheen of sweat glistened on his skin despite the chilly day and his hands trembled at his sides.

Good God, he was terrified and trying not to show it. Had

Zina's tirade brought on another flashback?

She wanted to reach out, entwine her fingers through his, let him know he had nothing to fear. No, dammit. She was supposed to be keeping her distance. For both their sakes.

She hurried toward the front door. "I'll talk to her."

She didn't wait for a reaction and ducked inside. Pausing in the foyer, she leaned against the cool wood of the door and swore under her breath. Keeping her distance was going to be harder than she thought. Seth Harlan had stolen a small piece of her heart two years ago when he stoically withstood the public lashing caused by her article, and she didn't want distance. She wanted to help him. Wanted to make up for the pain she'd caused him.

"Is he an American soldier?" a voice asked in Pashto.

Surprised, Phoebe pushed away from the door and spotted Tehani Niazi coming down the stairs. "Who?" she asked, even though she knew exactly who.

"I was watching from the window," Tehani admitted. "He looks like a soldier."

"He's…" How to explain the difference between Seth and the type of soldier Tehani meant? She didn't think she knew enough of the language to do so, in any case. "Yes. Yes, he is."

Tehani crossed the foyer to stand in front of Phoebe, her hands tucked behind her back. "Can you take me to see him?"

"Oh." She winced, imagining Zina's reaction. No, thank you. "I don't think that's a good idea."

But Tehani wasn't deterred. She lifted her chin, showing a glimpse of the stubborn streak that ran through her core. "I have something I *need* to give him."

Phoebe reached out and straightened Tehani's slipping head scarf. Such a strong, brave, determined girl. It was impossible not to love her. "All right. I'll introduce you to him, but let's keep it a secret, okay?"

Tehani nodded.

Phoebe started to open the door, but then thought better of taking an Afghan to meet a traumatized former Marine without first knowing what the girl meant to give him. Last thing he needed after facing Zina was to be surprised.

"Tehani," she said, pulling the girl's gaze away from the door. "First, can you show me what have for him?"

Tehani produced a battered folder from behind her back and held it out. Phoebe recognized it as the same one she'd carried with her few belongings from her village. She'd been so protective of it she hadn't wanted anyone to even touch it. That the girl now trusted her enough to let her see inside made Phoebe's eyes burn with suppressed emotion.

"Thank you." She opened the ragged cover and her chest seized. "Oh my God. Where did you get this?"

"Zakir gave it to me. He told me I had to give it to an American soldier. He said it was very important."

Phoebe leafed through the pages, then started at the beginning again and read more carefully to make sure she was actually seeing what she thought. No, she wasn't delusional. This was indeed a military report on at least two dozen arms deals and several suicide bombers, including the unidentified woman who attempted to bomb the American embassy three weeks ago. Dates, names, and places—all written by a precise hand and sometimes accompanied by photographs. And one particular name all but leaped off the page and smacked her in the face.

Jahangir Siddiqui.

The front-runner in Afghanistan's upcoming presidential election.

Holy. Shit.

• • •

Seth released a breath and consciously made himself relax as the door shut behind Phoebe. He shook out his hands, worked his jaw. He couldn't say what it was about the encounter that had bothered him. It wasn't that he thought Zina could hurt him, wasn't even that she was angry at him for disrupting the shelter's peaceful existence. She had every right to her anger.

Still, it had thrown him back into a very dark place. And now that he could think straight, that really pissed him off. What had happened to all of his fucking progress?

The shelter's front door flew open and Phoebe sprinted toward him with a girl on her heels. She didn't say anything when she reached him—just shoved an open folder into his hands and, wide-eyed, jabbed a finger at the pages.

"What?"

She gasped in a great exhale as if she'd been holding her breath. "Jahangir Siddiqui is Tehani's husband."

He tried to read the first page in the folder, but she was still jabbing at it wildly. "Okay. Who's Tehani?"

"I am," the girl said in Pashto.

He caught Phoebe's hand before she put a finger through the paper in her excitement. "This girl is Siddiqui's wife?"

"Yes, and he's behind the rash of suicide bombings. Look. He's using his wives. And look. He's buying arms, making bombs." She poked the papers again. "And we have proof! We need to tell someone. We need to stop him."

"No."

Her mouth snapped shut. "No?"

"No," he repeated. "Not yet, at least. It's too dangerous. Where did you get this information?" It read like a highly classified military report.

"Zakir gave it to me," Tehani said.

A little thrill curled in Seth's gut. "Zakir who?"

"Zakir Rossoul." She frowned in thought. "But I don't think that's his real name. I heard him talking on his radio in English when he helped me escape and he called himself…" She hesitated. "Sergeant Zak Hendricks."

Jackpot.

Seth closed the folder. "We need to get my team here right now."

"Wait," Tehani said and reached into the pocket of her dress.

Seth couldn't help the automatic tightening of his shoulders. Goddammit, this girl meant him no harm. He needed to stop jumping at shadows or he was going to make a mistake. And a mistake in this country meant death.

The girl held out her hand, a small flash drive in her palm. "Zakir told me it was very important I give this to an American soldier because my husband is trying to buy a nuclear bomb."

It took him a second to translate that last part and he looked at Phoebe for confirmation. "Did she just say nuclear bomb?"

"Yes," Phoebe breathed. "She did."

CHAPTER TWELVE

This was Seth's team, the men he was supposed to trust to watch his back?

They weren't what Phoebe expected. While the seven men filed into the courtyard, Zina ushered Tehani back inside before returning to stand guard by the gate like a mama bear. All of the men radiated varying degrees of disapproval as they passed Seth. One guy in a cowboy hat looked on with that assessing gaze doctors used while reading an X-ray, as if Seth were a broken bone that needed to be set. Another man with brutally short hair and a lean, mean face sneered like a high school bully in sight of middle school prey and, sure enough, he started right in with the taunting as soon as he cleared the front gate. "Hey, Hero. Thought you ran home crying."

Seth bore the ridicule in stoic silence and none of the others said anything to shut the bully up—not even the scowling man with the cane who appeared to be in charge of the motley bunch.

How could he put any trust in these men when they obviously didn't respect him? Didn't they realize he already thought of himself as subhuman and their coolness toward him only served to reinforce that belief?

No, probably not. They were men, after all. And this looked to be a power struggle that Seth had no hope of winning.

Phoebe ached for him.

Head held high, Seth positioned himself in front of the man with the cane like a prisoner facing off with his executioner. "Gabe, I have a lead on Hendricks."

"You're so good, you can do all of our jobs now, is that it, Hero?" the mean one sneered.

"Okay, Reinhardt," Seth said. "You want to share what *you* found out about Sergeant Hendricks first?" He waited a beat. When the only reply he got from the other man was a muscle twitch, he added, "Is that a no? Then fuck off and let me talk."

Way to go, Seth. Phoebe gave him a mental high five even as a little piece of her heart broke. She'd done this to him, made him an outcast among the very men who should be his support network. God, if only she could go back in time and tell her stupid younger self to burn that article because the notoriety she was going to get wasn't worth destroying a man's life.

Seth handed the folder and flash drive to his commander. "If this is correct, and they haven't moved Sergeant Hendricks yet, then he's probably being held at an old American outpost in the mountains."

The man with the cane—Gabe—opened the folder and his face turned to stone. "Where did you get this?"

"All right," Zina said, still standing by the front gate, holding it open. "You have your man. Now I'd appreciate it if you left."

Gabe faced her. "Where did this information come from?"

"A girl here at the shelter gave it to me," Seth answered. "She's Siddiqui's wife and she claims Zak Hendricks helped her escape the compound before he was captured. He could still be there."

Gabe nodded and turned to Zina. "You need to let me talk to this girl."

Zina crossed her arms over her chest. Her glare would have skinned a lesser man. "No. And who the hell do you think you are, coming onto my property and telling me what I *need* to do?"

"I'm sorry, ma'am," he said, but if he meant it, the sentiment didn't show on his chiseled face. "My name is Gabe Bristow. And you are?"

"Zina Ojanpura. I run this shelter."

"Ms. Ojanpura, I command a privately funded hostage rescue team and we've been hired to bring Zak Hendricks home. One of your girls knows where he is. We need her help to find him."

"No," she said firmly and let go of the gate. It fell shut with a *clank*. "If what you say is true and Tehani knows something about this missing man, then we'll take it to the proper authorities."

"With all due respect, the proper authorities in this country don't give a shit about a missing American. In fact, we're pretty sure those so-called *proper* authorities are the reason he's a hostage."

Zina shut her eyes and breathed out in a long, slow exhale. "I understand that and I wish I could help, but I can't risk the girls like that. I'm all they have, and they've been through enough. So I'm afraid the best I can do is take the information to the embassy."

Gabe nodded. "It's the right thing to do, but he still won't see freedom again anytime soon. The embassy won't act on your information right away. They'll sit on it, weighing the pros and cons of action, until something or someone finally forces their hand." His gaze shifted briefly to Seth. "Which can take months."

"Sometimes more," Seth confirmed softly. "And a month in enemy hands is a lifetime."

So what had fifteen months felt like for him? Phoebe shuddered to imagine.

Zina bit her lower lip. "I can't get involved. I can't risk reprisal from one of the local terrorist factions."

"I understand that," Gabe said, "but who is looking after Zak Hendricks's safety? There's only us."

Zina faltered, visibly torn between wanting to help and knowing she shouldn't take the risk. At last, her shoulders straightened. "I'm sorry. I can't help you."

"I can," Phoebe said into the following silence.

Seth's eyes cut to her, a clear warning, though she didn't know why he cared. She ignored him. "Tehani once mentioned that the compound she escaped from is only a few miles farther up the mountain from her village. I took pictures of the surrounding area as we left."

Gabe considered her. Damn, the man was intimidating even when she got the feeling he was trying to dial it back. "Who are you?"

"Phoebe. Phoebe Leighton. I'm a freelance photojournalist." She held out a hand and prayed he didn't see how nervous he made her. "I focus on human interest stories—women's rights mostly, which is why I was at the village with Zina. I'm working on a photo-essay about child brides."

"Okay," Gabe said. He had a strong grip and his hand all but engulfed hers. "Phoebe. Did you have contact with Hendricks?"

"No. Neither of us did. We're only now just hearing about him from Tehani. She hasn't said a word about this since she got here. I think she was too afraid of her husband to talk to anyone but an American soldier. She was adamant it had to be an American soldier, so when she saw Seth..." She shrugged. "And you know the rest. Here you guys are."

Finally, a softening showed in the big guy's features. "Can you protect the girl?" he asked Zina.

"We do our best," Zina said.

"Do you ever face retaliation?"

"If her husband found out we were keeping her from him? Yes, he'd come after the shelter," Zina answered with a calmness that belied the constant state of worry Phoebe knew she lived in. "And I can't count on the government to protect us like they're supposed to. Men like Jahangir Siddiqui have deep pockets and use them to pay off as many government officials as possible. The key to keeping Tehani safe is to make sure he doesn't find out she's here. Now do you see why I can't risk involvement with your mission?"

"Yeah, I get it. But that doesn't negate the fact that my team and I still have a job to do." He rubbed a hand over his face and for the first time, Phoebe realized how exhausted the entire lot of them looked. They were all bleary-eyed and sluggish, and if they tried to go up against someone like Siddiqui now, they'd get themselves killed.

"Listen," Gabe said, "I know you want us gone."

Crossing her arms over her chest, Zina nodded.

"And I understand, but I have a proposition for you. Our local contact has been compromised and we don't have a safe place to work from."

Ah, that explained why they looked like a casting call for a zombie movie.

"So," Gabe continued, "if you let my men stay here long enough to plan our mission, I'll make sure your shelter receives a sizable donation."

Zina's eyes narrowed. "From…?"

"Does it matter?"

"It does if it's blood money. I know your intentions are noble, Mr. Bristow. However, no matter how you and your team bill yourselves, you're still mercenaries."

"We only rescue people. That's all we do."

"And turn a profit while doing it?" Zina challenged, but Gabe was undaunted.

"No, not really," he admitted. "We're completely funded by our parent company, HumInt, Inc., which is a subsidiary of Quentin Enterprises. I'm sure even over here, you've heard of Tucker Quentin."

Phoebe laughed. "Who hasn't?"

Zina stared at her blankly.

"Oookay, apparently *you* haven't. Where have you been for the last ten years, Zee? Mars?"

Zina sniffed. "Busy. Who is he and why should I care?"

Phoebe took a second to call up details about the man from her memory. During her stint as a tabloid writer, she'd written plenty of stories about him and his troubled family life. "Tucker Quentin is the son of an action film star and a former model. He did some acting as a kid, but started getting in trouble early in his teens. He turned his life around in college, joined the military and had a short but illustrious career as an Army Ranger. When he left the military, he started his first business and is now a gazillionaire with eyes on a political career."

"Okay, Ms. Tabloid," Zina said with a roll of her eyes.

Heat bloomed across Phoebe's cheeks and she very carefully avoided Seth's gaze. If she looked at him now, she was liable to blurt out that she'd also written unflattering stories about *him* for that same magazine. "I, uh, assume when Gabe says 'donation' he means it's coming from Quentin." She glanced to Gabe for confirmation.

"I do," he agreed. "Tuc has set aside a hefty expense account for my team, which I'm able to put to use at my discretion."

"For bribes?"

Ah, that was Zina. Always suspicious. But given the current state of the country she'd adopted as her own, a little suspicion was healthy. Expected, even.

"For expenses," Gabe corrected. "Which, I'm not going to lie to you, can sometimes include bribes. But that's not the case here. This arrangement will be more like a donation as thanks for lodging—with the added bonus of a built-in protection force. We'll provide security for the shelter as long as we're in-country."

"How much of a *donation* are we talking about?"

"Let's say…" His gaze traveled over to the shelter, traced the side of the building. No doubt those sharp hazel eyes noticed the sagging roof and chipping, sun-faded mud walls, and he had to know if he priced it right, Zina would be helpless to say no. "A hundred thousand, American. That sound fair?"

"Oh my God." Zina actually swayed backward in shock like he'd dealt her a physical blow. "Oh…my God. How long will you need to stay?"

"Just a day to gather supplies and intel. We need to get up to that compound as fast as possible. Zak Hendricks is living on a very limited watch."

"It's an amazing deal, Zee." Phoebe couldn't believe she was hesitating. "Think of what you can do with that money. Hire the shelter a full-time security guard? Buy more books and clothes, new bedding? Medical care? Fix the roof?"

"Damn you," she said to Gabe and lifted a shaking hand to her temple. "You can stay if you pay the first half up front."

He nodded. "Fair enough."

"But if you bring danger to my doorstep, the deal's off. I don't care if you paid me a million dollars, understand?"

"Yes, ma'am." He motioned to the guys standing behind him. "Let me introduce you to the team. Zina, Phoebe, this is Quinn, my second-in-command."

A solemn looking man with short dark-blond hair nodded at them. "Ms. Ojanpura. Ms. Leighton."

Oh, so serious. Did he ever smile? From the hard line of his jaw, grim set of his mouth, and direct gray stare, Phoebe guessed not. Even so, he'd make a fantastic model and she itched to take his photo.

Gabe continued, "And Marcus, our hostage negotiator."

"Ladies." Marcus aimed a killer smile at both of them, and yet somehow, he made it seem like it was meant solely for her. She wondered if Zina felt the same way and glanced over. Nope. Zina was not impressed.

Nor was she impressed with the linguist, Jean-Luc—the blond man who had been with Seth at the market. He looked a little worse for wear, his face bruised, his lip split, but he still swept into a delightfully charming bow over Zina's hand.

Gabe went through the rest of the team. Jesse, a true and blue cowboy who apparently served as a medic. Ian, the scary dude with the constant sneer, who was their bomb expert—and why did that both terrify and not surprise Phoebe? He said nothing when he was introduced, which didn't break her heart. She'd seen the way he attacked Seth every time he opened his mouth and would rather not be on the receiving end of his bite.

Frowning at the thought, she glanced over at Seth. She'd rather he not be there either. He didn't deserve that kind of treatment after everything else he'd already survived.

Phoebe felt eyes on her and shifted to a find a young guy with glasses watching her. Crap. He'd caught her staring at Seth and he'd probably seen all kinds of emotions cross her face in that moment. But instead of making a deal of it, he pretended like he hadn't seen anything and turned on a wholesome grin when Gabe formally introduced him as Eric Physick, the tech specialist.

"Call me Harvard," he said and shook Zina's hand, lingering over hers for a moment longer than necessary.

Figures, Phoebe thought with an inward sigh. All the guys

falling for the pretty blonde. Cripes, it was high school all over again. Though she had to admit, if she were going to pick a guy for her friend, Harvard seemed like the better fit than Marcus or Jean-Luc. Obviously smart, a tad geeky judging by his COME TO THE NERD SIDE, WE HAVE PI T-shirt, and completely adorable. Hell, he was the kind of guy she'd pick for herself because she so wasn't into tall, broody, built-for-sex-and-fighting types.

She really wasn't.

She oh so casually slid a glance in Seth's direction and a jolt of awareness made her catch her breath. He was watching her and there was an indecipherable darkness in his eyes. Lust? Maybe anger? Or probably a mixture of both. He made eye contact without shame or apology. The same way, she imagined, he stared through a sniper scope before pulling the trigger. And she was his target.

Distance, she reminded herself as her pulse gave an unwelcome flutter. She had to keep her distance.

CHAPTER THIRTEEN

"Q, can I talk to you for a second?"

At Gabe's voice, Quinn straightened away from the satellite images laid out on the table and stretched. Winced. He'd been going over the images all morning with Harvard, trying to match them up with the photos Phoebe had provided of Niazi Village and the directions to the compound provided by Tehani. So far, no luck. There were just too many fucking mountains and they all looked the same.

Sitting still and concentrating on blurry images for so long had stiffened up his bad shoulder and given him a raging headache. He'd wanted to pop some of the pills his doctor had given him for the migraines, but he hadn't wanted Harvard to see it.

Yeah. He was regretting that decision now.

Gabe stood in the doorway of their makeshift war room and jerked his head in a *follow me* gesture.

Something was up.

He trailed Gabe into the hallway, through the building, and out into the backyard, away from where the guys were loading up the two SUVs he and Marcus had stolen yesterday. He bet if their host knew she had two hot vehicles sitting on her property, she'd kick them out, money or no.

The change from dim house to bright sunshine felt like needles stabbing through Quinn's retinas and he swallowed back a surge of nausea.

Gabe narrowed his eyes. "You okay?"

No. No, he wasn't okay. He hadn't been anywhere in the same postal code of okay since their car accident last year. "Yeah. Little dehydrated. What's up?"

"When we go into the mountains tomorrow, you're staying here at the shelter."

Oh fuck. Did Gabe know about the headaches, the blackouts? He scanned his best friend's features. Gabe was an inscrutable bastard on his best days, but he'd known the guy for so long, he usually had no problem picking out his tells.

But not this time.

Gabe's expression had closed down tight and not even a sliver of his thoughts crept through. If he knew about the blackouts, he'd straight-up say so, no pussyfooting around. That was Gabe's way. But if he didn't know, why leave Quinn behind on an op? Especially when he'd participated in several rescues in these very mountains while still a SEAL.

Goddammit, he wanted to argue. Wanted to rail against the shitty hand fate had dealt him. But what good would that do? Gabe would only think he'd lost his mind. Which, granted, wasn't all that far from the truth.

"Why?" he asked instead and every muscle in his body tightened in dread of the answer.

Gabe glanced toward the house. "A few reasons. If we all leave, the shelter will be vulnerable and protection was one of Zina's conditions for allowing us to stay here. I promised her we'd keep the shelter safe as long as we're in-country."

So this had nothing to do with his medical issues after all. Quinn told himself to relax and nodded. "Yeah, I wondered how we'd swing that."

"Someone has to stay behind and look after these girls."

"Understood." But he couldn't shake the sensation that Gabe was maneuvering him, tactfully keeping him out of the line of fire for some reason. Same this summer when Gabe had handed him the bodyguard assignment for a senator's family in El Paso, Texas—

Mara.

Quinn shut his eyes and pinched the bridge of his nose. If his skull wasn't already throbbing, he'd bang his head against the wall a couple times to shake loose the memory of that woman. Goddammit, he wasn't supposed to think about her anymore. It was one freakin' night.

Okay, true, his one-night stand with Senator Escareno's daughter hadn't been a shining moment of self-control on his part, but that was no reason for her to keep invading his thoughts.

But there she was. Shy smile. Big dark eyes. Curves like an old-time movie starlet. Soft black hair that had felt so fucking good between his fingers when he'd held her head still and took her tempting mouth with his...

No.

He forcefully shoved Mara Escareno out of his mind—he seemed to be doing that way too often lately—and refocused on the problem at hand. The shelter. Zak Hendricks. Siddiqui.

He opened his eyes. "You said you had a few reasons. What are the others?"

"Harvard," Gabe said. "He can't go up in those mountains."

Okay, definitely not the answer he'd expected to hear. "Whoa, back up. Harvard? If you'd have said Seth—well, I wouldn't like it, but yeah, I might have to agree with you. He's not handling this sitch as well as I had hoped he would. But Harvard?"

Gabe shook his head. "My gut tells me he's still too green. Hasn't gotten enough training under his belt yet and he's not ready for real combat. Besides, he's more useful to us on the computer."

"No doubt, but he's not gonna like getting left behind."

"And I don't like the idea of taking him home in a body bag. He's just a kid."

"He's no younger than we were on our first op," Quinn reminded him.

"And he hasn't gone through the kind of training we did."

"Got a point there." Despite their efforts over the last six months, the team was nowhere near where they wanted them to be training-wise. "I've said it before—we need to seriously consider buying a training facility."

"I know," Gabe said. "I've mentioned the possibility to Tuc, but a training facility's going to cost us millions and we need to hire a pilot first. Not to mention, we'd need to hire a staff for the facility. It's just not feasible right now."

Yeah, Quinn knew that. Still, it was frustrating. The guys all had potential to be excellent operators, if only they had the right training and equipment. But *if only* wasn't gonna get the job done now. "So," he said, getting back to the original topic, "if I'm staying here with Harvard, does that mean you plan on taking Seth with you?"

Gabe hissed out a breath through his teeth. "I should say no. All my reservations about him still stand, but I can't overlook his intimate knowledge of the enemy, either. As much as I'd prefer to leave him behind—hell, to ship him back to the States where he can get the psychiatric help he needs—part of me fears the information he has might draw the line between our success and failure."

"I still think you don't give him enough credit," Quinn said.

"Seth's a survivor. A fighter. When it hits the fan, he's gonna surprise you."

"I'll believe it when I see it," Gabe said, though his tone made it crystal clear he thought he'd see a flying pig first.

"Stubborn jackass," Quinn muttered.

"You're one to talk, asshole."

Out front, a peal of laughter split the air. A man's, low and rumbling, and one woman's, high and clear.

Gabe tilted his head toward the sound. "Any luck matching Phoebe's pictures up to the sat images?"

"Nope."

"Damn." Gabe dragged a hand over his face. "I'd much rather leave her behind. I don't want to run into another situation like with Audrey in Colombia."

Quinn snorted. "It better not be another Colombia. Audrey will castrate you if you come home with another wife."

Gabe punched him in the shoulder. His bad shoulder. Hard. It hurt like a bitch but somehow, it made him feel like all was right with the world.

"I was referring to Seth and Phoebe," Gabe said.

More laughter out front. A car door shut, and the voices faded. Apparently, the team was done loading and had gone inside. Which meant they had to cut this convo short and get in there for the pre-mission briefing.

"Yeah," Quinn said on a long exhale. "I've noticed it, too."

"Think I should be concerned about it interfering? I'm the first to admit I wasn't at my best in Colombia when Audrey knocked me for a loop. And I wasn't standing on shaky mental ground at the time, either."

Quinn gave the question some serious thought as he followed Gabe into the house. Gabe did have a point about the whole "knocked for a loop" thing, but at the same time...

They stopped outside the room they'd claimed as their base of operations and he noticed Seth sitting with his back to the corner, watching someone. After following the direction of his gaze, Quinn realized that someone was Phoebe. She sat beside him, flipping through a stack of photos, occasionally picking one out to show him.

Yeah. Something there all right. A spark. A sizzle. It was almost like watching Gabe and Audrey meet again for the first time.

"Hey, look." He elbowed Gabe in the side and motioned to the couple.

Gabe groaned. "It's worse than I thought."

"No," Quinn said, drawing the word out as he watched. "I don't think so. Look at him. He's...relaxed." Sure, his back was to the corner, but any operative worth his salt would choose the same position in the room. But Seth's shoulders weren't tensed up and he didn't appear to be ready to bolt at the first loud noise. His legs were bent, his arms resting casually on his knees, hands dangling until Phoebe pushed a photo toward him. He'd take it, study it, then hand it back. Sometimes he even murmured a comment.

But the biggest indicator he felt comfortable around her? The hood of his sweatshirt lay flat against his back, his head uncovered.

Quinn glanced over, watched all those same observations register on his best friend's face.

"Well, fucking A," Gabe muttered.

"Looks like she might keep him on an even keel."

"Fucking A," Gabe said again.

Quinn started forward, but Gabe caught his arm before he stepped into the room and pulled him back to the hall, out of earshot of the guys. "One more thing before we go in there."

"Yeah?"

Gabe ran his tongue along his teeth, seeming to weigh his words before speaking. "You read all of Hendricks's reports?"

"Yes, I did. Is there a reason we haven't briefed the men on that clusterfuck situation yet?"

"Because our focus needs to be one hundred percent on Sergeant Hendricks. The nuke…" He scrubbed a hand over his head and exhaled hard. "Frankly, we don't have enough manpower to handle something like that. We're a hostage rescue team, not an anti-terror unit."

Quinn nodded. "I completely agree, but what are we going to do about it? We can't let Siddiqui make that deal."

"I don't plan to, which brings me to the final reason you need to stay here. Our old team is at Bagram right now."

"Yeah, I'm not going to ask how you know that."

"Better not," Gabe said with a tight smile. "But it's good to know we have a sympathetic ear in this country. You can take Hendricks's information to Commander Bennett without telling him how we came into possession of it. Bennett should be able to put it in the right hands in time to stop the deal."

Quinn's stomach tightened uncomfortably at the mention of their former commander. He'd never cared for the guy on a personal level, but professionally, Bennett was a solid SEAL. So maybe it was only the idea of seeing the old team again. They had all been supportive since Quinn's medical retirement, but as time dragged on, they had drifted away. He hadn't been to Bagram since…well, since returning from the operation that rescued Seth. It promised to be an awkward reunion at best.

He nodded anyway. "I'll leave first thing in the morning."

CHAPTER FOURTEEN

"Oh, this one. Now there's an interesting story behind this one…"

Phoebe shoved another photo into his hand, but Seth couldn't tear his eyes from her to spare it more than the briefest of glances. And frankly, he didn't want to. Now that he wasn't chasing her down like a criminal and holding her prisoner—which he would never forgive himself for—she was so…vibrant. Animated. Full of joy and laughter.

His exact opposite in every way.

Her eyes sparkled as she talked about her photos and the stories behind them. A marriage ceremony in India. A Saudi woman in a burqa and high heels. A tiny girl from Nepal decked out in a red dress for her betrothal ceremony. She recalled the details of each photo with such vivid precision, he felt like he had been there with her, watching the events unfold.

"This one," she said and handed him another print. It showed the silhouette of a man tying a dog to a rusted-out tank. The setting sun lit the village behind him in a splash of pinks and oranges. "I took it right before we met Tehani. That's her village there."

"It's…" He couldn't find the right word to describe the photo.

"Breathtaking."

Her eyes lit up. "You think so? It's my favorite so far."

"Yeah. I mean, it's an amazing picture. You're very talented." And she had such a unique way of seeing the world, finding beauty and hope where there should be none. But that didn't mean she needed to go back up into those mountains.

He returned the photo to her. "You should stay behind."

She shook her head. "Not happening, so you can forget about trying to convince me. Tehani asked me to check on her family while we're there and I have no plans of disappointing her. Maybe I can even convince her sister-in-law to return to the shelter."

So much hope in her voice. How could one person contain that much optimism? Especially in a place as dark as this shithole of a country?

"Besides," she added, "it's not like I'm going all the way to the compound with you. I'll be safe in the village."

Movement at the door caught his attention, and his muscles instantly tightened out of pure reflex. He couldn't even recall the last time he didn't tense up at unexpected movement. Probably sometime before he'd left Bagram Airfield with his old team on his last fubar mission. A lifetime and a half ago, at least.

Gabe limped into the room, Quinn trailing in his wake. Shortly after, the rest of the team filed in, Harvard bringing up the rear with his ever-present laptop—the thing was like an extension of his body. He shut the door behind him and claustrophobia folded its clammy hands around Seth.

"Breathe," Phoebe reminded him softly.

Releasing the breath caught in his lungs, he pulled up the hood of his sweatshirt. He felt the guys' eyes on him and, shit, did they all know he used the hood like a security blanket? The back of his neck warmed. He pulled the hood off again and vowed to burn the sweatshirt at his first opportunity. From here on out, it was T-shirts, jackets. No more hoods to hide behind.

He wasn't a toddler in need of comfort, for fuck's sake.

Gabe broke the silence. "All right, gentlemen. Listen up. Here's how this op is going to work." He unfolded a large map and taped it up on the wall. "Phoebe, do you want to get us started with our itinerary?"

"Sure thing." She stood and uncapped the highlighter Harvard handed her as she walked toward the map. "Tomorrow morning, we'll drive as far as Asadabad in Kunar Province." She circled the city. "And that, unfortunately, is the end of the paved road. My fixer—"

"Fixer?" Marcus interrupted. "Sorry, but that sounds slightly illegal."

"Leave it to the former Fed," Ian muttered.

"Hey, lay off him," Jesse snapped. "At least he's got a conscience and not a black pit for a soul."

"Not illegal at all," Phoebe said, raising her voice only the slightest bit above the arguing. She handled them all with the grace and patience of a schoolteacher bringing an unruly class to order, and a sudden burst of pride caught Seth completely off guard.

"Fixer," she continued once she had silence again, "is journalist-speak for a local person who helps lubricate relations with the locals. I've already contacted my fixer in Asadabad and he's set up a place for us to spend the night in Akhgar Village, which is seven-ish miles into the valley"—she pointed to the map—"here. We'll have to take horses because there are no roads. From Akhgar, it's another ten, fifteen miles into the mountains to Niazi Village."

Gabe and Quinn shared a glance and a whole conversation seemed to pass between them in that instant. Quinn swore softly.

With a grim nod of agreement, Gabe returned to the front of the room and stood next to Phoebe. "Gentlemen, this is serious shit.

Quinn and I know this area. We've lost a lot of SEALs here and it is still very much under Taliban control." His looked at Phoebe. "I can't believe you and Zina went up there with only a police escort. Jesus Christ, woman. You should have gone up with a cavalry."

She blew out a breath, her frustration clear. "No, you're missing the point. We made it *because* we went up lightly. If we'd taken a cavalry, they wouldn't have thought twice about shooting at us. Instead, we looked like modest Muslim women traveling with our husbands and they left us alone. Which is why I suggest some of you wear a *chadari*." She left the room and returned seconds later with a handful of blue material. "The rest of you should wear local male clothing. We need to look as nonthreatening as possible. We go in with guns blazing, we're probably not going to make it out."

"You want us to dress like women?" Jean-Luc asked.

"Is that a problem for you?"

He grinned and took the veil she handed him. "Nah, *mon cher,* I'm always up for a little kink. Though I gotta say, gender swapping's a new one."

She laughed. "You're incorrigible."

"That's what Marcus's mama said last night."

The joke slammed into Seth like a punch to the gut and he watched through a haze as Marcus reached over and smacked Jean-Luc on the head. Except he didn't see Marcus and Jean-Luc. Rather, two of his former teammates, Aaron "Bowie" Bowman and Omar Cordero, ragging on each other in the chow hall at Bagram. The two of them never managed to run out of yo mama jokes, despite their ongoing war to one-up each other.

"*Hey, Cordero. Yo mama so dirty her bathwater's considered a chemical weapon.*"

"*Yo, Bowie! Yo mama so white, she make the Pillsbury Dough-boy look Puerto Rican.*"

Soft fingers brushed his cheek, jarring him back to the present.

Not Cordero and Bowie. Marcus and Jean-Luc. He blinked and stared up into Phoebe's worried eyes. She'd finished passing out the veils, leaving one for herself, and had returned to her spot at his side to set her veil down on top of her bag.

She didn't say anything, didn't draw attention to his mental slip in any way. She just smiled and tilted her head, indicating Gabe, who still stood by the map.

Right. Gabe was going over details of the op again.

He made himself pay attention and commit every word to memory. He wouldn't be going up into those mountains unprepared a second time.

Phoebe sat down beside him and, to his utter surprise, entwined her fingers through his. It was...comforting. More so than his hood ever was. Her skin felt soft against his scar-roughened flesh and caused all kinds of short-circuiting in his higher functions. What would it feel like to have those hands on his chest? And then sliding lower...

Gabe's team briefing became nothing but background noise as every cell in his being focused on the feel of Phoebe's hand, so small in his. Seemingly fragile, but he knew better. She was strong, probably even stronger than him. Nothing could break her, and with that knowledge came a strange sense of peace. There was no way he could damage this woman or corrupt her with his darkness. And maybe...

Was it possible the unbreakable had the ability to fix the broken?

Christ, with the way a simple touch from her lit him up, he almost believed it. She'd make him whole again and then—

No. Fuck, no. He shook his head and pulled his hand free from her grasp. Thinking like that was ridiculous. Dangerous.

Wrong.

And he needed to focus on the goddamn briefing.

CHAPTER FIFTEEN

The wafting scent of traditional Afghan dishes coming from the kitchen sent Seth's stomach churning, but he paused at the bottom of the stairs and glanced toward the sound of muffled voices in the dining room. He should go in there, but couldn't imagine sitting down at a table with the guys and putting food in his mouth like it was a big happy family dinner.

No fucking way.

"Hey, there you are."

He froze at Phoebe's voice from the top of the stairs and cast around for an escape. The front door sat straight ahead of him, the team's makeshift war room to the left, dining room to the right. Either of the latter two places would leave him trapped, so the door was his only option. He started toward it.

"Hey, wait. Seth! Where are you going? Aren't you hungry?"

"No," he answered and told himself no matter what, he wouldn't look back. If he did, she'd ensnare him again in that strange way she had.

"You have to be hungry. You haven't eaten all day."

Halfway out the door, he hesitated. The note of worry in her voice hit him dead center in his empty gut and some of his resolve to avoid her withered.

"Please," she said directly behind him and laid a hand on his shoulder. "Will you just stop for a minute and talk to me? You've been avoiding me since the briefing."

He opened his mouth to deny it but the scowl she gave him would have scared a pathological liar into spilling the truth.

"Yeah," he said instead, and her brow wrinkled.

"Did I do or say something to offend you? If I did, I'm sorry."

"No." Jesus, he hadn't meant for her to think that. Honestly, he figured she'd be relieved to be rid of him. He wasn't exactly glowing company on the best of days, and the last two had ranked among his worst. All the familiar sights, sounds, and smells of this fucking country had him so off-kilter he felt like a grenade just waiting for someone to pull his pin.

When he said nothing more, Phoebe's hand dropped off his shoulder. "Did Gabe talk to you about those reports?"

Thrown by the sudden topic change, he turned from the door. "Yes, he did."

She rolled her lower lip between her teeth. "Do you agree with his decision not to tell the others about the bomb?"

"He said he has it under control and he doesn't want anything taking the team's focus off the mission. I agree that Hendricks has to be our first priority, but I'm also sure Gabe wouldn't just sit back and do nothing if there was an imminent threat of the bomb going into play."

"You don't think there is?"

He hesitated. "I think there will be if nothing is done to stop Siddiqui."

Phoebe shoved her curls back from her face. It was the first time she'd worn her hair down and his fingers itched to sink into all of those corkscrews. "I still think we should make those reports public. Siddiqui can't go through with his plans if everyone knows. Plus, he won't get elected."

"You're forgetting the huge bull's-eye you'll paint on your back as soon as you go public."

"No, I'm not," she countered somewhat primly. "I'll report it anonymously."

"Nothing's anonymous. He will find out who's responsible and he will want revenge. And worse, at that point he'll have nothing to lose." When she didn't seem at all deterred, he gripped her shoulders. "Listen to me, this is not America. You are not entitled to safety here. Nobody is safe in Afghanistan."

She lifted her hands to cover his and gave his fingers a squeeze before backing out of his grasp. "You're very paranoid."

"Paranoia keeps you alive."

"And alone."

The verbal blow struck home and he sucked in a breath. "I'm good with alone."

"You shouldn't be."

"And you shouldn't be here," he shot back. She was hitting too close to the exposed nerve that ran right through the center of his being. "You should be in some nice suburb back home with a couple redheaded kids and a husband who adores you. Your biggest decision should be what to have for dinner tonight."

Phoebe laughed softly. "I don't want that life."

"Why the hell not?"

"I'm needed here. Someone has to tell these girls' stories or nobody will ever hear them."

"And those stories are important enough to risk your life?"

Something flickered behind her eyes — guilt? — and she glanced toward the dining room as the musical notes of girls' laughter drifted out. "Everyone has sins to atone for. I once believed that if I exposed the horrors of the world, if I saved enough women and girls by making people aware of what's happening to them, I could make up for mine." She shook her head, her curls bouncing. When she looked at him again, her smile was a little sad. "So, yes. Staying here and telling their stories is absolutely important enough to risk my life."

"Jesus. There's no karmic scale that lets you balance out bad deeds with good."

She raised a brow. "Isn't that what you're trying to do by coming back here?"

Another direct hit. She sure knew where to aim those sharp words. "No."

"And neither am I. I know I'll never do enough good to make up for the hurt I've caused."

How come he got the feeling those words were meant specifically for him? Considering they had only known each other a little more than a day, that made no sense. Probably his paranoia talking again. "I can't picture you hurting many people."

"You'd be surprised. And, yes, when I started on this path, I did see it as a way to redeem myself. But now? I'll gladly risk my life to stand up for these girls solely because if I don't, nobody else will."

"You can't save everyone, Phoebe."

"I can try."

Amazing. Foolish as all hell and probably a downright suicidal way to think—but, yeah, amazing. In all honesty, he didn't think he'd ever met anyone quite like Phoebe Leighton. He wanted to touch her, wanted to feel the softness of her skin under his fingertips. "You can't save me."

The expression on her face said she intended to do just that, and there was another uncomfortable sensation deep in the frozen recesses of his chest that he didn't want to name or explore. He turned back to the door. "I need to go."

"You need to eat," she corrected, grabbed his arm, and pulled with enough force that she caught him completely off guard. He hadn't been braced for it and stumbled after her.

The buzz of conversation and clink of dishware got louder. Inside the dining room, under Zina's gentle direction, several of the older girls twittered around, serving up plates of naan, a flatbread, and bowls of soup to the team. The men sat around the table, visibly uncomfortable with the service but trying to be polite.

Every eye in the room swung his way when Phoebe dragged him through the door, and the scent of the food hit him full force. A tremble worked through him, tap-dancing on something dark and twisted at his core. He wanted to punch someone. He didn't know why and fuck if he was going to analyze the source of the intense rage, but he wanted to pummel something until his knuckles bled and swelled and the buzzing inside his skull stopped.

Which meant he should go. He wasn't fit for public consumption right now.

He broke from Phoebe's grasp and backed away from the table. In his peripheral vision, he saw Ian's lip curl in disgust.

"Too good to eat with us, Hero? Or are you having another pansy-ass panic attack?"

That. Was. Fucking. It.

Before he realized he'd moved, he had his hands around Ian's throat. "Don't fucking call me Hero."

Girls screamed. Men shouted. Hands dragged at his arms, his shoulders, but he held on and watched the face in front of him morph into one he recognized and yet didn't quite remember. One of his torturers come back to life. The one he'd nicknamed Devil. The one who had gotten a kick out of alternately starving him, then forcing him to eat until he vomited and making him eat that, too.

Fear clawed up his throat and he tightened his grip. He wasn't going to be force-fed by this bastard. Not again. Never again.

Devil's features blurred and changed to Ian's, then back to Devil's, and Ian's again until he could no longer tell the difference between past and present. Ian. His torturer. They were one and the same and he had to make the pain stop.

Just. Make. It. Stop.

• • •

Chairs scattered as the men jumped up to contain the fight. Soup splattered across the floor, naan was smashed under several pairs of boots. The table scraped across the floor, shoved against the kitchen door by all the jostling bodies. Trapped in the kitchen, Zina pounded on the door and shouted. Several girls huddled in the corner out of fear.

Phoebe crossed to them first, shushing and consoling them as best she could.

Ian's face was turning bright red. Jesse and Quinn tried to pull Seth back while Jean-Luc and Marcus worked at freeing Ian. Gabe used his bulk to shove his way into the brawl, drew back his fist, and slammed into Seth's jaw.

"No!" Phoebe dove toward Seth as his legs gave out and he crumpled, but she didn't make it before he hit the floor. Going down on her knees beside him, she lifted his head and cradled it in her lap. His lip was split and bleeding. He stared up at her with dazed blue eyes—the gaze of a man who had no idea what was happening or why.

Jesse knelt down, but she shoved him away. "Don't touch him! I think you all have hurt him enough."

"*He's* hurting?" Ian croaked and straightened unsteadily, rubbing at the bright-red marks around his throat. "Lady, he just fucking tried to kill me."

"And you asked for it, didn't you?"

His jaw tightened.

"Yeah, I saw you poking at him all day long. All of you do it, in little ways, here and there, but Ian's the worst. And guess what? You poke at a snake long enough and the snake's going to bite back. I swear to God, I don't know how you plan on rescuing anyone when you can't even pull together for dinner without bickering and bloodshed."

She felt a tug on her hand and glanced down, surprised to see Seth squeezing her hand. "I'm sorry," he whispered.

"They should be apologizing, not you." She nailed the men with a glare and most of them had the grace to look ashamed. Ian, on the other hand, didn't appear to have a repentant bone in his body. He growled, shaking soup off his jacket. How anyone on the team managed to trust him enough to put their lives in his volatile hands, she had no idea.

On the other side of the room, Zina finally managed to open the blocked kitchen door with one powerful shove that moved the table several inches. She took one look at the scene before her, ducked under the table, and came up with her eyes spitting anger. "Get. Out."

Dammit. Phoebe tried to stand to go put out this newest fire, but Seth still had a hold of her hand like he didn't plan on letting go any time in the next fifty years.

Okay. She'd talk everyone back from the ledge while sitting on the floor. No problem. Just call her Wonder Woman.

"Get out!" Zina shouted when nobody moved, and her hair tumbled from its neat chignon. "I allowed you to stay in my home with my girls against my better judgment. Now you proved I should have listened to my instincts. Get out."

"Zina." She tried to get up again—but nope, not happening.

Seth stared up at her, transfixed, much the same way he had this morning, as if he wanted to memorize every detail of her features.

And she had to focus on the situation. Not on his gorgeous, sad blue eyes.

"Zina," she tried again. "Stop and think what you're throwing away. A hundred thousand dollars will do tremendous things for the shelter. For your girls. You only have to put up with them for a few days and this will not happen again, will it, boys?"

She got an emphatic, "No, ma'am," from everyone but Ian. And Seth, who was still staring at her.

"See? They'll behave."

As though to prove her point, Gabe ordered his men to start cleaning up the mess and everyone—including Ian this time— pitched in to right chairs and mop up spilled soup.

Interesting that Ian listened to Gabe and even seemed to respect his commander. Maybe that was why he was on the team.

Zina watched them, still trembling with anger. Then she glared at Phoebe. "Why do you trust them so much?"

Good question. One she didn't have an answer for.

Seth saved her from trying to come up with one. As if suddenly realizing he still lay with his head in her lap, he bolted to his feet and strode from the room without speaking a word to anyone.

She hesitated, glancing from Zina to the men, and then at the hallway Seth had disappeared down. She wanted to follow him, but would Zina try to kick the guys out again if she left?

"It's fine." Zina waved a hand. "Go after him. I know you want to."

That was all the encouragement she needed. She climbed to her feet, followed the path he'd taken through the classroom wing of the building, and found him standing in the back courtyard, a lone figure silhouetted by silver moonlight. His shoulders moved with a heavy sigh and the hood of his sweatshirt fell as he scrubbed his hands over his head, then knelt down in the dirt. She started toward him.

The man was so freaking lonely. How could the members of his team not see how much he needed someone? A friend. A confidant. Maybe even a shoulder to cry on.

But that shoulder could never be hers, she realized with a sharp stab of guilt, and froze. If he knew what she'd done, he wouldn't want to see her, not to mention confide in her. He needed a friend who hadn't already betrayed him.

Phoebe took a step backward, fully intending to leave and maintain what little distance still lay between them, but her heel crunched in the gravel. His shoulders tensed.

Crap. Now he knew she was behind him and she had to say… something. Anything.

CHAPTER SIXTEEN

"You shouldn't be back here."

Seth tensed at Phoebe's soft voice, so close behind him he could probably turn around and pull her into his arms, kiss her, and lose himself in the sheer goodness that made up Phoebe Leighton until all of his bad half memories disappeared.

He didn't.

Instead, he climbed to his feet and put more distance between them before facing her. "I'm not allowed in the courtyard?"

"No. I mean, yes, of course you are. But Afghanistan. You shouldn't have come back."

His gut twisted. No doubt she was right. His latest shrink even told him she didn't recommend exposure therapy for his PTSD treatment. He was too damaged.

And yet…

"I have to be here," he said. He wished he could better explain the deep-seated need, but there were no words, except for the same ones she'd given him in the foyer.

"Why? For those men in there?" She pointed toward the house. "They don't respect you. They don't trust you."

"Not them," he said softly.

"The team you lost?" When he couldn't manage a reply, she sighed. "Oh, Seth. That's it, isn't it? You think you're doing this for the men you lost."

He flinched. "Yes. For them."

"Do you think you're honoring them in some way by being here?" she asked and shook her head in answer to her own question. "You're not. You're just pouring salt into your wounds and for what? What are you trying to prove, Seth?"

Her words struck a painful vein of truth that she had no business digging into. "You can't understand."

"Maybe not. I didn't know your men, but if they were good friends, they'd hate to see you tormenting yourself like this."

She was right. Cordero had been big on forgiving and forgetting, and Bowie had always advocated living in the moment, looking forward, and not dwelling on the past. They'd probably both be kicking his ass all the way back to the States right now.

When he didn't reply, Phoebe took a step backward like she planned to leave, and a jolt of alarm rattled him to his core. He didn't want her to go. He didn't want to be alone.

He reached out and grasped her hand. "Thank you."

Her brow furrowed. "For what?"

She was staring up at him, the moon bathing her features in soft white light. Or maybe that was her internal light, shining so pure and bright. A beacon for a drowning man like him.

Awed, his hand lifted of its own volition and almost touched her cheek before he caught himself, his fingers so close, he felt the heat radiating off her skin in the cool night.

Her lashes fused and anticipation hummed from her. So many impossible possibilities charged the air between them.

Seth dropped his hand. Maybe he was a fucking coward after all, because right then, he feared touching her more than anything else.

Phoebe sucked in a breath and drew away. "Um, you still haven't told me what you thanked me for."

Backing up a step, he tilted his head. Indicated the door to the house. "You stood up for me in there."

"Of course I did," she said as if it was a given. "Someone had to."

"Not many people do."

"Well. Ian's a bully and if there's one thing I can't tolerate, it's bullies." Her expression softened. "But you were in the wrong, too. Answering a bully with violence only feeds the part of him that's broken. He keeps picking at you because he wants you to snap. Maybe to prove you're more damaged than he is or maybe even because he *wants* you to fight back, attack him, hurt him. Either way, you can't give him what he wants."

"Sounds like you know a thing or two about bullies."

"I do." A small smile tipped the corner of her mouth. "I was the nerdy girl in high school. Glasses, braces, frizzy hair—the whole stereotypical nerd package. Always had my nose in a book, didn't particularly care about how I looked, participated in things like chess club and debate team."

Her description put an image in his mind of a younger, awkward Phoebe with all the same spunk and even less tact. A light, foreign sensation overrode all of the poisonous emotions swilling inside him. It almost tickled at the center of his chest. Was it…amusement? It had been so long since he'd last experienced anything close, he had trouble placing it. But yes. Amusement.

He wanted to hang on to the feeling, extend this moment into forever, and searched for something to say to keep the conversation going. "I bet you killed at debate."

"As a matter of fact." Her chin lifted with a smug kind of pride he found adorable. "My team took the Massachusetts state debate championship three years running."

At some point during their conversation—he wasn't exactly sure when—they'd started walking, strolling around inside the walls of the shelter's property.

Seth spotted a ragged soccer ball on the ground and bent to scoop it up. He tossed it from hand to hand. "I was a jock in high school. Wasn't a sport I couldn't conquer."

"I know. You wouldn't have looked twice at me."

Unfortunately, she was probably right. But gazing at her now with her springy curls rioting around her head and her blue eyes full of amusement at the memory of her high school self, he couldn't see how he'd *not* notice her. "I don't know about that."

"Oh, please," she said with a roll of her eyes. "I bet you were the rich kid, quarterback, prom king, and had the prom queen slash head cheerleader on your arm. You wouldn't have talked to me unless you needed to buy an English paper off me."

Seth's jaw tightened at the reference to his ex-fiancée, but he refused to let the memory of Emma ruin…whatever this was. The first moment of light, easy conversation he'd had in a long time.

He hefted the ball and shot it in her direction. "I'll have you know, I had an A average in English."

She caught it easily and lobbed it back. "So you're the rare breed of smart jock? Aren't you on the endangered species list?"

"We're about as endangered as the nerd who can handle a ball." He tossed it down and kicked it.

"Oh, I know how to handle all kinds of balls." She stopped it with her foot and grinned. "Let's just say college changed things for me."

He froze as a long-forgotten heat fired his blood and filled areas of his anatomy that had no business being filled.

Was she insinuating…?

No. Couldn't be. He had to be reading her wrong. Her smile

was all sweet innocence and, really, why the fuck would she want someone as mentally and physically scarred as he was?

As he stood there debating, the ball rolled past.

Phoebe planted her hands on her hips. "Not a sport you can't conquer, huh?"

He fumbled for a response. "I was distracted."

"Oh yeah? By what?"

You, he wanted to say, but couldn't force the word past his lips. Everything about her was distracting. Entrancing. Gorgeous.

Christ, this woman.

Everybody had handled him with kid gloves since he'd returned to the States. Save for Ian, even the guys on the team treated him differently, walked on eggshells around him, which put him on edge as much as it did them. How many times had he wanted to shout at them to treat him just like a normal teammate? For fuck's sake, he wasn't going to break down if someone cracked a morbid joke, but all forms of joking always ceased whenever he entered the room.

But this woman. She didn't handle him like he'd break. She acknowledged his issues and let him deal, but she treated him like...like a human being. It was such a refreshing change from everyone else in his life these past two years, he could kiss her for it.

And that was the second time the thought of kissing her had crossed his mind.

No. Kissing wasn't on the menu. As intriguing as the idea was, even a sexless brush of his lips across hers seemed forbidden somehow. Like crossing a line he'd never come back from.

Phoebe closed the distance separating them and before he realized her intentions, she stood on her toes and pressed her lips to his. All kinds of sparks ignited in his blood, sizzling his nerve endings, at once freezing him to the spot with a cold kind of dread and blasting him with so much heat, sweat broke out across his brow.

She lingered with the kiss seconds longer than necessary and left the taste of sweetness and spices on his lips, like the chai tea Afghans were so fond of. His heart thundered in his chest and it took a tremendous amount of willpower not to draw her back in for another, deeper kiss.

She released a shaky breath that clouded in the air and rested her hands on his chest. She had to feel the pounding of his heart, but gave no indication.

"Tongue-tied?" she asked.

He stepped away from her. "This can't happen."

"Why not?"

"Because I'm…damaged goods. I'm crazy."

Her eyes closed as if his words pained her. "No, you're not. You're traumatized and you'd realize that if you just opened up and talked to someone. Anyone."

Now his heart was pounding for an entirely different reason. The thought of talking about his little slice of hell… "I can't."

"Someday you'll need to, and I'm willing to listen when that day comes."

Willing to listen…

The words shook loose a little nugget of fact he couldn't believe he'd forgotten: she was a journalist. Of course she was willing to listen. She didn't want to save him—she wanted a scoop. He couldn't trust her with any details. He'd made that mistake once before, telling pieces of his story—his *team's* story—to reporters, only to see it blown up into something grandiose or ugly or downright unrecognizable.

Never again.

He took another step away from her, his blood running cold. "Willing to listen so you can splash my name all over the headlines? Go on national TV and talk my story to death again? Or are you one of the so-called journalists who likes to dig up dirt?"

All the color drained from her face. "I—"

"Yeah, that's it, isn't it?" And here he'd thought she was special in some way. Maybe even someone he could grow to trust.

Disgusted with himself, he left her standing there in the middle of the yard. Trust her? What bullshit. You couldn't trust anyone but yourself in this fucked world.

And in his case, he didn't even have that.

CHAPTER SEVENTEEN

Phoebe stared after him. How did they go from chatting about their vastly different high school experiences to him accusing her of—well, exactly what she had done to him two years ago? But he didn't know that. He couldn't have known about the horrible things she'd written about him because she'd gone by Kathryn Anderson back then. *Nobody* from her new life knew. As far as she was concerned, Kathryn Anderson was dead and buried and never to be resurrected.

Still, she should tell Seth the truth. Judging by his reaction, he was never going to speak to her again—and God, the thought of his impeding anger opened a hollow ache in her belly. But he had to know.

She followed him inside and nearly ran into his back when she pushed open the door. He stood there, shoulders slumped forward, boots rooted to the floor as if he could not move any farther.

"I'm being an asshole again, aren't I?" He faced her, shame burning in his gaze. "I'm sorry. You make me…feel things I haven't felt in a long time. That scares the fuck outta me and I've had enough shrinks to know I have a tendency to lash out at things that scare me. So, uh…yeah, it was unnecessary. I don't want to hurt you. I…like you."

She opened her mouth to tell him he had every right to lash out—except "I like you too, Seth," emerged instead. Dammit. But she just couldn't tell him the truth. Not when his admission sent her heart fluttering like a crazy caged bird.

His lips twisted. "I can't imagine why. I'm not exactly likable."

On impulse, she stepped forward and wrapped her arms around his waist, hugging him tight. His spine was like a steel rod, immovable, inflexible. She laid her cheek on his chest and breathed him in, a masculine scent somewhere between leather and a spice rack. "You're too hard on yourself, you know that?"

His arms finally closed around her, albeit awkwardly. "I know."

She sank into the embrace, hoping it would relax him, and for the moment, nothing else mattered. "You've already taken more than your fair share of beatings from everyone else. Seems silly to dish it out to yourself, too, doesn't it?"

"Maybe," he admitted after a beat and rubbed his cheek against the top of her head. His tentativeness broke her heart. Where was the confident, cocky Marine she knew he used to be? Was he still in there somewhere, buried under the scars, battling demons and desperate for freedom?

She thought so and wanted to help him find his way out.

"There's no maybe about it, Seth." She lifted her head to smile up at him. "Cut yourself some slack. All I ask."

His mouth came down on hers, gentle at first, then coaxing. She hadn't expected it, and surprise filled her belly with butterflies. She opened to him and their tongues mingled, his invasion a pantomime of sex.

Crap, this was a bad idea.

Very bad idea.

No matter what her body wanted—no, demanded. She should put a stop to this because—because sex only caused problems.

His palms skimmed her spine, leaving a heated trail in their wake that sent a flash fire through her nerve endings. He hesitated at the dip at the small of her back as if debating the wisdom of continuing the southward path.

Oh hell. Why not? He needed a release as much as she did, they were obviously both attracted, and they were both adults. She'd never indulged in a fling before, but the need sparked by a simple slide of his hands convinced her that a fling was an awesome idea.

She rubbed against him, flattening her breasts to his chest, and the sound she made as he broke the kiss must have convinced him to keep going because he dipped his head again and backed her into the wall. His erection thrust into her lower belly and he gripped her rear, lifting her until she had no choice but to wrap her legs around his waist.

"Whoa." At the other end of the hall, Quinn about-faced so fast on his toes, he put ballerinas to shame.

Seth lifted his head, a classic deer-in-the-headlights expression on his face, his hands still gripping her bottom. He fumbled to set her down and cursed when his zipper, pushed out by a very obvious erection, caught on the hem of her sweater.

"Sorry. Carry on." Quinn waved a hand over his shoulder. "Glad to see you're okay."

"Yeah," Seth said, his voice rougher than usual. "I'm, uh, okay."

"Obviously," Quinn muttered and all but spirited back to the dining room.

Phoebe laughed and buried her face in Seth's chest. "He acts like he caught us naked."

Although if she were honest with herself, another five minutes and Quinn might have gotten an eyeful.

She backed away and glanced down at the zipper, still tangled in the weave of her sweater. Letting go of him, she ducked her head and tugged the sweater off, leaving her in only a tank top and the bandage around her arm. She straightened and burst out laughing. He looked ridiculous standing there with a sweater hanging from the front of his pants.

He scowled. "Not funny."

"Actually...yes, it is." She smothered another giggle behind her hand, but then let it loose when a muscle ticked in his cheek. He was holding back a smile and she wanted to see it, wanted him to realize he didn't have to hide his laughter from her.

"How am I supposed to go in there and face the team like this?" he asked. "You think they gave me a hard time before?"

"Oh, chill out." She knelt down and worked the sweater free. When she held it up triumphantly, she realized he was staring up at the ceiling.

"What?"

"Uh." He cleared his throat. "Sorry about..."

"What? Your erection?"

Color crept up his neck to his face. "Yeah."

"Why are you apologizing? It's a normal reaction when a guy kisses someone he's attracted to."

"Not for me. Not anymore."

This time, when he walked away from her, she didn't bother chasing him. She sighed and pulled her sweater on.

What would it take to get through to him?

• • •

Quinn had a headache.

Thank fuck the shelter had only been able to spare a few lamps for their makeshift war room or else the headache might have graduated from ouch-ouch-ouch to put-a-bullet-in-his-skull-just-to-make-it-stop. As it was right now, he could manage.

He glanced away from the spread of satellite images on the table in front of him because he was starting to see double—a sure sign of an impending migraine. He spotted the handful of photos Phoebe had provided of the village, which reminded him of what he'd caught Phoebe and Seth doing against the wall by the shelter's classroom. Which, in turn, made him think about why Seth and Phoebe had been in that hallway to begin with.

That scene at dinner had been a fucking disaster.

Hell, maybe it had been a mistake bringing Seth onto the team. Gabe seemed to think so, and after tonight, there was no denying the guy's head was fucked.

But going by that logic, Quinn shouldn't be on the team either because nobody's head was more fucked up than his. Of course, Gabe didn't know about the blackouts he'd suffered since waking from the coma after their car accident a year and a half ago. Nobody knew—except for Jesse, who had gotten a hold of his medical records back in July and had urged him to tell Gabe about the traumatic brain injury.

And he had planned on it. Hell, he'd even opened his trap to spill it on more than one occasion, but every time, the words stuck in his throat. He'd lost his SEAL team, the closest thing he'd ever had to a family. Now he had HORNET and, as much as they sometimes irritated him, he dreaded the thought of losing that ragtag bunch. What would he have then if he didn't have them?

Nothing.

No purpose. No family.

Besides, the only ops the team had gone on since May were training missions. And occasional bodyguard jobs, like this summer when they babysat Senator Escareno's family in El Paso—

Mara.

No. Jesus Christ, no. Why did that woman keep popping into his head?

Shoving away from the table, he paced across the cramped room and forced away the memories of Senator Escareno's gorgeous daughter. His focus had to stay 100 percent on this mission.

His last mission.

He stopped moving at the thought and scrubbed his hands over his face. It pained him that he'd never be out in the field again, but…yeah. It was the right thing to do. He couldn't keep putting his men—his friends—in danger. So when the team returned to the States, he'd have to come clean about his medical issues. And then…

Well. Honestly, he hadn't considered the "and then" part of it.

Footsteps creaked on the stairs in the foyer, dragging him away from his depressing thoughts, and he dropped his hands. He couldn't see any of the girls sneaking out in the middle of the night—they were all too frightened by one thing or another to leave the shelter—so it had to be one of the guys.

Seth appeared at the bottom of the stairs as a long, lean shadow. He had the hood of his sweatshirt up, and his head turned left, then right, eyes scanning, searching for threats. His entire body was as taut as a guitar string, vibrating with nervous energy.

Damn. He did not look like he was holding it together.

After an uncertain moment, he finally moved and stepped into the foyer and Quinn couldn't help but draw a mental comparison between the sniper and a deer he'd once seen on a hunting trip with his adopted father when he was fourteen. The buck had sensed their presence on that icy winter morning, but couldn't see them up in the tree blind. It had crunched through the snow one graceful, careful step at a time, freezing every other step, ears pricked, dark eyes scanning.

Seth moved with the same vigilant grace as that deer. As if he'd bolt at the faintest whisper of movement, just like the buck had when Quinn scooted forward in the blind to get a better look.

Christ, Quinn hoped he was making the right call about this guy.

He raised a hand in greeting. "Hey, Harlan."

Seth froze and for a long five seconds, Quinn thought he might make a run for it like the deer had. Then he drew a breath that moved his shoulders and turned toward the war room.

"You okay?" Quinn asked.

Seth swallowed hard and nodded. "Nightmares," he said, voice hoarse. "They've, uh, gotten worse since coming back here."

Quinn picked up several of the photos and flipped through them. It was useless. He wasn't going to match them up to the sat images, no matter how long he stared at them. He tossed them down again and said without thinking, "Man, the way they had you tied up, letting you just rot away…you're entitled to a few nightmares."

In his peripheral vision, he saw Seth go very still. "You were there?"

Fuck. Realizing the mistake, Quinn faced the guy. He knew Seth didn't remember him and he sure as hell hadn't meant to bring it up, but the cat was out of the bag now. "Yes. I was part of the mission."

"You're one of the SEALs that pulled me out of—of—" Seth's throat worked. "Is that why you keep going to bat for me with Gabe? Because you were fucking there?"

"Yeah. Partly." He'd never forget walking into that mud house, the scent of death like a smack in the face despite the brutal midwinter cold, and finding Seth Harlan chained to the wall in a back room, rotting away in his own filth. Seth's gaunt face had been a swollen, unrecognizable jumble of black, blue, and yellow splotches and someone had very recently sliced open his throat. At the time, the future hadn't looked promising for the young Marine. While the cold had kept him from bleeding out, he was hypothermic and septic, suffering from dehydration, and on the verge of starvation, and had infected wounds all over his chest, back, legs, and groin. In fact, Quinn hadn't thought he would survive the trip back to a friendly hospital, not to mention make a full recovery and try to find work in the private sector.

Seth had spirit. It might be broken like his shrinks all claimed, but he had it in spades, and that was rare. Plus, broken could usually be fixed.

And yeah, that hope was exactly why Quinn kept pushing to keep Seth on the team. He kept thinking of himself, how the Navy had tossed him to the curb for something beyond his control, how if it weren't for HORNET, he'd be lost right now. He'd gotten his second chance. How could he not offer the same to Seth?

Seth stared at some point on the far wall, his jaw locked tight enough to make a muscle twitch at his temple. No doubt he was reliving the rescue from his end, trying to visualize which of the faceless, white-clad rescuers had been Quinn.

Finally, he exhaled hard and refocused in the here and now. "I should probably say thank you for getting me out of there."

"I'm not looking for thanks."

"Good." He nodded once. "That's good. 'Cause I can't give it. I just…can't."

"Don't blame you." Quinn waited, giving him some time and space to pull himself together.

When Seth appeared steady again, Quinn picked up the photographs and held them out. "Do you recognize any landmarks in these photos?" It was worth a shot. The man had been dragged all over the mountains for fifteen months.

Seth accepted the stack, flipped through it, then shook his head and handed it back with a trembling hand.

God. A sniper with unsteady hands.

Quinn hesitated before putting the photos away. "Seth, man. Tell me truthfully, are you ready for this? There's no shame in it if you're not, but I need to know now. I need to know I can put a rifle in your hands and send you into the mountains without worrying about Gabe's safety, or yours, or the rest of the team's. I need to know right now you can handle this."

Seth stared down at his hands for a long time. So long, that Quinn figured it was game over and the sniper would be States-bound by morning.

Finally, his hands curled into fists. When he looked up, Quinn saw exactly what he'd hoped to see. Fire. Determination. Spirit.

"I can handle it," Seth said. "I'm going to bring Hendricks home, no matter what."

And Quinn believed him.

CHAPTER EIGHTEEN

As their two-vehicle convoy bounced through the desert, Phoebe peeked over at Seth in the seat next to her, using her head scarf to hide the action although it wasn't necessary. His gaze remained glued to the window, his hands fisted on his knees. He'd been silent since they left the shelter before daybreak this morning and she couldn't help but worry about him. What must be going through his head? Was he remembering the last time he made this drive through the desert toward the mountains?

After three hours, the silence was getting to be too much. She needed conversation, but Seth obviously wasn't in the mood to chitchat. That left her with only one other option.

She leaned forward in her seat. "Gabe?"

He cast his eyes toward the rearview mirror and briefly met her gaze in the glass. "Yeah?"

"I saw you give Quinn something before we left the shelter. What was it? If you don't mind me asking."

"I don't," he answered, surprising her. She'd expected the imposing man to shut her down for prying. "It was a note for my wife and one for my brother. It's a thing we do. In case."

Out of the corner of her eye, she noticed Seth's flinch. He'd probably delivered a note like that, hadn't he? Most likely one for each of the five teammates he'd lost. God, she couldn't even imagine carrying that kind of burden.

"I didn't realize you're married," she said, determined not to let the conversation end on that depressing note. "Was she in the military, too?"

Gabe snorted. "Hell no. She's an artist."

"Really? Do you have a picture of her?"

"Always," Gabe said and showed a quick a flash of a surprisingly handsome smile. He dug in the front pocket of his vest, the one closest to his heart, and held the photo up between two fingers. "That's Audrey."

Phoebe studied the woman with light-brown hair and caramel eyes. She sat on a white sand beach wearing a sheer swimsuit cover in a wild mishmash of animal prints that most women wouldn't have been able to pull off. Worked for her, though, and okay, Phoebe might have felt the tiniest pinch of envy for that. With her red hair and pale skin, animal prints were so not her friends.

In the picture, Audrey Bristow held her hand up by her face as if the photographer had caught her in the middle of pushing a windswept strand of hair behind her ear. A multitude of bangles hung from her wrist. Her big smile appeared natural and easy, like it was something she did often.

Phoebe wasn't sure what she'd been expecting Gabe's wife to look like, but this colorful, vivacious woman hadn't been it.

"She's lovely," she said and meant it. She passed the photo back to him, watched his eyes soften as he glanced at it before tucking it away again.

Aww. Under his gruff exterior, he was just a big old teddy bear and she kind of wanted to hug him for his unabashed adoration of his wife. She smiled over at Seth, expecting him to share in her amusement, but he hadn't even been paying attention to her and Gabe's conversation. He stared down at something in his hands, his shoulders hunched as if he didn't want anyone else to see it.

What was it?

She scooted closer, peered over his shoulder, and instantly wished she had stayed on her side of the car. The item he cradled so tenderly was a photograph, worn around the edges and severely faded, and he tucked it away when he realized she was looking. Even so, she recognized the gorgeous blond woman.

Emma. His ex-fiancée.

He still had her picture.

Phoebe stared out her window at the endless beige landscape of the desert, a lump sitting in the middle of her throat. No matter how hard she tried to swallow it, there it sat, hot and unforgiving.

It shouldn't matter that he still carried the woman's picture. Why did she care? He hadn't promised her anything and they'd shared nothing more than a few kisses. Besides, she'd wanted to keep her distance, right?

So why was she fighting back tears with every blink?

• • •

Seth knew he'd screwed up in the car. He shouldn't have looked at Emma's picture, shouldn't have let Phoebe see it. But Gabe's talk of "just in case" letters had sparked a fire of anxiety in his gut that he'd been unable to tamp down. Only one thing ever calmed him when he got like that and so, damn the consequences, he'd pulled out the photo.

Now Phoebe was avoiding him. It had been hours since they'd abandoned the cars in favor of horses and started their trek along the river into one of the most dangerous valleys in the country, but she still wouldn't speak any more than necessary.

How could he explain what the photo meant to him? He didn't keep it for the reasons she probably thought, but he'd never had any luck explaining his attachment to the damn thing. Would she understand if he tried? Or would she condemn him like Emma had for clinging to the ghost of a relationship long dead?

He studied the back of Phoebe's head as her horse plodded ahead of him. Her sometimes unruly hair was tucked away, hidden under the blue fabric of her *chadari,* and he wished he could see her curls. Touch them. He liked having his hands in them more than he should, and the way they always sprang back into tight ringlets fascinated him. He imagined playing with the locks far more often than he cared to cop to, but it was quickly becoming his favorite daydream. It soothed him and he sure as hell could use something soothing right now. Since climbing into the saddle, he'd been a bundle of raw nerves, every little sound setting his teeth on edge.

Maybe it was because the past was too close, hovering just under the surface, but when their little caravan followed a bend in the river and came up against a pile of boulders, all the air left Seth's lungs with a dizzying sense of déjà vu.

"Seth!" Cordero's voice. "We're under attack! Holy shit! There's hundreds of them."

"I got no comms, sir." Link's voice.

"Your orders?" Rey's.

"I'll draw their fire. Go, go, go!" Bowie.

Oh, fuck. He remembered this place.

And death.

So much death.

"Goddammit, we're not dying up here, Marines!" His own voice echoed inside his head, shouting those false words over and over even as he watched Bowie take a bullet through the leg and tumble over a cliff…

A hand settled on his thigh and he jerked hard enough that his horse trotted sideways off the trail, neighing a protest at the grip he had on its reins.

"Hey, it's okay." Phoebe flipped up the front of her veil. "It's just me."

Christ. He released the reins and scrubbed at his face with both hands, surprised to find his cheeks wet. The rest of the team hadn't yet realized he'd stopped and were already half a football field away.

Phoebe picked up his dropped reins and clicked her tongue, guiding both animals back to the relative safety of the trail. "Okay now?" she asked.

Not even. "Yeah."

She handed him the reins. "Where did you go?"

"Someplace I don't want to revisit."

"You said you remembered something?"

Had he said that? He swallowed hard and nudged his horse into a trot with his knees. He wasn't about to rehash his team's last stand with her or anyone else. He'd never even told his shrinks the whole of it.

Phoebe's mare easily kept pace beside him. "Have you been to this area before?"

"No."

"Seth." She positioned her horse across the path in front of him, forcing him to pull up or run into her. "Keeping that kind of trauma all bottled up will only make it worse. Talk to me."

Anger surged inside him, devouring the pain in heat, and he grabbed on to it, held it with both hands. Anger was so much easier to feel than...everything else. "That's all you journalist types ever want to do. It's always talk, talk, talk about stuff you know fuck-all about."

Her chin lifted in defense, but not before he noticed the flash of hurt across her features.

Aw, fuck him. She wasn't like those other journalists, the ones who had dragged his and his team's names through the mud. He knew that and, dammit, he was lashing out at her again out of fear. He had to stop doing it. She didn't deserve his anger and it wasn't going to change anything.

"Sorry," he muttered.

"I just…want to know you better," she said and urged her horse back, clearing the path. "And find out why you were crying just now. I hated seeing you like that."

An instant denial jumped to his lips, but wetness still clung to his lashes so it would kinda be like denying the sky was blue. Still, his ego took a major hit that she'd seen his tears.

"I remembered watching a good friend die," he said, gravel coating his voice. "More than one good friend, in an area much like this one. It's a memory I haven't let myself think about in a long time, but I saw those rocks back there and…" He trailed off.

"Will you tell me about your team? Not about their deaths," she added quickly. "Just…talk about them. Tell me about Aaron Bowman."

He saw Bowie falling over the cliff's edge again. And again. And again…

His chest tightened and he took a deep breath to ease it. "Aaron Bowman—we called him Bowie, like the knife. He was one of my best friends. Always smiling, laughing." If he closed his eyes and shut out the world, he could sometimes almost hear Bowman's distinctive laughter. "Bowie would whip out these hilarious one-liners and you just had to shake your head at the things he came up with. He and Cordero were always telling yo mama jokes. Actually, it got kinda annoying."

"What was Omar Cordero like?" Phoebe asked.

Talking about the guys like this should have opened up all of his wounds, should have made him hurt more. Instead something inside him eased as he answered her question. "Cordero was... solid. Reliable. Very proud of his Puerto Rican heritage. He had a huge family—brothers, sisters, aunts, cousins. His wife's family was just as big and still, they wanted a baby. They had been trying and he found out she was pregnant only days before..."

"And what about Garrett Rey?" Phoebe prompted when his voice faded.

Seth drew another breath, let it out. Focused on the feel of the horse plodding along, its bulk a solid reassurance under his saddle. "He and McMahon were both the new guys, first time in Afghanistan. They mostly kept to themselves, but they were nice kids. Just kids..."

"And Brandon Link?"

His eyelids felt gummy, his throat scratchy. He rubbed a hand over his face. "Link was smart. Loved gadgets, a lot like Harvard. He tried so hard to get us support that day..."

I got no comms, sir.

No. Couldn't do it, after all. Couldn't talk about this.

He snapped the reins and spurred his horse into a gallop, suddenly needing as far away from those rocks as he could get.

Again, Phoebe caught up to him easily but waited until he slowed to a walk before speaking. "It doesn't make you less of a man, you know. Crying for lost friends? Just means you have a heart. You're human."

Yeah, right. She really didn't have any idea what she was talking about. Just like every other journalist he'd ever met.

He leaned over and pulled on her horse's bridle until the animal stopped. "Let's get something straight. My humanity was stripped away a long time ago."

Instead of getting pissed like he expected, her eyes went soft. "That's not true." She reached across the space between them and cupped his jaw. "I wish you could see yourself through my eyes."

He opened his mouth with the intent to tell her how ridiculous she sounded, but all the little hairs along the back of his neck stood at sudden attention. The horses' ears twitched and Phoebe's sidestepped in agitation.

Not flashback-induced paranoia then. Couldn't be if the horses felt it, too. Someone was following them. He spun in his saddle in time to see two goat herders duck out of sight behind the rocks.

Goat herders with a disturbing lack of goats.

His heartbeat ramped up as adrenaline spiked his blood with the classic fight-or-flight response. And he was not fucking running from these people anymore. He whistled to get the rest of the team's attention. "Gabe!"

Phoebe's eyes widened and she turned too, but of course the herders had already disappeared. "What's wrong?"

Hooves thundered toward them and Gabe pulled his huge stallion to an easy stop feet away. "What is it?"

"A tail."

Gabe scanned the ridges above the valley and swore softly. "Where are their goats?"

"That's the problem."

"Let's go." He spun his horse and kicked it into a full-tilt gallop with Phoebe and Seth right behind him.

"Take cover!" Gabe ordered as they neared the team, but the command came a second too late.

Seth heard a whoosh overhead—a sound that replayed in his dreams every fucking night. By all rights, he should have been pissing his pants terrified, and reliving the moment when a rocket-propelled grenade exploded in front of his team's Humvee, instantly killing McMahon. That whoosh of sound and the following explosion had haunted him for years—but now, instead of shutting down, something like a missing puzzle piece snapped into place inside his brain and icy calm descended.

"Incoming!" He grabbed Phoebe right out of her saddle and kicked his horse into a run before the RPG round exploded against the cliff meters away from where she had been. Her horse freaked and took off like a shot toward the river at the valley's center. Rocks and dust exploded into the air and the whole mountain shuddered as the cliff began to crumble. Bullets followed the grenade in quick succession, sending up little clouds of dirt as they hit. Ian's mount bucked in panic, dumping him hard onto the ground.

Seth set Phoebe down behind a boulder, yanked his 9-mm pistol from its holster on his leg, and held it out to her. "Know how to use it?"

The veil of her *chadari* had ripped away from her face. She bled from a scrape along her temple, too much white showed in her eyes, and she trembled like a palm tree in a hurricane. She shook her head.

"Fuck." He did a quick demonstration. "Point—at the bad guys, not the good—and squeeze the trigger. Only if you have to protect yourself, got it?"

She nodded again and clutched the weapon in a white-knuckled grip. Kicking his horse into a gallop, he charged back into the battle and took stock of the situation as he rode.

Marcus had lost his horse, too, but he'd thrown off the *chadari* he'd been wearing, climbed to a good firing position high up one side of the valley, and rained bullets down on their attackers. Gabe and Jesse still had their mounts and used the animals' speed to draw enemy fire away from Jean-Luc, who was circling around behind the group of distracted fighters with a knife in hand. Ian still hadn't moved from the spot he landed. Injured? Dead? Seth couldn't tell from this distance and hesitated.

Help Jean-Luc get the drop on the enemy?

Or help Ian?

He debated for all of a nanosecond before jumping down from his horse. He grabbed his pack and his rifle drag bag, then sent the frightened animal running home with a smack on its rear.

He wasn't losing any more goddamn teammates. Even if this particular teammate was a massive pain in his ass.

He raced to Ian's side, dodging one bullet that came alarmingly close to his foot. Hooked his hand into the neck of the vest Ian wore under his loose-fitting Afghan tunic and unceremoniously yanked the man to cover behind a natural rise in the land. The slope didn't provide much in the way of cover, but it was better than nothing.

"You hit?"

"Wind. Knocked. Out," Ian gasped. "Bullet. In. Vest."

Seth pulled up the front of his tunic and sure enough, a bullet had burrowed into the one of the vest's Kevlar plates. He shook his head, dropped the tunic. "Lucky bastard." He unzipped his drag bag and shoved a high-powered scope into Ian's hand. "Gotta help Jean-Luc. Point me in the right direction."

As he assembled the pieces of his rifle in fast, well-rehearsed motions, Ian groaned and rolled to his stomach. Hissed in a breath. "Fuck, that hurts."

"Not as bad as it could've. Bad guys, Reinhardt. Where are they?" Seth flattened out at the top of the rise and jacked a shell into the rifle's chamber. "And don't point me toward Jean-Luc. I like the guy."

"You haven't heard him sing yet," Ian muttered and raised the scope to his eye. Seth looked through his own scope, which wasn't as powerful. Even so, he saw Jean-Luc take out one insurgent with a knife in the throat. Quick. Quiet. Deadly.

Who knew the laid-back Ragin' Cajun was capable of that?

"Tango, two o'clock. White turban," Ian said.

"What's the range?"

"Six hundred meters."

Seth judged the wind, mentally did the math, made the adjustments, and relaxed into position behind his rifle. Damn, but it felt good, a little like coming home. He breathed in. Breathed out and squeezed the trigger.

"Got him," Ian said with no small amount of surprise. He lowered the scope. "You blew his head off."

"One shot, one kill. Anything more is a waste." He ejected the fired cartridge, chambered a fresh round. "Find the others."

The corner of Ian's mouth kicked up in a sardonic half smile and he lifted the scope again. "This doesn't mean we're friends. I still think you're window-licking insane, Hero."

"And I still think you're an evil motherfucker, so we're even. Now find me another target."

CHAPTER NINETEEN

AKHGAR VILLAGE

Oh God, was Phoebe ever grateful to see civilization again—even if it was this tiny village along the river. But having used this place as a stopover in the past, she knew the people here, knew they would lay their lives down for their visitors if the Taliban came looking.

Normally, the Pashtun idea of *nanawatai* or "asylum" made her uncomfortable because it meant her presence put everyone in the village—men, women, and children—at risk. But not after today. No, now she was just so damn grateful to have that extra layer of protection. Since the Taliban didn't want to make enemies out of the locals, they usually respected when the villagers enacted *nanawatai*. That meant she and the guys had peace tonight before they pushed deeper into enemy territory tomorrow.

She planned to savor the peace.

The village's policeman—one of the men who had escorted her and Zina the first time—wasn't happy they were going back. He claimed to hear rumors coming out of the mountains about people dying up there by the dozens. For the sake of Tehani's family, she hoped that wasn't true.

Even so, the policeman gave up his home for their use. There wasn't much to the mud building—a main room with several smaller bedrooms in back. No running water and the bathroom consisted of a ditch out behind the house. Not five-star accommodations, but each of the rooms had an actual bed with sheets and blankets and Phoebe was so ready to collapse into one.

Jean-Luc and Marcus had already zonked out on bedrolls in the living room area. More power to them, but she wanted a mattress.

Jesse had set up a makeshift treatment center and was in the process of wrapping a bandage around a snarling Ian's heavily tattooed chest. Apparently the bullet had cracked a rib when it impacted his vest and he'd been in tremendous pain ever since, which had done nothing to improve his already sterling personality.

"Hey," Jesse said and eyed her as she passed. "You okay, darlin'?"

She smiled at him. "That charming drawl won't work on me, cowpoke. I'm a city girl."

He grinned. "Da-yam."

Ian merely grunted. He looked like he'd rather have his teeth dug out with a spoon than be anywhere in the same vicinity as the medic, and really, Jesse didn't appear all that thrilled with his patient either. Amazing they hadn't taken the other's head off yet, and she suspected they were tolerating each other only because Gabe had ordered Ian to get patched up. Definitely some history between them and more than a little bad blood. Maybe Seth knew why they hated each other.

Then again, Ian seemed to be an equal opportunity hater. She really didn't like the man all that much.

"Seriously, though," Jesse said, sobering. "Are you okay? No injuries?"

"I'm good." *Thanks to Seth,* she added silently. He had amazed her today. He spent so much time warring against his inner demons that, like the rest of the team, she'd feared how he'd react when faced with an actual enemy. But today, he proved they had nothing to worry about. In the heat of battle, he'd been more comfortable in his own skin than she'd ever seen him.

Which, honestly, was kind of terrifying.

"Have you see Seth?" she asked the two men and, to her surprise, Ian responded.

"Saw him go into one of the bedrooms. Said he needed space."

"Please tell me you didn't give him shit about it." One room was hers and by tacit agreement among the men, Gabe got another—probably because of the injury that forced him to use a cane most of the time. She'd heard the men good-naturedly arguing over the third and final bed, but Ian didn't have a good-natured bone in his body.

Ian's jaw tightened. "He pulled me outta the kill zone. Man wants space, he gets space." With that, he shoved Jesse away, grabbed his shirt, and stalked over to an empty bedroll already laid out on the floor.

Okay. Not the response she'd expected. Was it possible she had completely misjudged the cantankerous Ian Reinhardt?

Jesse huffed out a breath in exasperation and started packing up his medical kit. "Will you let me know if Seth needs any treatment? He wouldn't let me look at him."

Heat flooded Phoebe's cheeks. Was he insinuating she'd get close enough to Seth to see any injuries? Well, it was a nice thought. Not the possible injuries, of course. But as far as getting closer to Seth? Oh boy, did she want it. Despite her better judgment, the very idea of skin-to-skin contact with him filled her with the kind of feminine yearning she hadn't felt in years.

She promised Jesse she'd report any injuries and checked the rooms one at a time. Gabe was in the first one, the wooden door open to the hallway. He sat on the bed with his bad leg elevated and the photo of his wife in his hand. She decided not to disturb him and slipped past his door to the next, which proved to be an empty room. At the last room, the ill-fitting wood door sat slightly ajar and she peeked through the crack. Not to spy or anything, but if he seemed to really need space, she'd leave him to it.

Seth knelt by a shallow bowl on the floor, splashing water on his face, and she'd never in her life seen any man look so alone.

"Seth?"

At her voice and soft knock, his bare shoulders tightened and he straightened away from the bowl. "What do you want?"

"I'm sorry. I didn't realize you were getting cleaned up. I'll come back." Okay it was a little fib, but she didn't want him to know she'd been watching. She paused halfway out the door and glanced back. "But for the record, when someone knocks on the door, you say 'come in,' not 'what do you want?'"

He sighed and ran his hand over his head, wiping away the excess water that dampened his short hair. "Wait. You're right. I'm being an ass."

As he climbed to his feet, she faced him again and got an eyeful of nearly naked male. He wore only a pair of boxer shorts and he was…

Scarred.

Holy shit. She took several steps toward him before she realized what she was doing. Reached out, but thought better of touching him when he flinched. Battling a fierce rush of anger that brought tears to her eyes, she fisted her hands at her sides. Of course, she'd known some of the details of what had been done to him, but having it all laid out like a map of torture in front of her? Damn. She didn't even have half a clue of what he'd endured.

"Seth," she breathed. "I'm so sorry for what they did to you."

"Please don't." He turned away and reached for the clean shirt folded on the bed. "I don't—want you looking at me like that. I get enough pity at home. I don't need yours, too."

"I don't pity you." To prove it, she lifted her hands to his shoulders, let her palms slide down over the rough skin of his arms. "I'm amazed by you. Look at what you survived and yet here you are, back in the place it happened? I can't even begin to fathom the courage it must have taken to come here."

"It had to be done."

"No. It didn't." But that he thought so made him one of the most honorable men she'd ever met. She traced a raised C-shaped scar on his biceps. "Do they still hurt?"

He shook his head. "Not really. Sometimes it feels like my skin isn't big enough for my body, but it's more an annoying discomfort than pain."

"Do you see a specialist about it?"

"Not anymore. Nothing else for the doctors to do." He shrugged. "I'm healed up as good as I'm going to get. Just gotta live with it now."

But living with it shouldn't cause him discomfort. And now that she thought of it, she might even have something to help. "Lie down. I'll be right back."

Without waiting for a response, she hurried from the room and grabbed her pack from the spot she'd left it in the main portion of the house. She got a raised eyebrow from Jesse, and said, "He's not injured," before returning to find Seth hadn't moved. He still stood next to the bed, hands at his sides.

She pointed to the mattress. "Go on. Lie down."

The thin white scar across his forehead puckered as his brows drew together. "I'm sorry?"

"On the bed. On your stomach." She swung her bag off her shoulder and dug around inside for— Aha. There it was. She brought out the bottle of lotion her mother had given her before she left for Afghanistan.

His mouth opened then closed. Opened again. Closed. He cleared his throat and very casually fisted his hands together in front of his shorts, assuming a kind of parade rest stance as if protecting his goods.

"Uh, Phoebe, I'm not sure where you're going with this but—"

"Stop." She rolled her eyes at him. "I'm not going to jump you or anything." *Not unless you ask*, she added silently and immediately cursed herself for it. So much for keeping her distance. She motioned him toward the bed. "Go on. My mom's a massage therapist and I've picked up some tricks over the years. Plus, she gave me this really great lotion"—she wiggled the bottle back and forth—"that softens skin like you wouldn't believe. It might be able to help with that tightness you were talking about."

His expression eased, but he still didn't move. "You don't have to help me."

"I want to."

"Why?"

"Because you need it."

Again, his brows furrowed. "Is this some sort of compulsion of yours?"

"I just want you to feel better." She planted her hands on her hips and scowled at him. "Is that a crime? What's with the third degree?"

"I don't understand you," he muttered.

She flopped her arms in exasperation. "What's there to understand? I'm offering to give you a massage."

He said nothing more, but he didn't have to. That guarded look in his eyes said everything. Had he been so damaged by his captivity that simple kindness escaped his understanding?

God.

Her throat tightened. She'd show him kindness existed.

Starting with a massage.

CHAPTER TWENTY

She crossed to him, grasped his hand, and led him the few steps to the narrow bed. His lips flattened into a grim line, but he sat where she indicated and stiffly swung his legs up to the mattress. When he stretched out on his stomach, his feet hung over the end of the bed by several inches. He turned his head on the flat pillow to watch as she slid off her shoes and discarded her jacket and sweater. Unlike Kabul, where it was only in the forties, or up in the mountains, where it was even colder, this town sat low enough in altitude and far enough south that the temperature still hovered in the mid to high seventies. She'd been sweltering since they'd arrived here and it felt amazing to lose a few layers.

She knelt on the edge of the mattress and hesitated. God, his back. Even his scars had scars. "Will it hurt you if I sit on you?"

He lifted his head and...was that a twinkle of humor in his blue eyes? "Yeah, because you're a regular elephant."

Her heart did a happy little jig at his sarcasm, but as much as she loved that he'd finally relaxed enough to joke, she couldn't let him get away with that one. She whacked his hip with the back of her hand. "You wanted me to tell you when you're being an asshole? Well, there you go. Exhibit A."

Something that might have been a smile twitched at the corner of his lips. "Of course you're not going to hurt me, Phoebe. You're, what? Five three, one-ten, fifteen? What can a little thing like you do to me that hasn't already been done?"

Annnd there went the moment of levity.

"We need to work on your sense of humor." She swung a leg over his waist and straddled his back, sitting down hard because — well, damaged or not, he deserved it for the elephant remark.

He huffed out a breath, then sent her a scowl over his shoulder. "Easy."

She used her arm like a trunk and trumpeted.

"Smart-ass," he muttered and stuffed his face in the pillow. She suspected to hide a smile. Someday soon, she'd see his smile. And maybe he'd even give it freely, without feeling like he had to smother it. But for now, she'd mark that hidden smile as a point in the win column. It was progress.

Phoebe squirted some of the lotion into her palm, cupped her hands together, and blew on it to warm it up. She started at his neck and worked her way down his spine. Under the scars, he was all lean muscle, built like a runner. He used to be bulkier, she knew. She'd seen photos of him from high school, when he'd been offered a full ride to Notre Dame on a football scholarship. She'd also seen photos of him and his ill-fated team directly before they left for their last mission. And honestly, she liked his body better now, scars and all. Liked the way his muscles felt under her fingertips as she worked his skin.

Wait. No. She shouldn't be liking his body at all.

Except, dammit, she did. And in response, her body was heating up in all the right places and the groan of pure masculine pleasure that rumbled from his throat did not help. Her breathing shallowed until she was almost panting.

She was already wet for him, which was kind of embarrassing because she knew for a fact sex was the absolute last thing on his mind. At least he couldn't feel her arousal through her jeans.

Focus.

She simply had to focus, like when she did a nude portrait shoot. Only the subject was important. Their pose, the way the light played off their skin. Everything else was just background noise and she had to blur it out and focus.

On Seth.

Right. Focusing on him really hadn't been the problem since he barreled into her life. Focusing on anything but him, on the other hand? He'd gotten under her skin, invaded her every thought, and she couldn't shake him loose.

She traced the indent of his spine, fanned her hands out at the small of his back. Oh, but he had a beautiful body, even with the scars. Would she ever love to get him into her studio back home. He was determination and loyalty personified and would make an amazing addition to the *Naked Emotion* collection she'd been working on for the past few years.

Then again, she didn't want the world to see him naked. *She* wanted to see him naked.

No, no, no. Focus.

Needing a moment's distraction, she leaned over and reached for the bottle of lotion she'd leaned against the wall next to his head. His hand shot out, long fingers closing around her wrist. For a solid five seconds, he didn't move, didn't say anything, merely held on to her wrist, and she held her breath. Then, slowly, he lifted her hand to his mouth and kissed her palm.

Heat sizzled up her arm from the contact of his lips and she exhaled shakily. "Seth?"

His lips grazed her inner wrist and she gasped, her thighs involuntarily clenching around his waist. Who knew wrists were so sensitive? She certainly hadn't, but when he opened his mouth and added an experimental flick of his tongue, the caress rocketed straight to her sex.

As she swam in the heady, lust-drunk sensation, Seth changed their positions, and she suddenly found herself tucked underneath his body. She opened her thighs to cradle his hips, welcoming his weight and the growing bulge at the front of his shorts pressing against her core.

Was this really happening?

He answered her thought by lifting her up and yanking off her tank top. He made short work of her bra clasp and tossed the garment aside, then dipped his head to her breast like a man starving for intimacy and teased her nipple with his tongue. It was almost an assault—in the best possible way, with all of her senses humming from the bombardment. He was rough and impatient and she loved every second, moaning her encouragement to take what he needed from her.

And he did need it, same as he'd needed the massage. He was hyped up, tense, still high on the adrenaline rush of their close call in the valley. She had no illusions that this was anything other than an act of release and she was okay with that. More than okay if he kept using his teeth to tug at her nipple like he was right now.

"Seth!" She gasped his name, clutched his head to her chest, and arched toward him, riding the waves of heat pouring off him and into her.

He released her breast and pushed himself up to his knees. Blue eyes burning hot with unfulfilled lust raked down her body, but he didn't touch her again.

With a vicious curse, he jumped off the bed and paced by the foot. He made an impressive sight with his muscles and scars and the erection jutting from his hips, covered by only a thin layer of cotton. She watched him for several beats, dazed, still expecting him to return to her and send her flying with his mouth and hands. And more. Oh, yes, please more. Maybe he was looking for a stash of condoms, because they would definitely need those before things went any further.

The sheen of sweat on her skin started to cool and the haze of lust cleared from her mind. He wasn't coming back to bed.

She sat up. "What's wrong?"

He stopped pacing and stared down at his feet. "I've only ever been with one other woman." The back of his neck reddened at the admission and he wouldn't look at her.

"Um…" She struggled to wrap her mind around why that was a problem. "It's okay. I've only ever been with my ex-husband and one college boyfriend. So if you're nervous about—"

"No." If his neck got any redder it'd catch fire. "Jesus, no. That's not— I'm not a novice," he said roughly. "I know what I'm doing. Even used to be good at it."

Yes, she absolutely believed that. Just with his hands and lips, he'd brought her closer to climax than she'd ever been without the help of a vibrator. "I guess I don't understand what you're getting at." But as soon as the words left her tongue, his meaning became painfully clear: he was talking about his ex-fiancée. The woman whose picture he still carried around.

Yeah. That snuffed out any remaining spark of lust.

Phoebe found the edge of the blanket and drew it up over her naked breasts.

"This, uh, isn't going to happen between us, is it?" Resigned, she sat up on the edge of the bed and held the blanket to her front. She could still feel the lingering heat of his mouth on her nipple and her body hummed with anticipation, but she could also see the writing on the wall. He wasn't ready for intimacy yet. Had to wonder if he ever would be.

"No," he said and his shoulders slumped. "I'm sorry, Phoebe. I never should have started it in the first place, but I haven't…since before. The massage felt so good and the urge to—" He paused, cleared his throat. "Honestly, I don't even know if everything still works like it should."

A lump rose in her throat, but she swallowed it back and drummed up a smile. "It looks to me everything's working just fine."

He gripped his erection through his shorts like he wanted to hide it from her. "I'm disfigured. Scarred."

"I don't care," she whispered.

He stared at her in silence for so long, embarrassment warmed her cheeks.

"You're…" He seemed to search for the right word, but came up empty and shook his head. "How can you have so much compassion? Isn't it exhausting caring so much?"

"Not as exhausting as pretending not to care about anything."

Haunted blue eyes dropped to her mouth. A second later, he was leaning down, closing the distance between their lips. He kissed her reverently, like a man cherishing something priceless. And she couldn't help it—her heart melted into a puddle.

This man. What was it about him that made her go weak?

She shouldn't want him. Shouldn't allow herself to want him. Not with everything…

Seth cupped the back of her neck and tilted her head with the pressure of his thumb against her jaw, angling her mouth toward his to deepen the kiss. His tongue swept over her lower lip, asking gentle permission, and she opened to him, her fingers digging into his shoulders. Kissing him was…

God, she couldn't even find the words to describe the sensations he ignited with only a touch of his lips. All she knew in that second was the burning need to get closer to him. Feel more of his mouth and hands. Join with him.

No bad memories. No guilt. Just the two of them giving and taking pleasure from each other.

As he leaned over her, Phoebe lay back on the bed and dragged him with her. His muscles instantly stiffened and bunched under her fingers as if he were preparing to bolt, but she held on, unwilling to let him back away a second time.

"Please stay," she whispered in the millimeters separating their mouths and traced one of the scars on his shoulder. "I don't care that you have scars. I don't care what was done to you in the past or what you had to do to survive. It doesn't change anything for me. I still want you, the man lying beside me, right here, right now, in this moment. Can you live in the moment for me, just this once?"

Groaning, he buried his face in the crook of her neck. He stayed like that for a long time, unmoving, and she held him, running her hands along the curve of his back. All that lean muscle twitched under her touch. Then his lips, soft on the underside of her jaw, caressed the line of her throat to the edge of the blanket and a thrill jittered through her belly. He tugged the blanket away, exposing her breasts to the cool air. Her nipples immediately puckered and he swirled his tongue around one, and then the other, until she was arching off the bed.

"More." She reached between their bodies and found his length growing harder against her thigh. When she touched him, his erection bobbed in response and peeked out from the band of his boxers. She gazed down, anticipation like butterflies in her bloodstream.

Small, circular scars covered the flared head of his penis.

Burns.

She forgot everything else. The heat, the need, the promise of erotic pleasure. Tears blurred her vision. The man had suffered so much. And in that moment, she wanted nothing more than to give him pleasure to help ease away his pain. She circled her fingers around his shaft…

Seth froze, then lurched away from her like her panties had caught fire and he didn't want to risk more burns. "I can't do this." Without looking at her, he tucked himself back into his boxers, found his cargo pants, and yanked them on. Next came his shirt. Then he picked up his boots and was halfway to the door before she untangled herself from the blanket and jumped off the bed. She caught his hand.

"Seth, wait. What's wrong?"

He stopped, but wouldn't look at her. "I'm not a pity fuck."

She couldn't have been more surprised if he'd dropped a bomb at her feet. "A pity fuck? No! Seth, that's not—"

"Then why are you crying?"

Oh, God. She hadn't even realized the tears were dripping down her face. She swiped her free palm under her eyes, wiping the offending droplets away. "Because I hurt for you. For what you went through. But that changes nothing. I still want—"

"No." He pinned her with a dead, glacial stare. "If you're so desperate to get laid, ask one of the undamaged guys to do it. Jean-Luc's quite the ladies' man. Marcus, too, for that matter. Hell, I don't even care if you try for Ian." He freed his hand from her grasp and opened the door. "Any-fucking-one but me."

• • •

Seth hated himself the moment he turned away from her pale, stricken expression. He didn't know why he'd said that to her. It was an asshole comment that topped his already huge list of assholery and he should go back and apologize.

He couldn't.

In the hall, he stuffed his feet into his boots without bothering to tie the laces, then stalked toward the main room. He'd left his gear in the bedroom, but whatever. Not like he hadn't slept on a dirt floor before. Not like he even slept anymore.

"Hey, Seth," Gabe's voice called as he passed one of the bedrooms. He stopped, but wondered if he'd get away with pretending he hadn't heard.

Probably not.

In the end, he backtracked and leaned into the room. "Yeah?"

Gabe sat on the bed with his bad leg elevated and that was— hell, kind of a shock to see. True, Gabe walked with a cane unless the team was training or on a mission, but the handicap had always seemed almost like an afterthought. Never had it been as apparent as it was in this moment with the big man bedridden, his ankle enclosed in a soft cast and propped up on pillows.

"Nice shooting out there today." Gabe nodded in a show of approval. "I'm starting to see why Quinn's so adamant about keeping you around. He said you'd surprise me and you have."

"Thank you, sir." It took a huge amount of willpower not to salute the guy. After all, Lieutenant Commander Gabe "Stonewall" Bristow was the stuff of legends. He had a whole fruit salad of medals and would probably still be earning them if not for the car accident that ended his SEAL career last year. Had to wonder if the guy resented where he'd ended up. Didn't look it. He seemed at peace sitting there, content to be ordered to bed rest for the night by Jesse, the ever-sensible medic.

So what was his secret?

Gabe said nothing more and, not wanting to stand there like an idiot, Seth started to back away, sure he'd been dismissed.

"What do you think we'll be up against tomorrow?"

Gabe Bristow wanted *his* opinion? This was a change and he couldn't quite keep his shocked expression under wraps. "Uh... more of what we faced today. And they'll probably come down on us hard once they discover the bodies of their buddies in the valley."

Gabe nodded. "I agree. We did it Phoebe's way—tried to be quiet and respectful—but I think today proves we need a more aggressive approach. Tomorrow, we're going in like operators, not kids playing dress-up in their mother's clothing."

"Yes, sir."

"And I'm putting you in charge of Phoebe."

Another shock, and not necessarily a pleasant one. "Me?"

"She trusts you. She'll listen to you."

"Uh, sir, you have met her, right? I'm not so sure she listens to anyone but herself."

"She listened to you today," Gabe pointed out. "You told her to stay put, stay covered, and she did. It could have ended badly for her if she hadn't." His lips thinned into a grim line. "To be honest, I'd prefer to leave her here. It'll be rough going tomorrow and I don't want her caught in the crossfire. Is there any way you can talk her into staying behind?"

Seth winced, the memory of his final words to her filling his chest with heavy regret. "No. That won't happen. I just…kinda… pissed her off. She's not going to talk to me unless I apologize."

A wide grin split Gabe's face. "If she's anything like my wife, probably not even then." He sobered. "Apologize anyway. That's an order."

"Yes, sir."

Gabe settled against the wall behind him. His jaw tightened as he shifted his bad foot, but otherwise, he gave no indication that he was in pain. "All right, listen. I don't have to tell you this mission is personal for every man on this team. Hell, it's more personal for you than any of us, isn't it?"

Seth didn't dare speak, afraid of what might come out of his mouth, so he merely bobbed his head.

"And we're going to bring Hendricks home. I promise you

that, but"—he pointed in the general direction of Phoebe's room—"I don't want Hendricks's rescue to be at the expense of that woman's life."

A chill of dread crawled down Seth's spine. "Nor do I."

"So you do whatever necessary to keep her safe, you hear me?"

"Roger that, sir."

"Good." Gabe waved a hand in dismissal. "Oh, and, Harlan? Drop the fucking 'sir' already."

CHAPTER TWENTY-ONE

KABUL

"Paulie, wait!"

Quinn froze halfway out the shelter's front door as his surroundings snapped to sudden, vivid clearness.

What the fuck? Where was he? What was he doing? And what had Zina just called him…?

He spun and found her standing under the archway between the foyer and the dining room, chewing on her thumbnail.

"What did you just call me?"

"Um, Paulie." As if realizing she was gnawing her nail to the nub, she winced and folded her arms over her chest. "You've been insisting that's your name since you got back this morning."

"Paulie?" It felt like a foreign word on his tongue. Yeah, it had been his at one time, but he hadn't been Benjamin Paul Jewett Jr. or Paulie in nearly twenty years. Hadn't even thought of himself by that name since he legally changed it to Travis Benjamin Quinn, after his maternal grandfather and his adoptive parents. "No, I'm Quinn. Call me Quinn."

Her eyes all but bugged out of her pretty face. "Okay. I have to ask, are you all right? You've been acting…strange and insisting I call you by a different name for the last several hours. That's not normal and I don't want you around my girls if—" She seemed to search for the right words. "If you're not healthy."

"If I'm crazy, you mean?"

"I kind of think your whole team is crazy, so that's not saying much." She shook her head, huffed out a breath, and turned to go back into the dining room. "Just try to avoid the girls as much as possible, okay?"

"Not a problem." He'd rather shoot himself in the foot than deal with a flock of teenage girls.

He stepped outside and sucked in a lungful of cool, dry November air.

Fucking blackout.

He knew stress was a trigger and should have expected it after his visit to Bagram this morning. Commander Bennett hadn't welcomed him with open arms. In fact, Bennett's response basically boiled down to, "Thanks, but I know about your brain injury and I don't really trust a thing coming out of your mouth. Good seeing you again, though. Have a nice day."

Now he got what it must feel like to be Seth, to have everyone around you think you're crazy. And without being free to reveal how he came across the information about the nuke, he probably had sounded off his rocker.

Maybe he was.

Paulie?

What was that all about? Some kind of regression? His doctors had mentioned something about lapsing into fugue states, but they'd said it was a *possibility*. They'd also given him a lot of other possibilities throughout his recovery, starting with their first prognosis that he'd be a veggie for the rest of his life. Well, he'd shocked the hell out of them when he opened his eyes a month later, pulled out his IVs, and tried to get out of bed to find Gabe and make sure he was okay.

So fuck the docs and their possibilities. They even admitted they didn't know much about the area in his brain that had been damaged when his head had an up-close-and-personal encounter with the car windshield. He knew himself and even in a fugue state or whatever the blackouts were, he wouldn't return to the hell that had been his childhood.

Zina had heard wrong. Simple as that.

Unable to settle, he went back inside and made his way to the war room to check in with Harvard. Thank Christ the kid had been glued to his computer all morning. Last thing Quinn needed was another witness to his unraveling sanity.

Sure enough, Harvard was still in the exact position Quinn had left him, hunched over his screen. Only now, his hair stuck up from multiple passes of a frustrated hand. "Hey. Any luck locating Siddiqui?"

"None," Harvard said with a shake of his head. "And believe me, I have all of my digital ears to the ground."

"Where the fuck is he? He's running for president. Shouldn't he be out campaigning or some shit?"

"No, too early. The campaign won't start in earnest for another few months."

And in that time, he'll secure himself a nuke. "Fuck."

"Hey," Harvard called as he turned to leave. "What's going on with you?"

Quinn stopped dead in his tracks. Shit. Had Harvard been witness to the blackout after all? He schooled his expression into a blank mask before facing the kid again. "What do you mean? There's nothing going on."

"Don't give me that everything-is-fine act. I got enough of that from my parents when I was growing up." He took off his glasses and rubbed his eyes with his thumb and forefinger. When he slid his glasses back in place, he nailed Quinn with an exhausted glare that aged him well past his twenty-four years. "I'm young. I get it. But for fuck's sake, I'm not a child. I'm just as much a member of this team as you are and I know Gabe sent you to Bagram this morning. What was that about?"

So he wasn't talking about the blackout. Relief left Quinn light-headed. "All right. Point taken." Gabe hadn't wanted to tell the men about the possibly of the bomb—didn't want to divide their attention while they were deep in enemy territory—but Harvard wasn't up in the mountains and he needed to know. "This doesn't go beyond this room."

"Absolutely."

Quinn shut the door. "In Zak Hendricks's reports, he mentions Siddiqui is angling to buy a suitcase-size nuke. The deal is supposed to go down soon. Probably within the next few days."

"Which is why you went to Bagram," Harvard said, nodding. If the news rattled him, he didn't show it. "You wanted help dealing with the bomb."

"Yeah, but things didn't go as planned there. I couldn't tell them where I had gotten the information and they weren't about to take my word for it. Now, it's a possibility they'll still check into it, but I feel like this is all on us."

"We're not an anti-terror unit," Harvard said with a weary sigh. "But we can't sit back and do nothing. Shit." He straightened his shoulders and turned to his computer. "All right. Let me get back to work. I'll call you as soon as I have a lock on Siddiqui."

"Thanks." Quinn left the room and came face-to-face with a handful of giggling girls, led by Tehani. His blood went cold.

Jesus Christ. He'd rather face off with a thousand Taliban fighters than these four prepubescent kids. Especially since Zina told him to avoid them.

He tried to step around them, but Tehani blocked his path no matter which way he moved. The other three girls held their scarves over their mouths and giggled. Tehani's head was unabashedly bare, sleek black hair hanging loose around her shoulders.

"Hand-some," she said slowly in English and pointed at him, which set the other girls off again. "Pr—pretty yel-low hair." She patted the top of her head.

"Uh..." He scanned left and right. Dammit, where was an enemy ambush when a guy needed one? "Thanks?"

Tehani grinned. "You...make...good husband."

Whoa. Yeah. Definitely time to make a fast exit. He was starting to sweat and he had no doubt they could smell the fear on him.

Again, he tried stepping around her. "I have work to do."

She said something in Pashto. He knew bits of the language, enough to pick out the word "protector," and guilt sank its claws into the back of his neck. He stopped several paces away and faced the group again.

"Nobody's going to hurt you as long as I'm around, okay?"

He didn't think they understood him, but it didn't matter. Tehani grinned and the other girls jabbered excitedly behind his back as he strode away.

CHAPTER TWENTY-TWO

Oh, yeah, she was still pissed. Not that Seth blamed her for it. He deserved the silent treatment and probably more.

Phoebe had barely looked at him all day, even though they now rode the same horse since both his and Ian's animals had escaped during the firefight yesterday. The village had provided Ian with a donkey, which, as Jean-Luc pointed out, had the same shining personality as the bomb tech.

Phoebe had snapped a photo of the made-in-heaven pair and laughed about it with the guys—until Gabe ordered her to ride with Seth. She'd protested, of course, but it was either Gabe's way or the highway, and her arguments had died a quick death.

At least the trip was uneventful. No more run-ins with unfriendly locals, which was either a stroke of awesome luck or a sign of bad things to come. Seth suspected the latter, though he didn't say so out loud. No sense in jinxing it if they had just gotten lucky.

Seth tried to strike up a conversation with her several times during the daylong ride. Tried to apologize, too, but she wasn't having it. What did he have to do to prove he really was sorry?

Grovel? Yeah, probably, but that was kind of hard to do from the back of a horse when his passenger wouldn't speak to him.

He was mulling over ideas when their ragtag caravan cleared the top of a ridge and Phoebe stiffened up in the saddle, nearly knocking him in the chin with the top of her head. "Wait. Stop."

He pulled their mount to a halt and she climbed down.

"Oh my God. The dog's still here." She took off at a sprint toward the ruins of an old Soviet tank.

Gabe swung around as everyone else also came to a stop. "What is it?"

"She said something about a dog."

"What dog?" someone asked, but Seth didn't bother taking the time to answer. He handed his horse's reins to Gabe and ran after her.

Phoebe was on her knees in front of a scruffy dog and spoke soothingly to it in Pashto as she reached out a hand. The animal shivered wildly and got to his feet, his tail tucked between his legs. Though on the skinny side, he had the powerful build of a German shepherd with ears that stood upright. His body was a red-brown color and his face was completely black, as if he were wearing a mask.

"Oh, you poor thing. Someone bring me water," she snapped over her shoulder and rubbed the dog's head. "I saw his owner tie him here when Zina and I arrived. That was days ago."

Seth squatted down beside her and picked up the empty collar still chained to the tank's main gun. Apparently, the dog had slipped out of it, but hadn't run away. "Maybe his owner ties him here every day. Look, his bowls are right over there." But both of the dented metal dishes were empty and turned upside down, like the dog had pawed at them when he ran out of food and water.

Phoebe shook her head. "Something's wrong." She accepted

the bottle of water Jesse handed her and flipped the dog's dish over to fill it. "Do you think he can eat one of your MREs?"

Seth was already a step ahead of her, digging in his pack for the meal ready to eat labeled beef stew. He didn't bother with heating it and ripped open the pouch, dumping the contents into the second bowl. The dog devoured it, so he grabbed another one.

"Uh, Phoebe?" Jean-Luc called and they both glanced over. He stood at the edge of the hill, staring out over the village. "Did it look like this last time you were here?"

She gave the dog one last pat on the head and stood. "Oh. My. God."

"I'll take that as a no," Jean-Luc muttered.

Seth joined them and found himself looking down at a ghost town. Or no, not completely abandoned. Other animals roamed between the mud huts, including an untended herd of goats.

Really not a good sign.

"Oh, God. Tehani's family." Phoebe spun away and jumped onto their horse, urging it into a run with a "Hyah. Hyah."

Shit.

Seth grabbed Jean-Luc's mount and swung up into the saddle. He caught up to her easily at the edge of town, probably because their horse had been carrying two riders and was already exhausted. But when he grabbed her reins and eased her animal to a stop, she simply leaped down and continued running on foot.

"Phoebe, don't."

If she heard him, she gave no sign and ran toward one of the mud houses. She tore through the front door and went from room to room, shouting, "Darya! Nemat!"

Seth stood in the doorway without comment until she came back to the main room, a ragged teddy bear clutched to her belly.

"Phoebe, they're not here."

Tears streaked her dirty face. "Something's wrong. They left everything they own. They're not nomads. This is their home. Why would they leave everything behind?" She hugged the bear tighter and stared at a forgotten head scarf on the floor. "Maybe they decided to go to Kabul after all? Maybe they're on their way to the shelter to see Tehani right now." She sounded like she was trying to convince herself.

Seth struggled to find a comforting response—except no way Tehani's family was headed to Kabul without taking at least some of their belongings, and he wasn't about to lie to her. Something *was* very wrong here.

"Not liking this," Gabe said behind him and he glanced over his shoulder to find the rest of the team standing there in full view of Phoebe's breakdown. He faced them, but positioned himself in the doorway to offer her a modicum of privacy.

"Yeah, me either. She's right. These people aren't nomads. They wouldn't up and leave like this unless they were forced."

Gabe nodded and motioned for the men to go inside the house. After a second of hesitation and the reassuring touch of Phoebe's hand on his back, Seth stepped aside to let them pass.

Everyone was subdued and grim-faced as they packed into the small main room. Seth stuck close to Phoebe's side, unwilling to let her out of his sight.

Ian was the last to enter and the dog trotted in behind him, tail wagging.

"What?" he sneered when everyone gaped at him with expressions ranging from disbelief to suspicion. "I'm a bastard, not a monster. I wasn't about to tie him back up and leave him there. Nobody should be chained up like that." A beat passed in awkward silence before he lifted his chin and met Seth's eyes. "And I mean that. *Nobody*."

Seth opened his mouth, but wasn't quite sure what to say in response. At his side, Phoebe touched his shoulder and gave Ian a warm smile. "That was kind of you."

Ian grunted. "I don't do kind."

"All right, gentlemen," Gabe said. "Enough chitchat. I know you're all tired from the long ride today, but we need to keep pushing toward the compound. Now according to Tehani, we head three miles northeast from here. It's going to be a steep climb and we'll be on foot, so we should plan to reach the compound sometime in the middle of the night. We'll spend time on recon and if it looks like our objective is inside, we'll make plans to go in before dawn. Phoebe."

She looked up at the sound of her name.

"You're staying here."

She opened her mouth, no doubt to protest, but Seth caught her hand and gave it a hard squeeze in warning. It was enough of a distraction, giving her time to think before she started arguing, and she must have seen Gabe's logic because she agreed.

"Rehydrate and check your gear. Secure anything that might make noise," Gabe said to the team. "We leave in ten. And Phoebe, make sure that dog stays here with you."

She nodded and reached for the dog's reattached collar, giving the scruffy animal a scratch behind the ear. "I have him. You guys be careful up there."

The team filed out. Seth started to follow, but she let go of the dog and ducked past him, blocking his path.

"That goes double for you," she said softly. "I don't want to see you coming back with anything more than a bruise. And I plan to check, too. Thoroughly."

Her hands tracing his body, dipping inside his shorts…

Fuck. Heat gathered at the base of his spine and there was a sudden, noticeable lack of room in the front of his pants. He cleared his throat and stepped back, resisting the urge to adjust himself. "You're, uh, not still mad?"

"Oh, I am. You were a complete ass last night."

He winced. "I know."

Phoebe closed the distance between them and clasped his cheeks in her palms, forcing him to look at her. "But that doesn't mean I want to see you hurt, so come back in one piece, okay?"

He wasn't sure what to say to that—it had been forever since anyone besides his family cared enough about him to worry about his safety—so instead of replying, he bent and pressed his lips to hers.

Wasn't enough.

He gripped her hips and drew her against him, slanting his mouth to a better angle over hers. The kiss did a flurry of strange things inside him. Jacked up his pulse, made him aware of every heartbeat, every expansion of his lungs as he drew air in. Even the brush of his clothes against his skin was too much sensation. He felt at once hot and cold, covered with goose bumps, and the surge of heat along his spine coalesced in his balls as an aching need. It had been a long time since he'd been inside a woman. Given half an opportunity, he would have stripped her bare right there in the abandoned house, buried himself in her willing body, and spent the next several hours sating himself.

Okay, several *minutes*. It had been a *long* time and his staying power probably wasn't what it used to be, but it didn't matter right now because he had a mission and she was going to stay here where it was safe.

Maybe when this was over…

The thought had him jerking backward in surprise.

Phoebe opened her eyes and scanned his face. "What's going on inside that head of yours?"

That's what he'd like to know. In the three years since he was taken captive, he'd lived hour to hour, day to day, not thinking about the future. Because until HORNET, he had no future.

And even then he'd viewed his employment with the group like an unsteady bridge, always swaying, constantly on the verge of collapse. He'd woken up every morning expecting Gabe to call and tell him his latest screw-up was his last.

Phoebe was steady. She was solid and real, a focal point he could fixate on. He had a future with her. It probably wouldn't go any further than one night together, maybe a fling, but that didn't matter. She gave him something to look forward to.

He dipped his head again and put every ounce of reverence he felt toward her in his kiss.

"Harlan," Gabe called from outside. "We're moving."

Damn, he didn't want to move. He wanted to stay right here for the rest of his life.

When he finally drew away, Phoebe's eyes remained closed, but a small smile played around the corners of her mouth. "Hmm."

He brushed his lips across her temple. "Remember where we were. I want to pick up right here when I get back."

"Harlan!" Gabe called again.

"Fuck. Hang on!"

Her lids opened and her eyes went all soft as she traced the stubbled line of his jaw with one finger, ending at the indent in his chin. "Are you sure?"

"Yeah." He swallowed hard. His heart was thundering in his chest like he'd just run a four-minute mile. "I'd like to try last night again. Without the part where I freak out."

She smiled and started to say something, but Marcus popped his head through the front door. "Yo, Gabe's getting pissed."

Phoebe let go of him and stepped back, still smiling. "Better go."

He nodded and made it to the door before she added, "I'd like to try last night again, too, so please be safe out there."

He couldn't help the grin as he joined the team out front

and bent to pick up his gear. When he straightened, he realized they all stared at him as if he'd just walked out of the house stark naked. And even though he was fully dressed, in that second he felt stripped bare. Exposed.

"All right, gentlemen," Gabe said, cutting through the awkward moment in his usual no-nonsense way. "Let's go. We have a hike ahead of us. And, Harlan? Next time I tell you to move, you sure as fuck better move. Got it?"

"Yeah," Seth muttered and secured his gear on his back. He jumped up and down a few times to make sure nothing rattled or came loose.

The men fell in line behind Gabe.

Seth hesitated, glancing back as he brought up the end of the line. Phoebe knelt in front of the squat mud house, arms wrapped around the dog as she watched them go. Her head scarf hung loose over her shoulders, her hair a riot of copper in the dying evening sunlight. Already the temperature had dropped by a good ten degrees, and the night promised to be a chilly one.

"Find some blankets," he called. "Don't start a fire. You don't want to risk drawing attention to yourself."

She nodded and lifted a hand in a wave.

She was safe here.

Sucking in a breath, Seth forced the paranoia down and jogged to catch up to the team. He had a job to do and had to put her out of his thoughts for the next several hours.

Distraction equaled death in these mountains.

CHAPTER TWENTY-THREE

At first glance, the old military outpost appeared heavily fortified, backed right up against the mountain and surrounded by a high, barbed wire–topped mud wall on three sides. When it had belonged to the Americans, it probably had been damn near impenetrable, but now the wall had crumbled in several places and much of the barbed wire had been removed, probably for scrap. One of the five buildings inside the wall had been razed, and another stood in crumbling disrepair. Only the largest seemed to be in use at the moment, and the other two sat dark and silent. One narrow road snaked down the mountainside from the compound and a battered 4x4 waited at the front gate.

From Seth's perch in a tree some two hundred meters uphill, he counted six Taliban fighters around a campfire in front of the main building, which was lit up inside like Times Square. They seemed to be engaging in some kind of feast, which didn't make sense. This wasn't a holiday and these weren't rich men, but the layout on the blanket in front of them was a hearty one.

Unless it was a last meal.

Suicide bombers. Those six Taliban fighters were preparing to become martyrs.

And there were probably at least six more men inside the building, because each bomber would need a handler—someone to remote detonate in case the martyrs got cold feet at the last second. So, twelve men altogether.

Seth repositioned himself on his limb and scanned the narrow slits of windows, hoping to confirm an exact number for Gabe. The more information, the better the team's odds, but he couldn't see anything more than shadows and fleeting movement.

Every few minutes, the muffled *pop* of a gunshot rang out and the fighters sent up a cheer.

Seth's stomach rolled and sweat dampened his shirt along his spine. Whatever was happening inside that building was ugly.

He gave it another few minutes until the next shot sent a chill racing over his skin. Fuck, they had to get in there and see what— or who—these guys were shooting at. What if they were using Sergeant Hendricks as target practice? Or worse.

The missing villagers really bothered him.

And the paranoid buzzing in the back of his brain wouldn't let up, no matter how emphatically he told it to fuck off.

He had to talk to Gabe, but they'd been ordered to radio silence. They didn't have secure channels and couldn't risk the Taliban overhearing, leaving him with only one option: he had to make his way to Gabe's position.

Waiting any longer to raid the compound was a huge miscalculation.

Slinging his rifle across his back, he jumped out of the tree and landed with far more noise than he'd hoped. He crouched at the tree's base and held his breath, listening for anything out of the ordinary.

Save for another shot and cheer from the compound, the mountain was silent.

He moved slowly, picking his way through dense underbrush until another gunshot stopped him in his tracks. It was followed by a second, then a pause and two more in quick succession.

And was that…a scream? Faint, it swept through the trees like the wail of a ghost. The hair on the back of Seth's neck stood on end.

They were torturing someone down there—most likely Sergeant Hendricks.

And at the rate he was moving, he wasn't going to make it to Gabe before the shooter ran out of targets. He glanced around, searching for other options. In the dim light from the half-full moon, he spotted the grotto where Jean-Luc was supposed to be hiding. He dropped his pack and walked in a crouch toward the mouth of the small cave.

"Cajun," he whispered, "coming to you."

"Roger that." Jean-Luc's voice floated out, sounding like an echo.

A second later, he flattened himself against the cave's wall at Jean-Luc's side. A mountain stream rushed somewhere nearby, but without the benefit of moonlight, it was too dark to see the water. The cold spray of it misted his face, though, and the cavern amplified the sound, which provided perfect cover for their voices.

Jean-Luc touched his shoulder. "What's up?"

"I need your scarf."

"Can I ask why?" Even as he said it, he started unwinding the fabric from his neck. "I paid a pretty penny for this thing."

"I'm going to wrap it around my head and walk into the compound like I belong there."

Jean-Luc froze. "Say again?" No doubt he had that you're-completely-fucking-insane look on his face—too dark to tell for sure, and in any case, Seth was used to seeing the expression aimed in his direction. Didn't bother him anymore.

"You heard me."

Instead of trying to talk him out of it, Jean-Luc just clicked his tongue and handed the scarf over. "You have some balls, *mon ami.*"

Not really. The thought of walking into the hands of the same group that tortured him for fifteen months had him quaking in his boots, but he didn't see any other options. "We can't assault the place. You see that feast they've cooked up? It's their last meal. Those men are preparing to martyr themselves. They have nothing to lose and they'll slaughter us. But we have an advantage. I *know* these people. I spent over a year living with guys just like them. I can pass myself off as one of them long enough to get inside and create a diversion to give you guys a shot at grabbing Hendricks."

"You sure he's in there?"

"Yeah." He couldn't explain how, but he *knew* Zak Hendricks was being held somewhere inside that crumbling wall, just like he knew this was their only shot of getting him out.

Finally, Jean-Luc shrugged. "Hey, it's all good with me. Love a good suicide mission. But," he added, dragging the word out, "I doubt Phoebe will feel the same when I tell her you went and got yourself killed."

Phoebe.

Jesus, he hadn't even considered…

And he couldn't start now.

Hardening his heart against the sweet memory of her lips on his, he quickly wrapped the scarf around his head and face. "Just get word to Gabe. Tell him there are at least twelve men inside, possibly more."

Jean-Luc whistled through his teeth. "You do know if you survive this, he's going kill you."

"Yeah, well, he'll have to get in line."

• • •

No amount of training in the world could have prepared Zak for the amount of pain he was in. Moving hurt. Breathing hurt. He imagined blinking would even hurt, if his left eye wasn't swollen shut and his right eye wasn't taped open.

Whatever they were about to do, they didn't want him to miss it.

Bring it, he thought. They couldn't make him hurt any worse and he wasn't going to talk, so whatever they had planned…

Siddiqui's second-in-command, an ice-cold bastard who went only by the name Askar, or "soldier" in English, walked into the room, dragging something behind him.

No, not something, Zak realized as his good eye focused. Someone. A frail old man with sunken eyes and missing teeth.

Askar grabbed a chair from against the wall and placed it directly across from Zak's, then forced the man to sit down. He pulled a gun from under his tunic and pointed it at the sobbing man's temple, then watched Zak without even a flicker of emotion. "Who are you, traitor?"

So they'd given up on torturing *him* for information. Now they were moving on to civilians. Christ Almighty.

"Let him go." With his tongue so dry it stuck to the roof of his mouth, he found the Pashto words hard to articulate, but he'd die before uttering a word of English in front of these men. They couldn't know he was American. That was all there was to it.

Askar didn't even blink as he pulled the trigger. Zak tried to avert his gaze, but Askar grabbed a handful of his hair and forced him to watch.

On and on it went, one villager after another. A circle of questions, refusals, and death. And then they brought in a woman.

She was young and clutching a toddler to her chest.

"Don't," Zak whisper around the lump in his throat.

Askar pressed the gun to her temple. "Who do you work for?"

Zak almost broke. He opened his mouth to spill it all, tell them everything from his name to the reason he'd weaseled his way into Siddiqui's good graces. He could take all the pain and humiliation they dished out, but he could not sit idly by while women and children were murdered in cold blood.

But the look on Askar's face as he held the gun to the woman's temple stopped Zak from uttering a sound. The little boy and his mother were both already dead in that soldier's eyes. They all were, and nothing Zak said would change that fate. He could spill all the state secrets he knew, and he'd still be unable to save any of the villagers from a bullet.

"You fucking prick!" Tapping into a reserve of strength he didn't know he had, he kicked out with his chained legs. He unbalanced his chair, but he also nailed Askar in the balls, and the bullet meant for the woman went into the ceiling.

"Run!"

She didn't listen. She clung to her child, sobbing in big hiccupping gulps.

After a moment, Askar straightened. Wincing in pain, he ignored the woman and child and limped over to Zak's overturned chair. Still, there was no flicker of emotion. No anger, just a flat assessment. "Why risk death to save a woman you don't know?"

Zak gritted his teeth. The fall had sent his already-aching body flying to new heights of pain, but he wasn't about to let on how much damage he'd done to himself. He met the soldier's impassive stare with as much defiance as he could muster. "If you don't already know the answer to that, then you're incapable of understanding and I'd rather not waste my last breath explaining it."

Askar stared, dark eyes unblinking. The emotionally castrated bastard really didn't understand. He raised the gun.

So this was the end.

Zak expected the whole "life flashing in front of his eyes" thing to start, but he didn't really want to see it. He'd done a lot of shit he wasn't proud of, like sabotaging his marriage by leaving the country every chance he got because he was too much of a goddamn coward to tell Jillian it wasn't working. And then spending the last five years since his divorce losing himself with any willing woman who came along. He'd also killed more times than he wanted to count. All in the name of democracy and freedom, but sometimes the people at the receiving end of his assassinations hadn't been wholly guilty of threatening those values.

But he'd done a lot of good, too. He'd served his country to the best of his ability and hadn't betrayed her by spilling her secrets. When he was home, he tried to be a good son to his parents, a good brother and uncle. And he'd saved Tehani. That had to count for something, and he held the girl's face in the forefront of his mind as he waited for the bullet to end his life.

It didn't come.

"So you know," Askar said, "you didn't save the woman or her son. This entire compound and the village below are about to be razed by an air strike. And in case you're still entertaining heroic notions…"

The gun barrel shifted away from his head and aimed at his kneecap.

CHAPTER TWENTY-FOUR

Seth left Jean-Luc and backtracked down the mountain a quarter of a mile before finally stepping onto the road just out of sight of the front gate. He walked with cool purpose toward the compound, keeping his pace fast, but not panicked. His muscles ached with the effort to not fidget. Appearing nervous would be a dead giveaway to anyone watching his approach.

As it turned out, nobody was standing watch, all of them too busy with their meal or whatever was happening in the main building. At least he didn't have to worry about a trigger-happy guard ending him before he got inside. The gate was even cracked open about a foot.

Well, hell. Maybe the team could have raided the place without sustaining any casualties. These guys obviously weren't all that concerned with security.

Surprisingly, Seth's heart didn't beat out of his chest as he strode across the open courtyard a mere twenty feet from the dining wannabe martyrs. He was calm, focused. So focused on getting inside the main building, in fact, he nearly missed when one of the men shouted to him.

"What are you doing?"

Forcing himself to pause when all he wanted to do was run, he stared down the guy who had called out and infused his tone with impatience. "Siddiqui sent me to make sure everything is going according to schedule."

The men didn't seem to like that, grumbling in the same way men complained about their bosses the world over.

"Does he think we won't follow through?" one asked. He was so young, not even old enough to have a full beard, and yet so willing to die.

"No, he's knows you'll stay true to the mission."

"Then what did he say?" another demanded.

"He gave me a message for you," Seth blurted, sweat dampening his shirt despite the cold night. They all stopped eating and looked interested in what he had to say.

Shit. Now what? His gut response was to try convincing them the plan had been called off, but he doubted that would work and mentally scrambled for something else. Only one other thing popped to mind: "'And slay them wherever ye catch them, and turn them out from where they have turned you out; for tumult and oppression are worse than slaughter; but fight them not at the Sacred Mosque, unless they first fight you there; but if they fight you, slay them. Such is the reward of those who suppress faith.'"

The Quran passage elicited a round of cheers and he swallowed a surge of bile. Throwing up would not be a good plan, but those words had been beaten into him for four hundred and sixty long days and saying them now caused his stomach to threaten a revolt.

One of the men stood up. "We are honored to offer our lives if it means the end of the infidels' oppression."

"And Allah rewards the faithful." His lips were numb; his tongue felt like wood. "I have last-minute preparations to see to.

Go. Enjoy your meal."

Without waiting for a response, he ducked inside. As soon as he was alone, he bent at the waist, swallowing compulsively to keep from revisiting his last protein shake. His captors had used that verse and others like it to justify the things they did to him, same as the men out front now used it to justify the killing of who knows how many innocents.

After his rescue, he'd read the Quran cover to cover, and found comfort in the fact that it didn't actually promote terrorism. Same as Christian extremists who twisted the Bible to suit their purposes, his captors had taken those passages out of context and wielded them like weapons against all non-Muslims.

Straightening, he sucked in a breath through his nose and let it out in a long exhale. He still had a job to do, a diversion to create.

He reached under his baggy tunic and found one of the grenades on his belt. He pulled the pin, turned back to the door, and revisited his football days as he threw the grenade into the middle of the wannabe martyrs' dinner spread. He half thought he'd get some kind of perverse satisfaction from the act, but as he listened to the panicked shouts in the seconds before the grenade exploded, he pictured the young one's beardless face and wished like hell things could have been different for the kid.

Shots peppered the side of the building. And here comes the HORNET swarm, right on cue.

A man with a wild black beard tumbled out of a room up ahead, weapon in hand. "What's going on?" he shouted. "Has it started? It's too soon!"

Seth grabbed the guy by the tunic. "We're under attack!"

He blinked like he didn't understand and opened his mouth, but all that came out was an *umph* sound as Seth jammed a knife into his heart and let him slide to the floor.

Another man stepped into the hall and this time, Seth didn't bother playing the part of friend. He grabbed the dead guy's AK-47 and raised the weapon. "Put the gun down, fucker! Hands in the air!"

The man swung in his direction and their eyes locked. His finger froze on the trigger.

Something about those dead eyes, peering out over a bushy dark brown beard...

Catching himself before he slipped into the past, he tightened his finger. Bushy Beard dodged the bullet and sprinted deeper into the bowels of the building. Seth let him go and took a second to get his head back in the right space.

Fuck. That moment of hesitation could have been his last. Probably should have been his last, but for some reason, Bushy Beard hadn't pulled the trigger either.

The door rattled at his six and he swung around, ready to fire until he saw Marcus and Jesse. He lowered the muzzle toward the floor and held up one hand. "Friendly!"

"Dude," Marcus said, lowering his own gun. "You are fucking insane."

"Hey, we got in, didn't we?"

"Gabe's spittin' nails," Jesse said.

"Don't doubt it." He turned away from them and raised his gun again to push deeper into the building. "On me. I haven't cleared this area yet."

"Roger that," they said at the same time and stacked up behind him. One by one, they checked each room in the corridor. Most were empty with an occasional forgotten desk or other detritus from the building's former life as an American outpost. Sometimes they found bedrolls or stacks of gear, but no more Taliban fighters.

The hall ended in a set of double doors and T'd from there.

They cleared the two short wings, finding nothing but a side exit hanging open, which they secured, and then they met back in the middle. Going by the words printed over the doors, the room on the other side was the former chow hall. Some fan of *The Walking Dead* had long ago spray-painted DON'T OPEN. DEAD INSIDE on the dented metal doors.

"Wait," Marcus said as Seth reached to try the handle. "You don't think…?"

"Really?" Jesse smacked him on the back of the head. "You watch too much TV, pal."

"Just sayin'." He made the sign of the cross over his chest and took a large step backward.

"Didn't know you were a religious man, Marcus." Seth tried the door. It was jammed. He shouldered his rifle and threw his weight against it.

"I'm not," Marcus said. "I'm Italian. And if zombies come pouring outta there, you two are on your own. I draw the line at zombies."

The door gave a few inches and Seth found his flashlight, shined it through the crack. There were dead inside—just not the walking kind. At least ten bodies that he could see littered the floor. One of the men had lived long enough to crawl to the door, but had succumbed to his injuries inches from freedom and his body now blocked it from opening.

"Guys, I think we found the missing villagers. Help me push this open."

Marcus and Jesse added their weight and together, they managed to move the body enough to slip inside.

Jesse checked the man's pulse before shaking his head and stepping over the corpse. "Check for survivors."

"Nada," Marcus said a moment later.

"None yet." Seth straightened away from the body of an old

man, spotted another body chained to an upturned chair a few feet away, and started toward it. Surprise coursed through him when a small head peeked over the man's shoulder. "Wait, got movement over here. Fuck, it's a kid. A toddler. And a woman. I got two survivors."

Sobbing, the boy held out his arms. Seth scooped him up and passed him to Jesse, who handled the child as only an experienced father could, murmuring soft words of comfort as he checked for injuries.

"He's unharmed," Jesse said. "The mother?"

Seth squatted down in front of her and spoke softly in Pashto. She stared past his shoulder, uncomprehending. "Alive, conscious, but in a severe state of shock."

Jesse nodded and knelt to tend to her. "Marcus, get the kid out of here, then come back for the woman."

Marcus handled the boy with a lot less confidence but was careful to keep his face turned away from the carnage as he crossed the room.

"Has to be more villagers somewhere," Seth said after the boy was out of earshot. "Maybe even survivors. We have to keep—"

The man tied to the chair at his feet groaned.

Seth spun and used his foot to push the chair up on its side. Even despite the man's battered face, he recognized him instantly. "It's Hendricks. Jesse! Got Sergeant Hendricks here." He knelt and started working at the ropes securing Zak to the chair. The guy had taken a beating and one of his legs was a bloody, pulpy mess at the knee.

Jesse took one look at him and swore. "I need my bag. Keep him stable and talking." Then he scooped up the woman and was gone, leaving them alone amid the carnage.

"Hey there, Zak. My name's Seth. We're here to get you home, okay?"

One dark, bloodshot eye fluttered open. A piece of tape stuck to his lashes, and Seth carefully pulled it off.

"What branch are you?" Zak whispered.

"Marines," Seth answered automatically, then winced and added, "Well, used to be."

"They told me...fully deniable op. Thought...nobody...was... coming."

"Nobody official was, but we're not working for the government. Greer Wilde sent us."

A ghost of a smile showed on Zak's swollen and cracked lips. "Shoulda known he wouldn't leave me behind. Those Wildes are good guys. The whole lot of 'em." He winced as his bonds came loose and his hands dropped like stones to the floor. "Tell Greer I didn't give Siddiqui a fucking thing. No matter what his men did...I didn't talk. I didn't talk."

"I believe you." One look at the room and Zak's condition spoke volumes for his loyalty. Nobody who saw him now would doubt him, and Seth's respect for him shot through the roof. It wasn't easy to hold up under torture. Seth sure as fuck hadn't.

"Hey." He caught Zak's face in his dirty hands as the soldier's head lolled. "Hey, man, you'll tell Greer that yourself. All right? I know how easy it would be to give up right now. I *know*. I've been where you are. You feel safe and you think, 'It's in someone else's hands now.' But you stop fighting now and you're never going to see American soil again."

His lid peeled open, but he wasn't seeing Seth. He stared at a point on the ceiling and for a horrifying minute, he went so still Seth thought they'd lost him.

Then he blinked and sucked in a breath. "Safe?"

Oh, shit. Seth swallowed the lump in his throat. "Yeah, man. You're safe."

"No!" He surged into a sitting position, his fingers digging into Seth's biceps. "Not safe. Not safe at all. We need to leave. Get the villagers and the boy and get out. Siddiqui is bombing this compound and the village."

Every cell in Seth's being flash-froze. "What do you mean he's bombing the village?"

"He wants it to look like an American attack."

"On Niazi Village, where all these people came from?"

Zak looked at the bodies like he was seeing them for the first time and tears leaked from his good eye. "He's punishing them for hiding Tehani."

"When?"

Zak looked toward the narrow slits that served as windows. The sky outside had gone a pale blue-gray and he winced. "Dawn."

• • •

Askar plastered himself against a tree as the entire mountain shook under his feet. The air strike, happening right on time. He stole a glance upward, saw the compound take two more bombs, and wondered if the Americans were still inside—especially the one he hadn't been able to shoot. Everything in him had revolted at the idea of killing the man and he couldn't figure out why. Maybe because the face he'd seen on the soldier had belonged to a dead man?

With shaking hands, he lifted the edge of his tunic and swept away the sweat beading on his forehead, then stared up at the compound again.

A ghost.

He'd just come face-to-face with a ghost from…where? His past? But he didn't have a past. His mind raced, struggled to put together jagged pieces of memory that somehow felt both real and imagined.

A ghost.

A...friend?

No. No, that wasn't right. His friends were all dead, killed by the Americans. He shook his head and staggered away from the tree.

He had to report the attack to Siddiqui. And hope like hell he wasn't lashed for the breach in security.

CHAPTER TWENTY-FIVE

Seth's heart lodged in his throat as he crested the ridge where they had left the horses. He'd heard the bombs hit the compound behind him, could still hear the planes' engines droning as they disappeared over the mountain, but he'd hoped the village…

The village was gone, nothing more than a pile of rubble spread through the valley.

He was too late.

No. No, he wouldn't accept that. Maybe Phoebe hadn't been in the house. Or possibly not even in the village. She didn't have the best track record for listening to orders, so she could be wandering around, snapping photos, completely oblivious to how terrified he was right now.

And the dog was alive, pacing through the rubble. That had to mean Phoebe got out in time, too.

He cupped his hands around his mouth. "Phoebe!"

No answer.

He skidded down the hillside, vaulting over rocks and chunks of mud that used to be someone's living room wall. The dog chased him, barking, nipping at his heels as if telling him to go faster. He skidded to a halt in front of what was left of Tehani's family home. "Phoebe!"

Nothing.

Flattening himself out on the ground, he peered through a small hole the wreckage. He couldn't see a damn thing. "Phoebe!"

Still no response.

Shit, shit, shit.

Had to make the hole bigger. Had to go in there and get her the hell out. He started digging with both hands, pulling away chunks of wood and other debris. The dog danced around him, tugging on his pant leg.

The structure shuddered and big slats of dried mud fell from the walls, forcing him backward. The roof shifted dangerously, pieces raining down. A plume of dust shot into the air as the house shifted, collapsed in on itself, and settled.

Fuck it. He'd take the place apart piece by piece if he had to, but he was going to pull her out of there. He dug faster, his hands coated in dust and blood from the wounds opening on his knuckles and palms. Didn't matter. He'd had worse pain. All that mattered was getting Phoebe out.

He'd promised Gabe he'd look after her.

Several sets of hands locked around his ankles and dragged him away from the house. Away from Phoebe.

No, he couldn't leave her. Being with her…for the first time in years, he'd been able to just live. He'd felt alive and whole when he was with her and he wouldn't give her up. She was his connection to humanity, to life. The good to soothe the decayed pieces of his soul.

"Phoebe!"

No response.

Except the hands on him, yanking him somewhere against his will.

Inside his mind, past collided with present and he screamed until his voice gave out. He was still in captivity. He'd never been rescued and those hands on him weren't friendly. They were dragging him into the center of the village for more humiliation, more torture. Everything else—his new teammates, the mission to rescue a black ops soldier, the taste of Phoebe's kiss—it had all been nothing but a cruel trick of his imagination.

Someone crouched down in front of him and he lashed out. The man ducked and his cowboy hat went flying.

Wait. Cowboy hat? Not a turban.

Seth blinked.

For a long time, he couldn't make sense of the face his eyes showed him. A sharp jaw covered with several days' worth of stubble. Kind blue eyes. Brown hair pulled back into a ponytail. Not one of his captors. When his brain finally caught up and placed a name with the face, shame burned like a coal fire in his gut. Jesse Warrick. A friend. Sort of.

"Hey. Hey." Jesse snapped his fingers in front of his face. "Seth. Focus on me. You back with us? Don't make me sedate you, pal."

He was free, with friends. Free.

And yet his body refused to listen to logic. It took every ounce of self-control in him to stop struggling against their hold, and his muscles twitched at the forced inactivity.

Chest heaving, he stared at grim faces surrounding him. Gabe held his arms twisted behind his back at a painful angle and Jean-Luc and Marcus each had a leg pinned to the earth. Again, memories of being held down threatened to rip his sanity into shreds, but he held on, focused on the here and now.

Friends.

These were the good guys.

The. Good. Guys.

His gaze snapped to the collapsed house. "Phoebe?" he croaked in a voice that didn't sound like his own. "Where is she?"

Gabe's grip loosened. "We don't know," he said. And was that *understanding* in his tone? "But the house is gone, Seth. There's no getting inside."

"I'm good now. Let me go." The hands holding him lifted and he climbed to his feet, his eyes glued on the tiny opening he'd tried to make bigger.

C'mon, Phoebe. Come out of there.

What was left of the house shifted again, more slabs of mud crumbling inside.

Despair dragged him to his knees as a cold wind swept off the mountain and kicked swirls of dust into the air around him. His eyes watered, but he refused to look away.

The men murmured behind him. He ignored them. But then Gabe, of all people, settled down beside him in the dirt.

"I know what you're feeling right now," Gabe said softly. "During our last mission, I thought I lost Audrey."

Seth didn't bother glancing over. "But you didn't."

"No. I didn't."

"And I haven't lost Phoebe. She's still in there. I don't know why—why she won't answer me, but—she's coming out." He'd have hope, like she'd told him to, and he'd hang on to it with every cell in his being because that protective, intelligent, courageous woman was the first good thing that had come into his life in a very long time.

Stupid of him to take so long to see it, but he'd make damn sure she'd know if—no, he had to have hope. *When* they got her out.

"I'm so sorry, Seth." Gabe squeezed his shoulder. "We have to keep moving. Zak is in no condition to stay in these mountains."

"Go. I'm not leaving here."

The words conjured up another flashback, one he now realized he'd visited many times in his dreams. Fourteen months into their captivity, just him and Omar Cordero left. Awakening to blood-curdling screams that lasted all night until their captors finally flung Cordero's limp body into the room.

The rattling breaths of approaching death.

Seth assuring him they'd get free.

No. I'm not leaving here, Lieutenant. Tell Theresa I love her and I'm sorry.

Seth dropped his head into his hands. He never had gone to see Omar's wife. Had never told her that her husband's final thoughts had been about her.

He hadn't been able to save any of his men.

And he could do nothing to help Phoebe.

A horrible numbness filled him, similar to the cold detachment he'd felt for weeks after his rescue. "She's gone, isn't she?"

Gabe exhaled slowly, but didn't answer. He didn't have to. Too much time had passed without a sound from her and every one of the men standing there knew what that meant. If Phoebe were alive and trapped, she'd be calling out for help by now.

"But Zak?" Seth rasped. "There's still hope for him."

"Yeah," Gabe said. "There's still hope. He's in bad shape and will probably lose his leg, but if we get him to a hospital as soon as possible, he'll survive. Thanks to you."

Straightening, Seth wiped at his eyes. Nobody gave him shit about the tears, not even Ian, who was standing off to the side of the group, his arms crossed over his chest, staring at the ground.

Amazing. Somehow Phoebe had managed to win even that asshole over.

Just went to show how truly special she was.

He may have failed Omar Cordero, but, goddammit, he was going to do right by Phoebe. "We're coming back for her," he said. "She's not staying here. We're coming back with the right equipment to dig her out."

And if it was the last thing he did, he'd make sure the world mourned her loss with him.

CHAPTER TWENTY-SIX

KABUL

Quinn sat upright in bed, every trained sense he had going on high alert. He couldn't put his finger on what had tipped him off—the house was quiet, everyone sound asleep, and he heard no unfamiliar sounds.

But something.

Something...

What?

He swung his legs over the edge of the bed and checked the time on his phone: 0520. When he'd done his rounds twenty minutes ago, he hadn't spotted anything out of the ordinary, but he wasn't waiting another forty minutes to check again when every fiber in his being told him something. Was. Wrong. He grabbed his rifle and edged down the hallway to Harvard's door.

He rapped his knuckle against the wood. "Harvard."

A thunk. Voices. At least two, trying to be quiet. Scrambling.

What the fuck?

Quinn's heart rate jacked up and he raised his weapon, all

ready to burst into the room and take down whoever was on the other side.

The door opened and Harvard poked his head out. "Uh, Quinn. Hi. What's up?" He was shirtless, showing off lean muscles that the last few months of training had added to his once-broomstick-thin body, and his pants hung low on his hips, unbuttoned. His hair was mussed as if he—or someone else—had been running their fingers through it all night.

Well, shit. No wonder he hadn't put up a fight about being left behind at the shelter.

Quinn shouldered his rifle. "You can come out, Zina. I know you're in there."

Red bloomed across Harvard's cheeks as Zina came to the door in a bathrobe, her hair just as mussed, her lips puffy, cheeks reddened by stubble.

"Uh…" Harvard said, rubbing the back of his neck like a teenager caught in the act by dear old dad.

Quinn snorted at that mental image. Yeah, right. As if he'd ever qualify to be anyone's father. He held up his hands. "No judgment here."

After all, how could he cast stones after his one-night stand this summer with—

Mara.

Goddammit. There she was again. He'd been doing such a good job blocking her out of his mind too.

"Is there something wrong?" Zina asked, clenching the bathrobe to her chest. If she was at all embarrassed, she didn't show it, but maybe that was because worry lit her pretty features.

"I don't know," Quinn admitted. "I got this feeling…and it's probably nothing," he added when her eyes widened. "Still, I wanted Harvard to run a check with the security cameras he installed."

"Absolutely," Harvard said. "Give us a minute."

The door shut and Quinn heard their murmurs, the unmistakable sound of a kiss. Yeah, maybe he'd give them a bit more space. He walked over to the top of the stairs and peered down to the dark first floor.

Harvard reemerged a few minutes later. "Camera's showing no activity."

Damn. Wincing, he rubbed his temple where a headache was starting pound. If everything was secure, why did he feel so uneasy? Probably just head trauma–induced restlessness, but he still didn't feel right about going back to bed. "I'm going to walk the grounds. Just in case."

"All right," Harvard said. "And since I'm up, I'll check out a few things online. See if I can't dig up more intel on Siddiqui or the bomb he wants to buy."

Guilt prickled up the back of Quinn's neck. "No, don't do that. Go back to Zina."

"Nah, that's over."

He said it so offhandedly, Quinn gaped in surprise. He'd never pegged Harvard for the one-night-stand type. That was more Jean-Luc's specialty. And his own. "Didn't your relationship just start?"

"It's not a relationship. We had sex and now it's over. What?" he said defensively when Quinn continued to stare. "It's a perfectly natural stress release if both parties know and agree to the terms going in."

"You make it sound like a…loan contract. It's sex."

"Which is a kind of contract between two consenting adults."

Quinn blinked. He couldn't wrap his mind around— Where the hell did this kid learn about fucking, from a law textbook? "But it's sex. It never wraps up all neat and tidy like that. It's dirty and rough and the aftermath is—"

Now Harvard was blinking at him, owl like, and he realized he was giving away far more about his own fucked-up sex life than educating Harvard on what a healthy sexual relationship should be. "Uh, can we pretend this whole convo never happened?"

"Yeah," Harvard said, dragging the word out. "That works for me. I'll let you know if I turn up anything more on—"

A bell sounded from Harvard's room and he ran toward it. Quinn waited a beat, then started downstairs when it didn't seem like he would be back.

"Wait," Harvard said, coming to the top of the stairs. He waved a paper in one hand and grinned. "I got a lock on Siddiqui's car. It's sitting in a restaurant parking lot only two freaking miles from here. What do you say we go slap a tracking device on the thing?"

CHAPTER TWENTY-SEVEN

Christ, there was so much death in these mountains. So many bodies, enough to haunt Seth's already-troubled dreams for centuries.

His throat closed as he stood by his horse on the hill overlooking the destroyed village. As soon as Jesse got Zak stabilized and ready for travel, they'd be leaving. And then...

No. He turned away and continued saddling his horse. He couldn't think about Phoebe—had to focus on something else. Didn't have the capacity to deal with the sharp edge of grief threatening to cut away the numbness of shock.

Then he saw it. The saddlebag carrying Phoebe's clothes, her camera. She never had a chance to retrieve any of it...

So why was it hanging open?

Who the fuck had gone through it?

He did a visual sweep of the contents. Her scarf—the red one she'd worn during the drive from Kabul to Asadabad—was missing.

Movement in the village below caught his attention and he grabbed his rifle, peered through the scope.

Ian picked his way through the rubble toward the dog, who had still not left his spot in front of one of the half-collapsed houses, most likely the home of his former owner. And in Ian's hand was a length of…

Red scarf.

Moving fast and silently, Seth maneuvered down the hillside and reached the house just as Ian leaned over the poor, forgotten animal.

He lifted his weapon. "What are you doing, you sadistic son of a bitch?"

Ian glanced back with a raised eyebrow. "You got the son of a bitch part right."

"Yeah, you don't want to fuck with me, Reinhardt. I've had a really bad fucking day. Give me back the scarf or I end your miserable existence, and it'll be one of the few things I won't lose sleep over."

Ian sent him a wicked grin and knelt down.

Seth's finger tightened on the trigger, but then relaxed as the dog's tail wagged. Ian spoke softly and buried his hands in the animal's scruff, giving the dog a good rub that sent his bushy tail whipping, then he held the scarf under the dog's nose and said firmly, "Phoebe. That's Phoebe."

Seth lowered his rifle. "What are you doing?"

"Trying to give him Phoebe's scent." Ian stayed focused on the dog. "Thing is, I've worked with some bomb-sniffing dogs in the past and this guy's not trained, but he's smart and he already has an attachment to her. We might be able to use him to find her."

Seth's lungs ached, his chest so tight breathing became a chore. "She's dead," he said in a strangled voice that didn't sound like his own. He looked across the village toward Tehani's family home, now nothing but a pile of rubble. "Nobody can survive that."

"I don't think she was in Tehani's house," Ian said and jerked a thumb over his shoulder. "C'mon, this is Phoebe we're talking about. Do you honestly believe she'd just sit around and wait for us to get back? No. She was exploring, looking for the villagers, and I think she was in this house when the bombs dropped. That's why the dog won't leave this spot. He knows she's in there."

Seth stared at the semi-collapsed house. The wreckage wasn't as severe as Tehani's home and if Phoebe was trapped inside—Jesus, it could be survivable. A dangerous bubble of hope expanded in his chest. "Do whatever you need to. I'll stall Gabe."

. . .

Phoebe started awake to a loud scratching sound. Her ears rang and a pounding, dizzying headache made her nauseous. Blood, lots of it, caked her face, clogged her nose with the smell of copper and death. Her tongue tasted like dirt and was about as dry, pasted to the roof of her mouth.

What happened?

She shut her eyes, struggled to recall…something. Had she been in some kind of accident? Natural disaster?

No. No, that wasn't right. She was in Afghanistan…

With Seth.

He'd been the last thought to flash through her mind before unconsciousness sucked her under. Where was he? Was he okay?

She lifted her head. It hurt like hell, but at least she still had a head to lift—definitely a check in the plus column. Her arms and legs all seemed to work too, albeit painfully. Another positive check.

In the negative column—she couldn't move more than a few inches in any direction. Nor would her parched throat work enough to form a call for help. She tried, again and again, but produced no sound. Panic coated her tongue and she shoved at the debris blocking her in. She did not want to die. Not here. Not like this. Not when a scarred and tortured man would spend the rest of his life drowning in guilt over his perceived failure to protect her, even though there was no way he could have known...

Bomb.

That's right. She'd been searching through the empty homes, looking for clues to the villagers' whereabouts, when a plane had dropped bombs on the village.

And even though Seth couldn't have known it was going to happen, he was going to destroy himself if she died here.

And she didn't even want to think of what it'd do to her parents, her little brother. Nate was in high school—still so young—and he'd never admit it out loud, but he looked up to her with near hero worship.

She wouldn't let Nate down. Wouldn't let Seth self-destruct.

Desperate, she clawed at the mud. Dug for all she was worth and managed to move a chunk of collapsed wall. A hole opened up, almost big enough. Maybe—if she flattened herself out and moved slowly—she just might be able to wiggle through to safety. Or into another mud prison. She had no idea what lay on the other side, but she had to try and pushed forward with her legs.

God, what she wouldn't give for a bottle of water.

More scraping sounded from outside. It was the same sound that had awakened her and she strained her ears. Listening. Listening.

Seth?

She wanted to scream his name, but no matter how much air she pushed out of her lungs, the best she could do was a tiny whimper of sound.

No, wait. That whimper wasn't from her.

She shifted and her leg came up against a warm, furry body.

A…dog? Yes! He scooted in beside her until they were nose-to-nose and gave her a sloppy hello lick.

Joy burst through her. Tank the Wonder Dog. The amazing animal had come to find her. She hugged him tight, reveled in the warmth of his scruffy coat. He barked excitedly and the sound caused her head to spin, but she didn't care. She wasn't alone anymore.

Good boy, Tank.

With numb fingers, she unknotted her scarf from her neck and tied it around the dog's. She nudged him to go. It took a few tries, but she finally got the stubborn animal to shimmy out the same way he'd come in. She watched his progress, then wiggled herself around until she could see the path he'd used. He'd dug a hole under one of the heavy slabs of wall that had kept her trapped.

Oh, Tank. Such a good, brilliant boy.

She'd kiss that dog when she got out.

Every nerve ending in her body screamed as she pulled herself through the hole, but she saw light and it was enough to keep her going. Then she heard Seth's voice: "That's her scarf. She tied her scarf around his neck."

"Holy shit," someone else said—Ian maybe? But, no, she must be delusional because Seth and Ian hated each other for reasons she'd never been able to pin down. And she was going to talk to them about that, too. They could be friends. She didn't know much about Ian, but got the feeling they had a lot more in common than either of them realized. Maybe if Ian had a friend he wouldn't be such a jerk all the time. Silly, obstinate men.

Cripes, she was tired. And no matter how far she crawled toward the light, it seemed to move farther and farther away.

Wait. Wasn't she supposed to avoid the light? Going into the light was bad, right?

Her head spun and she paused, resting it on her forearm. She really wanted some water and a warm blanket, but she'd settle for a nap. A nap was good.

"We need Gabe. And everyone else. Somehow, we have to lift this house off her. Phoebe, if you can hear me, hang on, okay? We're coming in for you. I promise."

Seth.

She had to keep moving, if not for her sake than for his. He couldn't lose another person he cared about. And he did care about her, even if he wasn't ready to admit it yet. She cared about him too, even if *she* wasn't ready to admit it, either. But they had something. Maybe even something special, something worth pursuing.

She'd never know if she stopped now.

Gathering her last bit of strength, she pushed forward with everything she had and the light suddenly blinded her.

Sunlight.

She was free.

Strong hands gripped her wrists and Seth hauled her up out of the dirt and rubble and into his arms.

"I got her," he yelled and hugged her to his chest. "Guys, she's alive and I got her!"

She smiled and dug her fingers into the front of his shirt, burrowing into his strength and warmth. As she tumbled back into unconsciousness, the best sound she'd ever heard in her life followed her.

Seth was laughing.

CHAPTER TWENTY-EIGHT

AKHGAR VILLAGE

The next time Phoebe woke, she was warm. Cozy, wrapped up in blankets and the leather-and-spice scent of a familiar male. Safe in the embrace of strong arms holding her close to a hard chest. Under her ear, a heart thrummed slow and steady, lulling her back to sleep.

Seth had her. She was okay now. They'd both be okay.

When she woke again, the bed was empty, but she sensed a presence in the room with her. Not Seth. Somehow, she knew that instinctively before she opened her eyes. Still, it wasn't a stranger.

She turned her head on the pillow and found Ian seated on the floor, knees bent, back against the wall. His right hand rested in the scruff of the dog who had saved her.

Tank, she remembered naming him. Tank the Wonder Dog.

Ian glanced at her and for the first time she saw something other than a scowl or a sneer on his lean face. One side of his mouth kicked up and those nearly black eyes of his, usually so full of anger, softened.

"Hey," he said and got to his feet. Tank did, too, and stayed right on his heels, looking up at him adoringly like he was the most wonderful man in the world. And maybe he wasn't the *most* wonderful, but dogs were known to be good judges of character so he couldn't be all bad, right?

Phoebe pushed herself upright as he crossed to stand beside her bed. Tank put his big paws up on the mattress, but then glanced toward Ian as if asking permission. Ian whistled between his teeth and motioned toward the bed. The dog's tail wagged and he hopped up. He lay down and inched forward until his nose touched her arm. The dog looked clean now, healthy and happy. Ian must have bathed him.

Smiling, she rubbed his head. "I owe you a kiss, Tank." She rocked back in surprise at the croaking sound that came out of her mouth. Was that *her* voice? Holy crap, she sounded horrible and tried to clear her sore throat.

Without being asked, Ian crossed the room to a pack on the floor—Seth's—and found a bottle of water in one of the pockets. He even twisted off the cap before handing it to her.

Oh God, the water tasted amazing. It wasn't cold, but she didn't care and drank half the bottle in one breath.

"Tank?" he asked.

She nodded and wiped a hand over her mouth. "That's what I called him."

"I like it."

She handed the water back. "He seems to like you."

"Yeah, stupid mutt." There was a faint hint of affection in his voice as he re-capped the bottle and set it aside. He gave the dog's ear a scratch. "I tried to shove him off on the villagers but he won't stay with them. Doesn't know what's good for him, obviously."

Tank's tail thumped against her leg and he nuzzled her arm. She lifted her hand and he wiggled closer. "He's not stupid. He's loyal."

"Yes," Ian agreed. "He is."

They both stared at the dog for several long seconds until Ian shifted around uncomfortably on his feet. "I'll go find Seth. He didn't want to leave you, but that prick Jesse forced him to get some food. He hasn't touched anything since we found you."

Since they found her? Oh boy, that didn't sound good. "How long have I been out?"

"Most of the day. And while Jesse's an asshole, he had a point. Seth has to eat something, keep his strength up. We're hiking outta here tomorrow first thing."

"Where are we?"

"Back in Akhgar, but the villagers are starting to make noises about us overstaying our welcome and Zak is doing well enough to make the trip."

"You found Zak Hendricks?"

"Seth did." He hesitated. "We also found the missing villagers. They were all dead except for a young woman—her name's Darya—and her son. Do you think the shelter in Kabul will accept them?"

Darya was alive? Oh, thank God. Phoebe's throat closed up even as relief left her feeling shaky. "Zina won't turn them away. They're Tehani's family."

Ian nodded. "Good."

"I'd like to see them."

"They're safe and you should probably rest some more. We have a long hike out."

"Ian," she called as he told the dog to stay and turned toward the door. "Why don't you get along with anyone? Seth, Jesse. The only two guys you seem to tolerate are Gabe and Quinn."

"I'm not here to make friends."

"Why are you here?"

His hand, resting on the doorframe, tightened until his knuckles whitened from the pressure. He stayed silent for so long, she didn't think he'd answer. Then he glanced over his shoulder and in his dark eyes, she saw depths of despair she couldn't begin to fathom.

"Because I don't have a choice."

• • •

Seth ran into Jesse leaving the bedroom as he hurried in with his hair still dripping from his quick bath in the nearby river. "How is she? Is she okay?"

"She's just fine," Jesse said. He looked exhausted, but between taking care of Phoebe and Zak, he had every right to be. "She's bruised up and sore, but honestly, she's a million times better than we could've hoped for. She got lucky."

"Thank you."

Jesse gave him a tired smile and clapped him on the shoulder before heading back out to the main room.

Seth waited a beat before pushing open the bedroom door, taking time to smooth down his wet hair and straighten his clothes.

Phoebe sat up in bed with the dog's head on her lap. "Hi."

"Hey." Seth crossed to her side and momentarily wished he'd brought along a treat—the dog deserved hundreds of treats every day for the rest of his life. Without him and Ian's quick thinking, she probably would have died buried under the house.

But she hadn't died. And, dammit, he wasn't going to get hung up on all the shoulda, woulda, couldas of the past. She was here now, in this moment. With him. Safe.

He sat on the edge of the mattress, examining every inch of her face. Even though Jesse had just assured him her injuries weren't serious, he wanted to hear the words from her lips. "Are you okay?"

"I'm fine, Seth. I could really use a bath, though." When she smiled, the spring of tension wound so tightly inside him finally uncoiled and he dropped his forehead to her shoulder. She did need a bath—despite his efforts with a package of wet wipes while she slept, the scent of mud still clung to her, covering the sweet-citrus tang he'd come to associate with her.

Phoebe lifted a hand and stroked his cheek and he suddenly realized he hadn't shaved in… Shit. Well over a week. The stubble had to hurt her abraded skin.

He backed away, found her hand with his own, and entwined their fingers. "Would you like help getting cleaned up?" Her eyes widened and, dammit, he was screwing this all up, wasn't he? "Er, I mean, if you're not comfortable, I can find a woman from the village to—"

She shook her head. "I want you."

Seth didn't miss the double meaning packed in those three words, but chose to ignore them. For now. He'd come to realize something was happening between them, whether he was ready to give up the past or not.

No more shoulda, woulda, couldas.

What he felt for Phoebe ran deep, like an ache in his blood, and it scared the living hell out of him. Here was this amazing, courageous, beautiful woman, who wanted him despite his scars, despite his sometimes-shaky mental stability, and even despite his tendency to be a complete asshole.

Which reminded him…

He leaned in and pressed a kiss to her forehead. "I'm so sorry for what I said to you last time we were alone together in this room. It was a low blow and I—I'm ashamed of myself for it."

She untangled her fingers from his and reached to cup his cheeks in her palms again. He jerked away before she made contact. "Don't. I haven't shaved. You'll hurt your hands."

She snorted and clasped his face anyway, rubbing the pad of her thumb over his lower lip. "You are such a silly man sometimes."

"I know what I said hurt you."

"Doesn't matter now."

"It does. I didn't intend to hurt you, but when I get all knotted up inside like I was that night, a bunch of shit comes out of my mouth and I push away everyone who means anything to me."

Her hand dropped back to her side as if even that small motion exhausted her. "Is that what happened to your family? You pushed them away? I know you were close to them at one time. I saw the photo of them after they got the news of your rescue."

That photo. It was one of those pictures seen around the world—his mom, dad, and sister on their knees in a sobbing embrace—and it killed him a little more every time it was published or broadcast. He'd put them through so much grief— and he was still doing it because, even two years later, he couldn't work up the courage to go home.

He stared down at the dog, unable to look at her for the shame burning inside him. Of all the things he'd done wrong over the last several years, he most regretted the distance he'd put between himself and his family.

"Yes," he admitted. "It's my fault we don't talk anymore. I couldn't stand their pity, their worry. It just—" He sighed. Searched for a way to explain. "It wore on me until it was easier to move away and avoid their calls. Then they stopped calling as much. I'll still get one every few weeks, but it's always awkward, like they don't know what to say to me. And I have no fucking clue what to say to them. So we make small talk for a few minutes and that's that."

"Seth." Her voice was little more than a whisper and he finally sucked it up and met her gaze. She closed the distance between them and brushed her lips over his. "*Nothing* you say is going to push me away. So when you need to, throw your worst at me. I'm not going anywhere. Except," she added, and a slow, sexy smiled crossed her lips, "into the bath."

He hated to burst her bubble. "There's no running water here."

With a groan, she flopped back to the mattress. "Oh, not fair. I was so looking forward to soaking in a tub of hot water. I ache everywhere."

Damn this village and its lack of civilized amenities. He hated the thought of her hurting in any way—which reminded him of the massage she'd given him last time they were here, and a light bulb went on in his head.

He leaned over and planted a kiss on her forehead. "Give me a few minutes. I have an idea."

It took longer to gather the supplies than he'd anticipated and when he got back to the room, he found her sound asleep, her arms wrapped around Tank, who was perfectly content being her cuddle buddy.

Ian had once called him window-licking insane and yeah, he must be, because right now, he was envious of a dog.

He whistled softly. Tank ignored him. He whistled again, louder, and the dog gave an annoyed harrumph before wiggling out of her arms and plodding from the room.

"Go find Ian," Seth told him and shut the door on his sad puppy eyes.

When he turned, he caught Phoebe smiling sleepily at him. "You must be made of ice to resist that pathetic face."

"Nope. Just determined to give you a soothing bath."

Her eyes brightened. "You found me a bath?"

"Uh…sorta." He crossed to the heavy pot of warm water he'd set on the floor beside the bed and picked up a sponge.

Phoebe laughed. "You're going to give me a sponge bath?"

"Yeah," he said, his voice going raspy despite his best efforts to stop it. "I am."

"Well, what about you? Can I give you a bath?"

His throat worked as he swallowed hard. "I, uh, jumped in the river and washed up earlier."

"Oh my God. The river? Wasn't that cold?"

"Freezing." He reached down and tugged on the hem of her shirt. "Do you need help with your clothes?"

"Hmm, yes." A dreamy smile played over her lips. "I think so."

Seth sat down beside her to help pull her borrowed tunic off over her head. Don't stare, he told himself. Don't stare. Don't—

Oh, fuck. Her nipples stood out through the material of her bra, practically begging for his mouth. He wanted to yank the cups down and see those rosy peaks again. Wanted his mouth on them, and this time, he wouldn't let himself get all tied up inside.

With trembling hands, he untied the waist of her baggy Afghan pants. "Lift up."

She complied, raising her hips in a suggestive way that all but screamed, "Sex! Want! Now!"

No. Not going there. He shut down that dangerous line of thought and slowly drew the material down her legs. Then there she lay, wearing only a half-transparent bra and panties. And all but stripping him with her eyes.

All right. He could do this and be a gentleman about it.

Hah. Right. *Says the guy with every drop of his blood rushing south.*

This wasn't about sex. It was all about helping her feel better, and he planned to return the favor of her massage to soothe her aches and pains. Sure, he wouldn't be as good at it as she'd been. His hands were rough and his touch nowhere in the same ballpark as gentle, but he'd try. And if he could work even one knot of tension out of her, he'd call it a win.

Except, now that he saw the extent of her injuries, maybe a massage wasn't such a good idea. Bright purple and black bruises streaked her rib cage, dotted her arms and legs.

"Sweetheart," he whispered, gently brushing his fingers along her ribs. "Jesus, look at you."

"It doesn't hurt. Jesse gave me something. Actually, I'm feeling pretty good right now." She dragged a finger down the front of his chest. "And you're still wearing too many clothes."

He jerked back. A gentleman. He had to be a gentleman. Especially now that he knew Jesse had given her something for the pain, something that had obviously knocked her for a loop. He wasn't about to take advantage of her.

"Let's get you cleaned up before this water goes cold."

CHAPTER TWENTY-NINE

Phoebe rolled her eyes and flopped over onto her belly in frustration as he busied himself with the preparations for her bath. Now that her body no longer ached every-freaking-where thanks to the wonderful pills Jesse had given her, there was another ache she needed to tend to, one low in her belly that had been growing steadily for days.

She. Wanted. Seth.

Even more so now that she'd cheated death.

Still, he refused her. And after she'd pretty much thrown herself at him! For the love of all things sexy, what was it going to take to make him understand she needed this from him more than she needed a sponge bath?

Although…

He dipped the sponge in the steaming water, wrung it out, and ran it down her spine between her shoulder blades. And okay, that felt amazing. More than amazing. It was like chocolate if chocolate were a sensation. Decadent. Soothing. A little slice of heaven.

"Mmm."

"Like that?"

"Umm-hmm," she murmured into the pillow.

He dipped, wrung, swept the sponge across her shoulders, down her arms, then paused to unhook the clasp of her bra. The water sloshed as he dipped and wrung again, then the warm sponge traced her spine from the middle of her back to the waistband of her panties. Goose bumps raced along her skin in his wake and her nipples puckered hard, suddenly so sensitive the cups of her bra irritated. She squirmed out of the shoulder straps and rid herself of the thing, then snuggled in again, hugging her pillow and savoring every swipe of the sponge. Down her arms, her legs. Tickling her sides along her tender, bruised ribs.

"Turn over," Seth commanded and she smiled at the strain in his voice. Served him right. As much as she was enjoying the bath, they could be doing something else mutually enjoyable right now. She rolled and loved the way his gaze fell to her bare breasts before he remembered himself and shook his head.

Another dip of the sponge in the water. Another wring. Then he stroked the ring of her collarbone, taking his time as he worked lower to the valley between her breasts. He lingered over her nipples, circling each and watching with lust-darkened eyes as they puckered achingly tight at the attention.

Oh, God, he was torturing her. She was going to vibrate apart if he didn't touch her soon, *really* touch her, flesh to flesh, without the buffer of the sponge. Moaning encouragement, she arched into the caress.

The sponge left her breast and continued downward across her tight belly. She wanted to scream with frustration, but just as she opened her mouth, he reached the waistband of her panties and drew them down her legs. Then the sponge returned to her, warm as he traced it along her inner thighs. Her breath stalled in her lungs. Her body arched with each pass of the soft sponge over her most intimate parts. And when the sponge left her, she made a sound damn close to a whimper. "Seth."

"What do you want, sweetheart?" he asked in a sexy, roughened voice that had her wet with need. He tossed the sponge aside and it landed in the water with a splash. "Tell me what you want me to do."

"Touch me."

"Like this?"

She gasped as his fingers parted her and one plunged deep. "Yes." She pushed her hips toward him, needing more. "I tried to tell you before. I want you. So. Damn. Bad."

His thumb brushed over her clit, sending a tremble through her thighs. She clamped her legs shut around his hand, holding him there before he got any stupid ideas about stopping himself again. But he didn't back away. Instead, he slid a second finger in to join the first, stroking her closer to climax with a slow, teasing rhythm. He drew circles around her clit with his thumb until her hips rocked against his hand and a whimper escaped her throat.

"Please, Seth. Please."

He bounded off the bed and for one horrible moment, she feared he was going to leave her again. What was wrong with her? Was she really so inferior compared to his Emma? Why did she so desperately want someone who was unable to reciprocate?

But then Seth returned and sat down on the edge of the mattress to untie his boots. He laid several packages on the bedside table.

Condoms.

Thank God.

Grinning with relief, she picked one up. "Where did these come from?"

"Jean-Luc." One boot hit the floor. Then the other.

"Oh, I might kiss that man."

Seth stood up, pulled his shirt over his head. "Don't you dare."

"Why not?" She stretched lazily and enjoyed the show as he worked on the button and zipper of his pants. "You the jealous type?"

His pants hit the floor too and he hooked his thumbs in the waistband of his boxers. Only then did he hesitate, uncertainty creeping into his eyes.

Oh hell no. He wasn't stopping now.

Phoebe sat up, hooked her fingers into the elastic, and tugged the boxers down, all the while holding his gaze. Why didn't he get it? She didn't care what he looked like. It didn't matter because she wanted *him*.

All of him. Scars and everything.

She took his erection in hand, felt the ridges of scar tissue along his shaft, but never broke eye contact as she guided him into her mouth. He tasted of salt and male and she liked it more than she thought she would.

She flicked her tongue over the head of his penis, testing, exploring. He stared down the length of his body at her with an expression of pure awe on his face, but he wasn't writhing in ecstasy.

Was she not doing this right? She'd never taken a man into her mouth before, but was pretty sure she had the gist of the act down. There wasn't much to it, but shouldn't he be—

Crap. His scars.

Why hadn't she considered that sooner? The rough, thickened tissue probably made him far less sensitive than other men.

Experimentally, she used a little of her teeth, dragging them lightly over his shaft. His stomach muscles tightened and his eyes rolled back. Finally, he groaned.

That was more like it. She liked watching him come undone, enjoyed the heady rush of feminine power that came with knowing she played a part in his undoing.

The underside of his shaft had very little scarring and she traced her tongue along the unmarred flesh from root to tip. His back arched, a fine sheen of sweat broke out over his skin, and his hand shook as he threaded it through her hair. Yup, he liked that. She did it again and a tremble rocked through him.

Hand wrapped in her hair, he tugged her away and pulled her up into his arms.

"Need you. So damn much," he said between clenched teeth. He reached for one of the condoms and rolled it on. Before she could beg, he lifted her hips in his big hands and drove himself in to the root.

Yes. Finally.

Her head tilted back and her eyes fell closed as he filled her. He was large enough that she thought he might hurt if she wasn't so aroused. As it was, she just felt full, the pressure intense and delicious, and she wanted more. She circled her legs around him, dug her heels into his ass. Urged him to move.

"Please," she said.

Seth withdrew long enough to lay her on the bed, but she barely had time to miss the contact because as soon as they were both horizontal, he was inside her again. And, God, everything about this felt good—his weight pinning her to the mattress, his hips moving in lazy strokes between her thighs as if they had all the time in the world for this. When he leaned over and propped himself on his forearms, the change in angle thrilled her. The deeper, longer stokes built the pressure and it all erupted in a breath-stealing flash of heat and sensation.

He dropped his forehead to her shoulder and, with a shuddering groan, thrust deep one last time, joining their bodies so tightly together she wondered if she'd ever get him out of her system.

Or even if she'd ever want to.

She held him through his climax, her lips nuzzling his ear, until all the tension drained out of his muscles and he collapsed. He was heavy, but she couldn't have cared less and held him tighter.

She ran a soothing hand over his short hair, liking the rasp of the stubble under her palm. Even so, he should grow it out again. She'd seen pictures of the way he used to wear it before joining the Marines, rakishly long and perpetually tousled, and would love to run her fingers through the light-brown locks.

As their breathing settled, Seth lifted his head and found her mouth in an achingly sweet kiss.

"Okay?" he asked, his voice little more than a rasp. He brushed a lock of hair off her face. "Did I hurt you? I wasn't gentle. Or…" He winced. "Slow."

She laughed. Hurt her? Not even close. Not when her body tingled with the warm aftereffects of an orgasm. But he needed the reassurance. She got that. Her close scrape with death had aroused his protective instincts.

"No," she said, indulging him. "You didn't hurt me and I didn't want gentle or slow. This time."

He let go an explosive breath and rolled off her, freeing their still-joined bodies. She instantly felt bereft at the loss and wanted the connection back.

Seth disposed of the condom, then dipped a hand in the pot of her bath water, testing the temperature. It wasn't steaming anymore, but he must have decided it was still warm enough because he used the sponge to gently clean between her legs again. It was sweet. *He* was sweet.

"Thank you."

"You're welcome." He washed himself with considerably less care, then picked his pants and boxers off the floor. Something fluttered from his pocket. He froze and stared down at the creased photo, an expression of horror crossing his face before he grabbed it and rubbed the new crinkles out of it.

Emma's photo.

All of the after-sex warm fuzzies drained out of Phoebe, leaving her numb. For a short time, she'd forgotten the sex had just been about release and she had no right to an attack from the green-eyed monster. But dammit, he handled the woman's photo like it was the most precious jewel on Earth.

"Seth." Her voice came out more strangled than she wanted. She'd tried for casual, but the lump in her throat made that impossible. "It's okay."

He glanced at her, guilt all over his features, and hurriedly stuffed the photo back in his pocket. He yanked on the pants. "I'm gonna go."

"Wait." She climbed out of bed and tried to catch him, but he'd already disappeared out the door.

An ugly mix of shame and sorrow dragged her down to the edge of the mattress and she covered her face with both hands.

God, she could be such a naive fool sometimes. Because deep in a corner of her heart, and despite all of her reservations of getting too close, she had hoped for more from him than just sex.

CHAPTER THIRTY

Phoebe woke the following morning to a chorus of male groans followed by some good-natured cursing. She sat up in bed and glanced around, at first expecting to see Seth with her. The room was empty.

Right. After finding Emma's photo, he'd walked out and never come back.

She swung her legs out of bed and muscles that hadn't received a workout in a long time pulled tight, reminding her of last night. Seth's hands on her. His mouth. His body…

No.

Honestly, she didn't want the reminder.

She braided her hair and tied her scarf over the frizzy locks. One thing she loved about the country—the necessity to wear head scarves. Saved her loads of time getting dressed when she didn't have to fight with her hair every morning.

She slipped into the hall and heard Seth's voice among the others coming from the main room. She followed the sound.

Seth sat on the floor with Jean-Luc, Marcus, and Jesse, a deck of cards and piles of poker chips in front of them. Ian sat in the corner with his hand resting on Tank's back, watching the game in silence. Gabe wasn't in the room, but another man with dark hair and a beard was. An IV hung from a nail in the wall and drained into his arm. Must be Sergeant Zak Hendricks.

Seth's pile of chips was the biggest, the other three men down to their last few. He was taking them to the cleaners, which was probably what all the groaning had been about. Good for him. After the way they'd all treated him, he deserved a little payback.

He spotted her and his jaw clenched.

Okay. She drew a fortifying breath. Time to be an adult. Yes, last night had ended on a sour note and she didn't plan to sleep with him again, but that didn't mean they couldn't still be friends, right?

She walked over and smiled at the group. "Poker?"

"Seth's cheating," Jean-Luc declared.

Seth scowled. "I don't cheat."

"Yeah, right. You're hiding aces up your sleeve."

"I'm not wearing sleeves."

Phoebe did a double take. That was true—he wasn't wearing sleeves, the scars on his arms bared to the world. It was the first time she'd seen him around anyone but her without his hoodie.

Jean-Luc eyed his T-shirt like he still didn't believe it. "You're using voodoo then. No other explanation."

"No," Seth muttered, "just sold my soul to the devil."

"Close enough."

"I'm done," Marcus said, throwing down his cards. "If we keep going, Ace is gonna take my shirt next."

"Who says I'd want it?" Seth shot back.

Even though he had barely acknowledged her presence, warmth for him radiated through her chest. She liked seeing him banter with the group.

A few minutes later, Gabe strode in and the chatter abruptly died. The men ended their game without finishing and the entire mood in the room shifted from playful to all-business.

"All right, gentlemen," Gabe said. "We're going to do a quick briefing before we decamp." His gaze settled briefly on Zak, who gave a slight nod. Gabe released a breath and pinched the bridge of his nose. "There's something from Zak's initial report I haven't told you about. It was a conscious decision to keep it under wraps, but after debriefing Zak last night and speaking to Quinn via sat phone this morning, I realize it was a mistake."

The bomb.

Crap, Phoebe had forgotten all about it until this moment. She looked at Seth, saw the same realization dawn across his face.

"Zak?" Gabe said. "Do you feel well enough to fill them in? You know more about this than I do."

Even though he looked about a stone's throw away from death, Zak nodded. "Someone help me sit up."

Between Jesse and Marcus, they managed to pull him into a sitting position without jostling his ruined leg too much. By the time they had him settled against the wall with a pillow propped behind his back, he was breathing hard and a fine sheen of sweat coated his forehead.

It was another moment before he spoke. "I don't know how much Greer Wilde told you about my mission here, but I was basically put in place as a precautionary measure. My mom was born here and I know the language, the customs, so they sent me in to work for Siddiqui hoping I could find something to prove his tie to several recent acts of terrorism—or, if all else failed, I was to remove the problem at all costs. But when I got in there and discovered what he had planned…" He trailed off, obviously exhausted, and Gabe picked up the briefing.

"Cold War," Gabe said. "You're all familiar? Good, so you probably also know both sides have since admitted to producing suitcase-size nuclear warheads, several of which made their way into the black market after the collapse of the Soviet Union."

"Jesus Christ," Ian said. "Are we talking about The Suitcase here?"

"What's The Suitcase?" Phoebe asked.

"Most suitcase nukes aren't very powerful," Ian explained, "but that's not the case with this one. It's got enough juice to wipe out a small city, and that's not including the fallout." He looked at Zak. "I thought it was lost."

Zak opened his good eye and shook his head. "No, it was never lost. It's hard to keep track of because anyone can carry it anywhere. On a plane. In a government building. It's virtually undetectable, even with recent advances in security. Its last known location was Transnistria, a breakaway republic of Moldova, which is still very much living in the Soviet era. They allegedly have huge amounts of Soviet ordnance stockpiled in factories across the republic, including several of the missing nukes and The Suitcase. Even worse, a known Tranistrian arms dealer, Nikolai Zaryanko, has been in talks with Siddiqui for weeks now. Zaryanko has no political agenda, no loyalties. He's only out to make money and will sell to the highest bidder. And Siddiqui plans to be the highest bidder. They are going to make the trade in two days. We can't let that happen."

"Obviously," Gabe said after a heavy moment of silence, "we're not an anti-terror unit and don't have the manpower to handle something like this, but Quinn has already tried to bring the situation to the military's attention and they're not listening. So we'll have to handle this and I've called in some help. A helo will be arriving within a half hour to take us to Kabul so we can get Zak to a hospital and plot our next move. Any questions?"

Nobody spoke.

All right, if they weren't going to ask the obvious, Phoebe

would. "If we have the proof that Siddiqui is not only involved in all of these horrible acts, but also actively planning a terrorist attack, why not use my contacts and take the information to the press? Make it public and he won't be able to sneeze without someone watching. Won't that stop him?"

Seth glared across the room at her. "I already told you why that won't work."

"Why? Because it will put me in danger?"

"Yes."

"As opposed to the hundreds of thousands in danger if Siddiqui has possession of The Suitcase?"

A muscle ticked in his jaw. "You're not doing it."

Exasperated, she faced Gabe. "I know you see my point."

"I do," Gabe said slowly, eying Seth as he spoke. He hesitated, which was so unlike the big man, she knew she'd already lost this argument before he opened his mouth again. "But I don't think it's a good idea. We just got you back, Phoebe. None of us are willing to risk your life."

Oh, he couldn't be serious. "It shouldn't be *your* decision whether I risk my life or not. And it's not Seth's decision either," she added when Gabe sent another glance in Seth's direction. "He doesn't own me now that we've slept together. I make my own decisions."

"O-kay," Jean-Luc said, clapping his hands together. He stood. "And on that note, I need to hit the head and pack before the helo gets here."

The rest of the team followed him in quick succession, including Seth. Which left only her, Zak Hendricks, Ian, and Tank in the room.

Ian pushed to his feet and whistled for Tank to follow him. He paused at her side. "Cut Seth some slack, okay?"

Still fuming, she stared at him in complete disbelief. *"You're* telling *me* to cut him some slack."

"Yeah, I am."

As he left, she pressed her fingers to her eye sockets in an effort to relieve some of the building pressure there. "What an ass."

"Interesting team you have here," Zak muttered.

"They're not mine." She dropped her hand to her side and heaved out a breath. "Well, one of them is mine. Kind of."

"Seth?"

She didn't bother confirming or denying and he didn't press. Instead, he said, "You know, he's the reason I'm alive right now."

Oh, God. She turned to leave. "Please don't tell me the details. I don't want to know."

"All right. But for what it's worth," he added as she reached the door, "I agree with him. You don't want Siddiqui's bull's-eye painted on your back."

CHAPTER THIRTY-ONE

The noise from the helicopter's rotor had half of the villagers hiding in fear and the other half staring with awed fascination as the chopper landed in a clearing just south of Akhgar. One of the last people in the world Phoebe expected to see jumped off the bird.

Tucker Quentin.

Holy crap.

She instinctively reached for her camera, but Gabe sent her a glare that said *don't you fucking dare* and strode out to meet the billionaire. Still, her shutter finger itched to snap a photo. Sure, she'd turned over a new leaf and had gotten away from the sensational, paparazzi side of journalism, but the kind of money magazines offered for pics of Tuc Quentin would tempt even a saint. Especially pictures of Tuc Quentin in a war zone, where he had no discernible reason to be.

"Hollywood," Gabe said and held out a hand in greeting. "I didn't expect you personally."

"I was already in the area taking care of personal business," Tuc said and accepted the handshake.

Okay, maybe she hadn't *completely* turned over a new leaf, because excitement hummed in her blood at the possibility of getting the scoop of a lifetime. What kind of business would one of the richest men in the U.S. have in a war zone while dressed in fatigues with a rifle slung over his shoulder?

She felt eyes on the back of her head and glanced over her shoulder. Seth was staring at her. The open disgust on his face extinguished all sparks of excitement and filled her with a biting shame. He'd always hate that she was a member of the media, wouldn't he? And she hadn't even told him about the scathing pieces she'd written about him. When she did, he'd never speak to her again—which, yes, was exactly why she kept putting it off. She didn't want him to hate her.

God, but she should have told him before last night. It had been wrong not to.

Sick to her stomach with guilt, she folded her arms in front of her and refocused on Gabe and Tuc's conversation.

"This everyone?" Tuc asked, scanning the group. "We can't stay on the ground long here. Too many Taliban in these hills with RPGs."

"We have two more," Gabe replied. "Sergeant Hendricks, plus a woman and a toddler we're taking to the shelter."

"And the dog," Ian spoke up, his hand resting on Tank's head. "He's coming with us."

To her surprise, Tuc offered no protest. "All right. Let's pack them up and go."

"What about my guys at the shelter?" Gabe asked. "Did you bring them up to speed?"

Tuc nodded. "I did, and I sent a couple men to help them beef up security there. After we take Hendricks to a hospital, the rest of you will come with me to a safe house where we'll have better access to technology. Oh, and why didn't you mention my local asset had been compromised?"

"Last thing on my mind right now," Gabe admitted.

"Yeah, well, some forewarning would have been nice. I had to shoot my way out of an ambush at his house."

Phoebe started. Did *Tucker Quentin* just say he'd *shot* his way out of an ambush? Okay, yes, he used to be an Army Ranger, but he downplayed that aspect of his past so much that the mental image of him going all Rambo on some terrorists caught her off guard.

She must have made a sound of surprise, because Tuc turned in her direction, then he looked at Seth. His jaw slid to one side and for a horrifying second, she got the feeling he was about to spill all of her secrets.

But how could he know?

She bit down on her lip, her heart hammering as his gaze settled on her again. *Please don't.*

He ran his tongue over his teeth, then spun away. "Been here too long. We need to move."

• • •

When Tuc Quentin said "safe house" what he meant was a sprawling, multimillion-dollar mansion that Seth guessed was probably built off the profits of opium sales. Tuc confirmed as much as they piled into the elevator from the rooftop landing pad.

"Took it off a drug lord," he said casually and punched the down button when Phoebe asked about the house.

"Oh, I'm sure he was happy about that," Phoebe said.

"I'm sure he doesn't care one way or another. He went on an extended vacation."

Translation: Tuc and his men had made the house's former owner disappear. Seth wondered if she got his meaning and glanced over to see her staring at the billionaire in the same awed, somewhat greedy way she had back in the village when the guy first stepped off the bird.

Which pissed Seth right the hell off. Again. He'd barely restrained himself from stalking over to her and throwing her over his shoulder in a testosterone-fueled bid for ownership the first time. Now, in the close confines of the elevator, he gave serious thought to doing Tuc bodily harm.

So what if the tabloids had dubbed Tuc the world's sexiest man? And, yeah, so what if he was everything Seth was not. Wildly rich. Free of scars. And if he carried any baggage, he hid it well behind that Hollywood-bred smile of his.

Phoebe still had no right to stare at the guy like she wanted to lap him up.

When the elevator reached the main floor, Tuc held the door open and looked at Phoebe. "This is your stop."

She scowled. "Um, no. I don't think so."

"I know so." He nodded to Jesse, who passed the sleeping boy to her. "Zina's already with the kid's mother. She's worried about you. Take the boy and go talk to her."

Smart man, Seth thought with a tiny amount of grudging respect. Hit her with the one thing she couldn't refuse: Zina. Get her out of the way while keeping her safe. It was more than he had been able to do for her. Yet another plus in the Tuc column.

"Fine." She huffed out a breath, and cradling the boy, she stepped into what looked like a huge living room.

"And send Quinn and Harvard to the basement level," Tuc said before letting the door close. "She's a feisty one."

Several of the guys grunted in agreement. Seth just stared at the back of his head and tried to figure out if that was a compliment or an insult. Either way, he wanted to end the guy.

A few more floors down, the doors slid open again and Tuc

led the way to a long, windowless boardroom. Or more aptly, a war room. Screens covered one whole wall. A few of his people worked at the highest of high-tech computers, like something out of a sci-fi movie. Harvard would have a geek-gasm over all the fancy toys in this place.

Tuc picked up a remote, aimed it at the largest screen, and up popped a 3-D floor plan of a mansion almost as big as the one they stood in.

"My men," Tuc introduced, motioning to the two men standing behind the computer terminals. "Rex, my medic. Devlin, my computer guy."

The lankier of the two—Rex—gave a big, toothy smile like a crocodile considering its next meal. Devlin, with his dark, slightly slanted eyes, was one of those unreadable silent types. Actually, kind of like Quinn.

Speaking of, the elevator door slid open and Quinn joined them, followed by Harvard.

"How's Sergeant Hendricks?" Quinn asked and sat down at a long table in front of the screens. The rest of the team also took seats around the table.

"He'll live," Gabe said.

"Good. Another point in the win column."

"Not yet." Gabe joined Tuc at the front of the room to study the map. "What are we looking at?"

"One of Jahangir Siddiqui's homes," Tuc said. With a flick of his wrist, he turned the picture into an aerial satellite view.

Marcus whistled. "Why can't we have toys like this?"

"Because HORNET is meant to travel light and fast, get in and get out. You already have most everything you need to get the job done. Usually," Tuc added after a beat. "Not the case this time. You don't have the right equipment or enough manpower so we're here to lend you a helping hand."

"Thank you," Gabe said.

Tuc nodded once, then again flipped the view of Siddiqui's mansion. "Thanks to the tracker Quinn planted on his car, we know this is where he's staying and we think this is where he'll meet Zaryanko to make the trade for the bomb."

"Okay," Gabe said. "So let's talk logistics. What are we up against, force-wise?"

CHAPTER THIRTY-TWO

"What do you mean the compound was attacked? Wasn't that the plan?"

Cold as ever, Askar didn't flinch from Siddiqui's rage. He stood his ground and spoke as if he hadn't destroyed a perfectly good afternoon with his report. "It was a team of six Americans, sir. I believe they were after the traitor."

Muscles quivering, Siddiqui paced across the foyer of his home. Even though Zakir Rossoul hadn't talked, he'd figured the man had ties to the Americans. And he'd known they'd probably come looking for their comrade, but how could they have found the compound so quickly?

Unless.

He stopped pacing. "Tehani. She must have told them where to look."

"Makes sense," Askar said.

Siddiqui whirled on him. "Find my wife. I'm sure she's with that American whore journalist who has been snooping around. Find them both and bring them to me. They're ruining my plans."

"Yes, sir."

"Did the Americans get to Rossoul before you killed him?"

"I didn't kill him," Askar said without inflection. "I left him for the bombs to finish, but if they found him first, he wouldn't have lived long enough to tell them anything."

"Let's hope not. Go clean up, then meet me in my office in five minutes. We have a meeting."

He waited until Askar disappeared up the stairs, giving himself several minutes to calm down before he walked to his office and plastered a welcoming smile on his face. It was important that he didn't appear ruffled or overeager.

"Mr. Zaryanko," he said to his visitor in English. "It's a pleasure to finally meet you in person."

The man standing in front of his desk offered a wolfish smile. He wore a charcoal business suit and his long dark hair was pulled back in a ponytail at the back of his neck. "Please," he said, his English heavy with a Russian accent. "Call me Nikolai."

Siddiqui held out a hand. "Jahangir. Have a seat."

Nikolai sat. "If it does not offend, I'd prefer to use your last name. Easier for my Russian tongue to pronounce."

Siddiqui nodded and took the leather chair opposite Nikolai rather than put the space of a desk between them. A power move like that might offend a man such as Nikolai Zaryanko, and he needed to keep the man happy if his plans were to succeed.

"I apologize for my delay. One of my wives was giving me problems."

"Ah, you Muslims. I cannot imagine. One wife is too many and you have four."

"A Russian wife, perhaps," Siddiqui said, keeping his smile firmly in place despite the outrage roaring through him. "An Afghan wife knows her place."

"That they do," Nikolai agreed. "I've had several Afghan women in my brothels. They are always very popular with the customers.

Very…hmm, how do you say? Accommodating. You train them well."

Siddiqui relaxed into his chair. "If you don't mind, I'd like to talk business."

Nikolai waved a hand in an impertinent go-ahead gesture that turned Siddiqui's stomach. Still, he continued to smile. He needed this man, but he wasn't going to make that need known. That would only drive up the price.

His office door opened and Askar slid into the room, silent as a ghost. It would be so easy to give his personal attack dog the signal to kill and take what he wanted—except his window of opportunity was closing fast and killing Nikolai would only delay the deal. As much as it pained him to pay the exuberant price Nikolai was sure to ask, further delay would prove even more costly.

"All right, you have my ear." He leaned forward in his seat and linked his hands between his knees. "What will it take to have The Suitcase in my possession by the end of the week?"

Nikolai flashed that wolf's smile again. The price he named *was* exorbitant.

Siddiqui sat back in his chair. "That's robbery."

"It's the price of doing business." Nikolai stood. "And no, I will not negotiate. If you're not willing to pay, I know plenty of others who are."

Siddiqui watched him walk toward the door and didn't move, expecting to call Nikolai's bluff. But the Russian left the room.

He was serious. He really wasn't willing to negotiate.

Fuck.

Siddiqui pushed out of his chair. "Bring him back," he ordered Askar and a moment later, his soldier led an amused Nikolai through the door.

"Change your mind?"

"You have a deal," Siddiqui said. "But we need to make this happen today."

CHAPTER THIRTY-THREE

Two days.

According to Tuc's intel, they had two days to prepare. The team spent countless hours in the war room, running scenarios. What if this, what if that, covering all their bases. They spent just as much time running short training missions with Tuc and his men.

No room for error.

The afternoon before the raid, they performed one last training exercise, a mock run at an abandoned mansion similar to Siddiqui's.

It went off without a hitch.

Back on the helo, Seth relaxed into his seat, flying high on the job well done, feeling lighter than he had in years. He'd fucking done it. He hadn't frozen up once during any of the missions.

They actually had a shot at pulling this off.

He wasn't the only one revved, either. The mood on the helo had done a complete 180 from the ride in, the men now joking and laughing, releasing forty-eight nonstop hours of tension.

Quinn, in the seat across from Seth, smirked under the dirt

and paint coating his face. "Hey, Ace," he called over the rotor noise and leaned forward. "Nice shooting. Knew you'd show those motherfuckers."

"Which ones? The baddies or these assholes?" he asked, tilting his head toward the rest of the team.

"All of them."

"Oorah!"

Quinn held out a fist. Seth met him halfway and knocked their knuckles together as the bird started its descent. He glanced out the door and saw Phoebe standing on the roof next to Tuc Quentin, shielding her eyes from the prop wash. Her loose shirt whipped around her body, alternately showing flashes of skin at her belly and plastering itself to her curves.

All of his exuberance coalesced along his spine and nailed him in the balls. Instant. Hard-on.

As soon as the helo's runners hit the rooftop, he hopped out.

Tuc gave them a round of applause. "Nice job, guys."

But Seth's focus had narrowed to one person, the woman in front of him who looked torn between wanting to smile and wanting to smack him. And holy hell, that shouldn't have been a turn-on but if he got any harder right now he was going to have trouble walking.

She opened her mouth as he approached and he slid a hand around the back of her neck, dragging her to him, covering her mouth with his own. Claiming. Branding.

He swallowed her gasp and her fingers dug into his shoulders, but she didn't fight him. Perfect. He was sick of fighting with her. And fighting with himself about her. He wanted the easy intimacy they'd had together in the village before he'd gotten all screwed up in the head again.

He wanted her.

He backed her up into the elevator without ever lifting his

mouth from hers. Vaguely heard some cheers and lewd comments behind them and flipped the guys off over his shoulder. Laughter boomed as the doors slid shut.

Alone.

At freaking last.

He cupped her waist, skimming his hands under her shirt, filling his palms with her breasts. Her nipples stood erect under the fabric of her bra and he slid his fingers inside the cup, finding those gorgeous little peaks with his thumb. She trembled under his touch, broke her mouth from his on a moan as the elevator doors slid open again on the second floor.

Damn, was there any sexier sound than that?

Bed. He had to get her into his bed. Get her naked. And bury himself as deep inside her as he could.

"Whoa," she gasped and slapped a hand to his chest when he would have scooped her into his arms. "Hold on just a dang minute." She took a moment to catch her breath. Then she poked her index finger at his sternum. "For the past two days, you've treated me like I was contagious, avoiding me at all costs. And now you're trying to back me into a dark corner and have your way with me? I don't think so, buddy."

She ducked out of his embrace and caught the elevator door before it closed her in with him again. He wasn't quite fast enough and had to ride the elevator up a floor. He burst from the car as soon as the doors opened again and raced down the swooping staircase to the room she'd been given on the second floor, spotting her at her door. "Phoebe."

Chin raised with indignation, she ignored him and again, he wasn't quick enough. Got there just as the door slammed in his face. He tried the knob, found it locked, and scowled at the wood. "Phoebe, open up."

"Nope. You're being an asshole."

Oh, was he ever going to regret the day he told her to call him out on that.

"C'mon. Can we talk?"

"We could've if your tongue wasn't down my throat. Go away. I'm taking a shower."

He groaned and pressed his forehead against the door. Phoebe. In the shower. Not the mental image he needed when he could still hammer nails with his cock. Damn thing hadn't shown any interest in any woman for years and now suddenly it wouldn't behave when he needed it to.

Voices echoed down the hall and he shoved away from the door, following the sound until he found the rec room, where Jean-Luc and Marcus had started a game of pool.

"Hey, man," Marcus said and straightened from the table to chalk his cue. "That was a quickie. We figured we wouldn't see you until just before go-time."

"She shut me out of her room."

"Bummer. Well, we're not as pretty but you can hang with us for the evening. We're celebrating Zak's good prognosis. And taking advantage of our excellent accommodations while we can."

"Can't drink, though," Jean-Luc muttered and lifted a bottle of water in toast. "Orders direct from our esteemed *capitaine* since we still have a mission to complete. So, up for a game of pool? No, wait." He scowled. "You play pool like you play poker? 'Cause if so even I'm not stupid enough to play you."

"Pool's not my game," Seth admitted, eying the table. "Never was very good at geometry."

"All right then. I take that back. Care to join us, *mon ami*?"

"Nope." Struck with a sudden idea, he crooked a finger at Marcus. Like hell he'd let Phoebe shut herself away from him. Now that he had his head on straight again, they had to talk. "Need you, Deangelo."

"Well, I'm flattered, Harlan. But I prefer my partners a little more…I dunno." He tucked his cue under his arm and mimed an hourglass figure in the air. "Curvy."

"Mmm, and with longer hair," Jean-Luc said.

"Bigger lips," Marcus added.

"Legs for days."

"And no cock," Marcus said.

"Va-jay-jay all the way," Jean-Luc agreed and the two laughed like a pair of drunk frat boys, knocking their cues together.

Seth rolled his eyes, but found he was fighting a smile. Jesus, he hadn't smiled this much in years. Or laughed. Or scowled. Cried. Feared.

Loved.

Yeah, all kinds of messy emotions he'd kept locked up inside were suddenly bubbling to the surface. He wasn't quite sure what to do with them all, or even how to begin sorting through them. All he knew for sure was he had some groveling to do.

"No, you idiot," he said when the laughter died down. "I need you to pick a lock."

"Oh. That I can do."

As Marcus leaned his cue against the wall, Seth couldn't help but add, "Besides, you know you can't handle this much sexy."

Marcus stopped short and his mouth fell open. He exchanged a surprised look with Jean-Luc. The expression on both of their faces clearly said, *Holy shit, Seth Harlan cracked a joke.*

"What?" he said a little defensively. "I do have a sense of humor."

Jean-Luc finally laughed. "It's nice to see it make an appearance."

Annnd awkward silence.

"About that lock?" Marcus motioned for him to lead the way. "No cheating while I'm gone, Cajun."

"Wouldn't dream of it," Jean-Luc said and they heard the crack of his cue hitting a ball as they left the room.

Marcus shrugged. "Ah, he was winning anyway."

• • •

Phoebe left the en suite bathroom off her bedroom, still reveling in the luxury of hot water as sweet-scented steam followed her across the carpet. The heat had done marvelous things for all of the lingering aches and pains left over from her near-death experience and she felt somewhat human again.

Tuc's house was a palace next to the rundown shelter with its cold showers and stingy water pressure. And compared to the rustic living conditions in the mountains, hot water, soap, and even the plush carpet under her feet felt downright decadent. Admittedly, the shower had factored into her decision to stay here instead of going back to the shelter.

Well, the shower and Seth. Even though he shouldn't have had anything to do with it, since she'd spent the last two days convincing herself the abrupt end of their relationship had been a good thing. Which it was. Helpless against the pull of attraction, she'd been incapable of keeping her distance from him, despite knowing all the reasons she should. But as long as their awkward morning after continued to anchor a wedge between them, it wasn't a problem. He avoided her, and her secrets remained safe. *She* remained safe. There was no more risk of falling in love with him—which she'd been dangerously close to doing, dammit—and she'd never have to reveal that she'd once lambasted him in the press. She'd never have to hurt him.

Or at least that had been her plan until he kissed her on the roof. Thank God she'd come to her senses before things progressed past heavy groping. And thank God this bedroom had a lock on the door.

Stopping in front of a giant bureau, she opened the top drawer in search of panties, grateful Zina had dropped her belongings off when she picked up Darya and her son. It was nice to have her own clothes again. She'd just picked out a pair of functional blue cotton when the door burst open behind her.

The *locked* door.

She squeaked and dropped the panties. Nearly dropped her towel, too, but managed to catch the slipping terry cloth and tuck it around her breasts again as Seth strode in like he belonged.

She gaped at him. "How did you—?"

Marcus stood out in the hall, rolling up his lock-pick set. He gave a guilty wave. She glared. He shrugged. Seth pushed the door shut, blocking her view, but she continued to scowl at the wood.

Ugh. She was so going to take an unflattering picture of Marcus in a compromising position—wouldn't be difficult because, hello, this was Marcus Deangelo, by all accounts the second-biggest man-whore on the team. Then she'd blow the photo up to a life-size portrait and ship it to his mother. That'd show him for picking locks to ladies' bedrooms.

Seth moved into her line of sight. "We need to talk."

Oh, no. Talking was a bad idea. She clenched the towel tighter and turned her glare on him. "You need to leave."

"I'm not leaving until we clear some things between us."

A bubble of panic expanded in her chest and she backed away, stumbling a little on her own feet as she reached blindly behind her for the bathroom door. If she shut herself in there, he'd eventually take the hint and leave, right?

"Leave. Please." She spun away, but his arm banded around her from behind. He lifted her clear off her feet and turned her into his chest, holding her tight for a long time. His heart thudded under her ear, making her think of their time in bed together. The memories combined with the gentle slide of his hands down her back heated her from the inside out.

"Seth, no," she protested, but her voice came out faint and embarrassingly submissive and she didn't have the willpower to push him away when his arms felt so good around her. "Please, just…go."

"All right," he said after a moment, but didn't release her. "If you let me explain myself first."

"You don't have to—"

"Yes, I do. For several things." He drew a deep breath and finally set her back at arm's length. "Starting with that moment on the roof and in the elevator—it was a slip on my part. I was high on adrenaline and you were standing there next to Tuc looking so pretty, and your infatuation with him tapped into something—"

She gaped. "What on earth are you talking about? What infatuation with Tuc?"

"What infatuation?" he echoed incredulously. "Are you kidding? It's obvious. You salivate every time he walks into a room."

She knocked his hands away from her shoulders. "Because I want his picture. You know how much magazines pay for shots of him? Enough that I could set Zina and the shelter up in a place like this and have enough left over to travel the world. Twice!"

His mouth opened and closed like a fish. "Oh."

"Oh's right, you dummy."

"But you—" He shook his head as if trying to clear his thoughts. "No, never mind. That's not the point. We're getting off track. I need to apologize for the other day. For the way I left. It wasn't—I, uh, didn't mean—I couldn't—aw, fuck." He paused, rubbed a hand back and forth over his hair a few times, and winced. "Listen, I let myself get all knotted up again, but that was no excuse for walking out like you meant nothing to me. Because you do. Mean something." He lifted his gaze to hers. "More than something, actually."

"But…what about Emma?"

His brow wrinkled in an expression of genuine confusion. "Emma? She doesn't have anything to do with this."

"She does if you still love her."

"What? No, I don't love her."

She didn't bother hiding her doubt. "You don't?"

"No." But then he blew out a breath. "Okay, I admit I miss what I had with her and I like the idea of what we could've been. But that's it. I don't love her anymore. I haven't seen her in years and barely know her now."

"Then why carry her photo around?"

His hand covered the pocket of his vest before he caught himself and dropped it to his side. "It's…hard to explain."

"Try."

He said nothing. And more nothing. So much nothing, in fact, that she figured their conversation—and relationship—was officially over. Because despite all of her protests to the contrary, she wanted to talk with him. Without communication, they'd never have anything but sex. If she'd learned nothing else from her ex-husband, it was that harsh reality.

She bent to retrieve her dropped panties, then opened the bureau drawer to find something more substantial to wear than a towel. "Like I said, you need to leave."

Seth touched her shoulder. "I can't explain it. Just…know I don't love her anymore. I'm a one-woman man and right now, that woman is you."

Sighing, she gave up on trying to maintain her anger. How could she stay mad after an admission like that? It meant she'd have to come clean with him about her past, but not now. At this moment, she only wanted to hold him.

"What am I going to do with you?" She spun around and

walked into his arms. "You spend too much time and energy dwelling on all the bad parts of life—you miss out on the good. The two of us together, that was some of the good." She kissed his chin. "And we can have it again if you want."

"I *do* want," he breathed next to her ear. "That's gotta be obvious. I can't control myself around you. It's like my cock has a mind of its own."

She slid a hand between them, found him hard, and squeezed him lightly through the fabric of his pants. "Hmm. And explain to me why that's a problem?"

CHAPTER THIRTY-FOUR

Problem? What problem?

Seth shuddered violently at her touch. When she put her hand on him like that, his only problem was the clothes keeping him from burying himself to the balls inside her. He fisted the material at her lower back as she continued to stroke him, the caress maddeningly light, almost nonexistent between the numbing effect of his scars and the muffling of sensation through his pants. And almost too much. Wound as tight as he was and still riding the effects of adrenaline from the successful training op, he was about three seconds from exploding. And he *had* to be inside her when he did.

"Sweetheart." He caught her hand. Part of him wanted to pull her away. Another part never wanted the sweet butterfly caresses to end and he pressed his hips forward, thrusting into her soft palm. "If we do this, I can't go easy. Not this time. I'm too wound up, and I'm going to bend you over that bed and fuck you until you're screaming."

She inhaled sharply in the moment before his mouth covered hers. He showed her what he meant with the kiss, used his teeth to prove how hard he needed it, his tongue to show how he'd take over. When he finally released her, her breaths sawed in and out of her lungs and she looked up at him with dazed eyes.

"You promise?" She backed up a step and dropped her towel, exposing her bare body to him. She was too good to be true. All satiny white skin with a faint dusting of freckles over her shoulders. Her nipples plumped and darkened as he drank in the sight of her, and his mouth watered for a taste of those tight buds. She was slim through the waist and hips, with a thatch of hair at the apex of her legs the same copper as that on her head. She squeezed her thighs together as his gaze settled there and, hell no, she wasn't hiding her arousal from him. He wanted to see her glistening with dampness, ready to take him. He hauled her toward him, turned her back to his chest, and reached around to find her clit. She cried out with something that might have been his name and bucked her hips, grinding her ass against his cock.

Jesus.

He needed inside her.

He kicked her legs apart and used his free hand to unzip.

"Seth," she gasped. "I'm so...close..." She rocked faster against his fingers and a shudder of release took her knees out from under her. He caught her with a banded arm around her waist and maneuvered her to the bed, bending her over the mattress just as he'd promised.

"Hang on to something," he said and her fingers clawed at the blanket. He took himself in hand, found her entrance, and inched into her heat. She drenched his tip with her arousal, reminding him they needed a condom. Goddammit. He held agonizingly still as he searched through the many pockets of his pants. He knew he had one somewhere...

"Seth," she whimpered. "Move." She spread her legs wider, taking him in deep and almost making the condom unnecessary.

He held his breath as heat coalesced at the small of his back and his balls tightened.

Too close.

Condom, he thought again once he got the rising tide of his orgasm under control for the moment. He continued his search, all but emptying his pockets on the floor until he found the damn thing in a leg pocket and withdrew from her to slide it on.

"No," Phoebe cried and arched to keep him.

He flattened a hand on her lower back, holding her steady as he sheathed himself, then gripped her hips and slammed home again. And again. And again. She buried her face in the mattress and screamed, her sex spasming around him. He leaned forward and nipped the skin at the base of her neck and another shiver racked her, nearly undoing him.

Fuck, she felt good.

Straightening, he lifted her hips and set a pounding rhythm until his muscles quaked and she screamed again. Her orgasm clamped around his cock and ripped his own release from him with such force, it blurred the line between pleasure and pain.

Groaning, he pressed his face to the sweat-slicked skin of her lower back.

"Oh. My. God," she gasped, trembling with the aftershocks. "I'll never move again. And I'm good with that."

Seth dragged in a deep lungful of air and peeled himself off her. She was right—she didn't move. If anything, she started sliding off the edge of the bed like melting Jell-O. He gripped her rear and boosted her up until she lay across the mattress on her belly.

"I'll be right back," he told her, still breathing hard. "Have to take care of this."

"Mmm-hmm."

Yup, she was already well on her way to dreamland. Seth smiled, a primal kind of satisfaction filling his chest that had nothing to do with his own release and everything to do with satisfying his woman.

His woman.

He kinda liked the sound of that.

The air in the bathroom was still thick with moisture from her shower. He tossed the condom, but when he stopped at the sink to wash his hands, he caught a glimpse of himself in the vanity. He still wore his face paint and all his weapons. And she'd let him touch her looking like this?

He quickly shed the weapons and holsters, setting them on the bathroom counter. Then came his pants, his shirt. He ran through a shower, soaping himself up and rinsing off as fast as possible, his focus completely on returning to the bed, to Phoebe.

He had the evening free and he didn't plan on wasting a second of it.

Clean again, he shut off the water and stepped out of the glass-enclosed shower. Opened the linen cabinet to grab a towel—and came face-to-face with a full-length mirror on the back of the door.

Fuck.

There was a reason he only had one small vanity mirror at home. He hadn't wanted to see this, the whole view of his torture in a stark reflection.

He looked at his hands, almost like seeing them for the first time. His palms were rough from scrapes that had never healed properly. Raised welts covered the backs of his hands from the thin stick his captors used to smack his knuckles. He still had indents in his wrists from the cable he'd hung from for more hours than he remembered. Thin lines striped his ribs from the blades of multiple sharp objects. Circular burns from cigarettes. A brand on his hip—the Pashto word for infidel. The ragged ridge of scar tissue across his neck from when Devil sliced open his throat.

They'd intended for him to die before the SEALs got to him. By all rights, he should have. He didn't know how he'd lived and for a long time he'd wondered, why him? Why not Bowie or Link, whose bodies had never been recovered? Or Joe McMahon, who had been blown into such small pieces by the time the firefight was over all they'd had to bury was an arm and his dog tags? Garrett Rey, who had lasted only four days in captivity? Or Omar Cordero? Why couldn't he have just fucking hung on a few more days?

Why, out of all of them, had Seth Harlan survived?

Soft hands swept across his shoulders, down his spine, and then circled his waist. Phoebe leaned her cheek against his biceps and met his eyes in the mirror. Next to him, her skin was milky perfection and only highlighted how monstrous he truly looked.

"Are you okay?" she whispered.

Unable to manage an immediate reply, he swallowed hard. Shook his head. "How can you find this attractive?"

She took the forgotten towel from his numb fingers, gently dabbing his shoulders, chest, stomach. Then she looped the towel around his waist and tucked the end in before entwining her fingers with his. "Can we try something I've been dying to do since we met?"

Thrown by the subject change, he let her lead him into the bedroom without protest. They'd already done the most intimate thing two people could possibly do together. What else could she be "dying" to do?

At the edge of the bed, she pushed on his chest until he sat, then, ignoring her own nakedness, she dug her camera bag out of a large bureau.

Fuck that. He sprung to his feet. "I don't think so."

She frowned over her shoulder as she fitted a lens onto the

camera. "Trust me, Seth. Please."

She didn't think he trusted her?

Well, hell.

"All right," he said on a sigh. "On the condition nobody but us sees them."

She grinned and he got the distinct feeling he'd just been played. "Deal."

Man, what was he getting himself into? Self-conscious, he rubbed the back of his neck, which had gone hot to the touch. Now he was blushing. Great. "Uh, what do you want me to do?"

"Just lie down on your stomach. No, wait." She looped her camera around her neck and crossed to the bed. Considered it for a second, then yanked off the spread and rumpled the sheets. "There we go. Lie on your side here, arm tucked under your head. Oh, and get rid of the towel. There." She positioned him and stepped back. Darted forward, trailed the sheet over his cock, just barely covering it, and backed up again, head tilted, calculation wrinkling her brow. As if he were livestock she was assessing for purchase.

"What do I do with this?" He lifted his free arm. Kinda felt like it was in the way and he wasn't sure where to put it.

"Just act natural," she said and raised her camera, snapping a few shots of an area of his anatomy he'd really rather not be captured in a photo. "Where would you put it normally when you're up on your side?"

If she was looking to make him more uncomfortable with his body, she was succeeding. But two could play at this game. If he had to be uncomfortable, so did she.

"Between your legs," he answered.

A pink flush filled her breasts and crept up her neck into her cheeks. "Nice, Seth. But I'm not always in bed with you. Just relax. Forget the camera, forget posing. How would you naturally lie if you were going to sleep right now?"

He flopped over onto his back, spread his legs, rested one hand on his chest and threw the other arm over his head.

"There. Hold that."

He shut his eyes, breathed out. Heard the *click, click, click* of her camera.

"All right, perfect. Now roll over and get comfortable on your stomach."

He rolled, dragging the sheet with him, and wrapped his arms around one of the pillows. He felt Phoebe move to the top of the bed by his shoulder. More *click, click, click*ing. A few times, she had the camera so close to him, her breath skimmed across his skin and raised goose bumps as she looked through the viewfinder. His cock perked up, pressing painfully into the mattress.

And then, it wasn't just her breath, but her lips and tongue lightly tracing the scars crisscrossing his back.

He groaned and turned his head to capture her mouth. Kneeling beside him like she was, with her legs spread open just enough, he had a perfect view of the pink lips of her sex. He stroked his fingers through her slit, found her wet, and dipped inside. She broke from his kiss with a moan and arched her back, riding his fingers until she was panting, straining toward climax. Her camera still hung from a strap around her neck and bumped lightly against her belly with each rise and fall of her body. Shamelessly, she took her pleasure from him and his own grew with every soft, sexy whimper from her throat.

When he skimmed his thumb over her clit, she came on his hand. Head thrown back, eyes squeezed shut.

Christ, she was beautiful.

He lifted his fingers to his mouth and sucked, the taste of her arousal like honey in his throat. It wasn't enough. Gripping her hips, he lifted and repositioned her so that she was straddling his face. She gasped and tried to get up, but he held her still and tasted her. She vibrated over him and her protests faded into moans as his tongue flicked out, dipped inside her, then circled her clit. When she came again, his name was on her lips and a primal thrill shot through him, drawing his balls up tight.

Christ, he wasn't going to last much longer himself.

Phoebe laughed breathlessly and a pink blush filled her cheeks again as she stretched out beside him. "Well, that was unexpected."

He rolled up onto his side and took his cock in hand, stroking himself. She watched with hungry eyes, then covered his hand with her own and squeezed just hard enough. He cursed as his body jacked off the mattress and his release jetted into both of their palms.

"Shit." He scrambled upright and reached for the sheet. "Sorry. Let me—"

Phoebe waved him off and sucked the remnants of his orgasm off her fingers. And, fuck him if that wasn't the most erotic thing he'd ever seen in his life. If he hadn't just come hard enough to see stars, he had no doubt he'd burst again from the sight alone. He fell onto the bed, exhausted, sated, and yet unbelievably aroused again.

"Phoebe, you're…I don't have words. Gonna kill me probably."

Chuckling, she took the camera from around her neck and set it on the nightstand, then snuggled in beside him. Her head rested on his shoulder. "That'd be something, wouldn't it? After everything else you've survived."

"Death by sex." He tangled his fingers into her curls. They weren't soft, but springy, and he liked the way they felt around his fingers. He tugged on one curl. "No better way to go."

"Imagine the eulogy."

He swept a hand in a grand arc through the air. "Here lies Seth.

Survived a war only to be sexed to death."

She snorted and buried her face against his neck. "That's so wrong. I shouldn't laugh."

"I wanted you to laugh. That was the point."

Bang! Bang! Bang!

Phoebe started at the knock of a fist on their door. Seth simply lifted his head and scowled at the interruption.

"Hey." She smiled up at him. "An unexpected noise and you didn't jump."

"Progress," he said.

Bang! Bang! Bang! "Yo, lovebirds!"

"Fuck off, Marcus." He lay back again, content to ignore his teammate. He tugged another of Phoebe's curls until it was completely straight, then let it go and watched it bounce back.

She harrumphed. "Are you going to do that all night?"

"Yup." To prove it, he wound another around his finger and dragged it out.

"I'll look like a burning bush by the time you're done. A frizzy burning bush."

Bang! Bang! Bang!

"Hey, man, I feel ya," Marcus called through the door. "I hate coitus interruptus as much as the next guy, but Gabe told me to pick the lock again if necessary and I'd really rather not. So just get dressed and get your ass downstairs, okay? You have fifteen minutes."

Phoebe sighed. "That sounds kind of important."

"Unfortunately." He'd hoped for more than a few hours with her before the team headed out. Wanted to stay in this room and indulge in the warmth she caused in his chest and revel in the sense of peace just lying beside her gave him.

Yeah, it was selfish. And yeah, he felt like shit for even thinking it, but for the first time in years, he was...content. Relaxed even.

He propped himself up on his elbow and smiled down at her. Except she wasn't smiling back. She stared at the door, worrying her lower lip with her teeth.

"Hey." Dragging a finger lightly along her jaw, he guided her gaze to him. "If you're worried about the op, don't be. We got this."

"Oh," she said and released her lip as if suddenly noticing the nervous gesture. "No, it's not—I have complete faith you'll stop Siddiqui."

"Then what's wrong?"

She opened her mouth. No sound emerged.

Stomach tight with dread, he sat up. "Phoebe, what's wrong?"

She shook her head. "It's not important right now."

"Are you sure?"

"Yes. Absolutely. We can talk when you get back." She jumped from the bed. "I should shower again. I don't want to face the guys with sex hair." At the bathroom door, she glanced over her shoulder and finally smiled. "You're welcome to join me."

"Yeah, okay. Be there in a sec." He put his feet on the floor, but that was as far as he got. He stared into the open bathroom. Water came on, splashing against the tile floor. The shower door slid shut.

Still, he didn't move.

When he first cornered Phoebe at the market, he'd been so sure she was lying, hiding something. As he'd gotten to know her in the days since, he had convinced himself his initial impression of her was nothing more than his paranoia talking.

But the look in her eyes just now...

Goddammit. Should have trusted his gut.

CHAPTER THIRTY-FIVE

Seth never joined her.

By the time she realized he wasn't going to, the bedroom was empty. His gear was gone.

Phoebe stood in the center of the room, towel clutched around her, hair dripping onto the carpet, and replayed the last ten minutes in her mind. He'd been sweet and almost playful when Marcus knocked on the door.

So what changed to make him leave without a word?

As if she didn't know.

Damn. Phoebe grabbed some clean clothes and made quick work of throwing them on. She was out the door in the next instant, hair still dripping.

She shouldn't have opened her mouth to tell him about the article. At least not yet, but he'd looked so content lying next to her, playing with her hair, and she'd been overcome with a choking guilt. Her timing was shit, though, which was the only reason she'd pulled back from telling him. She couldn't hurt him like that only hours before he left to put his life at risk.

When she made it to the briefing room, she found the team

suited up, readying enough gear to wage a small war. A tremble jangled down her spine at the chorus of clicks from around the room—magazines snapping into weapons, bullets into chambers.

Oh, God. They weren't supposed to be leaving for another few hours. "What's going on?"

"Mission's a go," Gabe said, barely pausing as he shouldered his weapon and strode by her. "Let's move, gentlemen."

The team filed out.

"Wait." Phoebe grabbed Seth's hand. Sure the men had been training incessantly for this raid, but she couldn't suppress the bone-deep fear that gripped her. She stood on her toes to press a kiss to his mouth. "Please be careful."

He gave a tight smile and then he was gone without promising a thing.

Phoebe sank into one of the plush chairs at the paper-strewn table and the wall of screens at the front of the room flickered to life. Helmet cams, she realized when she spotted Seth on one. They were on the roof, climbing into the helicopter, and their voices came from a speaker somewhere as each of the men checked his radio. Her heart clenched at Seth's matter-of-fact "Radio check, over."

Please let him be safe.

"Ms. Leighton."

She stiffened at the sound of Tuc's voice from the door. "Mr. Quentin," she said, but didn't look away from the screens and watched as Seth ran through last checks of his gear. "Why aren't you out there with them?"

"Wish I could be. Unfortunately, I have one of those recognizable faces and according to the tabloids, I'm on my yacht somewhere in the Caribbean, sipping cocktails with a certain supermodel—I forget which one is supposed to be my flavor of the week. Still, I'd hate to disabuse anyone of that pretty notion."

Of course. Couldn't have the tabloids knowing about his

secret second life as a mercenary. A sour taste filled her mouth, but she decided not to comment.

Tuc strode in and picked up a keyboard. Seconds later, Seth's helmet cam came up on the big screen. "Better?"

A sickening apprehension filled her as Seth strapped himself into the helicopter and the camera began to shake with liftoff. Could she really sit here and watch him do this? No. But was she going to leave this room until he was safe again? Absolutely not. She would be with him every step of the way, even if it gave her a heart attack.

Needing a distraction, she glanced over at Tuc. "Back in the village, you knew me before we met. How?"

"I have my ways." He flashed his Hollywood smile and nodded toward the cameras. "So. You and Seth?"

On screen, Seth took a photo out of his vest pocket.

Oh, no. She couldn't watch him handle Emma's picture with such tenderness again. Not when the memory of making love with him was so fresh in her mind.

She spun her chair to face Tuc. "I'm assuming you also know about my former job."

"I do."

"Are you going to tell him about the article?"

"Yes," Tuc said without a blink of remorse. Heartless bastard. "That is, unless you plan to."

She opened her mouth to say that she did, but no sound came out. It was a lie anyway—she could admit to herself she was never going to tell him, despite her every intention. Look at how many opportunities she had already passed up. She shook her head. "I can't. He'll hate me."

"If you're sleeping with him, he deserves to know."

"Yes, but—it's not that simple anymore. When I wrote that piece, I didn't know him. He was just another juicy, tragic story.

And now—"

"Now you do," Tuc finished. "Which is why he deserves to know before things progress any further between the two of you. He's already on unstable mental ground."

"God, I hate how you guys all think that. He's not any more unstable than Ian. Or what about Quinn? 'Cause that guy's got some serious baggage. And you can't tell me Jean-Luc doesn't have a Disneyland of issues he's trying to rid himself of by sleeping his way through the female population."

Tuc smirked. "You think so highly of them all."

"I do," she shot back. "But Seth's not any more broken than the rest of them and I'm sick of hearing everyone tear him down time and again."

"And what about me? Am I broken? Do I have issues?"

She snorted. "You're the poster child for issues. You have a classic case of Hollywood child star syndrome, but instead of partying your way in and out of rehab, you've ramped the entitlement thing up to a whole new level of crazy."

"Maybe," he conceded with a little one-shoulder shrug. "But I save people."

"You move people around like chess pieces. All this?" She waved a hand at the room with its high-tech gadgets. "This is you playing God and it's disgusting."

Tucker's blond brows lifted. "You don't like me, do you?"

"No, I don't. I did like your father's movies, though. Hated yours."

"Ouch," he said without even a shade of indignation in his tone. "But I'll let you in on a little secret. I hated them, too. I never wanted to act. It was expected of me because that was my father's profession. But all this, what you call me playing God? This is what I'm good at. Strategizing, maneuvering. I use it to save people, to give good men second chances. What exactly do you do, Ms. Leighton?"

With that, he set down the keyboard and left her alone.

Fuming, she pushed out of her chair to follow and give him a piece of her mind. Yeah, she'd done some unethical things in the past, but that did not dictate her worth. She'd done a lot of good since then and if he thought he could get away with diminishing that good all because—

She stopped short, hand outstretched to shove open the door. Oh, was she a gullible idiot or what?

Tuc had said that on purpose, knowing it'd piss her off and she'd feel the need to set him straight. He didn't think she should be watching the mission and this was his way of distracting her.

Manipulative bastard.

Well, he had said he was good at strategy. No doubt about that now.

She about-faced and stalked back to her chair. Seth's helmet camera showed the guys all standing, Quinn by the door with his hand through a loop in the ceiling. He tossed a rope out of the helicopter and waved an arm. The first man grabbed the rope and jumped. Seth went third in line and she held her breath until his feet were on the ground, his rifle in hand, and he was moving toward cover.

Relief flowed through her in an exhausting wave and she sank back into the leather seat. This was going to be a long night.

Behind her, the door opened.

"Didn't work, huh?" Tuc said with a note of resignation. He handed her a mug of coffee then settled into the chair beside hers.

"Almost," she admitted and blew across the top of her mug before taking a sip.

"Can't blame me for trying. You don't need to watch this."

"Yes, I do."

"I suppose so." He faced the screen and raised his own mug. "Jesus, I wish I was there."

CHAPTER THIRTY-SIX

The sand-colored mansion looked empty through Seth's scope. Tucked into the side of a mountain, facing a desert dotted with little more than scrub brush, it was a very defensible position for anyone inside—*if* there was anyone inside—which was a major plus for the bad guys. The surrounding terrain did not offer a whole lot of cover for those looking to attack the place—not so great for the good guys.

Flat on his belly behind a natural rise in the land, Seth continued to scan for signs of life.

"Anything?" Ian asked. They'd been lying in the dirt for close to eight hours. Waiting. Watching.

"No. You?"

"Nada. This waiting sucks."

"You just wish you were in there so you could get your hands on that bomb," Seth said.

"Yeah, you're right. Bombs are what I do, so if anyone's going to handle it, it should be me. Instead, I'm stuck out here in the middle of the desert babysitting you."

"Maybe if you weren't such a volatile fucker, Gabe would

trust you to get closer to the action. Besides," Seth added and swiped a bead of sweat from his forehead with his sleeve, "I needed a spotter and you're surprisingly good at it."

Ian made a derisive sound. Several minutes ticked by in silence, then he asked, "Think we're jumping at shadows? If this deal was going to happen, don't you think it would have happened under the cover of darkness?"

"I don't know. Siddiqui's not in control of this. It's all on Zaryanko's watch. Maybe he tried to jump-start the deal last night and things fell through." Seth rested his forehead against his arm and closed his eyes for a second. He had to look away from the reticle before the image of crosshairs burned into his retina. "Sooner or later, they're going to show."

Ian grunted. "I'm starting to doubt it. We spent the last two days training to raid Siddiqui's house in Kabul and look how that turned out. We're sitting here baking our asses off watching an abandoned shithole."

"Plans change all the time, Ian. You know that, and Tuc's intel was solid."

"Yeah, well. Dunno how much I trust that guy."

"You don't trust anyone."

"List is a short one," Ian admitted.

"Yeah?" Seth fitted his eye back to his scope. "Name one person you trust implicitly."

"Like you're one to talk about trust, Hero."

He didn't have to look at the guy to know Ian's ever-present sneer was firmly in place. He heard it loud and clear in his voice. "I trust Phoebe."

"That's not trust, that's lust."

Says the man who wouldn't know intimacy if it bit him on the ass. Seth snorted, not bothering to argue over it because he'd only waste his breath. Ian wasn't capable of understanding his relationship with Phoebe.

"You still haven't named anyone," he pointed out. "And stop calling me Hero."

"You plan to harp on this all day, Hero?"

"You are one mean-ass mother," Seth grumbled. "And, yeah, I think I will. Nothing better to do but piss you off until the bad guys show up."

Ian hissed out an annoyed breath. "Fine. Tank."

"Dogs don't count."

"Yeah, they do. They possess a kind of loyalty most men can't even fathom."

All right. He had a point. "I'm talking about humans. I know you respect Gabe and Quinn, but do you trust them?"

Silence.

Seth let him stew on that and continued scanning for signs of life at the target building. Far as he could tell, there was nobody inside, and the hope he'd had after their final training op was starting to fizzle out. Maybe they were jumping at shadows.

"You," Ian muttered. "I trust you."

Startled, Seth glanced over at him. "Why me?"

"You saved my ass and you didn't have to, so you get my trust. And that's why I asked Gabe to let me spot for you. I owe you. Simple as that."

Seth opened his mouth, not exactly sure what he planned to say, but it didn't matter because the sound of approaching vehicles saved him from having to answer. He peered through his scope. A line of SUVs rumbled toward the abandoned house, kicking up clouds of dust in their wake. "Got three SUVs inbound from the east."

"Yeah, see them," Ian said and related the information over the radio. Gabe's voice came back, telling them to hold their positions and report if they got eyes on The Suitcase.

The SUVs trundled to a stop in front of the mansion and several men with scarves wrapped around their faces climbed out. They all carried M4s, except for one man who appeared to be their leader. He carried a sniper drag bag over his shoulder and motioned with one hand as he ordered his men to secure the perimeter. Then the sniper turned and seemed to look directly at Seth and Ian's position—but there was no way he could see them, hidden as they were behind the rise, under a camouflage net. More likely, the sniper was just scanning the horizon, possibly searching for Nikolai Zaryanko's vehicle, anxious to get the trade over with.

Still, a chilling sense of déjà vu clawed across the back of Seth's mind. He gave his head a little shake. Couldn't get sucked into the past now.

"Must be Askar," Ian said, still peering through his binoculars. "Can you get the motherfucker?"

"What's the range?"

"Four hundred sixty meters."

"Yeah, I got him. Ask Gabe if he wants to engage them now or wait."

Ian got on the radio. A moment later, Gabe's orders came back. Wait. Seth relaxed off the trigger and continued watching as Askar and his men began stacking duffel bags in the sand.

"Holy shit," Ian said. "That's a lot of money. Think it's American bills?"

"Don't go there. That's a slippery slope."

"I'm not." He sounded offended. "I'm more focused on making sure that bomb doesn't end up in enemy hands. If it does, 9/11 will look like nothing more than an appetizer to the main course."

Not a pleasant thought, but accurate judging by everything they'd learned about The Suitcase over the last few days. "9/11 is why I became a Marine."

"It's why I joined Navy EOD," Ian said, his native New York accent more apparent than usual. "I wanted to blow those motherfuckers from the map. Nobody attacks my city and gets away with it."

Askar and his men dragged the cash inside, then took up guard positions out in front. And for a long time nothing happened.

Wind kicked up sand, obscuring Seth's view to the point he feared they'd have to risk exposure and move, but eventually it settled and he had a clear shot again.

And still, nothing happened.

For a good hour they waited, baking in the desert sun. Even the guards out in front of the property started to fidget, tensions running high.

Despite the heat, a chill scraped claws along Seth's spine. He lifted his eye away from the scope, glanced over his shoulder. Not two hundred meters away, sunlight sparked off something reflective. He couldn't see anybody in the waves of heat radiating off the earth, but someone definitely waited out there with something metal. "Shit. We have company."

"Yeah, we do," Ian said and lifted his binocs as another SUV rumbled toward the house. "Zaryanko?"

"Looks like."

Seth swung his rifle around and used the scope to refocus on the area where he'd seen the flash. Movement. Slowly creeping forward. Two men. No, three. "We have three tangos on our six."

"Visual confirmation of Zaryanko," Ian said. "And he's got The Suitcase. You said three?"

"We gotta take them out. They're doing a sweep, looking for something. Probably us. We must have been spotted somehow."

"We can't take them out. We'll expose ourselves."

"If we don't, they'll expose us." Seth got on the radio. "Stonewall,

this is Ace. Be advised, we have three tangos coming up on our six.
We have to engage. Do you copy?"

"Copy," Gabe said after a pause, sounding none too happy
about it. "Fire at will."

Ian grinned. "Got something better. You were a football star,
right?" He held up a grenade. "Can you still throw?"

"Fuck yeah. Cover me." Seth pulled the pin and broke cover
to stand and lob the thing. It landed in the middle of the three
men and he dropped to the ground, losing sight of their mad
scramble to get away.

Bang!

"Got 'em," Ian said as chaos erupted down at the building.
"Now it's showtime."

Seth settled behind his rifle again. Zaryanko's men had
panicked at the sound of the grenade and started picking off
Askar's men. Zaryanko shouted at Askar until a bullet sent him
diving for cover, leaving The Suitcase out in the open.

After a quick, assessing glance at the firefight, Askar strode
over, plucked the metal case out of the sand, and booked it toward
one of the SUVs. One of Zaryanko's men plowed into him from
behind and tried to take the case. He righted himself and pulled
out a pistol. The other man backed off, hands raised, having lost
his weapon at some point in the confusion.

Askar shot the guy right between the eyes.

Jesus. It took a special kind of coldness to shoot an unarmed,
surrendering man point-blank like that.

As the body crumpled, Askar broke into a run.

"Have him?" Ian asked.

"Yeah."

"Then fucking send it!"

The first shot went high and Askar ducked behind the door of
the SUV, using it as a shield as he pulled himself into the driver's

seat. The vehicle's wheels spun, kicking up dust before finally gaining traction. He spun a 180 and hit the gas, headed straight toward Ian and Seth.

Ian cursed a blue streak. "He's found us. Do you have another shot?"

"No. He's staying low." Seth adjusted his aim for the driver's side wheel and squeezed the trigger. The tire popped and the SUV spun several times before crashing sideways against a sand dune. Askar scrambled out and over the dune, still gripping The Suitcase.

Seth had him. One hundred-fifty meters, a perfect head shot, one he could make with his eyes closed. Except he did have his eye to the scope and clearly saw Askar's face as a hot, dry wind whipped his scarf away.

And Seth froze, a chilling sense of familiarity keeping him from pulling the trigger.

"What are you doing?" Ian demanded.

Seth rubbed his eyes with one hand, sighted again, and took the shot, but he was too late. Askar had already claimed another vehicle and was bouncing through the desert at breakneck speed.

"Fuuuck." Standing, Ian watched the SUV until it was out of sight, then pounded a fist against his leg, sending up a small puff of dirt. "You had a fucking flashback, didn't you?"

"No." He couldn't explain what that had been, but it wasn't a flashback. "I just…hesitated. There was something familiar about him."

"Familiar or not, he's on his way to take that suitcase to Siddiqui. Fuck!" Ian said again and grabbed his radio. "Boomer to Stonewall. Be advised, we are not in possession of The Suitcase. I say again, we don't have the bomb."

• • •

Sometime during the long stretch of inactivity, Phoebe had fallen asleep in the comfy office chair. She hadn't thought sleep was possible — with each passing hour, her anxiety level climbed higher and higher. But eventually, exhaustion won out and her eyes closed of their own volition.

Bang!

She started awake, all but falling out of the chair, her arms and legs getting tangled in the blanket draped over her. She was alone in the war room, but had only a moment to wonder where Tucker had gone before a burst of gunshots rang out.

Seth.

Heart thundering in her throat, she scanned each helmet cam's feed, struggling to understand the jerky chaos unfolding in bits and pieces on the screens. Gabe and Quinn were taking fire, shouting military-ese at each other, both of them never looking more alive as when their lives were in imminent danger.

Oh God. Did Gabe's wife go through this stomach-churning apprehension every time he left for a mission? How did she stand it?

Jesse was taking shelter behind a vehicle, wrapping a bandage around someone's upper arm while Jean-Luc and Marcus provided cover fire. Seth? No, that was Harvard with the wounded arm, and as soon as Jesse was done bandaging him, he grabbed his gun. The four of them took off in a crouching run toward where Gabe and Quinn were pinned down.

She exhaled an explosive breath and finally spotted Seth on Ian's camera. He was lying belly-down in the dirt, stalled out with his finger on the trigger. He was in trouble and there was nothing she could do but watch, her nails digging half moons into her palms.

"C'mon, Seth," she whispered. "C'mon, baby. You can do this."

As if her words had reached his ears, he snapped out of whatever memory held him frozen and took the shot, but it was too late. The car he'd been aiming at was long gone.

Then Ian's voice came over the radio. They didn't have the bomb. They hadn't succeeded.

Which meant Siddiqui now had it.

Stomach churning, Phoebe turned away from the screens— and spotted the multiple copies of Zak Hendricks's original report scattered across the table. She grabbed one of the folders, tucked it into the waistband of her jeans under her shirt, and sprinted for the door.

The team had tried it their way and failed.

And if she didn't do something now, a lot of innocent people were going to die.

CHAPTER THIRTY-SEVEN

The debriefing sucked. The whole mission had sucked, and now they were back at square one. All because Seth had frozen up again.

If this didn't seal his fate in Gabe Bristow's eyes, nothing would.

He left the war room ahead of the rest of the team, needing a shower to wash away the stench of failure. Needing...

Phoebe.

Yes, Christ, did he ever need to see her.

As he waited for the elevator, Tucker Quentin emerged from the stairwell at the other end of the hall and approached like a tornado cell rolling in over the Iowa plains, dark and forecasting death. Seth made an effort to project fuck-off vibes. He didn't need another ass-chewing when he still hurt from the last one.

If Tuc noticed his vibes, he didn't care. He slapped a manila envelope against Seth's chest. "You need to see what your girlfriend's been up to."

Seth caught the envelope before it slid to the floor. "What?"

But Tuc had already stormed away, shoving into the war room

with enough force the door banged against the wall.

The elevator opened and Seth stepped inside, the sour taste of dread coating his tongue. He stared down at the envelope. He shouldn't look. Should just toss it out. Like old wounds, some things were better left unopened.

The car stopped at the living room, most likely where Tuc had been before he decided to use the stairs. Seth jabbed the button for his floor again, but a picture on the big-screen TV across the room caught his attention.

"...Afghan presidential candidate Jahangir Siddiqui has so far refused to comment on these allegations..."

What the fuck?

He nipped between the doors before they closed and crossed the room in several long strides to stand in front of the screen.

"Sources at the embassy," the reporter continued, a hint of excitement thrumming through the grave overtones in his voice, "say the evidence against Siddiqui is too strong to ignore and they expect that the current Afghan administration will have no choice but to respond. So far, no nuclear weapons have been found."

Phoebe.

Jesus Christ, what had she done?

Heat flashed through his body, but the anger didn't last as cold fear washed over it and his knees went to rubber bands. He sank to the coffee table and only remembered the envelope when it dropped from his numb fingers and landed with a soft *whap* at his feet.

He stared at it for a long time before finally moving to retrieve it. He opened the flap, upended it, and the article that spilled out threw him back in time to one of his darkest moments after his rescue.

Lies.

So many lies.

But lies twisted to make sense.

And Phoebe had written them.

* * *

Phoebe hesitated as she neared the room she'd shared with Seth. She'd done exactly what he'd told her not too—she'd taken Hendricks's information public and now Siddiqui's face was spreading across the major news outlets like a wildfire. Even though she'd told her source to keep her name out of it, she wasn't naive enough to think that meant she was safe. She had to leave Afghanistan. Probably should also go into hiding, at least until Siddiqui was caught.

But all that was in the future.

Right now, in this moment, she had to face Seth. And say good-bye.

The thought carried her feet the rest of the way to his door, each step closer filling her with an aching desperation to touch him one last time. She wished she had time to make love to him again, make one last sweet memory she could hold close when the ache of missing him got to be too much. Because she would miss him. Probably for the rest of her life.

Unless...

What if he felt the same way? Of course, he was going to be angry at her right now, but what if he wanted this thing between them to continue? It wouldn't be easy with her in hiding and his job sending him across the world, but maybe they could make it work. Even if it was just a physical relationship, she'd live with that. Better than not having him in her life at all.

Hope took root and blossomed in her heart.

His door was already ajar and she pushed it the rest of the way open. He sat on the end of the bed, still dressed in his combat gear, smeared with dust.

And he held Emma's picture. Once again, he'd turned to the ghost of a woman who didn't even love him anymore. A woman he claimed not to love.

Phoebe's steps faltered as a sob welled up in her throat. She viciously choked it back, but a dismayed squeak of sound still escaped.

His head snapped up.

"I'm sorry," she said, backing toward the door. "I can't."

"Can't what?"

"Keep pretending her picture doesn't bother me."

He gazed at the photo still clutched in his hand, guilt filling his face before he carefully blanked his expression. Didn't that just underline the stark fact that she'd never be as perfect as his idealized version of Emma? She'd never measure up to the pedestal he'd placed the woman on. And even as much as she cared about him, probably even loved him, she would not destroy herself by trying to live up to Emma's memory.

"You don't understand," he said.

"You're right, I don't." The words whipped out, barbed with anger she suddenly couldn't control. "I don't understand why you are so hung up on a woman who cheated on you, who was warming another man's bed when you were over here fighting through hell. A woman who left you almost as soon as you returned to the States and got engaged before you even left the hospital. What is so great about that woman? What makes her so perfect that you have to carry her photo around?"

What makes her so much better than me? She wanted to scream it, but didn't. Even so, the question clogged the air between them like a toxic smoke.

He didn't answer. Instead, he picked up a manila envelope and flung it at her. It slapped against her chest, but she didn't manage to catch it before it slid to the floor. Papers spilled out at her feet and every cell in her being turned to solid ice.

The headline. That damn headline.

How heroic is the "Hero" Sniper? Murder, corruption, and the cover-up of the decade.

"Want to explain that, Phoebe?" he demanded. "Or should I call you Kathryn Anderson? Imagine my surprise when Tuc handed me that envelope and I found out the woman I've been sleeping with not only lied to me about her name, but also publicly raked me over the coals."

Tears blurred her vision, coursed down her cheeks. "I didn't lie about my name. It's Kathryn Phoebe Leighton. Anderson was my married name." A ball of pain grew in the back of her throat and swallowing became an impossible task. "And I—I was going to tell you."

He scoffed. "Yeah? When? After you fucked me into submission?"

"No!" Sick to her stomach, she hugged herself and searched for the right words—something, anything to explain. But really, what was there to explain? She neglected to tell him something he'd deserved to know. "I'm sorry. Seth, I'm so sorry. I didn't want to hurt you. To hurt…us."

"I knew all along you were hiding something. Should have trusted my gut." He laughed, and it wasn't a pleasant sound. "There was a lot of shit said about me and my team and I was able to overlook most of it, but that article? That fucking article was the worst because it made sense. It was all bull, taking my men's deaths and twisting them into a political agenda, but it wasn't sensationalized. It was laid out like fact and people believed it. Omar Cordero's wife believed it and to this day, she won't speak to me. Because of you, I never got a chance to tell her that his last words, his last thoughts, were of her. And now you're at it again—taking Zak's reports to the media. Did you twist them, too? Make Zak look like the bad guy?"

Phoebe raised a shaking hand to her mouth, each new word hitting like a physical blow. "No, I wouldn't—I didn't say a word about Zak. I was just trying to stop Siddiqui."

"Yeah, well. He's not going to be president now, so there's that. But he still has the nuke and now he's gone to ground, so you only succeeded in stalling him. And pissing him off."

"You'll find him."

He made an ugly sound of derision. "It's not my job to find him."

Seconds ticked by and Seth didn't seem inclined to say more. He stood and crossed to the opposite side of the room, rolling his shoulders as if to shake her memory off. It was a completely dismissive gesture. No, not just dismissive, but a nonverbal *I never want to see you again.*

Phoebe didn't blame him for his anger, but after everything they'd shared, it couldn't end like this. All these vicious words couldn't be her last moments with him.

Trembling, she chanced a step forward. "Seth—"

"No." He whirled and pointed a finger at her face. His lips pulled back in an ugly sneer. "Do you want to know what makes Emma so much better than you? She *never* lied to me. Yeah, she started dating another man while I was gone, but she thought I was dead and Matt was there to help her through the loss. When I came home, she told me flat out she had fallen in love with him and wanted to marry him. And yeah, maybe I had trouble coping with the breakup, but that's on me, not her. She's not a liar, not a cheater, and even better, she never poisoned a whole population's views against a man who was too sick and injured to defend himself."

She winced, but took another step toward him.

"Stay the fuck away from me." He shouldered past her, but paused in the doorway to glance back. A shutter slammed closed over his expression. No more hurt. No more anger. His eyes turned glacial. "If I ever see *any* of your names on another article about me or my men, you'll sure as fuck hear from my lawyer."

Her knees gave out and despair dragged her to the floor. "Kathryn Anderson is dead."

"Good."

And so, she realized, was Phoebe Leighton. At least as far as he was concerned.

CHAPTER THIRTY-EIGHT

A light snow started falling as Phoebe climbed out of the car provided by Tucker Quentin, flanked on either side by Quinn and Harvard. None of the other HORNET guys had wanted to escort her back to the shelter. She couldn't blame them for that, but nor would she regret her decision to go public. She still believed it was their best option, not only because both the American and Afghan people deserved to know about a very real threat, but because it was also the fastest way to make sure Siddiqui's political career died.

And it had.

Under tremendous pressure from the UN and his own people, the Afghan president had finally renounced Siddiqui's seat on the National Assembly and his name had been removed from the presidential ballot. Whatever his plans, he was going to have a difficult time seeing them come to fruition now that the UN planned to launch an investigation into his actions.

So she didn't regret it. She only wished she'd had time to talk the guys over to her side before she went public.

She turned to the men and offered them a smile that probably looked as forced as it felt on her lips. "Thank you. I'll be okay from here."

Quinn shook his head. "I don't think so. We're going to see you inside and make sure the perimeter is secure."

"Besides," Harvard added, "I wouldn't mind seeing Zina again."

Quinn sent him a sideways glance that could only be described as smug. Or at least as smug as the poker-faced man got. "I thought that was over, ended all neat and tidy. Like a contract."

"Uh..." Harvard flushed bright red and scrambled ahead of them to open the gate.

"Yeah, that's what I thought," Quinn said.

"A contract?" Phoebe asked, but she was too tired and emotionally wrung out to be genuinely curious. She followed Quinn into the courtyard and waited while he did a visual sweep of the area.

The corner of his mouth kicked up in a tiny smile. "It's a long story."

"One he's not going to tell," Harvard added with a pointed look at his teammate as he shut and locked the gate. "Or else I'll turn him into an internet meme. With kittens. And unicorns."

Quinn actually shuddered. "No worries, H. You—fuck! Get down!" In a burst of motion, he grabbed Phoebe and all but threw her behind one of the shelter's ramshackle cars. She saw Harvard collapse where he'd been standing a second before she heard the actual shot that took him to the ground. Blood spread in a dark-red pool under him and he didn't move.

She scrambled to make sense of what just happened. One minute Harvard was standing there being adorably awkward and the next...

She pressed a hand to her mouth. "Oh, God."

"Stay here by the wheel," Quinn said. "Don't lift your head." Crouching low, he ran to Harvard's side and scooped him up in a fireman's carry, saving him from a second bullet that went into the ground where his head had been less than a second ago.

He laid Harvard behind the car and tossed her a cell phone. "Call for help." He leaned over Harvard, checked his pulse and airway, then pulled off his jacket and used it to stanch the blood flow. "Phoebe. Hey! Focus. We need help. Call Gabe. Seth. Someone."

She had been gripping the phone in both hands, frozen, staring at the blood. Help. Yes. They needed help. She ripped her gaze from Harvard's graying complexion and tried to dial. She shook so badly, it took two tries to hit the buttons, but finally, it was ringing.

A shadow fell over them and she looked up in time to see a man swing the butt of his weapon in an arc toward Quinn's head.

"Watch out!"

Her warning came too late. The rifle connected with a sickening crack and Quinn crumpled, unconscious, on top of Harvard's body.

Realizing she still held the phone, she screamed into it, not sure if anyone was even on the other line. "Seth! Help! We're being attacked! We're—"

The man grabbed the phone, threw it on the ground, and stepped on it. The crunch of plastic sounded like a bullet and she flinched, scrambling for the car's door handle. If she could get inside…

He caught her by the throat and shoved her against the car. The back of her head slammed into the door and her vision went white for a long five seconds. When it cleared, he was directly in front of her, so close she picked out hints of copper and green in his brown irises.

His chapped lips pulled back in a sneer, revealing teeth that hadn't seen a toothbrush in years. "Seth. Is. Dead."

Panic rocketed through her. Seth dead? How could he be dead?

No. No, he wasn't. Seth was at Tuc's safe house, angry but alive. "You're lying."

"Seth. Is. Dead." His fingers tightened around her windpipe— and she stopped struggling.

English.

He was speaking perfect English.

Perfect *American* English.

"Who are you?" She stared into those copper- and green-flecked brown eyes as tears started pouring into his wiry beard. He didn't seem to notice.

"Askar!"

They both jolted at the voice and all of the emotion in his gaze vanished in a blink. It was if he'd locked it all away inside his head, leaving nothing but an empty, breathing husk.

"I have the woman," he said in Pashto and hauled her upright.

"No! What are you doing? You're American! You. Are. American. Please, don't do this." He showed no indication he understood a word she said and shoved her toward the front door of the shelter, where Jahangir Siddiqui waited with a silver suitcase in hand.

CHAPTER THIRTY-NINE

"Seth! Help! We're being attacked! We're—"

The line went dead.

Seth's knees gave out from under him and he would have collapsed if two pairs of hands hadn't caught him.

"Seth!" Cordero's voice, so clear he swore the man was standing beside him again. *"We're under attack. Holy shit! There's hundreds of them."*

His men. They shouldn't have died. Shouldn't have even been on their way to the forward operating base in those mountains. He'd volunteered them for the mission when Jude Wilde's team was pulled out.

And they'd all died. All but him.

The hands on his arms lowered him into a seat and as his butt hit the leather, he came back to himself.

We're being attacked...

Not Cordero's voice this time. Phoebe's.

Phoebe.

Seth bolted out of the chair, knocking it backward into the war room's computer terminal.

"What the hell's wrong with you, Harlan?" Gabe said from his seat across the table, where he'd been trying to puzzle out a new plan of attack with Tucker.

"That was Phoebe." His mouth was so dry, he barely got the words out. "On Quinn's phone. She said they're under attack."

Gabe stood and leaned over the table. "Where are they?"

Chest tight, Seth gazed around the room, saw realization and dread dawn on each man's face. "Guys, I think Siddiqui's at the shelter. He's going after Phoebe."

For a beat, there was nothing. No reaction, no movement, no sound. Not even the whisper of an indrawn breath.

Gabe shoved away from the table. "Our guys need us. Let's move!"

• • •

Phoebe winced as Siddiqui tied a length of rope tightly around her wrists behind her back. He'd set up shop in the shelter's dining room and had both Zina and Tehani tied up, too.

God, how long had they been here like this, trapped, at this bastard's mercy?

After checking the knot on her binds one last time, Siddiqui straightened and his lips brushed her cheek, sending a shudder of pure revulsion through her. "You, Phoebe Leighton, have been nothing but a pain in my side since you arrived in my country."

God, she hated this disgusting man. She met his gaze with a challenge in her own. "I'm also the reason you're running scared right now."

"Do I look scared?" he scoffed.

"You should be. What did you do with Quinn and Harvard?"

"Phoebe," Zina said, a plea in her voice. "Please don't provoke him."

"Is that their names?" He laughed. "Don't worry. They're here, locked up with the whores from this so-called shelter. You'll all die together. I assume you know by now what that suitcase is behind you."

She would not look over her shoulder, refused to give him the satisfaction of her fear. "So your grand plan is to blow up the whole city of Kabul?"

The smile that slunk across his face was downright bone-chilling. "Once Askar returns with our helicopter, yes. This city—our government—is full of traitors and infidels, but if Kabul is decimated in a nuclear attack, who do you think will be blamed? America? Oh, I hope so. And then in the scramble to point fingers, the Taliban will come in, restore order, and take back the power the West stole from them."

Phoebe shook her head. "The only thing you're going to accomplish with this plan is killing a lot of innocent people. And how many of them were your supporters?"

He waved a hand. "Of course I regret Afghan lives will be lost, but this is war. I *will* detonate this bomb." He surged forward like a striking snake, gripped a handful of her hair, and yanked her head backward. "And guess who is going to be at ground zero?"

"Leave her alone!" Tehani shouted in Pashto and kicked out with her bound feet. Her legs were too short to reach him, but that didn't matter. In Siddiqui's eyes, the act of defiance was enough to warrant a punishment and he released Phoebe to backhand the girl. Her lip split open.

"And you, little whore," he said in Pashto, "were always more trouble than you were worth."

"I'd rather be a whore than be your wife." Tehani kicked out again and he caught her foot, squeezing her ankle until she cried out.

"That can be arranged." Siddiqui let go of the girl's leg and grabbed a roll of duct tape. "But first you're going to learn how to be silent."

"Oh my God," Zina sobbed as he started wrapping the tape around Tehani's head, muffling her screams.

Phoebe saw movement out of the corner of her eye and looked toward the foyer. Askar was just standing there, watching, and her breath caught in her lungs.

Oh God, this was it. He was back with the helicopter and he and Siddiqui would leave and—

Askar pressed his finger to his lips in the universal signal for silence, and she realized with a jolt he'd shaved off his beard.

American.

Askar was American.

She gave a slight nod to show she understood and he melted back into the shadows of the foyer without ever alerting Siddiqui to his presence.

Was he on their side now?

Her heart kicked into a gallop as Siddiqui blocked her view and pulled out a length of tape. Just before he pressed it over her mouth, she smiled at him. "You've already lost, Siddiqui. You just don't know it yet."

$$\cdots$$

Blurry, too-bright light stabbed into Quinn's retinas and he blinked against the assault. The headache was instantaneous, but whether that was from the blackout or his previous injury was anyone's guess. A bit of both, probably.

Good thing he had a damn hard head.

Soft dark-brown hair tickled his cheek and he squinted, trying to focus his bleary eyes. A woman was leaning over him, one with dark eyes and coffee-and-cream skin. She spoke, but he couldn't make out the words through the ringing in his ears. They sounded melodic, though. Like…Spanish?

"Mara?"

What was she doing here? She didn't belong here and yet he reached up and touched her face, unable to resist the temptation of having her skin under his fingers again.

Except, no, this wasn't right. Mara's skin was silk, not the coarse and scarred flesh under his fingertips now.

And Mara didn't belong here.

The woman jerked away from his touch and horror filled her features. Wait, not a woman. Girl, he realized as his battered brain came back online. One of the shelter girls. Her hair was uncovered and tangled. Her face—

Jesus Christ.

Quinn bolted upright. It was Saboora, the only girl at the shelter who refused to take off her burqa, even in the comfort of her own home. Now he got why. She was horribly disfigured, missing half her nose and her eyebrows. The pupil of one of her eyes was washed out and sightless. Old burn wounds, long healed over.

"Saboora," he whispered and his voice sounded like he'd inhaled an ash cloud. He coughed, then tried again. "Where's Phoebe? Harvard?" He couldn't think of the Pashto words he needed to communicate, but she seemed to understand just fine. She pointed across the room—one of the shelter's classrooms— and he stood, wobbling a little on his feet as he picked his way over to where Harvard lay. Two of the older girls sat on their knees beside him, working to stanch the blood flow. His skin held the same color and consistency of candle wax.

Quinn's heart took a nosedive into his stomach. "Is he breathing?"

One of the girls glanced up. Quinn couldn't remember her

name, but he recalled Zina saying something about her being one of the shelter's success stories, having just been accepted into nursing school.

"Yes," she said in English. "Needs hospital."

Quinn staggered and dropped to his knees next to Harvard. The kid's blood soaked into his pant legs and he cursed himself for blacking out when he was most needed. "Harvard, you hang on, kid."

To his surprise, Harvard's eyes opened a crack. "Gabe was right about me. Too...green."

"No, not at all. You're a born fighter and I'd want you at my six any day. Hey, Eric, you hear me? Any day. So you keep right on fighting and we'll get you help."

Quinn got to work putting his limited battlefield medical knowledge to use and checked the wound, a through-and-through that had gone in high on the left side and exited Harvard's back near his shoulder blade. Thankfully, the hole wasn't too ragged on either side and his bleeding had slowed considerably, but Christ only knew what the internal damage looked like. Lots of important shit in there the bullet could have ripped up.

Across the room, the doorknob rattled.

Quinn automatically reached for his weapon. Gone. Of course.

And he was in a fucking classroom.

Keeping his eyes on the door, he backed toward the teacher's desk and checked the drawers. The deadliest thing in there was a paper clip. He'd have to go hand-to-hand with whoever came in.

He pressed a finger to his lips, telling the girls to keep quiet, and soundlessly crossed to the door. It opened to the left, so he stacked up along the wall to the right and waited.

The door inched open—and then whoever unlocked it walked away.

What the fuck?

Sweat pouring down his spine, Quinn gave it a good five minutes before he moved, very carefully nudging the door farther back. He visually cleared the hall to the left, which led to a back door that let out in the courtyard. It was their best shot at an escape.

Opening the door a bit more, he glanced to the right and tensed at the shadow waiting at the far end of the hall.

Askar.

Quinn didn't know if he'd be able to take the coldhearted bastard in hand-to-hand. Maybe at one time, but he'd been too battered over the years and didn't have the reflexes he used to. But what other choice did he have? If he succeeded, he'd free the girls and they could take Harvard with them while he searched for Phoebe. If he didn't…

Well. He'd had a good run.

He stepped out into the hall, hands raised. For an endless minute, Askar didn't move. Didn't draw his gun. Just stood there, staring. He'd recently shaved off his bushy beard and, except for spots of razor burn, the lower half of his face was as white as an Irishman's ass in the middle of winter.

This was the weirdest standoff Quinn had ever been in. He got the sense the guy's head was more fucked than his.

He dropped his hands. Still, Askar stayed put.

All right. Keeping his gaze trained on Askar, he waved the girls out of the classroom and pointed them toward the courtyard door. The last to emerge were Saboora and Nurse Girl, who were dragging Harvard behind them on Saboora's burqa.

Smart girls.

Askar cocked his head slightly like a confused dog, but still didn't make any moves to stop them.

Quinn took a step backward. And then another. And another. Just as he was about to bolt through the door to freedom, Askar seemed to come to a decision. He raised his rifle in a *see this?* kind of gesture. Very slowly, he knelt and placed the weapon on the floor, then straightened and kicked it down the hall.

Quinn stopped it with his foot, disbelief roaring through him as Askar walked away. No fucking way that just happened.

Grabbing the rifle, Quinn checked to see if it was loaded and functional. It was and he didn't bother mulling over Askar's motives for helping them. He'd just give himself a worse headache.

Turning, he shoved through the courtyard door—and came up against the barrel of an M-4. The man on the other end, dressed in combat gear, was favoring one of his legs.

Gabe.

"Friendly," Quinn said and lowered his weapon.

"Friendly," Gabe echoed for the rest of the entry team's benefit. Then he added, "Fuck you, Q. How many times are you going to try to get killed this year?"

"At least two more. And you're one to talk, asshole."

"Fuck you," Gabe repeated, but there was a smile in his voice. "Tuc's men have Harvard and the girls secured. You good to go or do you need the medic?"

Christ, he wanted in on the raid, but his head still pounded in beat with his heart and his stomach churned. He didn't remember what happened in the moments after Harvard was shot, could only assume he'd blacked out again. And because of that, he'd put Phoebe in danger.

He held out his weapon. "I'm out."

Gabe hesitated. Although his face was mostly covered, Quinn knew his expression was broadcasting a whole lot of *what the fuck?*

"Got a concussion," he added, which might be true. "Vision's shit."

Finally, Gabe accepted the weapon, looped the strap over his head, and ordered the men inside with a hand motion. He gripped Quinn's shoulder and squeezed. "Go get your head looked at."

"Roger that," Quinn said although there was no point.

He already knew exactly how fucked his brain was, and no medic was going to fix it.

CHAPTER FORTY

After Gabe, Ian, and Jean-Luc fast-roped to the courtyard, the helo dropped Seth, Marcus, and Jesse on the roof.

Both teams waited for the helo to get out of range before moving, and the seconds it took drove Seth half crazy with impatience. He needed to calm down, so he used the time to soften his breathing, relax his shoulders, and lower his heart rate.

In a sniper's world, all impatience got you was dead.

Finally, Gabe's voice whispered, "Go," in his earpiece.

As the three of them headed silently for the shelter's roof access, adrenaline coursed through his blood, burning away the icy detachment he'd been functioning with since realizing Phoebe was in danger. He experienced a moment of worry—without the ice, would his demons get the better of him? Would he hear his men's voices screaming at him again?

But, no.

There was no paranoia. No more flashbacks. Only the knowledge that he had a job to do.

They weren't challenged at any point during their descent from the roof, thank fuck. Stairs could be a deadly place when you couldn't see who was waiting around the next landing. They emerged in the dark second-floor hallway, clearing each of the bedrooms as they went. Phoebe's room smelled like her and a lump rose in his throat.

She had to be okay. He wouldn't accept any other outcome.

As he left her room, Jesse caught the front of his vest. "You good for this, Harlan?"

Irritation blasted away the sharper edge of his fear. "Wouldn't be here if I wasn't, Sawbones."

Jesse's expression remained unconvinced. Seth shook off the medic's grip and moved toward the stairs. Hadn't he proved himself when they were attacked in the mountains? Or at the compound? What would it take for these guys to trust him?

Nothing he needed to worry about now. Right now, his objective was to find Phoebe.

Soft sounds floated up from the lower floor and Seth motioned Jesse and Marcus back with a wave as Jahangir Siddiqui crossed the foyer below, headed toward the dining room. He carried a small cell phone–shaped object.

Fuck.

Crouching by the wall at the top of the stairs, Seth beckoned Jesse and Marcus closer. "Siddiqui's here and I'm ninety-nine percent sure he has the bomb. He's carrying a dead man's switch. We can't shoot him."

"Gabe needs to know," Marcus said.

"Yeah, but do we risk using the radio if he's got it rigged to detonate by remote?"

The three of them stared at one another for a beat and came to the same conclusion. No choice. Except none of them wanted to do it.

"Rock, paper, scissors?" Marcus suggested and promptly lost. Twice. Wincing, he hit the talk button on the radio strapped to his vest.

Nothing happened.

"City's still here," Jesse said, exhaling hard.

"For now," Seth added. Listening with half an ear as Marcus reported to Gabe, he peeked around the wall and saw Siddiqui cross the foyer again. He moved like an agitated bird in a cage, impatient but unable to leave. Was he waiting for something?

Seth wasn't prepared to stick around and find out.

When Siddiqui disappeared into the dining room again, Seth made his move, taking the stairs as quickly and silently as possible. Marcus and Jesse stayed right on his six and they stacked up along the shared wall between the dining room and foyer. Seth grabbed a handheld mirror from his vest pocket and took stock of the situation.

Jesus.

Siddiqui had shoved the table and chairs out of the way, creating an open space in the middle of the room, where Phoebe, Zina, and Tehani sat huddled together, their wrists and ankles bound with rope, mouths gagged with several layers of duct tape that wrapped around their heads. The bomb was on the floor in the middle of them.

Tehani stared at Siddiqui's back with narrow-eyed hatred. The older women were holding it together well enough, although Phoebe had been crying recently. Her eyes were puffy and red, and her tears had left clean trails on her dirty cheeks.

Hang on, sweetheart.

As if hearing his thoughts, she lifted her head and stared in his direction. He let the mirror catch the light once. A risk, yeah, but he wanted her to know he was here.

Siddiqui noticed her wide eyes and whirled around. "What is it?" From his position on just the other side of the wall, there was no way he'd see anything, but Seth didn't dare take another risk.

He silently tucked the mirror away and motioned to Jesse and Marcus, telling them he had eyes on the girls and the bomb.

Siddiqui started toward the foyer, but paused when the front door swung open. "Ah, there you are. It's about time."

Fuck. Seth shared a glance with his team. Anyone coming through that door was going to spot them lined up on the wall and he motioned for them to be ready.

All hell was about to break loose.

• • •

Askar smiled when he stepped through the door and saw the three mercenaries already in position to take Siddiqui down.

Had to give them credit. They were good. He'd suspected as much when they raided the compound, but now he knew for sure.

Of course, he had all but laid out a welcome mat for them.

His gaze landed briefly on the first merc in the line and his chest tightened with a shockingly painful jolt of…something. He hadn't let himself feel emotions in so long, he couldn't even come up with a name for the experience now.

The merc lowered his weapon slightly.

Askar blinked in acknowledgment and didn't point them out as he strode past Siddiqui. Sick fuck held the three women captive around the open suitcase like Girl Scouts around a campfire.

Captive.

Suddenly that word had a whole new meaning, one he'd only recently realized still applied to him. Drawing a knife, he crouched and started cutting away the women's bonds.

The look of blank confusion on Siddiqui's face was priceless. He fumbled a gun out from under his tunic. "Stop!"

Once the women were free, Askar handed the redhead his knife. "Run."

She didn't have to be told twice. She grabbed the girl by the hand and bolted with the other woman right behind her. Siddiqui tried to catch them, but look at that. Between the gun and the dead man's switch, he didn't have any free hands.

"This isn't the plan!" Sputtering with outrage, Siddiqui swung the pistol in his direction. "You follow orders, Askar. What the fuck is this?"

"My revenge."

Siddiqui finally looked at his face—really looked—and his eyes bulged. The gun wobbled. "Askar. What happened to your beard?"

"I'm not your soldier," he answered in English that felt rusty on his tongue. "I haven't always remembered that." Still crouching, he grabbed the roll of duct tape Siddiqui had used for the women's gags and pulled out a strip. The sound it made was that of a life being torn apart. "But now that I do, I have something American to say. Fuck you."

He lunged.

The gun bucked and pain blazed through Askar's chest, but he grabbed the detonator and wrapped the tape around Siddiqui's hand.

The mercs burst into the room, weapons aimed. More than three of them now, but only one of them mattered. Askar searched for and locked eyes with Seth.

He remembered Seth Harlan now.

His strength began to leak out of his arms. He wasn't going to be able to hold Siddiqui much longer and he swung around, providing Seth with an easy target. "For fuck's sake, Lieutenant. Shoot him!"

. . .

Seth took the shot. The bullet tore through Siddiqui's heart, ending his life before he hit the floor.

Ian ran toward the detonator, but there was no need. The tape held. He crossed to the bomb and knelt down. Studied it for a moment, then released a slow breath and removed the trigger, a golf ball–size piece of metal. "Disarmed."

"Thank you," Askar said and collapsed, blood erupting from his mouth. He wheezed, his lips turning blue as he gazed up at Seth. "I really thought I was one of them. Then I saw you at the compound and started remembering…what happened to us."

Seth stared into the man's bare face. Studied every line, every scar. Leaner, older, leathered by too much time in harsh climates…but he knew that face and his knees gave out at the realization.

He sank to the floor. "Bowie?"

Blood stained Aaron Bowman's teeth when he smiled. "Yo mama so fat…"

Jesus Christ. It was him.

Seth choked on a sob and clasped the guy's outstretched hand. "Yeah, how fat is she, Bowie?"

"She so fat…she fell in love and broke it."

"Aw, man. Not your best one."

"I know. All…I…got." His eyes went out of focus and he started making an ominous rattling sound deep in his chest.

Seth sent a panicked look over his shoulder at Jesse. "Can't you do something?"

Jesse stepped forward and took off his helmet. He didn't have to say a word. His answer was written on his face.

"For fuck's sake, at least give him something for the pain."

Nodding, Jesse knelt down and administered a morphine injection with the steady hands of a tested battlefield medic. Then he stood again and backed away. "We'll be outside."

"Lieutenant?" Bowie whispered.

"I'm here." Seth tightened his grip as the hand in his went slack.

"I'm sorry."

"Nah. Don't do that."

"They broke me. The things I did…" His voice trailed away and his eyes took on the glazed, far-off look of a man already staring into the spirit world.

Seth's vision blurred. "Hey, Bowman, it doesn't matter. Aaron, can you hear me? I don't care what you've done, okay? I don't. No matter what, I'm here for you, buddy. I've got your six, okay? Semper fi."

His features smoothed out and he smiled again. "Oorah, Lieutenant."

A moment later, he drew in one last gasping breath. The rattling stopped and his chest stilled.

Seth let go of his hand and sat back, numb to his core. Hollowed out. He didn't think he could survive the grieving process a second time and waited for the anguish, the wrenching pain as if someone was ripping his heart from his chest.

Except it never came.

This man had Bowie's face and voice, but he was still more Askar than Aaron. Seth had already said his good-byes to the real Aaron Bowman, who was always quick with a joke and a smile, who had gone out of his way to keep from hurting anyone. Seth refused to remember him as this broken husk of a human.

Broken.

Yeah. This is what broken looked like. Evil so dark, it twisted a good man into someone unrecognizable.

And Seth realized that had never been him. He was damaged, maybe, but never broken. And he was healing.

Because of Phoebe.

And HORNET. His team. His friends.

He walked out of the dining room, leaving his past lying there on the floor with the man who had been one of his best friends. As the brisk night air stung his wet cheeks, relief filled his chest and for the first time in three years, his lungs opened and he could actually breathe.

Phoebe darted across the courtyard, her hair a streak of fire in the darkness. She slammed into him with enough force to shock all of that newfound air from his lungs. Her fingers clenched his shirt at his back and she buried her face against his vest as trembles racked her body.

Quinn broke away from the team and followed her at a slower pace, stopping several feet away. "I couldn't keep her back without hurting her. And figured you'd kill me if I did."

Seth rested his cheek on the top of her head. "Smart man."

A fleeting smile touched Quinn's mouth before his gaze shifted toward the shelter. "We're going to make sure Bowman's body gets back to the States. No matter what he's done, he's a POW. He's one of ours and he's going home."

Seth nodded, for a moment unable to articulate past the lump in his throat. "His mother will be glad to finally have him back. But she doesn't need to know all the details."

"No, she doesn't," Quinn agreed. "You holding up?"

"Yeah. I'm good." And, he realized with a mild jolt, he was telling the truth. "Hey, Quinn? Thank you."

His eyes narrowed in question. "For what?"

"Rescuing me from those mountains." Against his chest, Phoebe released a shuddering sob and he stroked a hand over her hair.

Quinn's lips flattened, his Adam's apple bobbed. His voice, when he spoke, held a note of strain. "I told you once before I'm not looking for thanks."

"But I'm giving it. You pulled me out of there, then gave me a second chance when nobody else would. I can't express my gratitude enough."

With a stiff nod, Quinn retreated. It was such a classic Quinn response, Seth chuckled and shook his head. Someday, that guy would have to face his emotions or he was going to end up like Askar—cold and unfeeling to the core.

And that was a disturbing thought.

Seth pushed it away, focusing instead on the woman in his arms. "Phoebe, are you okay?"

She drew back enough to gaze up at him. Tears spiked her lashes. "Yes. Scared shitless," she admitted with a half laugh, "but okay. What about you? I was so afraid this would bring back memories and—"

"It did," he said. "I remember more now than I ever have and I'm sure it's going to haunt me when I try to sleep, but I'll get through it."

As if suddenly remembering things were still troubled between them, she dropped her arms from his waist and stepped back. "You don't have to get through it alone."

"I know I don't. I have the team."

She flinched as if he had slapped her. "So that's it? I ruined us for good, haven't I?"

Seth reached to brush away her tears, but caught himself before touching her with his bloody hand. "Not for good," he said, wishing like hell he could just forgive and forget. But the wound was still too raw and that coupled with Bowie…

It was too much.

"Give me some time, okay?"

"Okay," she said and hugged herself.

"Okay," he echoed stupidly because he couldn't think of anything else. They stared at each other for several heartbeats.

Finally, she drew a breath, let it out, and stood on her toes to kiss his cheek. "Good-bye, Seth."

Shit, he thought as she walked away. That good-bye had sounded really fucking final.

CHAPTER FORTY-ONE

It was nearly noon by the time Seth returned to his room from the debriefing, and paper crinkled under his boot when he stepped over the threshold. He lifted his foot and glanced down.

Fucking manila envelopes.

His immediate gut response was to toss it in the trash. Nothing good ever came in a manila envelope. Then he spotted his name written in feminine handwriting on the front.

Phoebe's handwriting.

He'd only seen her write something once or twice before, but he already knew the bubbly lettering as well as his own nearly illegible scrawl.

He dropped his gear right there in the doorway. Even though Phoebe had slid the envelope under his door, he should still probably ignore it. He needed a shower and maybe he'd even give sleeping a shot—though that didn't sound nearly as appealing as it had when Phoebe was lying next to him.

Goddammit.

Call him a masochist, but he had to know what she'd left. He scooped it up and ripped the thing open without finesse, dumping the contents into his palm.

Photos.

No, not just any photos. The nude pictures she'd taken the last time they'd slept together.

Hands suddenly shaking, he slid down the door until his ass hit the carpet. His scars were front and center in the shots, but instead of the ugliness that greeted him every time he looked in the bathroom mirror, there was a stark kind of beauty and a grim strength reflected in the black and white photos. Love, too. Not only in his eyes as he indulged her, but in every carefully composed frame.

Jesus.

What was he doing? All that shit about needing time? That was him being an asshole, and why she didn't call him out on it, he'd never know.

He leaped to his feet, flung open the door, and found her standing on the other side, fist raised to knock.

"Oh my God!" She pressed a hand to her chest and stared up at him like he was a madman. Which he was. Then, regaining her composure, she backed up a step. "I know you said you needed time and I understand that. I'm leaving Afghanistan tonight, but I couldn't go without apologizing for—"

He held up the photos. "Is this how you see me? No, look at me." He gripped her chin, made her meet his gaze when she tried to glance away. "You said once you wished I could see myself through your eyes. Is this how you see me?"

She swallowed hard. Shook her head. "No. That's not how I see you. It's how you are."

"Are you in love with me?" he asked, point-blank, although he already knew the answer. He saw it in the photos, but he wanted to hear her say it.

Tears filled her eyes, spilled over. "Yes. Very much."

"Good." Seth pulled her into his body and claimed her mouth with his, instantly remembering the shape, the taste, the way her lips moved against his.

How could he think he'd be okay for even a moment without this? Without her?

She gasped when he finally came up for air and he hooked a finger under her chin again, stared down into her dazed eyes. "I love you, too, Phoebe. Which is why…" He left her standing in the doorway and found the article where he'd left it on the bed. He held it up for her to see and ripped the papers in half. "I'm done living in the past."

Again her eyes filled with tears. "But I hurt you."

"You didn't know me then. You were only doing the job you were told to do. Same as I was when I took my men up into the mountains. You told me I couldn't keep holding myself responsible for what happened to them and you were right. So now I'm saying the same to you. Let it go. Kathryn Anderson is dead. Let's keep her that way."

Crossing back to stand in front of her, he cupped her cheeks in his palms and thumbed away her tears. "Will you stay with me? Please. Last night opened up a fuck-ton of bad memories and I don't want to be alone. I don't need time. I need *you*."

• • •

How could she say no to that?

Without a word, she let him pull her into the room. Once inside, he released her hand to shut and lock the door. She should probably say something, but her mind was blank with shock. She hadn't expected this.

At. All.

He claimed to love her, and maybe he did, but she just couldn't see how he'd ever forgive her for the horrible things she had written about him when she couldn't even forgive herself. If she asked him questions now, would he wonder if she was digging for a story? Would he ever be able to trust her with his secrets? How could they build any kind of relationship with so much baggage between them?

Seth exhaled a half laugh and walked toward her. His big hands curled around her shoulders and rubbed. "You're thinking awfully hard."

"I just—this isn't going to work."

"Why not?"

"You'll never trust me again and I don't blame you for that, but—"

His hands paused. "Who says I ever stopped trusting you?"

Shock reverberated through her. "You didn't?"

"No, sweetheart. I didn't." He lowered his head, pressing his forehead against hers. "Here's the part you call me out for being an asshole."

"You had every right."

"No. All I had was a shitload of hurt pride. The mission went sideways and I was wallowing in all my failures, then you went and put yourself right in the crosshairs. I was not in a good headspace."

She swallowed. "What I said about Emma…it was wrong. I know she's important to you and she always will be."

"She helped me through the worst years of my life." Seth released a long breath and trailed his hands from her shoulders down her back. "My captors took fifteen months from me, robbed me of my friends, my dignity, my sanity. Emma's photo was the only thing they never took away and for a long time, I couldn't get rid of it."

"It's okay. You don't have to."

He shook his head. "Doesn't matter anymore." He reached

into his vest pocket and brought out a photo too small to be Emma's. He held it up between two fingers.

Her professional head shot, torn from a newspaper.

She sucked in a breath. "Me?"

"I've been carrying it since our fight yesterday," he admitted, his voice little more than a thick whisper. "I realized I was clinging to the past and it wasn't helping me heal. If I wanted a future, I needed to change and so the first thing I did was toss Emma's photo and replace it with one of the woman I love."

Oh, God. The sweet, sweet man.

She went into his arms, intending to hug him, but as soon as her body came into contact with his, she wanted more. So much more. She lifted her head to tell him how much she wanted him, but he was already a step ahead of her, his mouth coming down on hers in a branding kiss so hot she was surprised her panties didn't catch fire.

"I want you naked, sweetheart." His lips traced the line of her jaw to her ear and she shivered.

"Yes." Oh, yes, she wanted to be naked, wanted to be skin-to-skin with him. She broke away from him long enough to pull off her coat and shirt and tug at his vest. He chuckled softly and bent at the waist so she could strip him of it and his shirt.

"What's your hurry?" His fingers skimmed her bare shoulder, sending goose bumps racing over her skin. "We have all day."

"Just means we can go fast this time and slow the next."

"How many times do you think we're going to have sex?"

She pretended to think about it as she unbuttoned and unzipped his jeans, freeing his erection. "Well, like you said, we have all day."

"I'm not a machine. And I only have so many condoms." His soft laugh faded into a groan as she took him in hand and stroked him, massaging his sensitive underside with the tips of her fingers.

His hand weaved into her hair and gripped her head as his hips rocked into each stroke.

"Jesus," he gasped. "You can't keep doing that. It'll be over before it's started."

"Can't have that." She gave him one last lingering stroke before releasing him and shoving him down on the bed. "I want to be on top."

"Yes, ma'am." His gaze was fire on ice as he watched her strip off the rest of her clothes.

"Condoms?" she asked, swinging her bra around on her finger.

He moistened his lips and pointed to his bag on the floor. She found a string in the front pocket and grinned at him over her shoulder, knowing good and well he was getting an eyeful of her backside. "Well, it's a start."

He groaned. "You're going to be the death of me."

She tore one package open. "Lie back." Straddling him, she used one hand to steady his penis and rolled the condom on.

"Phoebe," he groaned.

"Had enough foreplay?" She lifted herself over him and sank down his length, inch by viciously slow inch until he was buried to the root inside her and they both shuddered.

"Lemme see you move, sweetheart," he whispered, skimming his hands along her waist to grip her hips.

She lifted herself up, sank down again, and rode him at a pace meant to drive him insane. And it was working. His jaw clenched and his fingers dug into her hips. He tried to hold her still and surge into her from underneath, but that so wasn't going to happen. Not this time. She laced her fingers through his and peeled his hands from her hips, pinning him to the bed. She leaned over, tracing her open mouth across his chest as the angle of his penetration changed so that each thrust brought his pelvis into contact with her swollen clit. Her entire body instantly warmed and tingled and she quickened her pace, her breath sawing out of her lungs, matching his.

She screamed with her orgasm, the force of it taking her by surprise and draining her of every last drop of energy. She collapsed onto his chest, heard a growl rumble under her ear and then she was on her back, Seth rising over her with her legs looped over his shoulders. Already sated, she watched through blurry eyes as he took his pleasure from her body.

Was there ever anything more beautiful?

The cords of muscle in his neck and shoulders stood out, his jaw clenched as he surged closer to his own peak. After one last thrust, he groaned with his release and his muscles relaxed, the tension slipping away. He dropped her legs and buried his face in the crook of her neck and she held him as he shuddered through the orgasm.

No, she decided and sleepily stroked her hands down his scarred back. There was nothing more beautiful than this man.

Absolutely nothing.

EPILOGUE

A buzzing sound startled Phoebe awake. She hadn't remembered drifting off, but she must have because Seth lay next to her, sound asleep, his arm a warm, heavy weight over her breasts, his leg wrapped intimately around both of hers.

God, she didn't want to move. Ever. Between their jobs and the long-distance relationship, it had been too long since they had been able to lie together like this.

Buzz buzz buzz.

Oh. Right. A phone was ringing in vibrate mode. She craned her neck to look at the nightstand, saw it was Seth's, and nudged him in the ribs until he finally stirred.

"What?" he mumbled, sleep roughening his voice more than usual. "I was having a good dream."

She smiled and kissed his cheek, knowing how rare good dreams were for him. "I'm sorry, but your phone's ringing."

He lifted his head and squinted at the clock on the nightstand.

"Is it after midnight?"

"No, not yet. Why?"

He shoved himself to his hands and knees, lingering a moment to trail kisses down her nose and chin before he reached across her for the cell. "Just something my dad always says. Nothing good comes from a phone call after midnight." He checked the screen. "It's Gabe."

With a sigh, he settled against the headboard and wrapped an arm around her when she snuggled in beside him. He scowled at the screen for a few more rings.

"Better answer."

"Yeah." He hit the phone icon and lifted it to his ear. "Hey, Gabe, what's up?"

Phoebe couldn't hear Gabe's end of the conversation, but whatever he was saying tightened Seth's jaw. His muscles went rigid under her hand.

"Yeah. I'll be there." He hung up and cursed, disengaging himself from her arm and swinging his legs out of bed.

"What's going on?"

"Gabe says the team has another mission."

Phoebe smothered a spike of annoyance. So much for having a whole week off to spend together. She'd been looking forward to sharing New Year's with him, even if it was in a hotel room in Washington, DC.

But she had to be understanding. He hadn't made a fuss when she went to Papua New Guinea last week to research the rampant women's rights abuses there. It was just…she was really starting to miss him. "Where are you going this time?"

"He didn't say." Finding his pants on the floor, he yanked them on, but left them unzipped. He leaned over to kiss her. "We're meeting at Wilde Security's office for the briefing."

Her immediate response was to insist he take her along, but

that was the journalist in her afraid to miss a big story. The woman, the lover, feared for him and she caught his face in her hands before he backed away. "Be careful and please call me when you can."

His brow wrinkled. "Gabe said he wants you there, too."

"Me?" Instantly alarmed, she threw off the covers and hunted for her clothes. "Why? Is Zina okay? Tehani? Zak?"

"Shit, I'm sorry. I didn't think to ask." Frowning, Seth grabbed his gun and jacket, but hesitated before putting them on and set them back on the bed. He pulled her into his arms, stroked a hand down her back. "I'm sure everything's okay. Gabe didn't sound alarmed."

"Oh, God, I hope so."

• • •

The Wilde Security office was located in a strip mall that had been closed for years. It wasn't exactly a pretty place, especially now that the far end of the building showed some fire damage from an incident that happened while they were in Afghanistan. Due to that same incident, the parking lot now had enough new lamps to light up a construction site—but where were the rest of the team's vehicles? Seth doubted he was the first to arrive. Everyone had been in DC to welcome Zak home, so nobody had to fly in from the far-flung reaches of the country.

Seth slid from his rental car and glanced around, unease creeping over his skin. His paranoia was clanging up a storm, telling him he was about to be attacked, which made no fucking sense.

Still, he nudged Phoebe behind him as he tried Wilde Security's front door. Unlocked.

He took a cautious step forward...

And realized what was happening a second before gallons of cold water splashed over his and Phoebe's heads. Phoebe squawked. Laughter sounded from the darkness and he swore, groping for the light switch.

The entire team—Gabe, Quinn, Jesse, Marcus, Ian, Jean-Luc, and Harvard, who was well on his way to making a full recovery from his wounds—stood around the room, laughing and congratulating each other on a prank well pulled. And they weren't the only ones enjoying themselves. Audrey Bristow was here. Jude Wilde and his wife, Libby, had also joined in the fun— hell, knowing Jude, he'd probably given the guys this idea in the first place. Greer Wilde stood in the back of the room next to Zak Hendricks, who was wheelchair-bound after losing his leg. Zak still looked pretty rough around the edges and he had a long road of recovery ahead of him, but he'd shaved and had gotten a haircut and he was smiling right along with the rest of the asshats.

Seth glared at them all. "Did you really just call me out of bed in the middle of the night to dump cold water on me?"

"It's New Year's," Jean-Luc declared and blew into one of those annoying horns before taking a drink from his champagne glass. "Who sleeps on New Year's?"

"Who says we were sleeping?" Which, yes, technically, they had been, but only because they were gearing up for a round three.

"Well, *mon ami*, I am sorry for that. But, c'mon, we had to initiate you and this was better than some of the other suggestions."

"Still say we shoulda made him wear a toga and dance to 'Sexy and I Know It,'" Marcus said, slurring his words a little. He did a hip-thrust dance move that caused another uproar of laughter.

Phoebe smothered a giggle behind her hand. "Oh my God. They're all wasted."

Gabe stepped forward. "No, I'm not drunk." At Audrey Bristow's disbelieving snort, he added, "Well, getting there now, but when we came up with this plan, I was sober."

Seth scowled at him. "I thought you said no hazing."

"It wasn't appropriate at the time. Now it is." He stuck out a hand. "You're officially off probation. Welcome to the team, Ace."

Holy. Shit.

As Seth accepted the handshake, Jesse let out a whoop fit for a rodeo-riding cowboy. Harvard gave him two thumbs up. Marcus and Jean-Luc slapped a high five. Ian, leaning against the wall with Tank faithfully at his side, smirked and gave a sardonic golf clap. Jesus. The fucker couldn't do anything light on the sarcasm. Once you got past the sneer, he had a sense of humor like a knife. Seth laughed and flipped him off, which made Ian grin.

"All right, enough of the mushy stuff," Jean-Luc said. "He's official, we all love him, and blah blah. Now let's give the man and his lovely lady some dry clothes and ring in this New Year right. Gotta feeling it's gonna be a good one."

An hour later, someone turned on the TV to watch the ball drop and everyone gravitated in that direction. Seth hung back, watching with a smile until Phoebe sneaked up behind him and wrapped her arms around his waist.

"I've never seen you laugh so much. Does this make you happy?"

He looked around the room at the guys, all of them grinning, some of them so drunk they couldn't stand straight. They put the fun in dysfunctional—and he wouldn't have it any other way.

"Yeah, it does. But…" He turned in the circle of her arms and pulled her flush against his body. Her fingers slipped under his borrowed shirt and played over the small of his back, sending a delicious shiver up his spine.

Up until meeting her, the only reason for his continued existence was to make damn sure his captors didn't win. It had been his way of flipping them a big fat "fuck you very much." But now he wanted more than existence. He wanted laughter. Friendship. Love.

Finally, he wanted life.

More than that, he wanted a life with Phoebe.

"But what?" she asked, smiling up at him.

He lowered his lips to hers, stopping just short of a kiss. "I love you, Phoebe. I want to make this work between us, whatever it takes. If that means I have to leave HORNET—"

"No." She slapped her hands to his chest and pushed. "Don't you dare. You need them and they need you. I would never ask you to give up another team."

"But where does that leave us? This long-distance thing we've been doing…it doesn't work for me. It's not what I want with you."

Her teeth sank into her lower lip. "So what do you want?"

"More than a week here, a week there. I sleep better at night when you're next to me. I eat better—"

"Only because I nag you."

"Yes, and I love it. I want you to nag me for the next fifty years at least."

She poked a finger teasingly at his stomach. "You know you're probably going to regret saying that sooner rather than later."

"No. Never." He caught her hand and lifted her palm to his lips. "Phoebe, you make me a better person. You make me whole."

She lifted a shoulder, trying for casual, but the telltale glimmer of happy tears gave her away. "Well, I guess I'm not tied to Boston. That's the beauty of my job—I can write and take photos anywhere in the world."

He grinned. "Key West is a beautiful place to write. Even Ernest Hemingway thought so. He used to live there, you know."

"Yes, I've heard that." She grinned back. "I'll still have to travel some."

"So will I."

"But we'll make it work," she said without a shred of doubt. "As long as you always come home to me."

Seth caught her chin between his fingers and turned her face up toward his. Her lips tasted of cool, crisp champagne and he took the kiss deeper, hugged her closer, let himself relax into her embrace.

Home.

After three long years, he was finally home.

Keep reading for three exclusive scenes from
HONOR RECLAIMED!

BONUS MATERIAL

PUTTING GABE IN HIS PLACE

The team wasn't happy to see him. Nobody said so out loud, but the good-natured ribbing and off-color jokes stopped whenever Seth entered the hotel conference room where they all waited for their travel arrangements to be finalized.

Not that he could blame them. After the botched training mission, he wouldn't be happy to see himself either if he were in their shoes.

Seth finally gave up on sitting with the team because the silence in the room fit like a too-tight boot. He got that they wanted to bullshit to blow off steam. He also got that they didn't feel comfortable doing it around him, so he grabbed his pack and left. He almost heard the sigh of relief at his back and the noise level shot up even before the door closed. In the hall, he sat on the carpeted floor and pulled out his deck of cards for a game of solitaire. Sleep weighed heavy on his eyelids. Dammit. He should have brought a thermos of his stay-awake concoction. He shook himself like a dog as he started to drift off. Got up and paced. Sat down again…

Someone screamed.

He bolted to his feet and looked for his rifle. It was gone. He was in fucking enemy territory, unarmed, without his team…

No. No, that wasn't right. Hotel. He was in a hotel in Miami. He wasn't back in Afghanistan. Yet.

He rubbed both trembling hands over his face. Cold, sticky sweat coated his skin and his breath heaved like a marathon runner's as the scream echoed through his memory. His? But, no, it wasn't his own. It was…Cordero's? Had Omar Cordero screamed like that before he died?

Bowie, Link, Cordero, Rey, McMahon. Bowie, Link, Cordero, Rey, McMahon.

No. He shut down the creeping sense of a returning memory. He didn't want it. For fuck's sake, he so didn't want it. He got flashes of images, snippets of sound, usually in his dreams, but mostly his captivity was just a blank spot in his mind. And honestly, he didn't think he wanted to remember it all. He recalled every detail about the day his men died, down to the smell of their blood. He had the scars from his captivity and they pretty much read like a goddamn road map of what had happened to him. How they got there was not something he particularly wanted in his head.

After a moment, his breathing eased and he was able to focus on the man and woman standing in front of him. Gabe and Audrey.

Shit on a motherfucking stick.

"Are you okay?" Audrey asked. Pity filled her light-brown eyes while her husband's expression radiated disapproval.

Seth nodded, not daring to speak, his shame all but choking him. Moments ticked by, nobody speaking until Audrey nudged her husband's side.

"Plane's ready," Gabe said. "So you have about ten seconds to unfuck yourself, Harlan."

Audrey heaved a sigh. "What he *means* is you have nothing to be ashamed of. Nightmares are normal."

Gabe narrowed his eyes at her. "I say what I mean, woman."

"Okay, caveman." She motioned to the conference room door. "Go grunt and posture with the other subhumans so Seth and I can have a reasonable, *adult* conversation."

Seth gaped. *Nobody* talked to Gabe Bristow like that. Man, he half expected the guy's head to explode and for lava to come draining out.

Except...

Gabe was grinning. He grabbed his wife around the waist, pulled her to him, and kissed her thoroughly, shamelessly right there in the hallway. "God, I love you."

She smiled and stood on her toes to kiss him back. "I love you, too, even when you act like a caveman. Try to be nice to him, okay? He's not like the other guys."

And he's standing right here, Seth wanted to say. He was a head case, not deaf. Instead, he bent over to pick up his scattered game of solitaire, wrapped a rubber band around the cards, and tucked them away in his pack. When he straightened, the lovebirds were just pulling apart from another kiss and the sight of so much happiness twisted a knife in his gut.

Emma.

Would he have been this happy with her?

No, his subconscious whispered.

A sour taste filled his mouth and he told his subconscious to fuck off. One of the things he did remember about his captivity was Emma. She'd been there with him, locked inside his mind, her memory the only thing his captors couldn't strip him of. She had kept him going for those fifteen months and to think of her as anything less than his guardian angel was...

No. He just wouldn't do it.

Gabe and Audrey opened the conference room doors and Seth trailed behind them inside, but hung back as everyone took seats at the large rectangular table in the middle of the room. Gabe broke away from his wife and crossed to stand in front of the men.

Much to Seth's dismay, Audrey walked back to him and pulled him to an empty seat at the table. Then she blew her husband a kiss and left the room in a swirl of color and activity.

What would it feel like to be that…light? Carefree? Comfortable in his own skin?

He couldn't imagine it.

HOW DID A NICE YALE GIRL LIKE YOU WIND UP IN A PLACE LIKE THIS?

"So...Harvard, huh?" Phoebe said and watched him set up his equipment in the room given to the team for their base of operations. The rest of the team were already downstairs at the dinner Zina had requested—okay, *demanded*—they attend to introduce them to the girls.

Phoebe had been sent to retrieve Harvard, which turned out to be easier said than done. It had taken three tries just to draw his attention away from the computers, and he'd said "one more minute" ten minutes ago. So might as well make small talk while she waited.

"Yeah. Harvard," he answered distractedly, connecting cables to the back of a small black box. "It's been my nickname for so long it's weird when anyone besides my parents calls me Eric."

"Is it just a nickname or did you actually attend?"

He smiled and it crinkled his eyes behind his glasses, but he didn't look away from his computer screen. "Both."

"Oh, that's unfortunate."

He finally glanced up. "Yeah?"

"Yeah, because you're a strangely appealing mix between nerdy and hot. But," she sighed, "I'm a Yale girl. We have no future together."

Harvard flushed a charming red to the tips of his ears and straightened his slightly crooked glasses. "I, uh, didn't realize there was even a chance. I was under the impression you had your eye on someone else."

"You mean Seth?" She huffed out a breath that fell somewhere on the scale between a laugh and an exasperated snort. "No. Absolutely not. You're more my speed. I don't go for dark, broody, mysterious, built-for-sex-and-fighting types."

"Uh-huh," he said, heavy on the disbelief.

"Okay," she admitted. "Maybe there *is* something about him I find…captivating. If he'd talk to me. But I don't see that happening, do you?"

"Stranger things have happened."

"Possibly." She trailed her fingers along the top of his computer and tried for casual interest. "What's his story, anyway? I mean, I know what happened to him here two years ago. Want I want to know is how he ended up back here with you guys."

"I'm afraid that's his story to tell, not mine." He returned his attention to his screen for a moment, but then closed the laptop and faced her directly. "And not to sound like one of Marcus's pickup lines, but how did a nice Yale girl like you wind up in a place like this?"

"Oh. That." She paced away from the table, circled the room. "It's a sordid story. Not the sort I tell to Harvard boys I just met."

But, she realized, she wanted to tell him. She felt a kinship with Harvard, and not only because of their shared Ivy League backgrounds. She genuinely liked him, more so than any of the other men on the team, save for Seth. He was real. No hidden agendas. No secrets. It was a refreshing change after spending the day observing the team and realizing every one of them harbored a secret or two.

Phoebe sat down cross-legged on the floor mat against the wall. "I was at Yale studying comparative literature and one of the requirements was a literature course in a foreign language. I choose Persian because I figured with everything going on in the world, couldn't hurt to have an understanding of the people and their language. That was the start of my interest in the Middle East, but it didn't gel into a calling until my senior year. Until then, I still thought I'd end up with a solid career teaching lit at an Ivy League school, living a normal American life with kids and a husband and all the stuff that's expected of a good, smart girl from an upper-middle-class family."

"So what happened?" Harvard stood and joined her on the mat, crossing his legs the way the Afghan people did, with his feet tucked underneath. She wondered if he knew it was the polite thing to do—showing your feet was considered uncouth—or if he was just copying her. Either way, she appreciated the gesture.

"A very good friend of mine—my roommate—was raped. It happened during a Halloween party. She was slipped something in her drink and I was too caught up in my own drama, I didn't realize she was more than drunk. When she came home the next morning, she was inconsolable. I confronted the guy for her and he laughed it off, said she begged him for it. She was too afraid to report it because she had a history of one-night stands and heavy partying, so she just let it go and ended up in this twisted relationship with her rapist. She started having nightmares and stopped eating and just…degraded in front of me. I couldn't help her."

Harvard reached over, covered her hand with his, and gave it a squeeze in a silent show of support. Such a good guy. She wondered why she couldn't be attracted to him for real. She'd joked about it, yes, but really, she felt little more than a growing fondness for him. He was best-friend material, which she bet he heard from the opposite sex far more often than he preferred.

"What happened to her?" he asked.

"We graduated and I didn't see her again until several months later. At her funeral. She, uh, swallowed a whole bottle of antidepressants and killed herself. I couldn't help her when she was alive, but I had to do something. I had to tell someone her story, so after her funeral, I asked her family's permission to write an article on the hidden rape culture of the U.S. It was picked up by several large news outlets, giving me the money and freedom to pursue the stories I wanted to tell—the stories of women who can't or won't speak for themselves. Last year, while investigating the stoning death of a woman in Iran, I met Zina in Tehran and learned about the epidemic of suicide by self-immolation among young women in Afghanistan. It's a devastating problem and most people back home have no clue about it."

"And so here you are," Harvard said.

"Here I am," she agreed.

SETH'S LAST MISSION

NOVEMBER 2010

If Jude Wilde went up into those mountains, he'd never come down, and Seth Harlan sure as hell didn't want to be the one to deliver that kind of news to his four brothers back home. Reasoning with the stubborn jackass was pointless, but the mission was so not fucking happening for him. Seth would make sure of it, even if he had to take his own exhausted team up to Forward Operating Base Delacour instead.

Seth stared down at his best friend, who lay shivering under a thin blanket on a bunk in the officers' quarters. When one of the second lieutenants tracked him down after his last mission debriefing and told him Jude Wilde was sick, he'd expected the typical cold that made its rounds among the men. Not a fucking plague.

"Shit, man. You're supposed to be oscar mike by 0400."

Jude nodded even as his teeth clicked together. "I'm good. I'll be there. Just…give me a few."

Frowning, Seth shifted his rifle to his shoulder and bent over, laying the back of his hand across Jude's forehead. "You're hot."

"Thanks, but I don't swing that way."

"Smart-ass motherfucker. You have a fever." And a wicked cough judging by the way he'd started hacking up a lung. His coloring wasn't good either, somewhere between paste and pea soup. "Any other symptoms? Puking, diarrhea?"

When the fit subsided, Jude blew out a breath and lay his head back on his pillow. "Yeah, got the whole package. Started about 1800."

Seth cursed. "You can't go on a mission like this."

"I'll get through it. Always do."

"You start coughing at the wrong time, all you'll get is your ass killed. Not to mention your guys." He pulled a bottle of water out of his leg pocket and shoved it in Jude's face. "Drink before you dehydrate."

The guy's expression twisted and his coloring shifted more toward the pea soup side of the scale. Seth backed up a step, just missing the splash of revisited dinner as Jude leaned over the side of his bunk and let loose.

Jesus.

He left the water on the ground within easy reach of Jude's bunk although he suspected the only fluids going into his buddy's body would be in the form of an IV as they shipped him to the hospital. Seth was no medic, but he was pretty damn sure Jude shouldn't be wheezing like each breath was a chore.

He stepped out of the tent into the dry, brutal cold of winter in Afghanistan. Beyond their camp to the north, ragged mountain peaks gleamed with caps of snow under a clear sky and the nearly full moon. Growing up in Iowa, he never got an eyeful like this. Everything was flat, uninteresting, and even after ten years of globe-hopping with the military, the raw beauty of mountains still blew him away.

But not this time. A gut-wrenching dread froze his boots to the hard-packed sand. The mountains loomed, dark and ominous, casting their deep shadows over the desert valley. He couldn't put his finger on the source of the feeling, but a chill that had nothing to do with air temperature raked down his spine.

Seth made a beeline for the Godfather's tent. Their commanding officer had gotten the handle from his real name, which was—honest to God—Michael Corleone, like the character in the films. Unlike some commanders who couldn't see beyond the big picture to all the moving parts underneath, Mike was reasonable and as fair as a guy could get in wartime. He'd listen. Didn't mean he'd agree, but at least he'd listen.

Seth found him under a nearby tent, bent over a beat-to-shit map, his mouth pulled down into a deep frown. He picked up a marker and circled a small section on the map, then tapped the cap to his chin a few times in thought.

"Sir."

Mike turned and his gaze swept over Seth's rigid salute. His brown eyes crinkled a bit at the corners, but the smile never touched his lips. "At ease. Can I do something for you, Lieutenant Harlan?"

He relaxed into the formal resting pose. "Thank you, sir. Permission to speak freely?"

"Go ahead."

"I believe Lieutenant Wilde is unfit for Operation Overload."

"Do you?" Mike set down the marker and gave his full attention to the conversation. "What makes you suggest that?"

Besides the fact Jude was puking his guts out at that very moment?

Seth bit back the sarcasm. Merely telling his commander about Jude's condition wouldn't have the same effect as an up-close-and-personal with the vomit geyser. "It's something you should see for yourself, sir. And we may want a hospital corpsman to meet us there."

Mike didn't move for a moment, but finally nodded and motioned for Seth to lead the way.

It took less than a minute with Jude for the Godfather to reach the same conclusion.

Cursing, Mike stepped out of the officers' quarters and reached for his radio to summon the hospital corpsman. "Shit's gonna spread like wildfire if we don't contain it now."

"Yes, sir. I'm no corpsman, but it looks like pneumonia."

Mike rubbed a hand over his face and heaved a tired sigh. "Fuck me. I can't risk sending his men up there, even if I find a replacement for him."

"I'll go with them."

"No. They've had the most contact with him. If they all end up like him, they're dead. No," he said again, almost as if talking to himself, and shook his head. "That's not happening under my command."

"Sir, then send my team up instead."

"You sure?" He pinned Seth to the spot with a steady, assessing stare. "You just got back to base."

"Yeah, and we're ready for more. Send us. We already know FOB Delacour," Seth said. "We've rotated up there before. And I know Operation Overload almost as well as Jude. We just have to bring my men up to speed."

Mike stayed silent, watching as the hospital corpsman ran toward them. Finally, he nodded. "All right. You're up, Harlan. Rouse your men and meet me for a briefing."

"Yes, sir." He waited until the Godfather ducked back into the officers' quarters with the medic, then strode across camp to the enlisted barracks to wake his team. They wouldn't be happy. Their first night back in relative safety, and they were already mobilized again.

"Bowie, Link, McMahon, Rey, Cordero." He tapped the butt of his rifle against each bunk with a resounding clang. "Get up. We're oscar mike."

ACKNOWLEDGMENTS

First and foremost, I have to thank my editor Heather Howland and her assistant Sue Winegardner for taking my hot mess of a manuscript and helping me turn it into a story that does Seth and Phoebe justice. What would I do without you guys? *hugs*

Tricia Leedom, my honorary big sister: I would have been so lost without your brainstorming sessions. Thanks for giving me all the great ideas for Ian's character. And thanks for letting me read Honor Reclaimed to you during our car ride to Key West—that helped so much! I know you're getting discouraged, but you're an excellent writer and someday soon, a publisher will notice your awesomeness. Just keep writing!

Of course, my family. You all are my rock. No matter how much I wander, I do it with the comforting knowledge that I'll always be welcomed home with smiles, laughter, and open arms.

Also, I want to give a special shout out to Zina Lynch, the winner of Seal of Honor's blog tour giveaway. Thanks for letting me borrow your name for a character!

Lastly, my readers, who I'm convinced are the absolute best fans in the world. You all are the reason I can live my dream. THANK YOU!

Discover the **HORNET** *and* **Wilde Security** *series...*

SEAL OF HONOR
a *HORNET* novel by Tonya Burrows

When Navy Seal Gabe Bristow's prestigious career comes to a crashing halt, he's offered the chance to command a private hostage rescue team. It seems like a good deal—until he meets his new team of delinquents that includes the sexy, frustratingly impulsive Audrey Van Amee. She's determined to help rescue her brother—or drive Gabe crazy. God help Gabe if he can't bring her brother back alive, because he's finally found something worth living for.

WILDE NIGHTS IN PARADISE
a *Wilde Security* novel by Tonya Burrows

Former Marine Jude Wilde's motto has always been "burn bridges and never look back." But when Wilde Security is hired to protect district attorney Libby Pruitt, the woman he loved and left, Jude can't ignore the heat—or the animosity—sparking between them. With her life on the line and a grudge to break, can he win back Libby's heart?

WILDE FOR HER
a *Wilde Security* novel by Tonya Burrows

Former homicide detective Camden Wilde craves more than friendship from his ex-partner, but Eva refuses to lose the only person she trusts, even after a scintillating night she's trying—and failing—to forget. But when a murder-for-hire contract on his head lands her on his doorstep, Cam refuses to let the delectable detective ignore what's between them, no matter how many demons from his past try to stop him.

Try these page-turning reads from Entangled...

QUEEN OF SWORDS
by Katee Robert

Ophelia Leoni grits her teeth and boards the starship that comes to seal her fate — to marry the Prince of Hansarda. When she's introduced to the ship's commander, it's none other than the gorgeous stranger she just spent a wild, drunken night with. Boone O'Keirna can't be in the same room with Ophelia without wanting to throw her out an airlock — or into his bed. Her marrying his sadistic half-brother is not an option. But while the fates may never lie, the truth is sometimes hidden between them...

EAST OF ECSTASY
by Laura Kaye

Devlin Eston, black-souled son of the evil Anemoi Eurus, is the only one who can thwart his father's plan to overthrow the Supreme God of Wind and Storms. But first, Dev must master the unstable powers he's been given. Distrusted and shunned by his own divine family, the last thing he expects is to find kindness and passion in the arms of a mortal. But Devlin's love puts Annalise in the path of a catastrophic storm, and in the final Armageddon showdown between the Anemoi and Eurus, sacrifices will be made, hearts broken, and lives changed forever...or lost.

A SHOT OF RED
by Tracy March

When biotech company heiress Mia Moncure learns her ex-boyfriend, the company's PR Director, has died in a suspicious accident in Switzerland, Mia suspects murder. Determined to reveal a killer, she turns to sexy Gio Lorenzo, Communications Director for her mother, a high-ranking senator — and the recent one-night stand Mia has been desperate to escape. While negotiating their rocky relationship, they race to uncover a deadly scheme that could ruin her family's reputation. But millions of people are being vaccinated, and there's more than her family's legacy at stake.

TANGLED HEARTS
by Heather McCollum

Highland warrior Ewan Brody always wanted a sweet, uncomplicated woman by his side, but he can't fight his attraction to the beautiful enchantress who's stumbled into his life. He quickly learns, though, that Pandora Wyatt is not only a witch, but also a pirate and possibly a traitor's daughter—and though she's tricked him into playing her husband at King Henry's court, he's falling hard. As they discover dark secrets leading to the real traitor of the Tudor court, Ewan and Pandora must uncover the truth before they lose more than just their hearts.

FIGHTING LOVE
by Abby Niles

Former Middleweight champion and confirmed bachelor Tommy "Lightning" Sparks has lost it all: his belt, his career, and now his home. After the devastating fire, he moves in with his drama-free best friend, Julie. One encounter changes everything and Julie is no longer the girl he's spent his life protecting but a desirable woman he wants to take to his bed. Knowing his reputation, he's determined to protect Julie more than ever—from himself. Can two childhood friends make a relationship work, or will they lose everything because they stopped fighting love?

SUNROPER
by Natalie J. Damschroder

Marley Canton joins Gage Samargo in tracking down the goddess who went rogue decades ago. Insane with too much power from the sun, she's selling that energy to Gage's younger brother and his friends. But Marley's ability to nullify power in those who aren't supposed to have it means that every time she nullifies someone, she takes on some of the goddess's insanity. Gage falls for Marley's sharp wit and intense desire to right wrongs. Once he discovers she's turning into her enemy, is it too late to back away?

Touch of the Angel
by Rosalie Lario

Night after night, Amara and her fellow succubi are forced to extract special abilities from the strongest Otherworlders for their psychotic master's growing collection. When Ronin Meyers, the gorgeous angel-demon hybrid she believed to be dead captures her, Amara is both stunned and elated. But the happily-ever-after Amara's dreamed about will have to wait. Before she and Ronin can find salvation, they must bring down the madman hell-bent on destroying everything—and everyone—they love. And Ronin and Amara are at the top of his list.

Dyed and Gone
by Beth Yarnall

When Dhane, a dynamic celebrity hairstylist, is found dead, Azalea March suspects foul play. Her friend Vivian confesses to the murder and is arrested, but Azalea knows there's no way she could have done it. Vivian's protecting someone. But who? Now Azalea and Alex, the sexy detective from her past, must comb through clues more twisted than a spiral perm. But the truth is stranger than anything found on the Las Vegas Strip, and proving Vivian's innocence turns out to be more difficult than transforming a brunette into a blonde.

Malicious Mischief
by Marianne Harden

Twenty-four-year-old college dropout Rylie Keyes won't be able to stop the forced sale of her and her grandfather's home, a house that has been in the family for ages unless she keeps her job. But that means figuring out the truth about a senior citizen who was found murdered while in her care. She must align with a circus-bike-wheeling Samoan while juggling the attention of two very hot cops. As she trudges through this new realm of perseverance, she has no idea that she just might win, or lose, a little piece of her heart.